JOURNEY

BOOKS BY THE AUTHOR:

Seasons of Harvest
The Awakening Land
Shadows on the Land
(A three-volume trilogy of the Corrales Valley)

Unlike Any Land You Know
The 490th Bomb Squadron in China-Burma-India

Coon Creek
A Novel of the Mississippi River Bottoms

Journey
A Novel of America

JOURNEY

A Novel of America

James M. Vesely

iUniverse, Inc.
New York Lincoln Shanghai

JOURNEY
A Novel of America

iUniverse, Inc.

For information address:
iUniverse, Inc.
2021 Pine Lake Road, Suite 100
Lincoln, NE 68512
www.iuniverse.com

JOURNEY is a work of fiction.
Aside from actual historic figures and historically factual events, All other names, characters, places, and incidents are either Products of the author's imagination or are used fictitiously. Any resemblance to actual events, locales, or persons, Living or dead, is entirely coincidental.

ISBN: 0-595-29441-3

Printed in the United States of America

For my parents, Joseph and Mildred.
And for my grandparents, Vaclav
Vesely, Lena Vosepka, and Josephine
Malovich—who had the courage to
make the journey.

Prologue

The Farm

Although she'd left her cat with a neighbor and boarded the Delta flight out of Los Angeles both excited and curious at the prospect of a family reunion on the first Fourth of July holiday of the new century, Lynn Novak found the solitude of her uncle's Montana farm uncomfortable—almost unnerving.

Stark, weathered, and lonely, the white frame two-story house and the rolling, rugged land that surrounded it seemed incredibly remote, so far removed from the life she was accustomed to—a lonely and forlorn place as distant from her small apartment in Los Angeles as the earth from the moon.

Driving out to it from Great Falls the day before, she learned they'd visited the farm once many years ago, a month or so after her father had come home from his tour in Vietnam, but Lynn had no memory of it.

"It was probably 1970," her mother told her at the airport in Great Falls as they talked and waited for Lynn's battered suitcase to appear in baggage claim.

Not having seen each other since Christmas, Jane Novak and her daughter had catching up to do. Lynn was still a Midwestern girl at heart and hadn't been much inclined to spend the Christmas holidays among palm trees and ocean breezes on the coast. But she'd decided to spend that summer in Los Angeles, taking two courses toward her master's degree. So it had been more than half a year since they'd been together. Most of their conversation was small talk, the latest news about friends and relatives.

But later, in the car, Lynn brought up her Uncle Harland and the farm. She couldn't remember any of it.

"Lynn, honey," her mother said, as the Buick rolled silently northwest on Highway 87 across the stark, rutted plains of eastern Montana. "You were too young to remember the last time we were here—why, you were just a baby."

It was late afternoon, almost evening, in midsummer—a day before the long Fourth of July weekend, with the heat still causing a reflective shimmer on the sticky blacktop. All around, as far as Lynn could see, were thick, waving fields of hard red wheat and Durham, flax, barley and rye, sugar beets and alfalfa.

As they drove, the flat and featureless landscape rolled silently past, looking like an empty, forgotten land with only the occasional farmhouse or tall grain silo to break the horizon. Some of the small towns they passed through—places like Floweree and Carter—looked to be drying up and withering away. Along the empty main streets, storefronts were closed—some even boarded up, and on the streets, few people could be seen.

My God, Lynn asked herself, thinking of Chicago's museums, clubs, and restaurants, and of the balmy beaches and neon nightlife of Los Angeles—how could Uncle Harland, or anybody else live out their lives in such a dismal place as this?

Along with a Beatles' *Abbey Road* CD playing much too loud on the car stereo, her mother had cranked up the air conditioning to maximum. "Your dad just came back from the war, and with you all bundled up, we drove out here for a few weeks. I still remember being bored near to death, but he needed to spend some time in a quiet place.

"God, your daddy was in such bad shape when he came back," Jane Novak went on, her voice just on level above the sound of the music. Reaching into her purse, she took out a pack of Salems, lit one, and gently shook her head as she remembered back to that time. "For almost a year, Bob slept with that damned hunting knife under his pillow."

Robert Novak had died of a heart attack three years earlier—just months before Lynn had left their comfortable home in the Chicago suburb of Westchester to become a graduate student at UCLA. She was taking political science, economics, and history at the university's Center for European and Russian Studies.

For most of her life, Lynn's ambition was to travel—hopefully as a teacher or even in a diplomatic post with the State Department once she'd obtained her Ph.D.

This midsummer's day, an early Delta flight had brought her to Salt Lake City, where she'd made a plane change and gone on to Great Falls by late afternoon. A week earlier, her mother had wired out the airfare, then pointed the Buick west from Chicago and was waiting at the airport to meet her.

At the picnic the next day, after greeting all the Chicago aunts, uncles, and cousins who'd come, Lynn was sitting alone, eating a delicious piece of fried chicken when one of her distant Montana cousins approached. He was a slight boy with freckles and blond hair the color of summer wheat, happily tugging a stubborn puppy around on a leash.

"My name's Curtis and that's Grandma Annie over there," he said boldly, pointing to an elderly woman slumped in a lawn chair. "Ma says she's almost a hundred years old, and carries her kidneys around in her purse, attached by a tube."

"Maybe so," Lynn whispered back conspiratorially, shaking the boy's hand and rubbing the excited, playful puppy behind its ears. "But you oughtn't to be telling people such things."

"Are you from around here?" Curtis asked, cocking his head. "I never seen you before."

"No," Lynn answered. "I'm from Chicago—and now I live in Los Angeles. Do you know where those places are?"

The boy nodded. "Uncle Harland says both of them stink."

"Really, why?"

Curtis shrugged. "He says Chicago's full of niggers and Jews—and Los Angeles has got too many Chinamen and fairies."

"Curtis, that's a terrible thing to say."

"You gonna scold me?" the boy asked.

"No, but I ought to scold Uncle Harland."

"*Hah,* you better not try it," Curtis laughed, pulling the puppy away. "Nobody scolds Uncle Harland—not even Aunt Mae."

As she watched the boy walk away, Lynn realized how little she knew about Uncle Harland Novak and the rest of the Montana side of the family. She'd heard their names mentioned from time to time in the course of growing up, but the names were just names—never connected to faces or personalities—just names and a casual knowledge that she had relatives somewhere in Montana, and that most of them owned farms.

Aside from those Novaks who'd flown out from Chicago, she felt almost as if she were among strangers—people who looked and spoke and acted so differently than her own side of the family. But it was the same blood, Lynn reflected. Most of these people relaxing and chatting in the big yard were kin to those Novaks who first emigrated from Czechoslovakia near the turn of the century.

She recalled seeing their names in an old journal, along with brown, faded photographs in a tattered album her father had kept. She could still remember the picture of a stern woman in a dark shirtwaist and a wide, feathered hat. Next to her in the picture were two young men, and standing behind them a fierce-looking fellow with a starched collar and a heavy mustache.

"Those are my great-great grandparents, Janicka and Valentyn Novak," her father had told her years ago, pointing at the man and woman in the photo. Then he'd moved his finger slightly. "And these were their sons, Joseph and Andrew. Joseph was my great-grandpa, and Andrew was my great-uncle—he went out west years ago to start a farm."

"A farm?" Lynn had exclaimed. "With animals?"

"With animals—sure."

"Can we go there?" Lynn had asked.

"You were there once. Can you remember?"

"No."

"Someday we'll go there again," Robert Novak promised. But it was never to be.

Lynn looked out beyond young Curtis, to a stand of tall, leafy cottonwoods where Uncle Harland was busy talking to some other men. She assumed them to be cousins or uncles, if not by blood—then by marriage. Earlier, her mother had said that Harland was the patriarch of this side of their family. He certainly looks the part, Lynn decided. Harland Novak was tall and wiry slim, with unruly white hair, a heavy, salt and pepper mustache that drooped down to touch the corners of his mouth, with a sunburned face and hands deeply creased by years of wind and weather.

Then a thought came to her. She needed a subject for a paper due by the end of the summer term and had been having trouble deciding on a subject. Why not the story of her family's journey to America, along with their lives and fortunes over the generations? For a moment she almost decided against it—much too ambitious a task for a term paper. But then she considered it again: such a project would dovetail nicely with her area of interest in European history; she could easily research the broader facts in the library and on the Internet, then flesh it out by introducing a personal narrative in the account of her own family's experience.

It was an interesting notion, she thought, looking at the crowd in the yard. Talk about personal histories, they're all here—right in front of me, growing old with their stories and their memories.

Lynn chuckled to herself, intrigued by the idea, and thinking for a moment that she never saw men in Los Angeles who looked anything like Uncle Harland Novak.

"He's quite the old bull, ain't he?"

Lynn turned to see a woman who was very old herself. She put out a hand and the old woman grasped it firmly. "I don't know the particulars about aunts, great-aunts, great-great-aunts and such," the woman said. "So I'll just tell you that I'm your Aunt Jo—that's short for Joanna. I'm married to Harland's brother, Walter."

"I'm so pleased to meet you," Lynn said. "I was just thinking how few people I actually know from this side of our family."

"Well," Aunt Jo said. "None of us is all that familiar with the city side of the bunch, either—so we can call it even, I guess. Your ma pointed you out and told me who you was—the last time I seen her, you was just an infant.

"That little feller with the puppy you was talking to belongs to Wendell and Angie Purvis," Aunt Jo went on to say, pointing to a younger couple drinking longnecks on the porch. "They're related, too. He's a dickens, that little boy."

"Curtis?" Lynn laughed. "Curtis Purvis? That's quite a choice of name."

Shaking her head, the old woman chuckled, too. "Wendell and Angie ain't skilled at naming children. The whole nine months that Angie was pregnant the first time, Wendell took a liking to grilled cheese sandwiches morning, noon, and night. And when the little girl was born, they went and baptized her *Velveeta*—Velveeta Ann Purvis—don't that beat anything you ever heard?"

"I'll say," Lynn agreed, fascinated. "What else can you tell me about the family, Aunt Jo?"

"Oh, I ain't the one to tell you, honey. I only married a Novak in 1939. Grandma Annie knows more than anybody, but she's too old." Aunt Jo twirled a finger next to her head. "Grandma Annie's a little confused. Rarely knows where she's at these days."

"That's too bad," Lynn said, genuinely disappointed.

"But your Aunt Mae—that's Harland's wife—why, she knows as much about the whole bunch as anybody. Come on, and you can ask her."

Mae Novak was a tiny, wisp of a thing. Lynn marveled at how much she resembled the late actress, Lillian Gish. Aunt Mae was cheerful and spry—her quick movements almost birdlike. Around her slim waist she wore a white cotton apron and laughed as easily as a sprightly young girl, but her eyes were always on the party, making sure no one lacked for food, drink, or comfort.

Pulling Lynn across the grass by the arm, Aunt Jo wasted little time introducing them. "Mae, you remember young Lynn—Jane's daughter from Chicago?"

"Of course," Aunt Mae said pleasantly, giving Lynn a warm embrace and then stepping back. "Why, we last saw you when you were a baby, and see what a beauty you've become."

"Thank you so much," Lynn said. "I was hoping you might be able to tell me about our family in Montana. I'm thinking of doing a paper on it."

Mae Novak nodded. "Well, I'm just about ready to go back in the house and fry some more chicken—maybe you'd care to come in and keep me company."

Although Lynn and her mother were sleeping in a small, airy room upstairs, she found the rest of the house to be dark and old-fashioned, mostly furnished with what looked to be locally-made wooden tables and heavy, upholstered furniture. On the tables were old copies of the *Reader's Digest,* seed and feed catalogues, the *Farm Journal,* and numerous other agricultural magazines, as well as a well-worn copy of the *Old Farmer's Almanac.*

Aunt Mae led her into a small foyer off the living room, where Lynn saw an old glass-fronted bookcase filled with ancient, dusty volumes of books on farming and livestock, as well as a number of thick scrapbooks and three bound manuscripts that were labeled *Family Genealogy.* They stood tight against an equally well-worn Bible; each consulted often and regarded as final, definitive cairns of both memory and truth, neatly stacked and tied like grain for the winter. Mae Novak opened the bookcase, carefully took out the three genealogy books and handed them to Lynn.

"If you're really interested," her aunt said. "This is how things were. This is what you need to know."

Dated 1905, half of the first volume was in Czech, penned in a rough and hurried hand by Ondrej Novak during his first winter on the Montana prairie—the second half had been rewritten in English by a woman named Irena—who, explained Aunt Mae, had married Ondrej Novak in the summer of 1906.

"Ondrej—that means Andrew," Mae said. "Was your Uncle Harland's *dĕdeček*—his grandfather, and this side of the family all traces back to him—he and Irena are both buried here."

As her aunt busied herself near the stove, tending great platters of fried chicken, Lynn sipped a beer and sat fascinated at the large kitchen table, pouring over journals, faded photographs, letters and pages from diaries written long ago. Both sides of the family were represented here; the Montana side in the genealogy books, and her own people, those who'd stayed in Chicago, in the fragile pages of scrapbooks and letters sent west over all the many decades of their lives in America.

"Aunt Mae, this is a treasure," Lynn said, astonished.

"Oh no, it's just old stuff," Mae said. "Not much of interest to anybody else but us, I expect—but it's all true."

Lynn took a deep breath. "Do you have room for me to stay a few weeks after the party is over?"

"Why of course, dear. It's just Harland and me rattling around this old place now. I expect we'd enjoy the company."

The next day, Lynn canceled her flight back to Los Angeles and told her mother she'd be staying on for a while.

"Why honey, whatever for?"

"How often did you write to the family out here?" Lynn asked.

"I rarely did," her mother admitted. "Your dad did though, and some of the other relatives back home did, too."

"Those letters are all still here, Mom," Lynn explained. "The last hundred years of our whole family is still inside this old house—even letters written almost ninety years ago by Great-Great-Great Grandma Janicka. Aunt Mae and Uncle Harland kept everything."

Jane Novak was surprised. "Well, I had no idea that you were so interested in these things," she said.

"I didn't either," Lynn answered with a sigh. "Until yesterday, when Aunt Mae took me inside and dropped all those scrapbooks and journals in my lap. At first, I was thinking of doing a paper on the family, but now I'm not sure—there's enough material in there to write a book."

"A book?"

"Sure, why not?"

Jane was slightly amused. She enjoyed mystery novels and the books of James Michener, and she usually kept herself informed of the newest bestsellers through the *Sunday Tribune* Book Section. Jane Novak had no illusions about being a literary critic, but she enjoyed reading, and she knew what she liked.

"Honey, you might not believe me when I tell you, but a book about our family, written by a graduate student, is not something for which the publishing world is holding its collective breath."

Lynn was unconcerned. "Then I'll print a hundred and we can send them out as Christmas gifts—I'm going to do it, mother."

Jane nodded and shrugged. She knew the discussion was over. Lynn was stubborn, had always been stubborn. She takes after her father, Jane thought. He had a wife and a baby daughter and it still wasn't enough to keep him from enlisting and going to Vietnam. It must be somewhere deep in the Novak blood, Jane had often told herself, this stubborn streak. She glanced over Lynn's shoulder and through an open window, staring at the cottonwoods, then to the lonely, empty land beyond. What else but pure stubbornness could have brought people out to this god-forsaken country in the first place, and then kept them here for nearly a century?

Two days later, after her mother and all her other relatives had left, Lynn phoned her professors at UCLA and explained that she'd be absent for a few weeks—doing research for a project. Then, she borrowed her uncle's Ford pickup to drive the seventy-five miles to Great Falls for some notebooks and a small tape recorder. At the last minute, Aunt Mae decided to go with her, planning to do some shopping at the big Walmart store on Smelter Avenue. Mae Novak sat in the passenger's seat and chatted cheerfully. She didn't often have company on her monthly trips into town. Harland usually refused to make the drive unless he was either seeing the doctor or thinking of buying a new truck or piece of equipment.

As she turned the pickup off a dusty county road and headed south on Route 87, Lynn asked her aunt a question that had been bothering her. "Aunt Mae, how does Uncle Harland feel about me being here? Is he angry about it?"

Mae turned toward Lynn, a puzzled look on her face. "Angry? Why of course not. Why would you think such a thing?"

Lynn laughed lightly. "Well, he barely speaks to me. The past two nights at supper, about all he's been able to get out is 'pass the potatoes, please.'"

Aunt Mae chuckled, too, then leaned back in the seat again. "Oh, that's just Harland," she said. "He doesn't talk much, period. To me or anybody else. He never did—I guess it's just his nature."

Lynn nodded, already sensing a problem. Harland Novak, a man reluctant to talk, would be a wealth of information. As much as Aunt Mae, his recollections of the family over the last seventy years would be so important if this book project was to be anything worthwhile.

Lynn's first week of research produced not much more than a dry, factual timeline of events. It was necessary, she knew, but that didn't make it interesting—she needed personal accounts, and for these she wanted the recollections of her aunt and uncle. Aunt Mae was cooperative, but Harland maintained his distance—remaining polite, but quiet, all through supper, then studying seed catalogues for most of the evening, and finally going to bed after watching the local news and weather.

The entire week was like that, and then on Sunday morning Mae Novak drove the truck to a neighbor's place to help with some canning, leaving Lynn and Uncle Harland alone together in the old house for the first time since she'd been a guest. Seated at opposite ends of the dinner table, they ate their meal in the middle of polite manners and awkward silence.

After supper, her uncle excused himself and left the house as Lynn cleared the table. Through the window over the kitchen sink she watched him stop on the porch, light a smoke, and then go into the barn. Ten minutes later, just as she'd started to wash the dishes, Harland returned, stepping gingerly into the kitchen.

"Miss Lynn," he said, somewhat urgently. "I've got a problem and I believe I could use your help. I'd ask my sons, but they're off in Great Falls on some bank business—and my closest neighbor is down with the shingles."

Hearing the concern in her uncle's voice, Lynn put down the soapy washcloth and rinsed her hands. The old man was holding a galvanized bucket and looked anxious, worried—a look she hadn't seen before.

"What's wrong, Uncle Harland?"

"I have a cow that's been calving since about four o'clock this afternoon," he said. "She ain't been gaining, and I expect she needs some help."

Lynn felt fear wash over her. Little more than a week ago, she was having a light lunch with friends at a trendy little restaurant in Malibu, and now a seventy year-old farmer she barely knew was asking her to help birth a calf in a Montana barn.

"Uncle Harland, shouldn't you call the vet or something?"

Harland shook his head. "Nope, ordinarily me and your aunt do our own animal doctoring," he explained. "But today Mae ain't here, neither, and this calf won't wait for her to come home—can you help me, miss?"

Lynn swallowed hard, wiping her hands on her apron. "Sure, I'll try to do whatever you need me to do."

He moved toward the sink. "First thing is to get this pail filled with some warm water."

As they stepped out onto the porch, Lynn saw that her uncle had already laid out equipment—a rope, a burlap bag that held a chain and snare, and next to it a tool that Harland called a calf jack. The jack was about six feet long. He said it was an instrument they sometimes used on hard-to-pull calves.

Approaching the barn, Harland admitted, "She was real tame when I brought her in, but now she's nervous."

"What's that mean?" Lynn asked.

"Means you need to be careful," her uncle grunted.

The oppressive heat and humidity, along with the smell of the barn almost made Lynn sick. As they entered, the milk cow looked at them warily but made no aggressive move.

Harland pointed to a small feed room. "That's where you head for should she get fractious."

"What about you?"

"Well, I'll be right behind you, miss."

Lynn watched, unsure of what to do, as Harland managed to get the rope around the nervous cow's head without alarming her, then snugged it tight around a support post. "Stroke her face and talk soft to her while I look things over," he instructed.

"What's her name?" Lynn asked, struck by the softness of the animal's large brown eyes.

"Mae named her Rosie," Harland said. "Don't ask me why."

Tied short, and with Lynn calming her, Harland moved behind the cow to take stock of the situation. After scrubbing his hands, he lifted Rosie's tail forward, tying it into position and washing both it and her rear end with warm soapy water and Betadyne solution. Then, reaching deep inside, he ran his hand over the calf, feeling it's front feet and its head. As best he could determine, the calf was a normal presentation, but it was a large baby, and Rosie's pelvis was extremely small.

"She'll need help," was all Harland said, coming back around to bring the obstetric chains out of the bag. "Just keep talking to her sweet and low."

"What will you do?" Lynn asked, nervously.

Harland sighed and his big shoulders seemed to droop a little. "I got to birth this baby," he said. "If a vet was here, he'd want to cut her open and bring out the calf that way—but I ain't got those surgical skills, and the vet's too far away.

"So we got to help Rosie birth this calf natural," Harland went on. "But it's risky. We could lose both her and her baby."

As Lynn continued to comfort the cow, her uncle plunged his arms up Rosie's birth canal and double-looped the chains around the calf's forelegs. "Now you need to pull them chains straight out a little, miss, while I feel what's going on in here."

Feeling lightheaded as sweat rolled down her face, Lynn put a steady pressure on the chains. Harland felt the calf's head forced back. He put a head snare on it and applied pressure, bringing the head back into line with the feet, then told her to pull some more as he manipulated the baby, gently using an up, up, up, down, down, down motion to help move the big calf forward.

"Don't pull too hard," Harland said. "Just keep a light tension on and if she starts to go down, let them chains go slack."

Both sweating now, they worked at it for ten minutes, before Harland swore and quit—pulling his arms back out. Shaking his head, he positioned the calf jack in place and attached it to the head and snare. With Lynn watching wide-eyed as her uncle tightened tension on the jack, the cow suddenly bawled and became frantic, lunging backward and snapping the restraint rope with the sound of a gunshot.

"Oh, shit!" Lynn screamed, jumping back.

Rosie was loose but the six-foot jack was still firmly in place, sticking from behind her like a heavy club. Harland grabbed Lynn by the shoulders and threw her into the feed room, then followed close behind. Frightened, Lynn crouched in the darkness, listening to the terrified cow bucking and slamming around in the barn.

"Oh God, the poor thing's going to kill herself," Lynn cried.

Rosie banged into stalls and upset feeders—while the calf jack sounded like a pistol firing every time it hit the floor. The swinging jack could have easily killed anyone it hit.

The more the jack banged, the wilder Rosie became, but after a few minutes of it the cow tired and began to settle down.

Harland crawled out of hiding, carefully took hold of the rope and retied her to the support. Rosie was all slobber and exhausted. The cow had spent herself in fear and had no more energy to resist. Surprisingly, the unborn calf was still alive.

"Rosie's played out," Harland said. "We need to do this quick now—otherwise we'll lose her."

As tremors and trembles ran through the shaking cow, Harland passed the chains back to Lynn while he held the calf jack steady, and with one final, determined effort, the face of the stubborn calf suddenly appeared and then with a gush of fluids, the entire body passed through Rosie's narrow pelvis.

Tears ran down Lynn's face. It seemed as if some miracle had happened—with a living, newborn calf flopping back and forth on the slippery wet floor of the barn. It was trying to get to its feet but kept falling back down on its side. Harland quickly knelt to blow and clean the mucous out of the calf's nose. When he was finished, he stood again and untied Rosie.

With surprised, blinking eyes the calf took one breath of fresh, sweet air, then another and another, lifting its head ever so slightly. Barely perceptible to Lynn, the newborn's efforts were enough to refocus Rosie from the discomfort and confusion of birthing to the attentiveness of mothering: she swung around and began to nuzzle the baby, licking it to stimulate the breathing while cleaning off the birth waters.

"I believe it's gonna be alright," Harland said, putting his big hand on Lynn's trembling shoulder. "She gave us a little bull. Now we can just step back and let nature take its course."

The male calf rolled up from it's side to a laying position, then jerkily stumbled up to take his first shaky, tentative steps, all to the gentle lowing and nuzzling of Rosie. Her maternal instinct had now kicked in. She was busy aggressively licking the bewildered calf, urging this little, new life to get himself going.

"Oh, look at them," Lynn cried excitedly, almost unbelieving of what had happened. "Just look at them, Uncle Harland."

"Well, ain't that something?" Harland said. "It was some little trouble, but it was worth it—it's always fine to get a live calf."

Her eyes still wet with tears, Lynn took a deep breath and saw that it was growing dark outside. There was no wind, and she felt a thin bead of sweat trickle down her neck.

To Harland it had been just another job of work, but Lynn was overwhelmed with a nearly mystical sense of continuity. It was as if she'd been suddenly blessed with some new understanding of the rightness of life on earth. To have had a hand in bringing the little calf into the world was like having had a hand in creation.

That one moment, Lynn recalled, that almost magical moment when the straining of the cow, their efforts with the calf jack and chains, and finally the emergence of the baby all seemed to gush forth in a rush of birth fluids, relief and wonder. It was a scene that played and replayed itself over and over in her head—birthing, new life, God at work.

Aunt Mae came home about two hours after the calf had been born, and Lynn was still bursting with excitement.

"Rosie dropped a bull," Harland told his wife.

"A bull? My goodness, any trouble?"

"Some—but Lynn was here to help. We made do."

Along with Harland and Lynn, Aunt Mae spent ten minutes in the barn tidying up and visiting her milk cow and its new calf, then announced that as long as she wasn't needed for anything, she was going up to bed.

"Me, too," Lynn said. "I'm beat."

"I believe I'll have a smoke before I turn in," Uncle Harland said. Then he turned to Lynn. "How about keeping me company on the porch?"

The night was warm and soft, with just the occasional hint of a breeze. As they sat on the porch steps, one of Harland's coon dogs—a bluetick hound named Sally—came out from under the porch and lay at their feet. Lynn glanced up and then stared at the sky, a sky that held more stars than she'd ever seen in her life. Suddenly, Harland Novak's farm on the banks of the Marias River, smack in the middle of Montana, didn't seem so lonely.

"You did real fine today," Harland said quietly, fishing in his shirt pocket for a cigarette. As he struck a wooden match to light it, Lynn noticed that he was missing the index finger of his left hand, just above the knuckle. Working with all the machinery he did, it didn't surprise her, but it was something she hadn't noticed before.

"Thanks, Uncle Harland. I was scared all through it, though."

"Yes, I seen that—but you never quit on me."

Lynn shrugged. He was right, she hadn't quit.

"How's your studies coming?"

"At UCLA?"

"No, I meant here—on all them books Mae showed you."

Lynn shrugged again, thinking there'd be no better time to ask him than this. "It's going all right, I guess. But I'll need a lot more first-hand memories from people like Aunt Mae—and *you*."

Uncle Harland nodded and gave his trademark grunt. Taking a long drag on his cigarette, he held the Winston up and stared at it. "The doc in Great Falls says these things are bad for you," he said, almost as if he were all alone and talking to himself. "But when my mother died at eighty, she was still smoking a pack of Marshall's Cubeb cigarettes every day."

"Cubeb cigarettes?"

Uncle Harland nodded. "Cubebs—I don't believe you can get them anymore. Best I recall, they mixed dried cubeb spice with the tobacco. Ma swore they relieved asthma and hay fever. Some folks even said they'd cure influenza."

Lynn perked up. It was the most he'd said to her since the day she decided to stay and go over the diaries and scrapbooks. It was almost as if what little help she gave him with Rosie was some sort of key that finally opened up the taciturn old man.

"See, that's the kind of stuff I need for my project," she told him. "Memories like that will bring it to life."

Another grunt. He wasn't too much for talking, and never had been, but he'd always held with the old saying that one good turn deserved another. Even if the poor girl did live in Los Angeles, this niece of his had been a help. If he could pay her back he would.

"Well, there's been some long, cold winters when I studied on those old books pretty good," Harland said as he lit another smoke. "And as near as I can make of it, the whole damn thing started with a pig—"

PART I

PASSAGE

CHAPTER 1

"*Být tichý*," Ondrej Novak whispered under his breath. "If you are not quiet, the animal will flee."

Normally a calm and unflappable man, Ondrej had finally lost patience with his younger brother, Josef, who'd grown bored with the hunt and could not stop complaining about his discomforts. His feet hurt, Josef protested, he was cold, and he had to shit. Hidden in a thicket of beech and oak—the two had been laying in wait for the approach of a large boar that was upwind of them, cautiously sniffing both sides of the narrow trail not sixty feet away.

As the pig came closer, popping its long, curved tusks, Ondrej slowly brought back the hammer of his father's old smoothbore, being careful to muffle its metallic *click* with his woolen gloves. Even though they'd both grown up as country boys, his brother had never been much of a hunter, Ondrej thought disapprovingly—nor for that matter did Josef have the soul of a farmer.

The life they lived on their father's small piece of leased land near Třeboň was not a life for Josef Novak. He was the son who'd always been restless on their poor farm and in the village, always dreaming instead of bigger cities—Prague and Plzeň, where Josef suspected the lights were always bright and the nights were filled with cheap beer and laughing, willing girls.

Both brothers were bachelors—Josef because his plans for his future did not yet include the encumbrance of a family, and Ondrej because he refused to marry until he owned his own land. It was an improbable ambition that would quickly become laughable if they were caught poaching this boar in their landlord's forest.

"Shoot it, damn you," Josef hissed, his breath turning to steam in the dark morning chill. "Shoot it and let's be out of here."

"I have powder and shot for only one barrel," Ondrej quickly explained, again in a whisper. "We must let him get closer."

The brothers were poor. For as long as each could remember, their family had scratched a meager living from a small parcel of leased ground that could barely be called a farm. In that winter of 1897, as the world was breathlessly moving toward a new century, Ondrej and Josef Novak lived in an ancient land rich in beauty, yet forever filled with hardship and strife—Slavic *Bohemia*—for three centuries, a reluctant part of the Austro-Hungarian Empire.

Their far distant ancestors had been tribal people of a peaceful nature, more enamored of farming than of war. Their documented history began in the seventh century, at which time they'd already extended their culture as far south as the Danube.

Known to the Romans as the *Boii*, they were an ancient race—and the westernmost branch of the Slavs living in what was then known as the Czech Lands—the name derived, it was said, from a noted ancestral chief. Their society was agricultural and pastoral, ruled by an early government almost republican in nature, under a chief, elected by an assembly of representatives of the primary classes of the people.

Later, their rule would grow and develop into a monarchy of hereditary kings, whose taking of the throne would nevertheless be ratified by the national diet. They were a people possessing a code of formal law, and throughout Europe they were known for their strength and physical prowess, their free spirit, love of poetry, and above all, a burning, passionate need for independence.

"Shoot the ugly bastard," Josef urged again, and this time his brother squeezed the trigger. The still of darkness was shattered by the smoothbore's roar. With a high-pitched squeal, the boar was knocked backwards and dropped to the ground like a sack of grain from a wagon.

"Is it dead?" Josef asked, once again excited.

"Yes, he's dead," Ondrej said with certainty. "I shot for the head, but now comes the hard work of carrying it home."

Help in hauling the dead pig home was the only reason Ondrej had brought his brother along. Some of the feral hogs in the woods belonging to their landlord could weigh up to four hundred pounds. This one hadn't been quite that large, Ondrej could see, but still too heavy for one man to carry.

"We must hurry *bratr*," Ondrej said. "If Herr Schwarzenberk or that bastard gamekeeper of his catches us, it will go hard on the whole family."

"*Pah,* Herr Schwarzenberk is still warm in his big bed," Josef snorted. "And anyway, that old man can kiss my ass."

"Nevertheless," Ondrej said, slipping his arm through the sling of the shotgun. "Help me lift the beast and let's be out of here—we must be home before daybreak."

Ondrej was unimpressed with his brother's lack of respect for their landlord—one of the most powerful men in Central Europe. They did not know Jakub Schwarzenberk to be necessarily a bad man, but rather a wealthy noble with a sharp eye for profit. He kept a close watch on all his interests, and a pleasant portion of those interests, dear to the landlord's heart, included his Rozmberk and Svet carp ponds along with the plentiful boar and stag that roamed his vast forests.

The dead pig was almost three hundred pounds and difficult to carry, but by both carrying and dragging it, Ondrej and Josef made it back to their parent's small cottage before the sun rose over the surrounding hills.

"*Ježíš a Maria,*" Valentyn Novak gasped, his eyes wide and his head shaking as he watched his sons drag the carcass across his modest threshold.

"And what is this?" Valentyn's wife scolded. Janicka Novak knew that she'd lost control of her sons long ago, especially Josef. Ondrej was hardworking and a good helper, but her youngest had always been lazy when it came to chores, a wild boy who had only girls on his mind and no use for life on the farm.

"What is this?" Janicka repeated, pointing a stern finger at the dead animal still bleeding on her floor.

"Christmas dinner, *Matka,*" Josef said, grinning. "And a lot of bacon for the New Year. Ondrej shot the brute and I helped drag it home."

"God in Heaven," Janicka snorted, casting a withering gaze at her husband. "Now our sons are poachers, too, as well as good-for-nothings. If Jakub Schwarzenberk learns of this, Valentyn—our whole family is in the stew."

"He'll not hear of it," Ondrej assured her. "It was dark when I killed the animal, and still dark when we brought it home. I'll dress and butcher it inside the cottage, and no one will be the wiser."

With Janicka Novak reminding them of the risk, they hung the pig from the ceiling, cutting its throat and allowing what blood was left to bleed out into a round metal washtub.

The dead hog was a big job, with Valentyn and Ondrej doing most of the work. The following night, once the animal had bled out, it was scalded to make the bristly hair easier to scrape away. Grunting and cursing while Josef watched, Ondrej and his father then hoisted the hog and hung it from a tree, working in the dark of night to remove the innards. When this was done, they carried the pig back into the house, out of sight of anyone who might pass by in daylight.

After their meager breakfast of rye bread and coffee, Ondrej planned to cut away the hams, shoulders, and side meat. He'd salt these parts and hang them in the smokehouse to cure for days over a small fire. He'd make sausage and headcheese from other parts of the hog, and souse by cooking the ears, head and feet together. Some small bit of lard would be rendered from what fatty parts there were on the animal—by boiling them in a kettle and straining out the crumbly renderings.

Lard was Janicka's source of cooking fat, and she would store it in a deep cellar pit—in wooden tubs. At least this was their plan, until a knock on the door interrupted the morning meal.

Janicka hurriedly draped a blanket over the hanging hog as her husband opened the door.

"*Dobré ráno*," the man standing outside said amiably. "Good morning, Mr. and Mrs. Novak—maybe we have a problem?"

Even though he'd just awoken, Josef recognized the voice of the man in the doorway as that of Radek Novotny, their landlord's gamekeeper.

Radek Novotny was a little man with a pinched face and a slight wheeze when he talked. "I heard a shot two nights ago," he said. "At first, I thought it to be only be some dirty gypsies passing through, but sadly this was not the case—in Herr Schwarzenberk's forest, I find a blood trail that leads me to your home."

Without invitation, Novotny prodded one of the Novak's gray geese from the doorway and stepped inside. He looked around the little cottage with the air of a man who loved the little authority he had, finally moving across the room and pulling aside the blanket that covered the dead boar.

"I see," he clucked. "There *is* a problem here. I am charged to protect the *výčnělek's* game, you see, and Herr Schwarzenberk will be very angry with this, Valentyn. He does not tolerate poachers."

"He did not poach," Josef interrupted. "I shot the pig, and my father knew nothing of it."

"No," Ondrej said. "My brother is lying to you. It was I who killed your boss's pig, Herr Novotny. No one else."

Novotny shook his head and clucked again. "It matters little who killed the animal. The carcass is here, in this house, and so is the guilt. This will go hard on all of you, I fear."

"Yes," Josef said sarcastically. "We are certain your boss will be rendered destitute by the loss of one wild hog."

"Josef, shut up!" Janicka hissed at her son. "You are a foolish boy whose head grows thicker every day. Can't you understand the trouble we're in?"

"Maybe, maybe not," Novotny said with a thin smile. "I too, might enjoy a few roasts for Christmas. Sometimes a man need not tell all he knows."

"I will have one of the boys bring them to you," Janicka said gratefully. "With our blessing, Herr Novotny, and our promise that such a thing will never happen again."

"Not so fast," the gamekeeper went on, glancing around the room at all of them. "You people must understand that I am a man who does not take his duties lightly. I fear it will take more than a few cuts of stolen meat to make this crime go away."

"I do not understand—" Janicka said.

"The bastard wants money," Josef spat.

Novotny shrugged his shoulders. "If a man is to compromise his honesty, such compromise should be made worthwhile."

"We are just poor people, Radek," Valentyn said. "You know this to be true. We have no money to give."

Novotny shrugged again. "Oh, not now perhaps, but next year when the harvest is in and you've peddled some of your hens and geese. Perhaps then, I might expect a portion of your profit."

"What portion?" Ondrej asked, furious enough to strangle this miserable, dishonest little man who held such power over them. In a year of generous rain and no disease or misfortune to the fowl, Ondrej knew they could still expect to earn just enough to get by. If this weren't the case, he could have just gone to market and bought a pig, rather than poach one in the dark of night.

"Fifteen percent, I think," the gatekeeper answered. "It's little enough to keep you on this land."

"You'll have your damned money," Valentyn sighed, to the irritation of his sons. Even though the land and the cottage did not belong to him, it was all that he had—all he and Janicka had ever had. How would they survive without it?

"Very well, then," Radek Novotny said, tipping his cap. "I'll expect payment after harvest, and the cuts of meat within the week. In the meantime, I wish your family a happy Christmas, and may the Infant of Prague grant you good fortune, Valentyn Novak."

CHAPTER 2

Just a week before Christmas, with most of the wild pig butchered and either smoked or packed in sawdust and blocks of ice cut from the carp ponds, Janicka received a large, heavily wrapped parcel.

"From America," the postman stated, grinning.

"Yes, from America," Janicka said with a smile. The postman carried it inside the house for her. In return, she gave him a cheese *koláčky* and a cup of coffee to take away the chill.

"From Matek?" the postman asked, munching the pastry she'd given him.

"Not that it should be any business of yours, old man," Janicka told him. "But yes, it's from Matek."

Janicka's younger brother, Matek Holub, had left Třeboň for America twelve years earlier, and at least once or twice a year, they received gift packages from him and his family—usually containing clothes and canned goods, and always some money. Matek was generous, and the money greatly helped to tide them over.

As a boy, her brother apprenticed as a cooper—a barrel maker—in Třeboň. He was hardworking and ambitious, and after leaving for America he'd prospered working for a cooperage in the city of Chicago, in the state called Illinois.

Yes, Matek had been the smart one to leave, Janicka thought, waiting impatiently for the postman to finish his coffee and be on his way again, so that she might open the package.

In Třeboň, and all the scattered villages of their district, people had long been rigidly divided into three social groups—doctors, tradesmen, and merchants were at the top of the heap, along with the large farmers, called *sedláci*.

Next in line, with varying degrees of success, were the small farmers, like the Novaks, called *zahradnici,* and at the bottom were the *podruzi*—poor day laborers just managing to scratch out a marginal existence. This pecking order had been in place for as long as any of them could remember, and there was nothing on the horizon that promised to change it.

Valentyn Novak and his family had never owned their two hectares. Like many others, they merely farmed the land and took care of it, each year turning over a percentage of their earnings to Jakub Schwarzenberk.

Janicka and many other struggling people in their district were dissatisfied with the way things were, and once, when she and her husband were much younger, she herself had brought up the idea of leaving Bohemia.

"America's too far away," Valentyn had told her. "This is our home and I don't wish to leave it."

There is no fire in his belly for a better life, she'd thought, as Valentyn dismissed the idea. These two poor hectares are where he wants to stay—growing cabbages and raising geese on property that will never belong to us—*this* is to be our life.

Janicka and most others throughout the country were aware of the fact that a steady flow of emigrants to America had been under way since at least the middle of the century. It waxed and waned as economic and social conditions in Central Europe improved or deteriorated. Yet, the thought of starting a new life in America had always appealed to her, and that notion turned to a burning desire after her older brother had actually done it—and was prospering there—sending her and Valentyn food, clothing, and money once or twice each year.

Valentyn was a good, decent man, Janicka told herself time and again, but because of his lack of adventure and ambition, the dream of going to America was one she'd never know.

Once again, she was forced to accept this sad fact as she waved goodbye to the postman and began to carefully untie the twine that secured her brother's charity.

They fasted all through Advent, and then attended Midnight Mass in Třeboň on Christmas Eve. Afterward, with Josef flirting and casting a lecherous eye toward all the single girls, the family took hot coffee and pastries while singing carols with their friends and neighbors as it lightly snowed outside the church.

The Christmas holidays came and went, and a week later they celebrated New Year's Eve.

"Think of it, brother," Josef said excitedly as they lifted steins of beer to toast the New Year at Havlicek's Tavern. "To be young and strong like us, and only two more years until the beginning of a new century."

Ever practical, Ondrej only sighed and shrugged. "Little about it will be new," he said. "There will still be planting in spring and harvesting in fall, and all the work to be done in between."

It seemed as if Ondrej was right. The family spent the next year working even harder to meet the bribe of gamekeeper Radek Novotny. Even Josef helped more than usual, all the while cursing and voicing distaste for the farm and all its work.

That one is so restless and unhappy, Janicka thought, listening to her younger son complain. And yet, she could hardly blame him. Although Ondrej rarely complained about anything, the futures of both her sons were increasingly gloomy. Their tiny house and two hectares of leased land were no inheritance, and as long as Ondrej and Josef owned nothing more than the work clothes they put on each morning, they'd spend their lives, just as their father was doing, as servants to a rich and powerful landlord.

One sunny autumn afternoon, soon after the harvest was over, Janicka went over the books only to find them short of money by the fifteen percent given over to Novotny. The shortfall came as no surprise, but it nevertheless brought sadness and frustration into the house.

Later in the day, Josef did little to help the situation—coming home drunk from the village. He was mumbling to himself and in his hand, he clutched a wrinkled sheet of paper.

"I am leaving Třeboň," he announced, placing the paper on the table and slapping it with his hand. "For New York, in America."

"You're drunk and a fool," Valentyn told his son. "A drunkard and a lazybones to boot."

"Nevertheless," Josef told his father. "I will borrow the money and leave as soon as possible."

Janicka shushed them both as she gently picked up the paper and read it. What Josef had brought home was an advertisement for the Hamburg-America Line. On the paper was an engraving of a modern, four-stacked steamship with the promise of comfortable, affordable passage out of Hamburg, Germany, to either America, Australia, or Africa.

"Where did you get this?" she asked her son.

"From Jirik Zelenka, at the tavern," Josef said, sitting down at the table with a loud belch. "He is going to America, too—as soon as we can get our papers in order."

"Zelenka is a fool as well," Valentyn threw in.

"Be still, husband," Janicka scolded. She hadn't thought about leaving Bohemia in years, but now found herself intrigued again. Her own hopes of emigration had been dashed years before, but her son might yet be able to realize the dream.

She'd always known he was dissatisfied with their village and the farm, and had long ago been convinced that someday Josef would leave Třeboň for one of the larger cities—Prague or Plzeň, perhaps—or even Vienna. But she'd never spoken of it to him, and so had no idea he'd even considered leaving Třeboň for a place as distant as America.

If Josef was truly serious, Janicka thought—her mind racing at the prospect of it—his Uncle Matek could sponsor him in Chicago. To hell with Valentyn and his fears of leaving home, she decided—the promise of a new century was only two years away, and she'd long ago convinced herself that a prosperous future for any of the Novaks would lay in America, not in Europe.

Janicka cooked and served the evening meal in silence. Ever since Josef had made his announcement about leaving, she'd been thinking of little else, and the more she thought about it, the more the old fires once again caught and flamed within her heart. She let them burn all night and throughout the following day—then finally broached the subject to Valentyn.

"Josef is determined to leave," she said, as they lay in bed.

"Let him leave, then," Valentyn countered with a shrug. "God knows, he is little enough help around here."

"I want us to go, too," Janicka said.

Valentyn sat up in bed and looked at her. "I told you long ago that I would not leave our country—"

"Our country?" Janicka said bitterly. "This is not our country, Valentyn. This country belongs to the politicians and the wealthy—men like Jakub Schwarzenberk and his family. We live on this land at his pleasure—and only so long as we profit him."

Valentyn stubbornly shook his head. "I will not go."

Janicka turned from him. "Then we will go without you," she said firmly. "Josef, Ondrej, and I—Ondrej is a born farmer, and America will give him land to farm."

Valentyn Novak did not sleep well; increasingly uneasy with the turn of events that suddenly seemed to be happening within his family. He was the head of the household, and yet he knew that his wife could often be a stubborn woman. Once Janicka made up her mind about something, that thing usually occurred.

If Josef and Ondrej truly wished to go to America, he thought, then let them go. It would be two less bellies the farm would have to feed. But his wife was another matter altogether.

In the darkness, Valentyn lay in bed with his eyes open. He did not think his wife would really leave him, but he wasn't certain of it, and if she did, he could barely imagine any life without her.

Early the next morning, Valentyn said little. As he finished his breakfast and went into town to pay some debts, Janicka kept both her sons seated at the table. After her husband had left, she looked at Ondrej first. "Your brother has said he wishes to go to America. Does my eldest son have such thoughts as well?"

Ondrej was confused. Like his father, he sensed that their lives might somehow, suddenly be changing. "I have not thought about such a thing," he said with hesitation. "This is my home. I know little else but helping you and father on this farm."

"You have read your Uncle Matek's letters," Janicka told him. "He always writes that there is cheap farmland in America, and he would be willing to loan you the money to buy it."

"Buy my own land—" Ondrej said, his voice trailing off.

"And you," Janicka said, turning her attention to Josef. "What will you do in America—besides drink beer?"

"I have read Uncle Matek's letters, too," Josef said firmly, as if he'd been thinking about it for a long while. "I will work—I will work hard in a land where a man's labor is fairly rewarded—where I wouldn't have to steal another man's pig to enjoy a fine dinner on Christmas—America has made Uncle Matek rich, and someday I will be wealthy, too."

Janicka nodded and poured another cup of coffee. "Now I will tell you both something," she said. Her sons sensed a seldom-heard excitement in their mother's voice. "Years ago, when I was much younger, I too, wanted to live in America—but your father refused to go.

"Josef's steamship advertisement has once more reminded me of those days when the two of you were just babies," Janicka went on. "Now, I have put it in front of your father again, and threatened to go without him if he loves this poor farm too much to leave it."

"You would leave Father?" Ondrej asked, unbelieving.

"No, I would not," Janicka admitted. "My place is always with your father."

Then she winked. "But he needn't be so sure of it. We've just enough money to get by should we stay here and scratch out our living for another miserable year. But without the expenses of this meager bit of land, we can all afford passage to America."

"Mother, you're certain of Uncle Matek's willingness to make such a loan?" Ondrej asked.

"He has made the offer every time he's written."

"Then I would be a fool not to go."

"We would all be fools to stay here," Janicka told them. "Now you both must help me convince your father of that fact."

CHAPTER 3

❀

Valentyn could easily argue with his wife or either of his sons, but he was unaccustomed to arguing with all three of them at once.

"Father," Ondrej said at supper the next night. "We've decided to leave—to go to America, where Uncle Matek will help us."

"You too, Ondrej, *eh?*" Valentyn said. He shook his head and leaned back in his chair, hooking his thumbs in his suspenders. So Josef has convinced his brother to be a part of this foolishness, he thought. Well, so be it. With both of them gone, the money from the farm would stretch even further.

"Well, go then," he told Ondrej. "I'll not stop you. If both my sons wish to run away to America and live off their uncle's charity, it is certainly none of my concern. Your mother and I can run this place ourselves."

"No, I will go with them," Janicka stated, staring deep into her husband's eyes. It was a bluff, but he didn't know it. "I meant what I said last night," she reminded him.

"Goddamnit," Valentyn Novak swore, smashing his big hand down upon the table. "What will you use for money to get there? It is a costly journey across the ocean."

"We will borrow it from Matek if we have to," Janicka said.

"But there is another way, Papa," Josef quickly added.

"And how is that, *výčnělek?*" Valentyn said scornfully, using the word for boss. He was angry with his son. After all, it had been young Josef and his big ideas that had started all this nonsense.

"You can go with us," Josef pressed. "Aside from what went to Schwarzen-berk and Radek Novotny, damn them, we have all the harvest money for the year—more than enough to get all of us to New York—and from there to Chicago."

"Goddamnit," Valentyn swore again. "I am fifty-one years old with no education. What would I do in America?"

"Live as a free man," Josef argued. "Beholden to no one."

"If I can just up and go so easily, my thickheaded son, am I not a free man already?" Valentyn countered, proud of his logic.

"No," Janicka interrupted. "Your own fear is what kills your freedom and keeps you prisoner here—servant to a man who cares little if your family prospers or starves."

Tired of arguing, Valentyn finally threw up his hands and left the table, walking out into the cool of the night to smoke his pipe. He'd been stung by what Janicka said, but somewhere deep in his heart, he suspected she was right. He'd known other restless men who'd emigrated and always secretly envied them.

Their life was hard, Valentyn always told himself, yet it was a life that at least offered some security. Just the thought of leaving Bohemia for a strange new country, a place where he could neither read nor write the language, much less speak it, terrified him.

A few moments later, Janicka joined him in the yard. She was wrapped in a shawl against the coolness of the night, and glancing at her, Valentyn saw for just a moment the pretty girl he'd married twenty years before.

"You would leave me, then?" he asked.

"Yes, husband, I will leave," Janicka said, knowing that if the situation were reversed, such words would be as painful as a sharp knife drawn across her heart. She would never leave this man, yet she was determined to carry the bluff just a little further.

"A man's life takes strange twists," Valentyn said, drawing on his pipe. "He works day and night to feed his family, and then one day wakes up to find them gone? It is a thing I cannot understand."

Janicka felt tears welling in her eyes. She reached out and took her husband's rough hands in hers. "Then do not let it happen," she said softly. "Come with us to America, Valentyn. Do not be afraid of a different life—a better life. I have watched you labor hard all the years we've been married, and still you have little more than when we started.

"No matter what we do or how hard we work," she went on, "We will always be subject to the whim and greed of our landlord. If we remain here, you and I will die poor people, owning only the clothes we are buried in. Husband, you must realize we will never own the land we live on, nor will our two sons. It is for them that we should quit Třeboň for America."

"I think I would be afraid," Valentyn mumbled as he tamped out his pipe. It was a hard, shameful thing for a man to admit, but he suspected his wife already knew it.

She moved closer, cradling his worn and weathered face in her hands. "Do not fear change, Valentyn. Change is a part of life. You are a good, strong man, and you can do anything you wish to do."

"Except stay here," he said softly.

Janicka nodded. "To stay here is foolish."

Valentyn sighed deeply, rubbing his eyes for a moment before looking at his wife again. "We have enough money?"

"To get there, yes—more than enough."

"And we would pay Matek back for any help he gives us?"

"Of course," Janicka said, her heart racing.

Valentyn sighed again, this time nodding his head. "Very well then, we shall go to America—all four of us—together."

Janicka stood and pressed his head to her breast, and only then did she allow herself to weep.

The first thing she did the following day was to write a letter to her brother in America. Sometime after the New Year, she told Matek, they would take the ship to New York and then a train to Chicago. Could he be so kind as to meet them at the station?

Although they owned little, Janicka quickly learned that going to America was not just a matter of packing their bags and leaving. Instead, they were to spend tedious and frustrating weeks dealing with officials in Třeboň and the church to secure birth certificates, travel visas, and emigration permits.

At one point, it seemed to Janicka that their entire enterprise might come to nothing. "How old are your sons?" asked one minor bureaucrat in the offices of the District Authority—a bespectacled little man named Hanus Skala.

"The oldest is twenty-four," Janicka replied, adding the years in her head. "And the youngest just twenty-one."

"Have either served in the army?" Hanus Skala went on.

"They have both reported for conscription," Janicka told him. "They drew high lot numbers and were released."

Skala smiled thinly and shook his head. "Yes, well I'm afraid it is not so simple as that, missus."

"I don't understand," Janicka said, increasingly nervous as the little man continued to smile at her, stroking his mustache with his thumb and forefinger.

"The Austrian government requires them to draw lots again next year," Skala explained. "And, if still not drafted, then once more the year after that. If they are so lucky as to not be drafted in the third lottery, then your sons must still serve in the military reserve for ten years."

"Ten years—" Janicka felt the words catch in her throat.

"Yes," the little clerk said. "Perhaps you should have applied five years ago, when your sons were underage."

"We didn't know."

"Are you or your husband disabled in any way?" Skala asked. "If so, a dispensation might be given—after payment of a special military tax, of course."

"My husband has a slight limp," Janicka said, truthfully. "The result of an accident years ago."

"Well, that might do it," Hanus Skala said with a shrug. The clerk then glanced around and added, in a conspiratorial whisper: "That is, if someone in authority made the infirmity out to be more severe than it actually is."

Janicka suddenly realized what Skala was about. Government officials were respected for the most part, but poorly paid. This one was out to feather his nest.

"I see," she said wearily, thinking back to Radek Novotny and the gamekeeper's price of silence for the poached hog. "And what might such a tax amount to?"

The clerk hurriedly scribbled a number on a sheet of paper and pushed it across the desk to her.

"Done," Janicka said with a deep sigh. The amount Skala was demanding would bite deeply into their funds, but any thought of staying on their poor, rented farm for another ten years was more than she could bear.

Gainfully employed as a tenant farmer, Skala scribbled on a form, *the husband drags a leg and cannot work without the help of both his sons.*

"Well, there you are missus," the little man said, stamping the document vigorously. "Your family should be free to leave, with no military obligations to fulfill—and all for a pittance."

"A pittance for you, perhaps," Janicka said. "Not for us."

"Be thankful you have dealt with me," Hanus Skala scolded as he dismissed her. "Others might not have been so generous."

Early in February, she received a reply from her brother. Her hands trembled slightly as she opened the thick envelope, fearful that now that they'd made their decision, Matek might be unable to help them, or might even attempt to discourage them from coming. Relatives could often be unpredictable, Janicka knew, and it might not take much to make Valentyn change his mind.

As she opened the envelope, money fell out onto the table—American money—along with a photograph, the first that Matek had ever sent. It was a picture of her brother, formally posed with his wife and children. Matek had put on a little weight, she could see. His wife was pretty and his two children, a boy and a girl, looked happy and healthy. She studied it awhile, then laid it on the table and carefully unfolded the letter.

February 6, 1898

My Dear Sister,

It is with great joy that we received your news. My Anna is excited to finally meet you, and the children are as well. My job goes well and we are all in good health here.

We have a bit of money put away, and I will use some of it to help you all I can. The American inspectors will want each of you to have at least fifty dollars apiece, so I am enclosing two hundred dollars to cover that expense. I assume you have enough for your passage and train fare to Chicago. If not, please let me know and I will send you more. Of course, I will expect to be repaid, with interest, for any loan I make—for this is the way things are done in America.

The journey across is not an easy one, dear sister, so you will need to keep your spirits up, as well as those of Valentyn, Ondrej, and Josef. Take courage and wire us from New York City when you know what train you will be on, and the time of your arrival.

May the Infant of Prague bless you and watch over you.

Matek

It would take two more months for everything to be approved by the emigration authorities in Prague, as well as the Ministry for Land Defense, located in Vienna. When the necessary documents of Emigration Consent finally arrived, Janicka hurried into town to get them, and stopping on the way home, purchased four one-way train tickets to Hamburg, as well as a like amount of steerage fares to New York City aboard Hamburg-America Lines.

"They are the best of the lot," the ticket agent assured her.

That evening, while the rest of her family packed trunks and worn valises, Janicka butchered and cooked the big gray goose that over the years had given them goslings to sell. She roasted the fat bird to a crisp turn, and served it with bread dumplings and a large bowl of sauerkraut. Later, before going to bed, she would pack her own suitcase for the journey.

"In the morning," Valentyn announced at supper. "I will pay a call on Herr Schwarzenberk, and tell him we are leaving."

"Why not clean the house and yard, sell the goat and chickens, and just go?" Janicka asked, becoming nervous that their landlord might somehow change her husband's mind.

Ondrej and Josef agreed, but Valentyn shook his head. "No," he said. "The Schwarzenberk family—for better or worse—have provided a home for the Novaks for three generations. I feel that I at least owe Jakub Schwarzenberk some explanation."

"What is there to explain?" Janicka asked. "We are going and that is that."

"I will see the man tomorrow," Valentyn repeated, glancing up at his wife with some annoyance. "And *that* is that."

Janicka offered no more objection. Even though he'd given in to her and her desires to go to America, Valentyn told himself, he would still remain the head of his family.

CHAPTER 4

✿

"You are going to America, *eh?*" Jakub Schwarzenberk asked, as Valentyn nervously stood before him.

Schwarzenberk was a large man, bewhiskered and big-bellied, befitting his station in life. This marked the first time that Valentyn Novak or anyone else in his house had ever spoken directly to their landlord. In all the years that he'd labored on the man's land, any dealings with Herr Schwarzenberk had been done through assistant managers and other assorted underlings.

Earlier that morning, as a brace of nervous wolfhounds snarled and barked at his unexpected appearance, Valentyn stood quietly before the Schwarzenberk estate's great iron gate until a uniformed guard quieted the dogs and came out to meet him.

"What's your business, here?" the man had asked curtly.

"*Statkář*," Valentyn said. "I wish to see the landlord."

"About what?"

"My family and I plan to vacate his property."

"Wait here," the guard grumbled. Then he'd turned on his heel and marched back toward the doorway of the huge estate.

Ten minutes passed before the guard finally returned to escort Valentyn into the house. "You have interrupted my breakfast," the uniformed man complained. "My coffee has grown cold."

Valentyn found himself annoyed by the guard's overbearing manner. "That is too bad," he told the man. "You should take your breakfast earlier—as a farmer does."

He was brought into a large wood-paneled room, whose dark walls were covered with the stuffed heads of stag and boar, shields, broadswords, and a wealth of other ancient weapons from Central Europe's long history of war and conflict. As the guard announced Valentyn, Jakub Schwarzenberk rose from an overstuffed leather chair to greet him. The landlord had been oiling the walnut stock of a fine German double-barreled shotgun.

"*Ach,* Herr Novak," Schwarzenberk said amiably, offering his hand. The big man spoke with a slight German accent. "It is good that I meet you after so many years."

"I am honored, sir," was all Valentyn could think of to say.

"What brings you to see me?"

"My family and I will be leaving."

"Leaving?" Schwarzenberk smiled. "Leaving for where?"

"America, sir."

"Going to America, *eh?* You have decided to emigrate?"

"Yes."

"I see," Jakub Schwarzenberk said, surprised.

"Yes, of course," he went on. "Why not? Everyone wishes to go to America these days." The landlord grunted, rubbing a finger up alongside his nose. "Once or twice, I have had occasion to visit America, and I must tell you it is a very large country—but rough-edged, I'm afraid, and greatly lacking in tradition or manners."

"I would not know about that, your honor."

Schwarzenberk invited Valentyn to sit, as a servant brought in cups of hot coffee and a plate of freshly baked apple strudel. Even though Herr Schwarzenberk paid little daily attention to his many tenant farmers, he carefully examined the ledger each winter to determine those who were profitable and those who were not.

The Novaks had lived and farmed on Schwarzenberk land for three generations—ever since Jakub's own father installed Artur and Jaruska Novak in that same small cottage and two hectares in the spring of 1821. They had been good, productive tenants, and Valentyn and Janicka Novak were more of the same—even though there was always talk in Třeboň about the youngest son, Josef, who was rumored to be lazy and too fond of the girls.

Herr Schwarzenberk munched on a piece of strudel and looked at the man sitting across from him. He knew they were about the same age, but Valentyn Novak looked much older. The farmer had always been a hard worker, Schwarzenberk recalled, and he did not like to lose such men.

"How was your year, Valentyn? Did you profit?"

We might have, Valentyn thought briefly, if it had not been for the business of the boar and Radek Novotny—but he couldn't tell this to his landlord. "A small profit—not much," he lied.

"Yes, well, some years are better than others," Schwarzenberk offered. "But let's be down to business, what can I do to convince you to stay?"

Valentyn shrugged. "Were it only myself, your honor, I'm not sure I would go. But it is my wife who has such ideas. Janicka is convinced that America will offer a better future to our sons."

"And what will they do there?" Jakub Schwarzenberk asked. "Do they have the guarantee of jobs? Do they even speak English? Valentyn, my friend, I must tell you that America is often harsh on those who journey to her shores expecting the streets to be paved with gold."

"None of us are expecting that," Valentyn shot back, suddenly annoyed at what seemed to be Herr Schwarzenberk's poor opinion of their decision. "Ondrej has been promised a loan to secure his own farmland, and I am certain that Josef will find gainful work in Chicago—we are to meet my brother-in-law there."

The landlord sighed. "Very well then, if you are determined to go, I will no longer attempt to convince you otherwise. Are you in debt to me for any reason?"

"No, sir," Valentyn said. "We have paid your honor the tenant fee and the percentage for last year's labor. The land is productive and the cottage in fine repair."

Schwarzenberk nodded and instructed a servant to bring him pen and paper. "In America, the authorities may ask to see letters of character," he told Valentyn. "You and your family have always been good tenants and hard workers, and I would be pleased to provide a letter to that effect."

"Thank you, your honor."

"Is your family *Katholisch?*"

"Yes."

"Then I suggest you obtain a similar letter from your priest," Schwarzenberk said, extending his hand. "Well then, you are free to go, Valentyn Novak, but you must understand—should you decide to return to Bohemia for any reason, the house and land that your family has occupied for so many years will be in the hands of another. As far as the House of Schwarzenberk is concerned, your journey to America is a one way trip."

"Yes, your honor—we understand."

"The guard will take you back to the gate," the landlord said with finality. "I wish you and your family good fortune."

It was as simple as that, Valentyn thought, a hollow feeling in the pit of his stomach. Politely dismissed, he now found himself an emigrant possessing neither home nor land—just his own uncertain future across a great ocean in a city called Chicago.

"Herr Novak, you are as old as I," Schwarzenberk called out, shaking his head as Valentyn moved toward the door. "And neither of us are spring chickens anymore. What will a man your age do in America?"

Valentyn stopped and turned. He briefly thought of the other night and his wife's tears of relief and happiness, then straightened his shoulders and threw out his chest, staring across the length of the room at this man whose powerful family had overseen his life for as long as he could remember.

"I will be an American," Valentyn said simply.

CHAPTER 5

Along with the geese, chickens, and a single goat, they managed to sell everything that would be left behind—netting at least a small amount of extra money for the journey.

Then, a week after Valentyn met with Jakub Schwarzenberk, and after they'd bid farewell to friends and neighbors, the family struggled with their luggage and trunks, and boarded the morning train out of Třeboň, bound for Hamburg.

"I've never been on a train before," Josef said, quickly finding a seat at the window.

"Nor have I," his brother offered.

"Well, none of us have," Janicka said, smoothing her skirt and glancing at Valentyn who was craning his neck to look around the upholstered coach. "So it's about time."

They all settled in as the train slowly steamed out of Třeboň's station. As it picked up speed, Janicka stared out her own window—watching as Třeboň passed by—barely able to believe that it just might be the last time she'd ever see the town in which she'd been born and raised. The thought frightened her for just a moment, the awesome finality of it, and suddenly made her realize the real fears with which her husband had been forced to deal. She reached down and gently squeezed his arm.

"Well, we are on our way," Valentyn said, looking at her with a thin smile on his lips.

"Yes, *vážení jeden*, we are on our way," Janicka said quietly, taking his big hand in hers.

It was a pleasant trip north toward Prague, the countryside passing as the steel wheels clacked along. The coach shook and swayed as an old woman entered their car and came down the aisle selling pastries and small sandwiches.

"*Chodíme do Amerika*," Josef said at one point, grinning and leaning forward to grip his mother's hands. "Can you believe it, Mother? We are going to America—to Chicago, Illinois."

"Well, we're not there yet," Janicka sniffed. "You mustn't jinx it with too much talk. Look around you, Josef, and tell me where is Jirik Zelenka? He, too, boasted of going to America."

It was true. Jirik Zelenka had also applied for all the necessary emigration papers, but was turned down because of his unfulfilled duties to the Austrian military. He'd had the misfortune of no extra money to offer as a bribe.

"Jirik was unlucky," Josef said, shrugging.

Janicka nodded and stared out her window, remembering the bribe she'd had to pay so that her sons could be aboard this train. "Say a prayer to the Infant of Prague," she told Josef. "That we are not unlucky as well."

With two Austrian flags flapping on its locomotive, the train passed through the countryside, stopping briefly at every village large enough to have a station. The name of each town was painted on a sign as they slowed and approached the platforms—Soběslav, Tábor, and Votice—towns whose names the Novaks knew, but had never traveled far enough to visit. At every stop, more and more people boarded—many carrying huge, tied bundles and trunks—obviously other emigrants traveling toward Hamburg or Bremen.

They finally reached Benešov—just south of Prague, and the last small town on this stretch of their journey—taking on even more passengers there. As she looked about her, Janicka saw that the train had suddenly become cramped and short of space.

An hour later, they began to slow again, approaching Prague Station. Josef was amazed at the size of the old historic capitol—a place he'd only dreamed about, but never seen.

When the train finally screeched to a stop, Valentyn, Josef, and Ondrej briefly got off to stretch their legs—leaving Janicka behind to save their seats and watch over their belongings. The three men sat on a wooden bench and shared a hurried lunch of rye bread, cheese, and stale coffee purchased from a station vendor.

"Prague," Josef exclaimed excitedly. "I never dreamed it to be so big. Can New York or Chicago be anywhere near this size?"

"Prague is ancient," Ondrej told him, remembering something he'd once read in a book. "The first settlement here has been traced to the second half of the 9th century—New York and Chicago are just babies compared to that."

Stopping again at Nový Bar, their travel papers were carefully examined by German immigration officials.

"Czechs, *eh?*" a uniformed guard asked. "Bound for America, are you?"

"*Ja,*" Valentyn answered in German. "My family and I are going to Chicago, Illinois."

"Do you enjoy good beer, Daddy?" asked the guard, thumbing through Valentyn's papers.

"Of course—what Czech does not?"

"Well then, you should have a last taste of it in Hamburg," the guard advised with a laugh. "People who have returned tell me the beer in America isn't worth a damn."

"Then maybe I'll drink wine there," Valentyn replied. "For we do not plan to return."

All the adult passengers were questioned, and once the border authorities were satisfied, the train was waved on to continue.

They were soon across the border and Josef leaned against the coach's window, staring in amazement as tidy, landscaped little homes and farms blurred past. This was Germany, he told himself, astonished that until just a day ago, no one in his family had ever traveled far beyond Třeboň—and now they were rattling across the picturesque countryside of southern Germany—all of them bound for new lives in a new land.

They stopped in Berlin in the middle of the night, but Janicka was the only one that woke, looking out her window on a dimly lit platform mostly filled with tired, disembarking passengers. Both of the boys were sound asleep and Valentyn was hunched in his seat, snoring loudly next to her. Her eyes burned and still felt heavy, and once she'd satisfied herself that nothing was amiss, she pulled her wool shawl close around her shoulders and let herself fall back to sleep again.

By morning, the train was approaching Hamburg and once it entered the station and came to a stop, another uniformed German official climbed aboard. With spectacles down on his nose, the ruddy-faced fellow walked slowly through each coach, calling out instructions for the confused and anxious passengers.

"All emigrants," he announced in German. "Will be detained for at least five days while being examined by the Emigration Authorities. Any person put in quarantine will be with us for two weeks or longer."

"Five days," Josef murmured angrily. "How can they waste our time like this?"

"Be still," Janicka said sharply, although she too, was irritated with the thought of almost a week's delay. "These are rules that we must obey—so be patient. America is not going anywhere."

"Once off the train, you and your luggage will be put aboard wagons," the official went on. "You will be taken to the Emigrant Barracks on the American Pier, and there you will find clean and comfortable quarters. Those sailing on the Hamburg-America Line will be taken to that company's own specially-built facilities."

"That is us," Janicka said, looking down at their tickets.

The Hamburg-America barracks were crowded and noisy, full of anxious, impatient passengers crowded together and waiting to be examined before being allowed to board the ships. A fine of one hundred dollars per passenger, plus the expense of return passage, Janicka learned, was being levied against any shipping company that transported someone with a communicable disease that might be transmitted to others during the voyage.

"They treat us like animals in a barn," Josef complained. "We are pushed this way and that, waiting in line for everything."

"No one said it would be easy," Janicka scolded. "Even Matek said the journey would be hard."

"It's not only that," Josef retorted. "Look around you, Mother. We are not all Czechs here. There are Germans and Slovaks, too, and that is fine—but look there, over in that corner."

Janicka followed the direction of her son's nod. In one corner of the barrack was a large family of ten, huddled closely together. The oldest man among them wore a long beard, their poor clothes looked very different and all of them seemed frightened.

"*Židé*," Josef said with some distaste. "*Polský Židé.*"

"Yes," Janicka said. "Polish Jews, and so what? Do you think only Bohemians and Germans wish to emigrate? If so, Josef, you are in for a big surprise when we reach America."

Janicka knew that in Třeboň, as well as much of Europe, Jews were less than highly regarded. Yet, like so many other things, she suspected, it might be different in America—and if so, Josef would be foolish to bring such intolerance with him on the journey.

"You are going toward a new life in a new land," she told her son. "If you are wise, you will leave such feelings behind."

Keeping to themselves and with a close eye on their baggage, they lived in cramped quarters and ate poor food for three days before it was their turn to be examined.

First, their eyes were looked at, the doctors searching for signs and symptoms of trachoma, a chronic conjunctivitis that was slow in the initial stages of development, but which eventually resulted in progressive scarring and total blindness.

"It seems the American Immigration Authority is terrified of this affliction," the examiner, a portly little German doctor, told Janicka. "But I see no signs of it among your family."

She was relieved—the first hurdle crossed.

"And I assume your sons are neither idiots nor lunatics," the little man asked, as Janicka took a deep breath and exhaled, letting him listen to her lungs.

"I have thought as much once or twice," she said with a small laugh, attempting to make light of the situation.

"Yes, madam," the examiner said, nodding as if he'd heard the same answer many times before. "I have two sons myself and often think that to be the case with them, as well."

"Your husband has already cursed at my assistant for looking in his ears," the man told her. "He seems a man of foul temper."

"My husband is not accustomed to having such things done to him," Janicka replied. "He has never seen a doctor in his life."

The examiner grunted. "Yes, well, he has a limp and I hesitate to question him about it. Perhaps you might tell—"

"A farm accident," Janicka explained. "It happened more than fifteen years ago."

"I see—he is able to work?"

"He has farmed ever since."

"*Ach, gut, gut,*" the doctor said, scribbling something on his clipboard. "They will want to know that in America."

With the first series of examinations behind them, the Novaks were listed on the Hamburg-America passenger manifest and each received boarding passes to the ship they'd been assigned.

"*Graf Waldersee,*" Josef said, looking at his. "I wonder what size she will be?"

"Big enough to get us there," Ondrej offered.

The *Graf Waldersee* was a relatively large vessel, built by the Blohm and Voss Shipbuilders in Hamburg three years earlier. She was almost thirteen thousand tons, five hundred eighty-five feet in length, with a sixty-two foot beam and built to accommodate over twenty-five hundred souls, most of whom would cross in steerage.

With her four tall masts and single stack, the *Graf Waldersee* was the largest thing the family had ever seen. Josef marveled at her size as they inched closer to a gangplank, part of a long, slowly moving line of people waiting to board.

Recalling his mother's words, Josef glanced around him at the crowded docks, seeing anxious, confused knots of people pushing and shoving—many of them speaking different languages.

There were other people from the Czech Lands—as well as a great amount of Slovaks and Poles, Austrians, Hungarians, and Dutch. Mixed in among them all, Josef quickly noted, were large and small groups of gypsies and poorly dressed Jews—everyone, it seemed, wary of everyone else—all searching for new beginnings, a better life across the gray and windswept North Atlantic.

CHAPTER 6

❀

Once aboard, Janicka decided their quarters in steerage were not worth the money they'd paid. Their sleeping space was small and crowded, privacy was lacking, and aside from being situated near the rumbling engines, the portion of the ship allocated to steerage smelled rank and sour.

Below decks, a few of the Jewish emigrants had sought out the head steward, bribing him with a fee to give them as good a berth as possible.

The Novaks were assigned an apartment, a narrow aisle with two rows of beds on either side, originally meant for twenty-four, but now occupied only by twelve persons, which allowed each an empty berth to stow baggage. Janicka found it difficult to guess what they would have done with their trunks and valises otherwise.

A close neighbor was a Slovak woman, with exceedingly dirty habits and unkempt appearance; she had a penchant for using her lap as a dish for the sauerkraut and potatoes she'd brought aboard. Three other women occupied the rest of the beds in the cramped apartment, as well as two young married couples.

"Two weeks cooped up in here?" Ondrej complained. "How will we stand it?"

"We'll spend as much time as we can on deck," Janicka told him. "There the air is fresh."

"And cold," Josef quickly added. "And blowing wind and rain as well."

Janicka shrugged and shook her head. Her two sons were able to find something to complain about every minute of the day, she thought. It seemed as if only Valentyn didn't complain—ever since her husband was finally convinced to make this journey, he'd been able to take any inconveniences that had come their way without undue grumbling.

At noon a steward came through, serving chunks of rye bread and bowls of cabbage soup for the midday meal, while late in the afternoon they heard the loud clank of the anchor being drawn up. The monstrous engines began to shudder and clank as well, as the pilot brought *Graf Waldersee* slowly out of her berth, pointing her bow into the busy, widening estuary of the Elbe River.

"Let's go on deck," Josef suggested. "We can watch Germany fade away into the fog."

"How far is it to open ocean?" Ondrej asked.

"I heard a man say four or five hours," Josef said. "We'll be there by night-fall."

To starboard, as Janicka and Valentyn did their best to settle in below decks, the brothers watched the barge and steamship harbor traffic, staring in fascination as their own vessel slid past the river towns of Blankenese, Dockenhuden and Mühlenberg.

They'd left Bohemia a week ago, Josef thought with wonder, and now were actually watching Germany disappear behind them. Soon there would be only ocean, and both wondered—strange as it might seem—when, if ever, they'd again set foot in Europe.

When the docks of Hamburg were out of sight, those that had remained on deck were driven down narrow iron stairs where they were instructed to present their tickets to an officer. The last Josef or Ondrej were to see of Hamburg, before the heavy fog rolled in, was the complex of shipyards and repair facilities in Steinwerder.

Almost five hours later, just as it was growing dark, the river pilot shook hands with the captain and returned the bridge to him. A small tug had eased up against the giant hull, and climbing down a ladder from the lowest deck, the pilot eased himself down onto the slippery deck of the smaller vessel.

As the tug steamed away in the night, *Graf Waldersee* passed the winking lights of Cuxhaven to port, and then set out upon the gray, uninviting swell of the North Sea.

Ondrej and Josef went below to find their parents and many of the others terribly ill from seasickness. Annoyed, the steward was bustling about, cursing under his breath as he reassured all those who were sick that the affliction would pass. Unable to help, and becoming ill themselves from the stink of vomit, the brothers again made their way topside.

"Do you know what you will do in America, Josef?" Ondrej asked as they stood at the rail. He tasted salt spray on his lips and shivered a bit as the night grew damp and chill.

"Find work," Josef said confidently. "Some sort of work." He lit a cigarette and flicked the wooden match over the rail. The hiss of the sea could be heard against the hull as Josef inhaled the sweet smoke and let it out again.

He'd been assured there were all kinds of jobs in America. If a man were willing and able to work, he or anyone else might find a job paying well enough to support a family.

"One thing is for certain," Josef told his brother. "I will never again feed another goddamned chicken, or shovel goat shit from a pen. Whatever I do in America, it will be city work."

Ondrej laughed and ran a hand through his hair. "We are city mouse and country mouse, I think. For my part, I will borrow from Uncle Matek to buy a farm—my own farm."

"Where—a farm?" Josef asked.

Ondrej just shrugged. "In the state of Wisconsin perhaps, or in Minnesota. I heard men on the docks speaking of North Dakota." He gripped the rail with his big hands and leaned backward. "Who can know? Wherever the soil is good and the land is cheap."

"Then you'd best get married quickly," Josef suggested. "And fill up your house with brats to help you with the work—because I'll not be there to do it."

Both began to laugh then, grasping each other by the shoulders and first shaking, then embracing one another, totally absorbed by the heady realization that they were young and healthy, strong and free—and reaching toward the promise of America.

Three days later, Janicka and Valentyn still kept to their beds, but could at least take food and keep it down. Because of the close quarters and utter lack of privacy, the family resigned themselves to the fact that the pleasure of giving one's self a good washing or changing one's underwear would most probably be denied them throughout the voyage.

"You'll have to get by with the steerage food," remarked the steward when he saw Janicka feeling better one night at supper. He was ladling watery pea soup out of a huge pail, yet even with her seasickness vanishing, she couldn't manage a full bowl of it.

The food in itself was plentiful enough, she thought, although oddly taste-less, being cooked by steam. The overworked steward was constantly plagued by passenger complaints. Most of them had little better on land, and after so many trips across he had come to suspect that the overwhelming grumbling against the steerage food could be easily explained by the fact that most steerage passengers confined below and crowded so closely together simply lost their appetites at sea, and would experience an aversion for even first-class fare.

Sipping his soup, Valentyn glanced at his sons with an impish grin. "You two boneheads might have been smarter to go into the army," he said. "The food would surely have been better."

That night, Janicka was awakened by the loud complaint of a Polish woman across the narrow aisle. This woman surpassed her Slovak neighbor in dirty appearance, and Josef suspected her to be possibly harboring vermin.

"The stupid bitch is wetting her bed," the Polish woman was screaming. "She's pissing down on me."

The cause of the sudden outburst was a bottle of wine brought aboard by the Slovak woman sleeping above her. The wine bottle had been carelessly corked and was now slowly dripping down into the bed below.

The Slovak's efforts to explain matters and offer excuses were in vain, for the Polish woman was furious. The other occupants, annoyed at being awoken, split evenly on the sides of both women—quickly turning into two hostile camps, with a brief flurry of invectives and cutting sarcasm. Order was finally restored with the intervention of the annoyed steward, who was on watch all night.

The *Graf Waldersee's* captain was Jürgen Schroeder, a thirty-year veteran of the long run between Hamburg and New York—first under sail and later steam. Schroeder was a cautious man who kept a good eye for weather—fully understanding that in any two-week period, one could expect bad storms.

On every ship venturing forth on the North Atlantic there was a special load-line mark painted on the hull. It was the lowest and most cautious of all load lines, and it was identified simply as "WNA"—Winter North Atlantic. This was the line beyond which a vessel must never be loaded in that season, on that ocean.

The Pacific, with its shrieking typhoons, produced greater waves and much higher winds, while the Indian Ocean, cursed by implacable monsoons, played host to more sustained storms, and the southern seas around Africa and South America could be harsh beyond reason. Yet Captain Schroeder knew, from experience, that for sheer unremitting menace, with every horror known to the sea—from fog, ice, and the interacting furies of wind, wave and current, the

North Atlantic had earned its reputation as the most dangerous body of water in the world.

Early the next day, the skies grew dark, and the seas began to roll. Janicka and Valentyn seemed to have gotten their sea legs, but all around them, groans and sighs indicated that many of the others were faring poorly. The air was close and foul, as the sea smashed against the groaning hull and cold water splashed in at many of the portholes, soaking beds and robbing the occupants of the last hope of comfort. The rush of frigid seawater caused the ventilators to be closed, adding to the stink and distress.

Already dressed, the Novaks quit their berths and groped their way above decks and into fresh air. The decks were streaming with water, the storm-tossed sea stretching to the horizon, and the dull sky above seemed all steeped in a sickly gray, while a few seagulls holding in the wind, screeched and fluttered over the ship.

As the *Graf Waldersee* pitched and rolled, an officer wearing sealskins made his way toward them and smiled. *"Gewöhnen sie sich daran,"* the fellow said in German. "You must get used to it—this is a large front and the bad weather will be with us for awhile."

The next three days were days of misery. The newly acquired sea legs of Janicka and Valentyn crumbled once more against the onslaught of the storm. Even Ondrej and Josef became ill, unable to take food or hold it down.

The sea beat on the decks, drenching everyone to the skin. The slanting rain fell in torrents and the ship's violent beating made life unbearable. Those emigrants who sought fresh air on deck stood for days in wet shoes and stockings that failed to dry overnight and had to be donned wet and cold each morning.

Their clothing was damp and ill smelling from being worn wet to bed. Chilled, many of them racked with fever, they could find only poor rest on their hard mattresses and short beds.

With the noise of so many congregated in so small a space and the odor of people who have not changed their garments for days, without a breath of air in the tightly closed space, Janicka's misery was made only worse by seeing the plight of the smaller children aboard. During the stormy weather they silently crept away from sight, pale and deathly sick. No play or encouragement from their parents could brighten them—they could eat nothing, and lay about wherever they could—filthy, soaked, and softly crying.

After three full days, the terrible storm came to an end and the dreadful seas and gray skies were followed by calm and sunshine. Some passengers emerged in holiday attire, while the little children began to play again, and the portholes were reopened.

Appetites also increased, and it became a serious question as to how individuals and groups could bribe, coax and induce the stewards to bring them better rations. Those steerage passengers with the needed bribe money had better food smuggled to them. It was termed "cabin food," but was only the same meal served to the ship's lower officials.

Selling of food by members of the crew was prohibited, but as the pastry cook also wished to make money, those with the means to pay were well provided with cakes and biscuits.

To Janicka's continuing surprise, once he'd made up his mind, Valentyn seemed to have entered this adventure with no thought of complaint. He merely laughed at things that irked the rest of them, often making a joke of their situation.

The thing that proved most interesting to Valentyn was the study of his fellow passengers. The Austrians and Germans kept an air of superiority, even though they too, were traveling in steerage. The few Dutch aboard rarely laughed or joked, preferring to keep their dour demeanor to themselves. There were some Poles in gray suits of peculiar cut, with baggy pants and high-heeled boots, as well as a small group of Hungarian gypsies with dark, dusky skins and large slouched hats, looking for all the world like brigands and highwaymen.

Also staying to themselves were small groups of Polish Jews dressed entirely in rags. Some were old women with hooked noses and witch-like faces, while many others were younger women and beautiful large-eyed children. Valentyn thought the Jews to be an amusing bunch; they lay around on deck, stretched at full length, huddled against each other under heavy, wool blankets—jabbering, quarreling, and eating raw onions and smoked fish—all the while arguing over questions of money.

The good weather also brought another pleasure. The captain thoughtfully ordered a hand organ to be played; yet even though an energetic little sailor ground away at it for hours, dancing among the emigrants remained half-hearted.

The fair weather held, and going into a second week at sea, all interests became centered on the end of the voyage, while one calm morning, the final leg of the journey introduced Josef Novak to the most beautiful young woman he'd ever seen.

CHAPTER 7

Josef spent a restless night. Stiff from the cold, he crawled out of his berth early, taking care not to wake the others, and took coffee from the morning steward who informed him that they were three days out of New York.

"It's almost done with," the steward said. "Another few days and we'll sight Sandy Hook Light in New Jersey."

"*Gerade rechtzeitis,*" Josef answered in German, which had, over centuries, become a second language in Czechoslovakia. "Not a moment too soon. I am sick of this ship."

"You have relatives in America?" the morning steward asked, attempting to be friendly.

"An uncle," Josef grunted. "In Chicago, where we will go."

"*Ah gut, das ist gut,*" the steward said. "I have not seen that city myself, but others have said it is a fine place."

Putting on his cap and winter coat, Josef made his way up the narrow ladder to the main deck. Bracing himself against the chill bite of the air, he leaned over the deck rail and lit a cigarette, then began to sip from the steaming metal cup. Drawing smoke into his lungs, he turned and watched a beautiful dawn break over the stern of the *Graf Waldersee.*

"Pardon me," a voice behind him said. "Do you perhaps speak Czech?"

"*Ovšem,*" Josef said, turning about to face a young woman in an oversized heavy wool coat, her lovely face framed by a shawl. "Yes, of course. We are from Třeboň."

He'd seen her before—on deck in the early morning, but had never clearly seen her face. Now, her beauty stunned him.

"Ah," the girl smiled. "And who are *we?*"

"Why, my parents and my older brother," Josef answered with some hesitation. He'd never in his life seen a girl quite so beautiful as this one. "We are traveling to America."

"I see," the girl said, smiling and offering her hand. "My name is Lia Stepanek—from Tábor."

"And I am Josef—Josef Novak." He took her hand in his and was surprised at the firmness of her handshake.

"I saw you on the docks at Hamburg," Lia told him. "You had a look of nervousness about you—and I thought there is someone here as frightened as I am."

"No, not frightened," Josef said quickly. "Just confused by all the goings-on. It was my idea to emigrate."

"Yes, leaving Tábor was my choice as well."

"Are you with your family?" Josef asked, pausing a moment before pressing on. "A husband, perhaps?"

Lia laughed—a light sound. "No, I'm unmarried, and traveling alone. My father died when I was little, and my mother just a year ago. I am going to Chicago, where my aunt—my mother's sister—has offered to sponsor me."

"We too, are going to Chicago," Josef said excitedly. "So you and I can no longer remain strangers."

To that, she said nothing, but nodded toward the stern. "What a beautiful sunrise."

"Beautiful, perhaps—but it hardly rivals your own."

"*Ah,* those girls in Třeboň must already miss you terribly," Lia said with a smile and an amused shake of her head. "Josef Novak, you are a man with sugar on his tongue."

As the sun rose higher and the air warmed a bit, Josef and Lia strolled along the open main deck. There were few people awake in steerage at this hour, and aside from a few working seamen and busy stewards, they had this part of the ship to themselves.

Even though the *Graf Waldersee* was not considered a luxury ship, the smaller, tightly restricted smaller decks above, where first and second-class passengers dwelled, were a world unknown to the steerage passengers—and strictly prohibited as well.

"In steerage, we are males and females," Lia observed wryly, as she and Josef made their way along the rail. "But up above, they are all called ladies and gentlemen."

Above, they'd been told, were spacious suites and comfortable staterooms for those passengers with means to afford them. Life in first and second class offered a dance floor and orchestra, smoking parlor and lounges, drawing rooms, small library, deck chairs and entertainment, an elegant dining room featuring a varied choice of entrées, a cold buffet, and a vast selection of delicacies.

"What will you do in Chicago?" Josef asked. With no husband to support her, he knew she'd have to find some type of work.

"Clean people's homes, I expect," Lia answered. "My aunt has assured me that there are many wealthy families there—the type of people who don't care to do their own housework."

"You'll be a servant, then?" Josef asked.

Lia nodded and shrugged. "Yes, I suppose so—at least until I have a home of my own to care for."

"And when will that be?"

She laughed lightly. "Why, when I manage to snag a husband, of course."

Josef laughed as well. He liked this girl very much. She was smart, honest and she spoke her mind. He was flirting with her and she knew it, yet she didn't blush or let it fluster her as did so many of the young girls he'd known in Třeboň.

Hunching over to light a cigarette against the morning breeze, Josef turned serious as he straightened up again and looked at her. "I did not mean to offend you, Lia, when I suggested we might see each other again—in Chicago."

Lia sensed the change in him and understood instinctively that their pleasant little game was ended. She moved closer against him as he leaned on the ship's rail, touching his hand with hers. "I took no offense, Josef Novak," she said quietly, smiling. "I am pleased to think that I will have a friend in America."

Except for the worsening weather, which had turned gray and blustery, the next two days at sea were uneventful.

Rising before anyone else, Josef and Lia had agreed to meet on deck early each morning. They strolled the main deck together, laughing and chattering all the while, happy to pour out their hopes and dreams to one another. They spoke of little else, but they could make no firm plans, for neither knew for certain what would await them in America.

"I don't yet know what I shall do in Chicago," Josef admitted. He had his coat collar turned up against the chill and sipped coffee from a metal cup. "But I am healthy and strong, and I can work."

"My aunt has written that there are enough jobs for cooks and housekeepers," Lia said. "I hope she is right."

"Why would she say it if it wasn't true?" Josef questioned.

"What will your brother do?" Lia asked.

"Ondrej?" Josef laughed. "Ondrej is a farmer. He will not stay in the city. My brother has plans to own his own land—a farm."

"A farm? Where?"

Josef shrugged. "He's not certain. He's talked of Minnesota or North Dakota—where the land is cheap."

Then, as they walked the deck and talked on the morning of that third day, they began to see birds.

Only a few at first. Although neither Josef nor Lia could name them, they spotted a large albatross just as the sun began to break through the overcast. Then came small numbers of storm petrels, and finally far-ranging terns and gulls, screeching and wheeling off the ship's stern, drawn by the *Graf Waldersee's* night galley crew who'd been throwing the kitchen garbage overboard.

"Do you know what it means, Lia—those birds?"

She shook her head no.

"Land," he said excitedly, placing his hands on her shoulders and drawing her to him in a happy embrace. "It means land."

Their last day at sea turned fair, and late in the afternoon, as the big liner approached landfall, the Novaks, with Lia Stepanek at Josef's side, along with hundreds of other steerage passengers, gazed through a faint, thin haze to stare with both wonder and apprehension. As if by magic, all around them land could be seen at a distance—it was far off, but nevertheless, it was land.

"New York? *Ist dass Neu York?*" Josef called to the German steward, excitedly pointing towards landfall in the direction the ship was headed.

"*Nein, nein,*" the steward answered, shaking his head. "That is only New Jersey—Sandy Hook Light. It will still be awhile before any of you see New York."

Twenty minutes more and Staten Island was off the port, with Brooklyn to starboard. Nearing Verrazano Narrows, they watched a number of small tugboats approach the *Graf Waldersee.* One of them carried their assigned harbor pilot, along with two other men.

Following the pilot, as the big liner slowed almost to a stop, the two other passengers aboard the tugboat clambered across a bobbing ladder and through an open hatchway in the ship's hull. Both were there to accept delivery of two huge, tightly wrapped bundles of German newspapers—*Die Werks Zeitung* and *Das Abendblatt*—to take back ashore for those recently arrived and still homesick German immigrants starved for news of the old country. In the German settlements of New York City, these two week-old papers would fetch ten times their normal selling price.

"Why on Earth would anyone who went through the trouble of leaving Europe care about what's happening back there?" Janicka asked when she learned of the enterprise. "I'd call it nothing but a waste of good money."

Then she stepped away from the ship's rail and moved back a little, motioning Ondrej to follow with a nod of her head. "Who is that girl your brother has become so friendly with?"

Ondrej looked toward Lia and shrugged. "Just a girl I suppose, Josef is always friendly with girls."

"He's said nothing about her?"

"No, not to me, Mother."

"*Humphf,*" Janicka snorted. "Nor to us."

Underway again, with tugboats on either side, *Graf Waldersee* began a slow crawl through the narrows towards New York harbor. Less than an hour later, a strange hush fell over the crowded deck of emigrants, followed by an almost collective gasp. People rushed to the port rail, crowding against those already there—then they began to cheer and shout, fingers pointing, grownups laughing and weeping as the children watched, not quite understanding why.

All of them saw it at last—the Statue of Liberty—appearing out of the mists off Jersey City, proof that their long voyage was ended, that the dream had become a reality.

In awe, Janicka Novak studied the statue's classic face—its flaming torch representing liberty, with flowing robes, and spiked crown whose seven rays symbolized the seven seas and continents—and she, too, began to weep.

"Almost all my life," she choked, wiping away tears and a bit embarrassed to be crying. "I've dreamt of this day."

"Then why be so sad?" Valentyn asked. "It should be a happy time for you."

"Oh, I am happy, you old fool," Janicka laughed, shocking her husband by throwing her arms around his neck and kissing him on the lips as ardently as she ever had when they'd both been young. "Thank you, husband, for letting us come," she whispered.

"What choice did I have?" Valentyn said with a shrug. "Had I said no, I'd have been a poor bachelor again, pestered and sought after by every old maid and widow in Třebóň."

They both laughed again, and turned back toward the statue as it passed to port, their arms around each other's waist.

"And now comes the most difficult part of your journey," the steward whispered to Josef and Lia. "You've reached the United States, but you must now knock on the door and hope that they let you in."

"Why wouldn't they?" Josef asked. "We're all healthy."

The steward shook his head and sighed. "*Sind sie verheiratet, Fräulein?*" he asked Lia.

"No," she said. "Not married."

He shrugged and looked at Josef. "She is unmarried and alone. The authorities may not let her onto the streets of New York City as a single woman without a family member to escort her."

Lia's hand came up to her mouth. "Oh, my God."

"No," Josef said, taking her by the shoulders. "You must not be frightened. We will figure out a way."

The steward pointed past the copper-clad Statue of Liberty to a looming, red brick building beyond it. The imposing structure was huge; three gracefully arched windows overlooked its entrance and four tall, spired towers reached up at each corner. It stood on another small bit of land at the mouth of the Hudson River.

"*Dass ist Ellis Insel*," the steward said. "That is Ellis Island—the United States Immigration Station—and it is there, my young friends, that America will decide if it wants you or not."

CHAPTER 8

❁

United States Immigration Inspector, Artemus Bunt, had earned his livelihood helping poor emigrants arrive in America since before the station at Ellis Island had even been built. His rheumatism had bothered him earlier in the day and he wondered how many more years he'd be able to do this job—the only one he'd ever had.

They'd brought them in first through Castle Garden, Artemus recalled, back in the old days when he'd still been a young man—himself newly arrived in New York from a farm in Ohio.

That morning, feeling the pain in his back and knees, Artemus had approached the Battery Park Barge Station to board the Ellis Island ferry. Throngs of people, most of them friends and relatives of emigrants detained on the island, or scheduled to arrive on the ships today, had pushed and jostled each other to board.

By late afternoon, the *Calabria* from Naples, the *Cymric* from Queenstown, the *Ivernia* from Liverpool, and the *Rotterdam* from Le Havre had been unloaded and their passengers processed. Only the *Graf Waldersee* remained out in the harbor—her steerage filled with anxious, frightened emigrants waiting their turn to enter the United States.

It had been a long day, Artemus thought, and it would still not be ended for a while—another night he'd miss supper at home.

Late in the afternoon, as the *Graf Waldersee* lay at anchor in the harbor's deep silt, the Novaks watched immigration officials clamber aboard. They had come from the Quarantine Station at the river's mouth. The bursar turned over the manifests, documents providing detailed information on the emigrants that filled the big ships on their return passages from cargo deliveries abroad. The manifests would be turned over to the Ellis Island inspectors, who would then confirm their accuracy.

On that morning, as they did every morning, the United States immigration officials that came aboard conducted examinations of first and second-class cabin passengers on board ship. Cabin-class citizens and eligible aliens in these two groups were then taken to the pier, free to leave after passing through customs.

Lia and the Novaks, however, were instructed how to make their customs declarations, then put aboard barges for Ellis Island. Three barges, filled shoulder to shoulder with loads of weary men, women, and children who'd just endured two weeks at sea in dirty, cramped quarters with no privacy, bad food, and no place to bathe, took them across the final stretch of water to the Ellis Island slip.

They would be the last emigrants of the day to go through the series of examinations required for admission into the new country.

As Josef watched with some amusement, immigration officers tagged each passenger—assigning them numbers and letters from their manifest positions. Over the years, it had proven itself a simple, efficient method of checking them through the inspection process.

"Will we have to wear tags to live in America?" Lia wondered out loud. She was becoming frightened as they slowly gathered on the pier. Frightened first that the authorities might deny her entry, and second, that she might somehow be separated from Josef. She clung tightly to his sleeve.

"Don't be silly," Josef told her. "It is just what they do to keep everyone in order."

Aboard the crowded barge, he'd finally introduced Lia to the rest of his family, describing her as a new friend who was traveling alone from Tábor to meet her aunt in Chicago.

Lia smiled and shook hands with all of them. Valentyn and Ondrej took her hand and pumped it enthusiastically, but Janicka remained stiff and reserved.

"It's odd, is it not?" Janicka commented. "For a young woman to be traveling across the ocean alone?"

"Perhaps," Lia said nervously. "But I had no other relatives or friends to accompany me."

"Except for Josef?"

"Yes, *Pani* Novak, except for Josef. He has been very kind."

Then Josef stepped forward and looked at his mother. "Lia has been told that she may not be allowed to enter America unless she is accompanied by a husband or a family member."

Janicka shook her head. "So? What does that matter to me?"

"I am going to say that Lia is my cousin," Josef told her.

"Then the two of you must stay separate from the rest of us," his mother demanded. "If you are caught in such a lie, the officials may send the both of you back."

"We will take that chance," was all Josef said.

The weather was unusually warm for April. Crowded together under the entrance to the main building, the emigrants milled about under a large canopy—protected from the sun.

Janicka glanced around and saw that even in the heat, many of them were dressed in everything they owned—sweating in layers of coats, jackets, and petticoats—trying to minimize the amount they had to carry. One man, out of breath and soaked with sweat, carried a goose feather mattress on his head, while an Italian with a long, flowing mustache clutched bundles of grapevine cuttings to transplant in America. Still others carried tools, cooking utensils and family heirlooms.

As Artemus Bunt entered the building earlier that day, he was greeted by the odor of disinfectant, turpentine and kerosene. The cleaning women and porters had already finished the first of their frequent, daily scrubbings of floors, benches and spittoons, beds, walls and showers. It was almost as if the emigrants represented some loathsome form of life, dangerous to other people. But they had reason to be cautious—emigrants indeed often carried germs and vermin from their time in steerage. Many were afflicted with lice, and lice carried typhus. American public health officials knew that the thoroughness and frequency of the sanitation protocols guarded against a major epidemic of typhus and other diseases.

Climbing the stairs to the second floor, Artemus grimaced at the pain of the arthritis in his back and legs. At the top of the stairs he'd greeted the waiting medical inspection teams and entered the registry room—often referred to as the Great Hall.

All throughout the day, the waiting ships in the harbor would disembark their steerage passengers. Artemus and the others were braced for the task, for soon the Great Hall would fill with people. Two thousand or more each day, the statistics said—emigrants of all ages, the majority between the ages of eighteen and thirty.

Then the growing noise would begin—a babble of shouts and curses, pleas and questions, crying infants and disparate languages that would soon echo up to the fifty-six foot ceilings.

And soon there was the smell—of steerage passengers unable to bathe for days, the odor of sausages, bread, and cheese, mingled with the ever-present stink of disinfectant.

"Move along now!" a gatekeeper shouted, attempting to direct each newcomer to the inspection line that had been assigned for his or her ship's manifest. A heavyset porter holding a broom trailed behind the gatekeeper, sweeping the pavement behind the confused emigrants as they shuffled along.

Soon, representatives of different religious denominations and charity organizations made their way through the growing crowds. Were there Jews, Lutherans, or Catholics seeking assistance, they asked, perhaps a Bible to take with them when they left?

Interpreters worked the long lines of people, assisting both inspectors and emigrants. Social workers representing Italian and Jewish welfare societies often stood by the inspectors, waiting to accompany unescorted women to the second floor dormitory area or the dreaded detention room. Busy clerks were positioned near each inspector. They entered information as tallymen kept track of the numbers—and so the lines slowly passed.

Artemus Bunt and many of his fellow immigration officials often appeared outwardly gruff, but that demeanor was foreign to his nature, and now and again he found himself smiling at some minor human incident or patting a small child on the head—always careful to wash his hands afterward.

Those unfortunates who were detained had to remain behind, housed in dormitories on the third and second floors, rooms packed tight with rows of iron beds. Most would remain only a day or two, until ticket money, a sponsor or a relative arrived.

Sick detainees were quickly sent to the general hospital or the contagious disease wards that had been established on the island. Other detainees waited to appeal their various cases to the Special Boards of Inquiry in operation daily. If their appeals were rejected, they were forced to wait at the expense of the steamship company until deportation could be arranged.

The United States Immigration Authority employed Artemus Bunt as an inspector. Years earlier, the Immigration Authority had sent him to school to learn German, Polish and Czech. Aside from his normal duties of interpreter for these people, he was called upon to use his language knowledge to act as interpreter for any special Boards of Inquiry set up to consider the cases of those emigrants detained by medical and legal problems. That morning, after eating a donut and drinking a hurried cup of coffee, Artemus took his place beneath a huge American flag at one of fourteen "line inspector" desks set up on a platform against the west wall of the registry room.

Lia and the Novaks checked most of their heaviest baggage in the first-floor baggage room and prepared to mount the stairs to the Great Hall. Back in Hamburg, questions had already been put to them concerning their health and personal status, and now they'd be subject to another medical and legal examination.

As the weary emigrants made their slow way up the stairs a Public Health physician observed them in what Artemus Bunt and other Ellis Island officials referred to as the *six-second exam.*

The doctor was looking for telltale signs of diseases that were automatic grounds for deportation or short-term detention at the island's contagious disease hospital. Next, the newcomers lined up in front of a man using a buttonhook to turn eyelids up, intent on finding trachoma or other contagious eye diseases that might be immediate grounds for refusal of entry.

The physicians placed chalk marks on many emigrants, a sign to report to the medical examination rooms for further scrutiny: an E for eye problems, an H for heart, L for lameness, SC for scalp, and X for mental disease.

Almost two hours after they'd entered the building, one of the medical examiners, after studying the manifest and noticing his slight limp, placed an L on Valentyn Novak, and Artemus Bunt was called over to give his assistance.

"This one's a *bohunk*," the examiner said. "Novak."

Nodding, Artemus glanced briefly at the manifest, then spoke in poor but understandable Czech. Smiling, he placed his hand on Valentyn's shoulder. "Well, what's the trouble, old fellow? You don't walk so good?"

"Who the hell are you?" Valentyn growled, shaking off Bunt's hand as Janicka moved quickly to step in.

"This is my husband, your honor," she told Artemus. "He has a foul temper, I'm afraid, but he means no insult."

"Is he crippled? Can he work?" They were the same questions she'd been asked by the examiner in Hamburg.

"Yes, yes, he has farmed all his life."

Artemus looked at the entire family. "Are all of you together?"

Josef and Lia were standing together, a little apart from the rest of them. "Yes," Janicka suddenly lied. "The two young men are my sons and that girl is—my niece."

When the official said nothing to challenge it, Josef sighed and squeezed Lia's hand. He would never be able to thank his mother enough.

Artemus grunted and held up a picture of a broom. "Tell me, missus," he inquired of Janicka. "Would you use this to sweep the stairs from the top down or the bottom up?"

A stupid question, Janicka thought, suddenly allowing her own temper to almost get the best of her. "From the top down of course, but I did not come to America to sweep stairs."

Artemus laughed and nodded his head. This woman had pluck, he thought. In fact, the whole family appeared healthy enough. "I'd pass Mr. Novak," Artemus told the examiner. "And when you've looked over the rest, assign their manifest to my line."

Once the Novaks finished their medical examinations, Josef insisted on staying near Lia until hers, too, was complete. It was only then that the two joined the rest of the family in line.

"*Pani* Novak," Lia whispered. "I don't know how to thank—"

"*Tichý,*" Janicka said. "I am not the witch I often seem."

Josef kissed his mother on the cheek, and noticed she had tears in her eyes. He wondered briefly if he'd ever understand her.

Now they stood and slowly shuffled through fenced off aisles, waiting to appear before Artemus Bunt once more. When they finally reached his station, Ondrej was the first to be questioned.

"What is your name?" Bunt asked, in the best Czech he could muster—good enough to be understood.

"Ondrej Novak, sir."

"Have you ever been hospitalized for insanity?"

"No sir."

"Have you ever been imprisoned?"

"Never," Ondrej answered, thinking back to the boar he'd poached that Christmas. That would have landed both he and Josef in the *vězení* had not the gamekeeper suggested a bribe.

"Are you an anarchist?" Artemus Bunt went on.

"Oh, no."

"A polygamist?"

"What is that, sir?"

"Do you have more than one wife?"

"No, I am a bachelor—no wife at all."

"Who paid your fare?"

"My mother, sir."

"Where are you going?"

"To Chicago, to meet our Uncle Matek—"

On it went. Each passenger's name was followed by his or her response to the identical twenty-nine questions.

When Artemus was questioning Janicka and asked her about prison and anarchy, she proudly drew forth the letters of character given them by both Jakub Schwarzenberk and Father Honzik, their priest in Třeboň. "We are good respectable people, your honor, and we will be good Americans, I can assure you."

Checking his pocket watch to see how late he'd be for supper, Artemus Bunt questioned Lia last. After finally nodding approval, he stamped the manifest, and gave her one more tag to hang from a button on her blouse. She excitedly passed through his station and found Josef, sporting his own set of tags, waiting anxiously for her on the stairs. They were almost euphoric, giddy with happiness—they had passed the final barrier and now considered themselves nothing less than Americans. Laughing and joking, they descended the stairs two at a time, looking to find the rest of the Novaks at the railroad ticket office.

Together again, the five of them approached a dour little man behind the screened ticket window.

"Deutsch? Slovak? Czech?" the ticket seller asked, looking at them over his spectacles.

"We are Czechs," Janicka said. "Bohemians."

"Bohemians, *eh? Kde jdete?* Where are you going?" He asked it as if he had the question memorized.

"To see my brother in Chicago, Illinois," Janicka answered.

"Five one-way tickets to Chicago," he said, taking the money she slid beneath the window. Lia stepped forward and added her own. The ticket seller counted out change in American dollars and pushed it back to them, along with the tickets and five tags with the word CHICAGO printed in large, bold type. "*Ukazovat k pestovat vúdce,*" he said, pointing at the tags. "Show to train conductor."

The ticket man's Czech was extremely poor. "Do you speak *Deutsch*, too?" Janicka asked him in German.

"Yes lady, much better than Czech."

"Good," Janicka said. "We will speak German. How many days is the train?"

"Two days and a half—maybe three."

"We must send wires to Chicago."

He pointed toward the small Western Union office. "You can send it out from there, missus. They speak German, too, and they will help you do it."

Janicka thanked him and took Lia's hand. They walked over to the small Western Union office and each gave the clerk an address, explaining the messages they wished to send. Both were similar. Another young fellow sat at the telegraph, read Janicka's message and translated it into English, tapping the key rapidly.

Matek Holub
1422 Cullerton St.
Chicago, Illinois

Brother—we will arrive by train in three days. Can you meet us? All is well.

Janicka

With the clerk's help, they gave him enough money for the wires, then joined Valentyn, Josef, and Ondrej in a search for their jumbled baggage. The railroad ferries were still shuttling back and forth, transporting the daily crowds from Ellis Island to the trains—each immigrant ticketed now, with the name and tag of the route that would take them to their destinations.

On the ferry over, they could relax a bit. Josef and Lia stood at the bow, arms about each other. They had finally made it through. For them and for the rest of the Novaks, the ordeal was ended, the long journey over, a new life about to begin.

The plain, nondescript barge office gate was their entrance to the trains and to the wonder of America, but it was also where the government would finally let them go. Once through the gate, they would have only themselves to depend on.

PART II

CITY ON A LAKE

CHAPTER 9

❀

To Janicka's delight, the Baltimore & Ohio steam train from New York to Chicago was faster and more spacious than the one they'd taken to Hamburg. A tall Negro porter, the first black man they'd ever seen, came through their coach every twenty minutes, with a tray of various snacks and sandwiches one could buy. He also took orders for both hot and cold drinks—coffee, iced tea, lemonade and beer.

"*Jak se vám říct pivo anglicky?*" Valentyn whispered to her as the porter appeared at the door. "How do you say *beer* in English?"

Janicka had bought a Czech-English dictionary before they'd left Třeboň. She quickly thumbed through it, finding the section on food and drink.

"*Pivo* is pronounced *beer,*" she told him.

"Beer." Valentyn repeated. "Like the German—*bier?*"

"Yes, do you want some?"

"I thought perhaps I might try an American beer," he said as he repeated the new word. "Can we afford it?"

"I suppose so," Janicka said. "But only one. If the boys want beer, too—you must share it with them."

As the porter neared their seats, Valentyn took a deep breath, held up a finger and asked: "Beer?"

"A beer?" the porter said. "Yessir—what'll it be, Budweiser, Pabst, or Schlitz—Milwaukee's finest, you know."

Valentyn suddenly felt a sense of panic, suspecting that he was expected to tell the man something more than merely *beer.* He was highly embarrassed listening to Janicka and the others chuckling at his predicament.

"*Já nemluvim anglicky—spravedlivý* beer," Valentyn blurted out in Czech. "I do not speak English—just beer."

The porter was used to such situations. He'd been working the coaches for twelve years. "I don' know that language," he grinned. "But I'll bring you a Schlitz beer, sir, it's our most popular."

Once the porter had written down the order and passed their seats, Janicka was still laughing. She poked Valentyn in the ribs and handed him the dictionary. "You'd better study this, old man," she told him. "Unless you want people in America to think you are a simple-minded fool."

Valentyn grunted, failing to find humor in the situation. Less than ten minutes passed before the porter returned with a tall glass and a cold bottle of Schlitz. Janicka gave the man money and after counting out change, he returned some to her.

"What is this?" Valentyn asked his wife in a whisper. "Beer in a bottle—and so cold? I have never tasted cold beer in a bottle."

"Well, drink it anyway," she said. "Perhaps it is the way they do things in America."

"Such a thing," he said, holding the bottle up and admiring the colorful label. All his life, Valentyn had enjoyed beer—heavy and flavorful pilsner beer, brewed in or near Plzeň, in west Bohemia, from the great, ancient breweries of Chodovar, Prazdroj, Karlovy Vary, and Domazlice. The Czech beer industry's fame dated as far back as the early Renaissance, and Czech hops were shipped up the Elbe River to the special Hamburg hops market as early as the 12th century. But never before had he drank it from a bottle.

Valentyn poured the pale amber brew into his glass and waited until the frothy head settled then eagerly tilted it up to his mouth. "*Pah!*" he exclaimed, grimacing with disgust after he'd swallowed a mouthful. "That German in Hamburg told me the truth—a glass of piss couldn't taste much worse than this."

"Husband, watch your foul language," Janicka scolded. "We are in America now, would you have people think us coarse?"

And they *were* in America.

The Baltimore & Ohio coach jerked from side to side, rattling through the marshlands of New Jersey, click-clacking across the rural landscape of western New York State, full of small towns and prosperous farms, rolling hills and soft, green meadows.

Even though it had grown dark, none of them could sleep. As the train slowed to approach each station, Janicka made it a point to watch for the names of the towns they were passing through. As the signs came into view and swept lazily past the window, she'd roll the odd names across her tongue, amused and delighted at their sound—Oswego, Elmira, Jamestown—they were American names, so strange and different from those she'd known in Europe.

The next morning, Janicka studied the phrasebook portion of the dictionary and learned to ask *what is that?* Whenever the black porter was in their coach, she would tug his white sleeve and pester him with the same question in broken English: *What is that?*

"Why, tha's a hay silo, ma'am."

"You lookin' at a John Deere cultivator—finest in the world."

"Yes ma'am, we passin' over the Allegheny River now."

And on it went as they traveled west—black night had taken them through New York and by morning, they were crossing the wide Allegheny River. Soon they were in Pennsylvania, passing through small towns named Harborcreek and Brookside. Although Josef and Lia were staring out their window with rapt attention, she had to shake Valentyn and Ondrej awake from their fitful sleep as the largest body of water any of them had ever seen, except for the Atlantic Ocean, gradually crept into view.

"Is it the ocean again?" Ondrej asked.

"Mister, what is that?" Janicka asked the porter, excitedly.

"Why, tha's Lake Erie, ma'am—leastwise it's the south shore of it."

They paralleled the great lake all day, passing through a small portion of Pennsylvania and on into Ohio, where all the countless small towns—Ashtabula, Unionville, Painesville—would bring the train to a stop for five or ten minutes. Soon the landscape began to change from faded red barns, white-painted farmhouses and rolling cropland to more crowded homes, stores, mills and factories that seemed to grow thicker as the train clacked west.

"*Cleve-land,*" the porter called out. "Next stop—Cleveland."

Their train was in the bustling Cleveland station for almost an hour. Although Janicka and Valentyn were concerned that the train might leave without them, Josef, Lia, and Ondrej left their seats and stepped out onto the platform to stretch legs and backs tired from sitting. Amazed, they watched and listened to those who were leaving the train in Cleveland. Many of the faces they remembered from the immigration lines on Ellis Island—some of them Poles, Jews, Germans and Ukranians, while others gathered their baggage and spoke to each other in Czech, Hungarian or Slovenian.

"But there are so many from so many countries," Ondrej said, shaking his head and marveling at it. "How can there be room for all of us in America?"

Josef laughed and slapped Ondrej on the back. "We have been traveling a night and a day, *bratr*, and still we are nowhere near our destination. This is a big country—it has room for everyone."

Their second night of restless sleep in the cramped seats of the coach brought them through Sandusky and Toledo—where Janicka slept through their stops.

Once past Toledo, the train whistled across the Maumee River, pushing west through the darkness toward Indiana.

As Josef awoke during the night, he found Lia staring out the window into the darkness. In the distance, they could occasionally see yellowish-orange lights flickering—farmers perhaps, drinking their early morning coffee by the light of oil lamps.

He reached over and gently touched her. When she turned to him, her eyes were red from weeping.

"What is wrong?" Josef asked. "That you cry?"

"I am frightened," Lia whispered, moving closer to him in the darkness of the coach, now filled with the sounds of snoring, and a sour smell of people needing to bathe.

"Frightened? Frightened of what?"

She sighed, shaking her head. "My new life in America. What if I cannot find work, Josef? Uncle Anton died a year ago. He was a laborer—a bricklayer. Aunt Emilka is a widow and not a wealthy woman."

"Lia, you will find work. She has promised you."

"Have you no such fears?" Lia asked him.

He thought for a moment and shrugged. "I don't think so. I am young and strong, and not afraid to work. What country would not welcome such a new-comer?"

"A *greenhorn*, you mean," Lia sniffed, giggling a bit. He and his confidence had already made her feel better.

"Greenhorn? I do not know that word."

"It is what they will call us, Josef," she told him. "My aunt has told me in her letters. Greenhorns, and bohunks, and DPs—none of them are good names."

"Who says such things?"

"The Americans," she explained. "Not all of them are friendly to those like us, who've come from the old country. Many wish we would stay home and not come here at all."

It was the first time Josef had ever heard such a thing. He said nothing, but sat staring into the darkness and thinking about what Lia had told him. Could it be true? He wondered. Why wouldn't a country the size of America want new people to live in it? People who would work hard in the mills and factories and ask for nothing more than the chance to earn a fair wage. Perhaps the aunt is a lazy woman, Josef told himself, and that is why the Americans call her bad names. In any case, he decided, he would never allow Lia to be called such things.

As the morning sun rose behind them, the porter came through and attempted to tell his passengers that the train had crossed the state line and was now passing through Indiana. Most had no idea of what he was saying.

Ondrej rubbed a stiff neck and stared out the window, noting that the land, hilly and rolling the day before, had turned as flat as a *bramborové lívanse*—one of his mother's potato pancakes—and that as far as his eye could see, the neat fields were already plowed and carefully furrowed.

A man could have a wonderful farm on such land, Ondrej told himself. If the land in Minnesota or North Dakota were similar to this, and cheap enough to buy, he felt sure that someday, with hard work and a bit of luck, he would prosper.

Just as she'd been doing for most of the trip, Janicka spent the morning studying her dictionary and phrasebook. Although they were heavily accented when she spoke them, she was beginning to more easily memorize English words and phrases. When she grew weary, she'd pass the book to Valentyn, who was having difficulty with it. Speaking Czech *and* German, he maintained, was enough for any man in one lifetime—and the need to learn English at his age was a bit more than he'd bargained for.

"Your brother wrote that Czech is spoken where he lives," he said. "Everyone speaks it, Matek says—there are even newspapers in Czech. So why must I learn to speak English?"

"Do you plan to spend the rest of your life sitting in the house with my brother? Reading newspapers and speaking only Czech?" She shook a finger at him. "No, *manžel*, the language of America is English—no matter what Matek says."

Grumbling, Valentyn took up the phrasebook once more. With Janicka's stubborn help, he managed to learn a few words and even to memorize four or five phrases by the time the porter came into the coach to announce they were nearing South Bend.

Less than an hour after chuffing out of the South Bend station, they began to once again see the shoreline of the enormous blue lake. Janicka had memorized its name the first time they'd seen it, and now she quickly called the porter over—pointing toward it and stating very proudly: "Lake Erie."

"No ma'am, 'fraid not," the porter said, grinning. "We passed Lake Erie a long time back—that one's Lake Michigan."

"Lake—*Michigan?*"

"Yes'm, the south tip of it. It's a big one, too."

Along with everyone else in the rocking coach, she peered out the window, awed at the size and number of these huge American lakes. There was nothing like them to be seen anywhere in Europe, she marveled, certainly none that she'd ever heard of. Even Jakub Schwarzenberk, as wealthy as he was, could merely boast of a few small carp ponds.

Nearing the shores of Lake Michigan, they could make out the dark shapes of steamships far out on the water. Traveling further west, they began to glimpse long, sandy beaches through a thick forest of trees—oak and elm, maple, hickory and beech.

Now and then, the train would rattle across a narrow, dirt road and on one such crossing, Janicka saw a bearded farmer in a heavy wagon, the man's two dray horses sidestepping as they nervously waited for the train to pass.

Then the forest began to thin, changing into drab, increasingly crowded areas of small homes and factories. They couldn't see the lake anymore, and gradually, the blue of the Michigan sky turned a dismal gray. After not much longer, both Janicka and Lia felt their eyes burn and their skin begin to itch.

Although the porter had no idea of how well they understood, he offered them cotton handkerchiefs for their eyes. "It's the soot from all them steel mills," he offered. "The train comin' into Gary, now, ma'am. Why, ain't too much further an' we be in Chicago."

CHAPTER 10

Josef and Lia peered out the windows, in awe of the city they were slowly approaching. Railroad tracks had appeared everywhere, all converging toward a central point. Chicago was considered to be the railroad center of the nation. The jumble of tracks Josef and Lia were marveling at made possible convenient freight and passenger connections to every part of the country.

Josef shook his head. "I have never seen such a thing."

"Where do all the trains go?" Lia wondered aloud. Even in her home city of Tábor, even larger than Třeboň, there had been only the one morning railroad train passing through.

There were roads, too, reaching from Chicago to all points of the east and Midwest, but those roads and the vehicles using them were vastly inferior to rail and water transportation, little used by travelers going for more than a day's ride—fifteen miles or so by wagon—occasionally a bit farther by bicycle. The major traffic on the thoroughfares leading in and out of the city took place before dawn, local farm wagons from nearby rural areas bringing produce to market in the city.

As the train made its way around the bottom of the lake, they could see both steamships and a few wooden sailing vessels on the water. Most of the lake trade loaded or unloaded on the busy docks along the river, providing both freight and passenger connections to all the Great Lakes ports, and even to a few overseas, just as the Illinois and Michigan Canal provided access to the sprawling river basin of the Mississippi.

Janicka was pointing toward a small complex of factories that stood near the railroad tracks, when suddenly a man appeared in the aisle, standing next to their seat. *"Odpuštìní mne,"* he said in a polite, but slightly accented Czech. "You folks are Bohemians?"

"Yes," Janicka said. "We are the Novaks—from Třeboň."

"My name is Drago Kosek," the man said, handing Janicka his business card. "From *Ljubljana*—in Slovenia."

"We are pleased to meet you," Janicka said, studying the card. "I take it you are not an immigrant, Mr. Kosek—like us."

"Oh no," Kosek told her. "I arrived in Chicago from the old country more than twenty years ago, when the city was not so big as it is now. I'm returning from an important business meeting in New York City." When traveling, Drago Kosek preferred to ride the immigrant trains—often a rich source of new customers.

"I am a vice-president of the Czech-Slovak Protective Society, Mrs. Novak," Kosek went on. "We are a long established, not-for-profit organization, and quite reputable, I assure you—providing low-cost life insurance to Bohemian and Slovenian immigrants."

"Life insurance?" Janicka replied, shaking her head. "I am not sure I know what that is, Mr. Kosek. My husband and I are not city people. We were just farmers in Třeboň."

Kosek nodded and cleared his throat. "Yes, well, perhaps I can explain it to you, missus—"

Drago Kosek went on to tell her that if they were to take out a ten thousand dollar life insurance policy on Valentyn or each of their sons, at a nominal monthly cost—if any of them died while the policy was in effect, the family would receive a payment in the amount of insurance originally pur-chased—ten thousand dollars.

"Ten thousand dollars," Janicka said, even though she had no clear idea of such a sum. "So much money?"

"Yes, Mrs. Novak. How old is your husband?"

"He will soon be fifty-two."

"Is he healthy?"

"Like a horse," Janicka laughed.

Drago put on spectacles, reached deep into a leather briefcase and brought out a thick set of tables—proceeding to study them with great care. Finally, he grunted, nodded, and told Janicka what the monthly cost would amount to for such an insurance policy on Valentyn Novak.

Janicka let out a sigh and shook her head. "We are not wealthy people, Mr. Kosek. We sold everything but our clothing and were able to bring just enough money to get to America in some degree of comfort—and much of that was borrowed from my brother. My husband and sons still need to seek work in Chicago."

Kosek cleared his throat once more. "Yes, of course," he said, knowing it was always the same with the greenhorns—no jobs and little money—yet sooner or later he managed to sell most of them a policy. "But keep my card, missus. In addition to life insurance, we offer many other generous benefits to our Slovenian and Bohemian newcomers—most of them at no cost. Have your husband and the boys come see me before they look for work—perhaps I'll be able to help."

Even as Janicka thanked him, Kosek's eyes were searching the coach for more likely insurance prospects. He saw none. Most of the emigrants aboard the train had left in Cleveland, and the few that stayed on he'd already talked to—it seemed the Novaks would be his last prospects before reaching Chicago.

"You are very kind, Mr. Kosek," Janicka said. "Perhaps some day, when we have more money—"

"Be careful, missus," Drago Kosek told her as he settled into a seat and lit a fat cigar. He'd attended his meetings and worked the train. Now he was through with work for a while. He'd relax for the last few miles into the station. "Life is fleeting—often *someday* never comes."

"The city is so big," Lia said. "It seems to never end."

"Yes, miss," Kosek agreed. "And getting bigger every day." By nature, Kosek was a friendly, affable man. When not working, he liked nothing more than a good cigar and amiable conversation. In all the years he'd sold insurance, he'd found no better way to turn prospects into customers—eventually.

"Where will you folks be living?"

Janicka passed him the envelope with her brother's address on it, and Lia did the same.

"Ah, Pilsen," Drago said. "We will be neighbors."

"Pilsen?"

"Yes missus, an entire section of the city, populated by people like ourselves—Bohemians, Slovaks, Poles, and some Italians just to make things lively."

Kosek liked to talk, and in his accented Czech, he began to tell them about the city they were about to adopt as their own—even as the train crept ever closer into the heart of Chicago.

"Most folks walk," he said. "Especially in Pilsen, most people live close to work and shopping. If you've got further to go, there are always the streetcars—some pulled by horses and others by cable, even some that are electrified. They charge five cents a ride—each time you get on. There are the elevated cars, too—trains that ride high above the streets—also a nickel a ride."

"What about work, Mr. Kosek?" Josef asked.

"There's plenty of it, young fellow." Hoping to establish good relations with the immigrants, Drago's company was always busy helping newcomers find work—consequently he himself made it a point to know as much as he could about Chicago industry—and about work opportunities on the west side.

"This city makes a lot of things," he went on. "We're second only to New York in manufacturing."

"We barely saw anything of New York," Janicka said, but to her increasing surprise, Josef's mind lately seemed fixed on work.

"What kinds of things?" Josef asked.

"Chicago has over a quarter of a million people who work in manufacturing, my young friend," Drago said, leaning forward to emphasize his words. "Clothing mostly, along with rail cars such as this, farm equipment, furniture, carriages and bicycles—almost anything you can think of—including beef and pork."

"Chicago *makes* beef?" Janicka said, looking at Drago Kosek as if he were mad. She'd farmed all her life, and certainly knew where beef and pork came from.

He laughed. "We don't make it, missus—but we slaughter it and pack it, and ship it all over the country."

"You talked of shopping, Mr. Kosek," Lia said. "Where do we do our shopping?"

"All along 18th Street, young lady, and of course there are the Montgomery Ward and Sears, Roebuck catalogues—have you ever heard of them?"

Lia shook her head.

"Well, they sell merchandise through books," Drago Kosek explained. "Big, thick books where people can buy anything from hatpins to milk wagons."

"What about beer?" Valentyn grumbled. "Is there decent beer to be had?"

Familiar with Bohemians and their love of beer, Drago shook his head and laughed. "No, Mr. Novak—the beer here in America is nothing like in the old country. I'm afraid you may have enjoyed your last *real* beer before getting on that Hamburg ship."

CHAPTER 11

Except for the reception hall on Ellis Island, none of them had ever seen anything to rival the size of Chicago's Grand Central Station—from its great, cavernous steel arch looming above six sets of track and four wide passenger platforms, to the station itself—with its huge central waiting room full of polished wooden benches and frantic passengers rushing in every direction.

Soon after gathering their luggage and entering the station, Lia suddenly became frightened of being lost. Her eyes were opened wide as she clung tightly to Josef's arm. The family marveled at the relentless crowds rushing this way and that, jostling each other to make rail connections or to find a hack or an omnibus out on the equally crowded streets.

"Welcome to Chicago," Drago Kosek said, looking about the great, noisy room. "I'm certain it is nothing like Třeboň.

"We are going in the same direction," he added. "I would be pleased to accompany you to your destination."

Janicka thanked him. "We are to meet my brother here," she explained. "And Lia's *teta* is to meet her as well."

Kosek tipped his hat and lifted his suitcase. "Very well then, missus, the best of luck to you. You have my card—do not hesitate to call on me if I can be of help."

Once Drago Kosek was gone, Janicka had the men take seats on a bench, watching the luggage while she took Lia by the arm and began to search the crowded waiting room for both Matek and Lia's aunt. "Don't be so frightened," she told Lia. "This is not so bad as steerage aboard the ship."

Once, twice, three times they walked slowly through the huge waiting room. According to her latest letter, Lia's aunt would wear a single red rose in her hat—but so far, there was no sign of her.

"It has been many years since I saw *Teta* Emilka," Lia said. "I was just a little girl. I do not know if I will recognize her."

"You worry too much, child," Janicka told her. "That is what the red rose is for—just look for that."

Finally, they heard a woman's shout. "Lia, *múj neteř*—is that you?"

Janicka and Lia turned to see a short, rather stout woman who was dressed in a stylish skirt and jacket. She wore black, buttoned leather boots and a single red rose was pinned to her hat. Standing at her side was a tall, well-dressed gentleman smoking a cigar. The man's face was pockmarked, his complexion dark. He sported a thick, neatly trimmed mustache and he, too, wore expensive shoes and a fashionable suit.

"*Teta* Emilka?"

"Yes, of course, it's me."

Lia's aunt stepped up and hugged her briefly. "I am sorry we are late. The traffic on the streets is terrible." She backed away and slowly studied her niece—looking her over from head to foot, then introduced her companion: "This is—my friend. Mr. Levine, Sol Levine."

"Solomon Levine, my dear," the man said, shaking Lia's hand. "*Vítáme vás k Amerika.* Emilka has taught me a bit of Czech, you see."

"Thank you Mr. Levine." Lia was finally beginning to relax, relieved that her aunt had come. "Aunt Emilka, I would like you to meet Janicka Novak, from Třeboň. Her son and I are friends, and Mrs. Novak has been very kind."

"We expected Lia to arrive alone," Emilka Kovar said. "I hope she was no trouble, Mrs. Novak."

"Of course not," Janicka replied evenly. There was something about these two she didn't like—something she couldn't quite put a finger on. For being the widow of an immigrant bricklayer, Lia's aunt seemed unusually fashionable, and Sol Levine carried himself too smoothly. He was Jewish, and no Jew Janicka had ever known dressed in fancy suits and wore patent leather shoes.

"We better be going," Sol Levine said. Now he was looking at his watch and sounded impatient.

"Wait, please," Lia asked them. "I must get my bags and say goodbye to Josef." Excited, she hurried off through the crowd, in the direction of where the Novak men still sat, leaving Janicka to make conversation with Emilka Kovar and her companion, both of whom seemed increasingly ill-at-ease.

"I have never seen such fine clothing," Janicka said, looking at the couple. "It must be that everyone in America is wealthy."

"Mr. Levine does quite well," Lia's aunt said. "And he is very generous. He speaks German better than Czech."

"*Was machen sie beruflich, Herr* Levine?" Janicka asked, raising her voice above the noise in the vast waiting room. "What do you do?"

Sol Levine cleared his throat and glanced at Emilka. "I make a living as—I'm a businessman, missus."

As he helped her gather her things, Josef was relieved Lia had found her aunt, yet he felt gloomy as well—understanding that she was now in someone else's hands and they'd be parted for a time.

"I must know where to find you," he told her. "Once all of us are settled again."

Lia took out her aunt's letter. Separating it from the envelope, she gave the envelope to Josef. "This is Aunt Emilka's name and address—Emilka Kovar, at 1650 W. 18th Street. Call on me there."

They held each other closely for a moment and Josef felt tears, warm and moist, on Lia's cheek. He stepped back and wiped them from under her eyes. Even though she wept, Lia was smiling.

"You have become a good friend, Josef Novak."

"I hope it will be much more than that," he told her.

"And I as well," Lia whispered. Then she was out of his arms and gone—vanished into the crowd. With his heart pounding in his chest, Josef stared at the name and return address on the envelope she'd given him, then folded it carefully, and placed it in his coat pocket.

More than an hour later, Janicka found her brother—with his entire family in tow.

Matek looked older, his hair graying, but he still walked with the purposeful stride Janicka remembered. Her brother had come to meet them dressed in his best suit—it was nothing as fancy as Sol Levine's—but stylish and serviceable, nonetheless.

His wife, Anna—whom Janicka had never met—was a pretty woman, plump and smiling, with a sense of easy familiarity. She'd immigrated as a young girl from a small village in Bohemia named Chomutov, near the Polish border. Having lived in Chicago most of her life, Anna Holub spoke English almost as well as her two children—Eddie and Margie. Both were in their teens, healthy and smart. Young Margie Holub was fascinated at how hand-some both of her older cousins were—even though she considered Josef and Ondrej to be only Bohemian DPs, wearing poorly made shoes and ill-fitting clothing.

"*Vítám, milovaná sestra*—" Matek said, enveloping Janicka in a crushing bear hug. "Welcome, dear sister—welcome to Chicago. I am sorry we're late, the streetcar was slow."

"Thank you, Matek," Janicka said, first speaking English then slipping into Czech. "You must remember my husband, Valentyn, and our two sons, Ondrej and Josef."

"Yes, of course I remember," Matek replied, shaking hands all around. "And this is my Anna, and our two children—Edward and Margaret."

Everyone embraced, and when they were done, young Margie Holub declared: "No more Ondrej and Josef—from now on, I will call my cousins Andy and Joe."

Anna laughed and shook her head. "These children of ours are as American as President Roosevelt, I'm afraid."

"Just not so rich," Matek added. "You look wonderful, sister, but tired. How was the journey?"

"It seems as if we've been traveling for months," Janicka said. "The ship was terribly overcrowded and we all became seasick."

"Then things have not changed much since I came across," her brother laughed. "But you and your family are here now, and that's the most important thing—so we can go home."

Struggling with baggage, they boarded a horse-drawn trolley and proceeded west on Harrison Street, away from the station, first crossing the south branch of the Chicago River, then turning south onto Halsted Street, past both residential and commercial buildings—storefronts and shops, and row upon row of two and three-storied brick tenements.

Although the newly arrived Novaks couldn't yet read English, all of them stared out the open windows of the car with their eyes wide, marveling at the great city as it passed. To Janicka, at first, it looked to be one vast signboard. On each street, hardly a façade or surface existed that hadn't been used as a ground for conveying a message. Each building, from the poorest to the newest, seemed either a sign in itself, or a vehicle for signs. The buildings were all of varied size, and the taller ones presented blank brick surfaces on their sides, left for the most part windowless—in anticipation of yet taller structures that would someday flank them. In such a city these empty surfaces could not long be left devoid of purpose, so they were rented—let out as signboards, their messages painted directly on the brick.

If the building walls were busy, Chicago's streets were even busier. To the Novaks, accustomed to the quiet pace of business in Třeboň, it seemed all manner of commerce was being conducted along the busy length of Halsted Street. Street vendors plied either side, calling out their offerings: fried oysters were to be had, and catfish, too, freshly baked buns, hot spiced gingerbread, berries, and flavored ice cream, as well as cooked sausages, frankfurters, baked apples and boiled peanuts.

"The people along here are *sheenies*," Matek said. "They buy and sell most anything."

"Sheenies?" Valentyn asked. He'd never heard the word.

"*Židé*," Matek answered. "Jews—you'll see more of them here than you did in Europe."

Ondrej and Josef watched ragpickers maneuver through the crowds, using the long handles of their pushcarts to jangle rows of little bells that were strung upon them. Knife grinders blew horns to announce themselves. Young boys sold neckties, pocketbooks, and photographs of the city. Little girls sold matches, toothpicks, songsheets and flowers—and almost forty years after the American Civil War, the crippled veterans still living, along with those who were missing limbs, made a meager living selling shoestrings, as well as cheap books and periodicals.

Among block upon block of tenements Janicka saw itinerant umbrella menders, tinkers, whitewashers, washtub menders, hod carriers, glazers, pavers, and men with bandanas tied around their mouths and noses, men who carted heavy baskets into the street, dumping the contents into open horse-drawn wagons.

"*Bratr*," Janicka said, craning her neck to get a better look. "Those wagons—"

"Yes—filled with *výkal*—excrement," Matek stated matter-of-factly, not bothering to look himself. "Some of these places do not have toilets. They used to haul it away and throw it in the river, but people became sick with typhoid. Now the city is building a canal for it—the Drainage Canal—to be opened two years from now."

Josef was stunned that in a country like America, men would make their living doing such a thing. Once each week, either he or Ondrej had cleaned the family's outdoor privy off in back of their rented farmhouse, digging a hole and shoveling the accumulated mound of turds down into it. Such a thing was normal work for the younger members of a farm family, but for a grown man to earn a living gathering other people's shit was hard for Josef to imagine.

Suddenly, almost as if they'd crossed some invisible line, the signboards and window signs became familiar and readable. Here they were surprised to see: *Břízová Maso, Svěží řezat maso, klobása a sýr*—a Bohemian butcher and cheesemaker; *Pavlík Soukup, Pivo, Víno a Tabák*—a beer, wine and tobacco store; *Červenka Potravinářské zboží a svěží zelenina*—groceries and fresh vegetables; *Pekařství z Nemecka, Čerstvě péci dort a pečivo*—freshly baked cakes and pastries.

"Why, it is almost as if we were back in Třeboň," Janicka said, her eyes wide.

"Yes," Matek agreed. "We are nearing 18th Street. This is the quarter known as Pilsen—where Anna and I live, dear sister, and it will soon be your home as well."

CHAPTER 12

They transferred to another trolley going west on 18th Street and finally gathered their baggage and stepped off the streetcar when it reached Racine Avenue. With Matek in the lead, tipping his hat to others who passed them on the street, they walked west along the avenue, before turning west on the street named Cullerton.

Walking another half block, they finally stopped in front of a brown frame two-flat with white trim. Only the varying colors of trim kept every building on the block from being identical to every other. Along with trimmed hedges, there was a small, neatly kept plot of grass in front and a vegetable garden in the back yard.

"*Tuto je naš dům,*" Anna Holub said with a smile. "This is our home. This is where we live."

Janicka stared at her brother's house. Two stories high—it was huge compared to the poor little farmhouse she and Valentyn had left behind in Třeboň. Whatever could Matek be doing, Janicka wondered, to earn enough money to buy such a house?

"It is grand," she told Anna, astonished. "It is a palace."

Anna laughed. "No, no—not a palace, just a house like many others have. We live on the first floor and rent out the second floor to the Staneks. They are a young couple from Kralovice, quiet and hardworking. Marika Stanek is expecting a baby this autumn."

"But then you have no room for us," Janicka said, suddenly confused and fearful. From the start, all of this had been based on the assumption that Matek and Anna would take them in until they were settled and financially sound. But now—

"Of course we have room," Matek said quickly. "You will live in the basement. Cool in summer, warm in the winter. We have put some furniture down there for you—a sofa, table and chairs, and some beds."

"What about food and cooking?" Valentyn asked. "What are we to do about that?"

"You have enough money to buy groceries for a few weeks?" Anna asked.

"A few weeks," Janicka told her. "Not much more."

"Very well then," Anna said. "Tomorrow, you and I shall go out together, and I will help you do your shopping. By this time three weeks from now, the men will all have jobs and be earning more money."

"But the cooking—" Janicka began.

"Matek has built you a small kitchen," Anna told her. "He has worked on it at night all last month. You will be comfortable down there—and it is only for a while. Someday, you and Valentyn will have a house of your own."

The basement *was* adequate, Janicka thought, certainly more comfortable that any place they'd ever lived. Looking around, she decided that once she put lace curtains on the small windows and a few flowers in the kitchen, her brother's basement would be as fine a place as any to make their start in America.

With the promised help of the insurance man, Drago Kosek, Josef quickly found work at the Chicago, Burlington & Quincy Railroad yards. He was hired as a section hand, working with two Irishmen, two Polish immigrants, and another Bohemian—Milos Sykora from Kežmarok. All six of them were supervised by a tireless Russian section boss named Pavel Barshukov—who, it was rumored, had been forced to flee the Caucasus twenty years earlier after killing an officer in his Cossack unit in a quarrel over a woman.

Pavel Barshukov carried a small pistol in his coat pocket—a .38 caliber Smith & Wesson revolver that he'd won in a game of dice. Except for his father's old smoothbore, Josef wasn't used to seeing firearms. When he asked the section boss why he carried such a weapon, Barshukov only grunted and said: "Who knows? Maybe somebody looking for me some day."

The tools of Josef's trade were the hammer, pick, and shovel. The days were long and the work was hard. Barshukov's section crew was responsible for the length of track between the Chicago yards and west to Cicero Township. Each day, the gang roamed their section by handcar, replacing ties and rails, bolts and spikes, shifting ballast and cutting weeds.

At first, Ondrej made no attempt to find work. He wished to go west and buy his farmland, and was confused that his uncle had as yet made no offer to lend him the promised funds.

Finally, unable to be patient any longer, he approached Matek who was busy making repairs on the backyard shed.

"*Strýc* Matek, I am anxious to begin farming."

Matek stopped what he was doing, sat on a small stool and lit a cigar. "Ondrej," he said. "I don't know how you will be able to find farm work here in the city."

"No, no," Ondrej said. "I mean my own farm, in Minnesota or Wisconsin. Perhaps North Dakota."

"Ondrej, you cannot expect to have your own farm—be your own boss—just a month after coming here," Matek said.

"But uncle, mother said you would lend me the money."

"Yes, of course, and I will lend you *some* of it," Matek went on. "But you would do well to earn and save some of it yourself—while at the same time you learn all you can about America."

Ondrej shrugged his shoulders. "I know only farming. It is all I have ever done."

"There are good paying jobs for strong young men," Matek assured his nephew. "At the packing yards."

Uncle Matek had been right, Ondrej thought a week later, after collecting his first week's wages at the paymaster's window. It was more money than he'd ever seen before. Yet, even though both he and his brother had been raised with the farmer's necessary lack of compassion for animals meant for the table, Ondrej's first week at the Union Stockyards, laboring in the killing pens of Armour and Company, had been a cruel and brutal exercise.

His age, inexperience and lack of seniority led Ondrej to be hired as a floater—an all-around laborer who'd be trained to work wherever needed. Ondrej's foreman was a middle-aged German butcher named Max Stroh, a man who wore a heavy, leather apron cracked and stained by dried blood, with forearms as thick as tree limbs. The solid German studied his new charge with a practiced and slightly disapproving eye.

"*Böhmisch?*" Max Stroh asked with a raised eyebrow.

"Yes sir," Ondrej mumbled in German. "From Třeboň—it is south of Prague."

"*Ach,* shit," the foreman cursed, shaking his big head. "The Polacks are hard workers, the Irish, too. But bohunk greenhorns—sometimes they don't work so good. How about you?"

"Good worker," Ondrej answered.

Stroh only grunted. "Maybe, maybe not—we see. You ever butcher animals?"

"Of course, I was a farmer—and a hunter, too."

"Well boy, these hogs and cattle not like little chickens and ducks," Max Stroh pointed out. "But we will see."

Ondrej's first job was on the hog line—as a sticker.

He labored in the pork plant of Philip D. Armour, a building that covered fifty acres of land—only a small part of the immense and sprawling Chicago Stockyards. Here, a force of twenty-five thousand workers, mostly Poles and Irish, processed close to fourteen million animals each year.

In the holding pens, lines of squealing hogs were driven up an inclined chute to a small open door leading into the building.

The doomed animals ended up in the catching pen, grunting and screaming in fright as if they knew what was to come. For hogs, the instrument of death was a great spokeless wheel with chains hanging from its rim. As it moved, the chains dragged on the floor—which was sticky and covered with a rank, bloody mud. Each chain had a hook at its end, and with speed and dispatch, a man fastened the hook around the hind leg of each hapless pig. When the wheel rotated, the helpless creature was jerked off its feet and into the air where it hung upside down. Terrified, the animal was carried by the wheel, screeching and squealing, kicking and biting, to an overhead railway that ran the length of the building.

Hanging by its feet from the trolleys, the hog was carried by gravity towards Ondrej and others like him—men equipped with a thin razor-sharp blade. With a quick thrust of their knives, they cut the soft throat of the animal and a gush of blood, almost jet black, hot, and as thick as Max Stroh's arm, rushed out.

After Ondrej made his cut, the creature gravitated downward for ten yards, bleeding into a catch basin that preserved its contents for fertilizer. Then the bled-out hog, still twitching and often still alive, passed over a vat of boiling water, was released from the guide rail and disappeared with a splash. The scalding water softened the hair and bristles, and the pink carcass was then scooped from the tub by a rake-like device and lifted onto a table. A strong chain was then attached to a ring in its nose and the animal was pulled through a scraping machine—to emerge ten seconds later cleanly shaved from nose to tail.

The hog's head was then almost completely severed, and left hanging only by thin gristle and cartilage. The body was hitched up again to the overhead rail where it passed over a long table flanked by a cutting gang—six men to a side—each working against time to perform a series of cuts and scrapes as the shaved and scalded carcass glided past. Hog parts flew everywhere, and each of the cutters was sprayed with blood from their head to their heels.

As the cleaned pig passed down the final stretch, it was cut down the middle by expert "splitters" with the halves pushed into enormous chilling rooms—thirty or forty acres of them at the Armour works—where they'd hang suspended for twenty-four hours to cool and grow firm.

The entire operation, from killing wheel to cooling locker, took less than ten minutes to accomplish.

When he returned home each evening, exhausted and still smelling of meat and gore, Ondrej could barely eat his supper, wanting only to rest and fall into a deep, untroubled sleep.

He'd been cutting the throats of hogs for less than three weeks when Max Stroh came up and jovially slapped him on the back. "Jesus, boy," the German laughed. "For bohunk greenhorn, you do good job. Maybe next week we see how you do with cattle."

In the Beef House the following week, the method of killing was both different and difficult to stomach. Ondrej was to take the place of a burly Irishman named "Knocker" Reilly who missed his home in County Kerry and decided to return to it. Here there were no squeals or shrill cries from the animals, and unlike the pork plant, the work was limited to a single floor, but to anyone with eyes, it looked a cursed, dark inferno of blood, steam, and sweat.

Taking Reilly's place, Ondrej was to be a clubber, and quickly found himself standing on a narrow catwalk, holding a ten-pound sledgehammer. The bawling cattle were led up a gangway by an old white "Judas" steer that a few of the Irish butchers had oddly named Old Vic—in honor of the late Queen Victoria. When Old Vic disappeared through an escape gate, the following cattle were driven into narrow chutes, one or two to a chute—penned in so tightly they couldn't move. Standing on a wooden platform above, the sweating clubbers guided the edgy, confused animals into the stalls, touching them gently with the handles of their hammers to calm them as the scent of blood was in the air.

Then, with such sudden brutality that it first caught Ondrej by surprise, the shirtless clubbers lifted the great hammers above their heads and brought them down with a crunching thud—smashing into the forehead of each dumb beast.

If the blow was well delivered, the steer collapsed in a lifeless heap. One side of the pen was quickly raised, and the unconscious animal, breathing heavily and bleeding from its nose and mouth, was hauled by a chain onto the killing beds. Here, its hindquarters were shackled, and with the press of a button the heavy beast was lifted by a steam hoist, placed on an iron railway, and sent down the line to the slitter. A man with a knife then plunged his blade into the steer's heaving chest and in one skilled slash, severed all the major arteries. The animal was left hanging to bleed out, and then a butcher called the "headman" severed the head with two or three well aimed blows.

In his first day on the job, Ondrej learned that if the pig men had been spattered by gore, the steer butchers would end their shift covered in it. The thick, dark blood of the cattle was slippery and almost an inch deep, despite the tireless efforts of Negro laborers who shoveled it into holes cut in the floor.

The butchery was as quick and efficient as that of the hog factory, except here hung multiple lines of carcasses, and instead of the dead animals being brought to the men, the men moved from one carcass to the next, working against the foreman's clock.

Each had his specialized task to perform. When he was done, another would follow with a different job. In this way, a gang of two hundred men could stun, kill, gut, scrape, clean, and cut up over eighty steers per hour.

After vouching for his brother-in-law's honesty and ambition, Matek managed to get Valentyn a job at Trilla Cooperage, where he himself worked at the barrel maker's trade. It was menial labor—sweeping floors, stacking barrels, and cleaning tools, but after his first payday, Valentyn was stunned. He'd made more in a week of sweeping floors at Trilla than in three months of work on the farm in Třeboň.

"We will soon be rich," he told Janicka excitedly. "If you save and spend our money wisely, it will not be long before we are able to repay Matek and have a house of our own, as well."

"It is not so easy as that, *manžel*," Janicka sighed, shaking her head. "In the stores along 18th Street, the cost of goods is dear. We spend more than we save."

"Well, you must find ways," Valentyn insisted. "I will not live in my brother-in-law's basement forever."

Janicka was determined to do the best she could. She bought rabbit or mutton for Sunday dinner instead of beef or pork. If she served her family bakery or pastries, it was baked at home—never paid for in a store. Janicka soon learned to take the Halsted Street horsecar north to Maxwell Street—where the Jews had their open market, their little shops and pushcarts, selling everything from steaming frankfurters to patent medicines, and where it was both possible and expected to bargain for every cent. The smells were of cooking food, mixed with the rancid odors of rotting garbage. The sounds were of accordions playing and of men shouting, hustling: "Right here, missus, look, I got whatever you need." "Come in ladies, see what ten cents will buy." "How much you wanna spend, lady, for such a beautiful coat?"

On occasion, Anna would go along with her, buying whatever the Holubs might need that week, but always holding back a nickel or a dime to have her fortune told by the Gypsy clairvoyants.

"They're wonderful," she'd tell Janicka, who refused to spend Valentyn's hard-earned money on such behavior. "They will never tell you anything bad—just good things."

"For a nickel, I will do the same," Janicka said. "One does not need to be a Gypsy to tell people what they want to hear."

Anna began to giggle. "The Gypsy once told me I would have a second child. For some reason, Matek came home from work that night eager for the bedroom. We put little Edward to bed soon after supper, and nine months later our Margaret was born."

Janicka laughed and rolled her eyes. "For that reason alone, I would not talk to the Gypsies—that is all I need these days, to have my Valentyn coming home with such ideas in his head."

CHAPTER 13

To Lia, the city had been frightening at first, a confusing maze of streets, buildings, crowds and traffic. Two days after she'd arrived, Emilka took her to an agency that found jobs for maids, cooks, and housekeepers—for ten percent of what they earned.

Lia became part of the great army of female domestic servants that toiled in Chicago and its distant suburbs. She wore a uniform consisting of a gray shirtwaist, ankle-length black skirt and white apron. The cost of the uniform and its cleaning would be deducted from her pay.

All of Lia's assignments were far from the two-flats of Pilsen. The wealthy people who paid the agency for her services also paid for her transportation. With written directions clutched in her hand, she rode the streetcars to assignments in fashionable Hyde Park, to the great mansions along Michigan Avenue, and even the North Shore railroad as far north as the green and idyllic suburbs of Lake Forest and Winnetka, where she'd often stay overnight.

The city's Park District maintained boulevards such as Lake Shore Drive. On her first assignment there, Lia saw the wide street was exquisitely landscaped, flanked by the residences of the upper class. Freight vehicles were prohibited, leaving the street clear for the carriages, buggies, bicycles, and the fine riding horses of those with money.

Even in such lovely surroundings, it was dreary, unsatisfying work—cleaning the dirt from other people's homes. With the 19th-century discovery that diseases like tuberculosis and plague were spread by bacterial microorganisms, many of her wealthy clients were obsessed with cleanliness, but even those who were wealthy and lived in the best of circumstance were forced to contend with a world covered in soot.

Indoor gas lighting from surrounding neighborhoods of poorer homes would create a layer of dust that added an extra week to the average spring-cleaning. From those same poor homes, ubiquitous coal-burning fireplaces gave up clouds of smoke and small cinders—coating the landscape and entering the homes of both the rich and poor alike through open windows or tracked in on the bottoms of shoes.

The homes Lia found herself cleaning were often magnificent residences—great, rambling structures three stories in height, with every room offering exquisite Victorian furnishings and fine works of art—from bright tapestries to dark, somber oil paintings. As she cleaned and dusted each big room, Lia couldn't help remembering those castles she'd seen from a distance back in the old country—could they have been any more grand than these wondrous homes along Michigan Avenue?

Often, in addition to cleaning, she would do laundry. Rubbing, pounding, boiling and wringing. Mostly, outerwear was merely brushed down to save time, but otherwise laundry of all sorts was soaked in boiling water and then scrubbed by hand with soda crystals. The process was slow and always sent Lia home with her hands raw, cracked and burning.

In some cases, the people had children at home, being tended by young Irish nannies, or taking lessons from private tutors of one sort or another. By a certain age, the children were generally spoiled and impolite—viewing the cooks, maids and butlers to be more slave than paid domestic help. More than once, Lia had been ordered to do something by an eight or ten year-old child and then called a "stupid polack" or "dumb DP" when the task wasn't done to the youngster's liking.

But more often, those families wealthy enough to contract for her services were gracious enough. The work itself paid a decent wage, more than Lia had expected, and she was often sent home with items of clothing—last year's cast-offs by the people who gave them—but always finely made, and new to her.

Less than two months passed as one Sunday Sol Levine made another of his frequent calls. It was still early in the day when he arrived, and Lia noticed that he was as finely dressed as always.

Sunday was Lia's only day off, and although Emilka had said nothing about it, Lia suspected her aunt had been expecting him—as she'd spent all morning making *ovocné knedlíky*—fruit-filled dumplings that were *Pan* Levine's favorite.

After he'd eaten his fill, Sol Levine sat in an overstuffed chair and clipped the end off a cigar. Their small parlor was immediately filled with sweet-smelling smoke.

Lia was busy cleaning the kitchen when Emilka called out to her: "Come in here, *neter,* Mr. Levine wishes to speak to you."

She had been thinking of Josef, and the fact that she hadn't heard from him since they'd parted at the railroad station. He had promised to call when everyone was settled, but as yet, she'd had no word. Was he all right? Lia wondered. Had he found suitable work? Was he still in Chicago? She had no way of knowing, and could only be patient and wait for him to finally come to see her.

When Lia dried her hands and walked into the parlor, she was surprised to see Aunt Emilka smoking a cigarette. Both Emilka and Sol Levine held water glasses half full of slivovitz plum brandy in their hands.

"Tell me Lia," Sol Levine said, speaking German to her as Lia sat down in a chair. "How do you like your work?"

Lia shrugged. "Work is work," she said. "Most of the people are nice to me."

"Yes, I'm sure," Levine said. "But being a cleaning woman is no way for a smart young woman to get ahead in the world."

Lia shook her head. "I do not understand, Mr. Levine."

Levine took a long pull on his cigar, glanced briefly at Emilka, and then looked back at Lia. "I own a club," he told her. "A place where gentlemen go to relax—businessmen mostly. Politicians, too—some of the most important men in town."

"A club?" Lia asked.

"That's right," Sol Levine said, smiling. "It's called the New Century Club—on Clark Street, and I can use a pretty girl like you. Work for me and you'll make more in a single night than you can in a month of scrubbing floors and cleaning rich people's toilets."

Lia looked to her aunt.

Emilka merely shrugged and smoked her cigarette. "Soon you must move out," she said matter-of-factly. "I am a widow and not a wealthy woman. You must understand. How can I afford to feed and keep you for what little you pay?"

Lia was suddenly confused and frightened. She'd never heard her aunt talk like this. "But *Teta*—"

"Shut up," Emilka snapped. "Mr. Levine has made you a good offer of a job. You would be a foolish girl not to accept it."

"What would I have to do?"

"Just be nice to the customers," Sol Levine said. "Act as sort of a hostess."

"When would I have to work?"

"Anytime," Levine told her as he sipped his brandy. His eyes were narrow as he stared at Lia, with a coldness in them that made her afraid. "We're open every day but Christmas and the Fourth of July—around the clock."

Lia looked at Emilka again. "How could I do it?" She asked. "The cars do not run at night."

"I think the position offers free room and board," Emilka said. "Is that not so, Mr. Levine?"

"That's right, Lia. As my hostess, you'd live there."

"It is very grand," Aunt Emilka insisted. She was acting nice again. "It is like the finest palace—much nicer than this poor flat."

A hostess, Lia thought, what is wrong with that? If Sol Levine was willing to pay her as much as he said, perhaps she should do it. But why did she feel afraid? Lia wondered, her feelings confused. If it was true that Mr. Levine's eyes were hard and cold, it was also true that he'd never hurt her or treated her badly.

At Aunt Emilka's urging, less than a week later Lia gathered and packed what little she owned, and boarded the streetcar to the address that Sol Levine had given her—the New Century Club on Clark Street. "*Teta*, you will tell Josef Novak where I am when he comes to call?" she asked Emilka before leaving.

"Of course, of course. Go now, before Mr. Levine gets upset. Be a good girl and do what he tells you."

Sol Levine's New Century Club was a three-story brownstone in the middle of the block, with no sign to identify it. On all three floors, the curtains were drawn—as well as the one that graced the large glass oval in the entrance door.

Lia had arrived around three in the afternoon. A police officer stood in front of an iron fence surrounding the house's small front courtyard. He was a short, chubby man with a red Irish face, and when Lia approached, he held up his nightstick.

"Hold up a moment, lass," the officer said. "Would you be one of Sol's girls, then?"

Lia struggled with her English. "I am—I am a friend—of Mr. Levine. He calls on my—aunt. Mr. Levine has offered me job."

"Who's your aunt, lass?"

"She is—Emilka Kovar," Lia told him.

"Emilka—Millie Kovar?" The officer shook his head. "You're Millie Kovar's *niece?* Jesus, Mary, and Joseph, don't these people have no bloody conscience?"

"I am sorry," Lia said. "I do not understand English so well."

"*Ah,* nuthin' miss," the policeman said. "Just talkin' to myself, I am. Go on then, but see that you ring the bell first."

Lia was met at the door by a Chinese maid. Of indeterminate age, the oriental woman held a feathered dust mop in one hand and a cigarette between the fingers of her other. "Who you want to see, girl?" the maid asked, her attitude one of boredom and disinterest.

"Mr.—Mr. Levine," Lia stammered. It was the first time she'd ever spoken to a Chinese person.

"Oh, Mr. Levine no home," the maid said, drawing deeply on the cigarette. "You come here work for him?"

"Yes."

The Chinese woman peered out the door, turning her head first in one direction, then the other. Seeing only the officer outside and no one else, she seemed satisfied and beckoned Lia to follow her inside. "You sit down. Wait here. I get Flora come see you."

With that, the maid was gone. Battered suitcase at her feet, Lia sat in a large overstuffed leather chair and looked about the room. With the drapes closed, it was cast in a dim, gloomy light.

Although the room had long shelves of books along one wall, to Lia, it looked more like a waiting room than a library or a parlor. She'd seen both in her brief time as a housekeeper, and none of them had been as crowded with chairs, sofas, and ashtrays as this room seemed to be. For a moment, Lia was tempted to look at the many rows of books, even though she suspected the text and titles would be in English, and impossible for her to read.

Just before she could stand and move toward the bookshelves, another woman entered the room and Lia was relieved that she'd hesitated. The woman was tall and well dressed, perhaps in her fifties, but still slim and shapely. She too, smoked—yet seemed to prefer, instead of cigarettes, a long, thin cigar.

"I'm Flora Thumb," the woman said, introducing herself as Lia quickly got to her feet. "You the new girl?"

"I am Lia Stepanek. You must be—wife of Mr. Levine."

"Sol's wife?" the woman laughed—it was a hard, brittle laugh with no soft edges to it. "No, not hardly honey. I just work for the little bastard, same as you—except you work for me now, too."

When she was young, Flora Thumb had earned her living as a whore—first in San Francisco, then in the scattered mining towns of Colorado when her looks began to fade. Her last years in the profession took her north to the Klondike gold fields, where looks barely mattered at all.

Flora took up with a gambler in Skagway, and killed the man after he'd beat her once too often—then she fled east until she ran out of money in Chicago, working for a time as a dealer in one of the Chicago Levee District's gambling houses. Sol Levine saw her and was impressed by her skill at cards and her efficient manner with customers. He bought Flora some new clothes, spruced her up and hired her to work in his New Century Club—as a general manager and housemother to his stable of young girls.

"I am to be hostess," Lia announced proudly. "For club that he owns."

"Sure, honey," Flora said. "Come on, I'll show you around."

Unlike Ada and Minna Lester's notorious, gaudily furnished Everleigh Club on South Dearborn Street, the New Century Club boasted the ambience of a gentleman's quiet retreat. Its walls were paneled in dark oak, the bar was solid mahogany, and it had both a chef and private dining room equipped to obtain and prepare most any dish for any taste. In addition, the brownstone mansion had a respectable art gallery, a modest library, a steamroom and a skilled Swedish masseuse. Each of the ten individual rooms was tastefully decorated and soundproofed, with mirrored ceilings, large, velvet divans and wide, brass beds.

Even though Sol Levine's New Century Club was a brothel, it was nevertheless positioned at the high end of Chicago's infamous Levee. His small, select list of clientele included many of the city's most powerful politicians and wealthy businessmen, and twenty percent of Sol's gross went to pay off police, firemen, and the First Ward Democratic organization run by "Bathhouse John" Coughlin and Michael "Hinky-Dink" Kenna.

Most of the Levee was a cesspool—a rundown neighborhood of brick or wood framed buildings between South State and the river. Here, in one small area, existed no less than forty brothels—including the infamous "dipping houses"—narrow closets in which victims were set upon and mugged by pimps or toughs. Along with out-and-out whorehouses, there were almost fifty saloons that were also frequented by whores, as well as pawnshops, peep shows and dirty, narrow streets haunted by thieves and pickpockets.

Some of the Levee's houses charged their customers a mere twenty-five cents, while others, such as the Everleigh and the New Century Clubs, were much more elaborate and expensive.

Many of his customers craved variety and for this Sol nurtured a stable of dependable procurers in various ethnic neighborhoods of the city. In the middle of the South Side "Black Belt" he found an old woman who did abortions and sent him young, dark-skinned beauties that Sol billed as tribal princesses from the Belgian Congo or dark Bechuanaland. None of the club's clients actually believed it, but it helped fuel the fantasy they sought.

It was the same with other varied tastes. Smuggled concubines from "Far Cathay" were present in the form of shy, young Chinese women supplied to Sol Levine by an opium dealer in the small but growing Oriental ghetto on Harrison Street.

An olive-skinned Arab grocer near Division and Wells was his source for pretty Middle Eastern girls, some as young as twelve or thirteen. Dressed in shear, diaphanous pantaloons, they were Sol's "daughters of Ali Baba," his *houris,* his dark, almond-eyed slave girls from the sultan's harem.

And then there was Emilka Kovar, supplying the New Century Club with immigrant beauties from Pilsen. Czech and Polish girls with strong accents if they spoke any English at all, presented to Sol's eager clients as genuine royalty—young countesses or duchesses exiled from small kingdoms in Eastern Europe because of some salacious scandal whose details were only limited by Sol Levine's erotic imagination.

Since her husband died of tuberculosis, living a decent life had become hard for Emilka Kovar, hard enough that she wasn't above selling a blood relative, her dead sister's daughter, to the proprietor of a Levee whorehouse.

Except for the old Negro woman who seemed satisfied with a mere twenty, Sol paid his procurers a hundred dollars per girl, and because most of them were used often and worn out quickly, fresh faces were necessary and turnover was high.

"This is your room, honey," Flora said, opening a door on the third floor. "This is where you stay when you ain't working."

Lia peered inside. The room was large and bare, except for ten or twelve beds, washbasins, and a few scattered dressers. Lia could see a few girls laying on the beds, one or two of them asleep, while the others were enveloped in a haze of rich, sweet smoke.

"What is smell?" she asked Flora.

"That's opium, honey. Some of the girls can't do without their poppy. But if you're smart, you'll stay clear of it. Otherwise, that stuff will eat up all your earnings."

CHAPTER 14

Less than three hours after choosing a bed and unpacking her bags, Lia learned what her role as Sol Levine's hostess was to be.

"Downstairs, Lia," Flora called. "There's a gentleman down here wants to meet you."

Josef, Lia thought—her heart suddenly racing. It must be him. Who else would be calling on her? It had to be Josef. He'd talked to *Teta* Emilka and she'd sent him here!

"A moment, please," Lia answered. "I must freshen myself."

But before she could even start, Flora Thumb was up the stairs and in the room—holding up as fine a dress as Lia had ever seen.

"It's silk brocade," Flora said. "The sport thinks you're every bit a duchess—and we can't disappoint him."

A duchess? Lia asked herself. That is silly. Josef knows who I am and where I come from—certainly not a duchess.

After quickly brushing her hair, putting on the fancy dress and going downstairs, Lia was disappointed. The man who'd come to see her wasn't Josef at all. Instead, he was short and stout, with a graying mustache and cheeks that looked flushed and red.

"This is Mr. Brannigan," Flora said. "He's an alderman and a very important man."

Lia put out her hand. "I am pleased to meet you."

"Yeah sure, honey," the red-faced man wheezed, taking her by the arm. "Which room, Flo?"

For the rest of her long life, Lia would remember the hour that followed with horror and loathing. Although still a virgin, she was not uninformed about sex, seduction, and the many pleasures that occurred beneath the sheets of the marriage bed. She'd been raised among too many aunts and female cousins to be unaware of what went on between grown men and women.

Yet, until that day, Lia remained wholly ignorant of the sheer brutality and terror of rape. Ignoring her tearful cries of protest and pleadings for pity, Alderman Brannigan had only grunted and used her as if she were some sort of animal. The fat, wheezing politician forced her, over and over, to submit to sexual acts and perversions never even whispered about among her aunts, her cousins, and her young, marriageable girlfriends back in Tábor.

In her pain and fear, Lia was barely able to resist. When she did, the alderman cursed under his breath and struck her, bruising her face and bloodying her nose. For a time, he held her pinned to the bed, on her back and on her stomach, roughly moving her one way or another to accommodate his appetite. At first, in confusion, Lia called out to Flora Thumb for help. This caused the alderman to laugh—a snorting, pig-like sound. When no help came, she began to pray, beseeching the Infant of Prague, and when nothing came of that, she suddenly just wanted to die, to escape into black nothingness, away from the fear and hurt that was tearing at her body and her heart—away from everything.

When he was finished, Alderman Brannigan dressed quickly, as if he too, wished to be somewhere else—away from all that had occurred in the small room.

Lia lay sobbing, with her face buried in the pillow. She could not look at the man who'd inflicted so much pain and humiliation on her. For a moment, her mind attached itself to a vision of Josef, but she banished it immediately. After what had happened here, he was lost to her forever.

"Sorry I busted you up, lass," the alderman wheezed, throwing three extra dollars on the bed. "But we pay Sol Levine good money and Flo needs to teach some of you tarts better manners."

After Alderman Brannigan left, Flora Thumb came back in the room to wash Lia's face and tend her bruises. "I'm afraid you was broke in hard, honey," Flora said, wiping Lia's nose. "They ain't all as mean as that one. You'll see."

But Lia could not stop sobbing.

On a crisp autumn evening three weeks later, Josef studied the creased and wrinkled envelope in his hand, comparing the address written on it with the one painted over the doorway. *1650 W. 18th Street*—yes, this was where Lia lived. He was trembling with the excitement of seeing her again. It had been almost three months since they'd parted on the teeming floor of Grand Central Station. In that time the Novak family had gotten settled. His brother was bringing home good wages from the stock yards, his father worked at the same place Uncle Matek did, and he himself was putting in long, hard days on Pavel Barshukov's CB&Q section crew. So far, America had been good to them all. They were slowly prospering in a modest way, and Josef was convinced that it was time for him to finally turn his attention back to the lovely young woman who'd managed to steal his heart.

"Good evening, *Paní* Kovar. I am Lia's friend, Josef Novak, come to call on her." Josef held his hat in his hand as Aunt Emilka stood shakily in the doorway, rheumy-eyed and very drunk.

"Lia's not here," Emilka slurred.

"Not here?" Josef questioned. He was confused.

"She doesn't live here anymore."

"Where, then?" Josef asked. "So that I might see her."

"I don't know," Emilka said, attempting to close the door. "Go away and leave me alone."

Something was wrong. Josef knew it at once. This woman was Lia's aunt—her only relative in America—for her to be ignorant of her niece's whereabouts was impossible to believe. Josef extended his arm and forced the door back open.

"You *must* know where she is," Josef pressed.

"Get out, get out," Emilka Kovar began to shout. "If you do not leave, I will call the police."

With two short steps, Josef forced his way through the door and closed it hard behind him. "I don't wish to make trouble, *Paní* Kovar, but I must know where Lia is."

Stumbling backward, Emilka drew an umbrella from its stand and began to swing it at Josef, striking him hard on the arms and shoulder. "Get out, you pig, get out!" She continued to shout.

Now angered, Josef grabbed the umbrella and broke it over his knee. Moving forward, he grasped the woman by her shoulders and shook her roughly. "Tell me," he threatened. "Or I'll beat you."

"She is gone," Emilka gasped again, fighting to catch a breath. Her voice was heavy with whiskey, and her breath was foul. "Lia is with Sol Levine now, at the New Century Club."

"Where is that?"

Coughing and wiping her mouth, Emilka gave Josef the club's address on Clark Street. "You are no longer in the old country, *Pan* Novak," she advised. "Interfere with Sol Levine and he might just kill you."

"How is she employed?" Josef asked, afraid of the answer.

"As a whore, of course," Emilka replied. "It was her choice."

"Filthy bitch—you sent her to him. Your own niece."

Emilka shrugged. "I am not proud of it, but a widow must earn her living. The city is hard."

Fueled by rage, it was the first time in his life that Josef struck a woman. Stepping back and balling his big right hand into a fist, he struck her full in the face, as hard as he'd ever hit any man.

"God might forgive you, Emilka Kovar," he choked, as Lia's aunt went limp and dropped to the floor unconscious and bleeding. "But goddamn your black soul, I never will."

CHAPTER 15

"We will search for her together," Ondrej insisted, after Josef had told him of Lia's plight.

"No, *bratr*," Josef told him, shaking his head. "Emilka Kovar told me it could be dangerous, and a man should not involve others in his troubles."

"Others?" Ondrej exclaimed, his eyes flashing angrily. "Josef, are we not brothers, bound by blood? Such a bond demands that I do nothing less. To refuse my help would be an insult—one I could not easily forgive."

Josef sighed and nodded. Ondrej was undoubtedly right. They would be at cross-purposes with Sol Levine—who Josef suspected to be a powerful man—in a city that favored powerful men. As he thought about it, Josef realized that he might need all the help he could muster. If there was trouble, perhaps they should go after Lia armed. With clubs, or even a gun. Where could they get a pistol? Josef wondered, then suddenly remembered—his Russian section boss, Pavel Barshukov.

"Why you need gun?" Barshukov asked casually as they sat on the sidecar eating their lunch. "Someone chase you?"

Using some broken English, Czech, and what little Russian he'd learned working for Barshukov, Josef attempted to explain the situation as best he could.

The Russian grunted. "You would kill Jew to get girl back?"

Josef nodded. "Yes, if I had to."

Pavel Barshukov began to pick his teeth with a thin sliver of wood and shook his head. "I don't give shit for Jews," he offered. "Gypsies or Chinamen, too—I will help you, Josef."

"You will lend me the pistol?"

Barshukov laughed and shook his head again. "No, Pavel will keep gun, but I will go with you and brother to get girl."

It was raining two nights later, as Josef and Ondrej, along with the old Russian Cossack, pulled up their coat collars and boarded the streetcar that would take them across the city to Clark Street. After Emilka had reluctantly given him the address of the New Century Club, Josef carefully wrote it down on a small slip of paper and was carrying it in his coat pocket. Unknowing of what might happen this rainy night, each had armed himself with a two-foot length of galvanized pipe hidden in their sleeves. In addition, Pavel Barshukov carried his revolver.

After getting off the streetcar, the rain had let up a bit and they were able to locate the Clark Street address with little trouble. The tall, well-kept brownstone building, surrounded by its iron fence, looked respectable enough, and Josef had to remind himself that this was indeed a Chicago nevěstinec—a whorehouse, and Lia was somewhere inside.

They noticed a stout policeman standing in front of the gate. The man wore a helmet, a rain slicker, and carried a nightstick. In order to get into the house, Josef knew, they'd first have to get past the guard.

As they huddled in the shadows of a dark alley watching the policeman, Barshukov rubbed his chin and whispered: "I not want to kill policeman, so this is what we will do—"

Standing wet, cold and miserable in the rain, Officer Clarence Dooley had served on the Chicago Force for almost twenty years and was no stranger to either side of crime. Dooley's own father had come of age on the muddy streets of The Valley—one of the first Irish ghettos in Chicago, a low level stretch of land, partial to flooding in the winter while scorching hot and humid in the summer. Throughout most of its existence, it had offered a dreary landscape of paint-peeling warehouses and shacks, weather-beaten shanties, overcrowded tenements, empty storefronts, and packed, noisy saloons.

At least ten years before the Civil War, The Valley became the center for Irish immigration into the city, most of its immigrants coming from the barren western coast of Ireland.

After coming to Chicago from Castlemaine on Dingle Bay, and after serving in the 23rd Illinois Infantry, of Mulligan's Irish Brigade, Dooley's father mustered out, returned home and became a policeman himself.

Growing up, young Clarence was a street tough, a member of the Valley Gang—becoming an expert at pickpocketing, mugging, and robbery. Like Clarence, much of the gang was made up of sons of policemen and low level politicians whose city hall connections kept their sons out of any serious trouble with the law. Using that influence, the gang was able to transform itself from a ragtag group of street urchins who stole fruit off vendors' wagons into a working criminal and political organization.

Growing older, Clarence realized soon enough that dishonest profit, influence, and respect could all be more easily acquired by the man who wore the uniform and the badge.

On this rainy night as on most others, Officer Dooley earned ten extra dollars a shift by limiting most of the time spent on his beat to an area outside the front gate of Sol Levine's New Century Club—keeping tabs on who went in and who went out, as well as keeping riffraff from the door. It was an easy way to make money, and because most nights were uneventful, Dooley was unprepared for what happened.

He'd looked down to glance at the time on his railroad watch when the wet, cold barrel of a pistol was suddenly pressed into the flesh above his collar and under his chin.

Dooley moved his head slightly, noticing that the man holding the pistol wore a bandanna over his face, as did the two others with him. "Go easy, laddybuck," Dooley said calmly. "You don't want to be shootin' no cop, now."

"Be still," Pavel Barshukov whispered, reaching down to take the nightstick from Dooley's hand. "You got gun?"

"Aye, in my coat."

The Russian grunted and nodded to Josef, who reached under the slicker and into Dooley's uniform coat. He brought out a small .45 caliber Webley Bulldog revolver.

"Careful," Dooley said. "All them chambers is loaded."

"Shut mouth," Barshukov growled, removing Dooley's helmet and bringing the nightstick down hard on the policeman's balding head. Knocked cold by the blow, Clarence Dooley groaned and dropped like a bag of wet sand. Ondrej and Josef dragged him back into the alley, then tied his hands and feet.

"I stay here watch cop," Barshukov told them, glancing down both sides of the empty street. "Cop wake up and yell, I knock him again. You two go in get girl."

Their faces covered to the eyes by bandannas, and with Josef holding the policeman's revolver, the brothers walked through the heavy gate and climbed the few steps to the glass-paned oak door. Josef slowly tried the doorknob, but the door was locked.

"How can we get in?" he asked Ondrej, who was nervous and watching for traffic on Clark Street.

"Knock or ring the bell, I suppose," Ondrej whispered. "Just like anyone else."

The Chinese maid hadn't been expecting customers on such an unpleasant night. When the doorbell rang, she was surprised and a bit annoyed. Only cur dogs would go out in the rain to couple, she thought as she came out of her small room to answer the door—cur dogs *and* Americans.

As the door was opened, Josef thrust the short-barreled pistol into the Chinese woman's startled face—then both he and Ondrej pushed her aside and forced their way into the foyer.

"No rob, no shoot," the maid cried out. Her slight frame was shaking.

"Sol Levine," Josef ordered.

"No, no, Mister Levine he no here," the maid said, shaking her head and suddenly relieved that this didn't seem to be a robbery. "Only Flora Thumb." She began to call out down the hall: "Missee Flora, you come quick! Missee Flora!"

"What in hell is going on out there?" Flora Thumb shouted as she hurriedly tied the belt of her robe—an exquisite silk kimono created by a skilled Kyoto seamstress and purchased from a San Francisco store catalog. Flora was thankful they had no customers this evening—their regular clientele weren't accustomed to such noisy goings on.

When she came into the foyer and saw two masked men, one of them nervously pointing a pistol at her Chinese maid, Flora was determined to calm the situation. Her years as a prostitute in the mining towns and gold fields of Colorado and the Klondike had left her singularly unimpressed by men brandishing weapons. But when they were as jumpy as these two seemed to be, Flora knew that anything could happen.

"There's no need for that pistol, mister," she said quietly. "Yu Jie ain't no threat."

Looking at her, Josef nodded and slowly lowered the revolver. "Are you whore here?" he asked indelicately.

"No, honey," Flora Thumb said with a brittle laugh. "I expect I aged out of that profession some years back. Are you two sports looking for a whore?"

"We look for Lia Stepanek," Josef said.

"Lia?" Flora asked, lighting one of her thin cigars. "If you're here for Lia, you men made a trip in the rain for nothing."

"She is not here?"

"Oh, Lia's here," Flora told them. "She just ain't too keen on practicing the trade, is all. She went crazy after the first time. Told me I could shoot her before she'd go with another customer. And he was a big shot, too, not all ratty and poor like you fellas look. I had to put her to work scrubbing floors and washing sheets.

"How'd you boys get in anyway?" Flora added. "Was Officer Dooley asleep, or what?"

"We knock him on head," Ondrej told her.

"Did you kill him?"

"No," Josef said. "But he'll have damn big headache."

Flora nodded, drawing on her cigar. "That's good. You fellas was smart. It don't do to kill a cop in Chicago. Besides, Dooley's a good Mick—just trying to earn his living, like everybody else."

"Where is Lia?" Josef asked again.

"What do you want with her?"

"She's not whore," Josef said. "I want to take her away from this place."

Even though she was annoyed at having these two break into Sol Levine's place, Flora was still impressed. Not many of the girls had men coming in to take them *away* from the New Century Club.

"No, she ain't a whore," Flora agreed. "Some girls ain't suited for it, and Lia's one of them. She threw her money back at me that night. I couldn't make her keep it.

"I'd of sent her off right then," Flora added. "But she wouldn't go back to her aunt. So's I put her to work scrubbing floors. It ain't the Palmer House, but it's a roof over her head."

"We will take her," Josef said. "If Mr. Levine comes for her I will kill him—you must tell him that."

"Hell, Sol ain't goin' to come after her. One girl don't mean nothing to him. You were smart not to kill that cop, though."

Finally, Flora Thumb told the frightened Chinese woman to go about her business, then led Josef and Ondrej to the upstairs room where Lia slept. She knocked on the door. "Lia, it's Flora, there's two men out here for you."

Josef heard something crash against the door, then Lia's voice—a combination of anger, fear, and desperation. Even though he was hearing her voice for the first time since they'd parted at the railroad station, Josef could tell she was crying. "*No men, please.* I just wash floors now. Make them go away or I will kill myself."

"It ain't that, honey. These two are fellas you know."

The door slowly opened. When she saw Josef, Lia's legs went weak, her knees buckled and she would have collapsed if he hadn't been quick enough to catch her.

"*Můj milánka*, Lia—My dearest Lia," Josef whispered over and over, holding her tightly, and letting her sob into the rough cloth of his coat.

"Oh Josef," she sobbed. "At first I prayed you would find me, and then that you never would. I am so ashamed."

"Hush," he told her. "Ondrej is here with me, and another man outside. We have come to take you home."

Tears streaming down her face, Lia looked up and shook her head. "Where is my home? I have no home, Josef. I cannot go back with *Teta* Emilka."

"No," Josef said, gently wiping her cheeks. "You have a new home now, *miláček*. A home with me—for always."

CHAPTER 16

Father Hruska, a stern Jesuit priest, had been made aware of Lia's grim experience in the Levee. She went to see him a week before the wedding, intent on making confession. Father Hruska spoke briefly to her after leaving the darkened confessional. "Our Savior forgave Mary Magdalene her shameless behavior, just as Josef has forgiven you. Count your blessings, girl, and cherish such a man."

"Father, I've done nothing willful to be forgiven for," Lia said, her temper flaring. "I was forced—Josef knows as much and he is marrying me because he loves me."

"*Být tichý*," Father Hruska retorted angrily. "Do not take upon yourself to argue with your priest."

Be still yourself, you old fool, Lia thought briefly. But she bit her lip and said nothing. What would this self-important old priest know of what could happen to immigrant girls alone in the city?

By tradition, Josef and Lia were married on a Tuesday, and the celebration was to last for three days following the wedding.

Because she had no blood relatives except for Emilka Kovar—who by Josef's order would be now forever shunned—the upstairs neighbors, Marika Stanek and her husband Rudi, took the place of the bride's family. The night before the wedding, Marika and some neighborhood friends gave Lia a crown of rosemary to represent wisdom, love, loyalty and remembrance.

The next morning, the day of the wedding, Anna Holub and her daughter, Margie, made themselves busy fussing over Lia.

Many traditions from the old country were to be observed that day, while others would be discarded—thought to be inappropriate to both Lia's circumstance and a growing feeling of independence among these new Americans—independence from the old life, the old ways.

When Josef appeared, dressed in his best, the women hid Lia and it was his traditional duty to make a big show of trying to find her, while at the same time failing at the task.

Only then, did Janicka bring the bride forward. Speeches were in order, with the couple thanking the guests for their presence and their parents for their upbringing.

A neighbor, Vera Sykora, laid her infant son on Josef's bed, blessing it to ensure the couple's fertility.

Anna put out a table of small refreshments, and after this, the entire wedding party began the short walk to St. Procopius Church for Mass and the ceremony itself.

On the steps of the church, as the excited bridesmaids bustled about pinning pieces of rosemary on each guest, Janicka's brother stepped forward to present the couple and then give them a stern lecture on their duties as husband and wife.

Following these formalities, inside the church, stern and frowning in his vestments, Father Hruska celebrated the Mass. When it was ended, he stood with Josef at the altar as Rudi Stanek, dressed proudly in his only suit, brought Lia down the aisle.

On the groom's side of the aisle, Janicka fought back tears as she watched her youngest son become a married man. At the same time, her heart ached that young, orphaned Lia had no one across the aisle to weep for her.

At the altar, Father Hruska noted that Josef had Lia genuflect after he did, thereby assuring her that she'd have the upper hand in their marriage. A foolish thing to do, the priest thought to himself, this young man has much to learn about life.

As Father Hruska performed the Sacrament of Marriage, both Janicka and Valentyn saw Josef quietly pass a coin to his bride, an old country custom that was said to ward off poverty in their future life together.

Once the ceremony was ended, the newlyweds along with the wedding party and their guests returned to Matek Holub's home. As they walked along, men from the neighborhood tried to stop them with lengths of rope or brightly colored ribbons tied around them. It was expected of Josef and Lia to free themselves by small monetary payment or by offering drink at the reception. It was an old custom known as *zatahovani,* or closing the passage.

At Matek's, Josef now sat at the head of the table, next to Lia. After the grace and a toast, liver dumpling soup was served. The bride and groom ate with spoons bound together with thin rope.

Served by young neighborhood boys, the first course consisted of roast pork loin with cabbage and dumplings. During all the festivities, Lia was admonished to be quiet, eat very little, and not laugh at all. Otherwise, Anna Holub sagely advised, she might be unhappy in the marriage.

After one or two more courses, a desert and a cake with coffee was served and then the music and dancing began. All night long, the party continued. In her wedding gown, Lia spun and twirled to the polka music of accordion, fiddle and harmonica.

Finally, the bride was formally brought before her husband. This was a serious procedure, when all the women gathered around Lia in a separate room, dressed her over and informed her of the secrets of the marriage bed. She sat as they took off her veil and her wreath of rosemary, replacing them with an ornamental bonnet symbolizing the transformation of Lia Stepanek Novak from a girl to an adult woman.

The dancing continued. Jokes were told, along with ribald stories out of earshot of Father Hruska who was, by this time, slightly drunk. Flushed with wine and whiskey, Matek could be heard calling above the noise in the hot, crowded house, urging everyone to eat, drink, and dance. Presently, at a subtle signal from one of the women, Josef put down his wine, excused himself and made his way down to the basement.

Upstairs and throughout the rest of the house the merriment continued. Fueled by wine, beer and whiskey, voices sang and shouted while the musicians played the old songs. Above it all, the pulsing throb of the celebration was like the muffled heartbeat of joyful, mindless life in the darkness of the Chicago night.

In his small basement bedroom, the women admitted him and Josef found himself at last alone with his bride. Lia sat in a chair in the corner of the small room. When she looked up at him, he could see tears in her eyes.

"Do you regret your choice already?" he asked, concerned.

"No, no," she said, shaking her head and rising to meet him. "I am remembering that morning aboard the *Graf Waldersee* when first we met—it seems so long ago."

"And this gives you cause to weep?"

"With happiness, yes."

"I too, am happy," Josef told her as she came into his arms.

He held her tightly and felt her tremble—slightly at first, then more and more. Stepping back, he looked into her eyes and wiped the tears from them. "Are you truly all right, *miláček?*"

"Oh Josef, as hard as I fight against it, as much as I tell myself that I was forced, I am still ashamed of all that happened and how you found me. Perhaps it is you who should regret his choice."

"Never," Josef said, shaking his head and holding her firmly by the shoulders. "At first I too, was ashamed. But then I was taken aside by people wiser than myself, people who love you almost as much as I do. They showed me the wrong of my shame. What has happened has happened, Lia. It cannot be undone, but let us go beyond it and grow old together, like Janicka and Valentyn. I wish never to speak of these things again."

She stepped forward and held him about the waist. "I wish to be a proper bride for you, Josef—but I am frightened. Please do not hurt me."

Choking back his own tears, he removed her marriage bonnet and ran his fingers through her soft, brown hair. "For as long as we may live, my Lia, I swear I will die before I ever hurt you."

By custom, the following morning marked the day that the bride followed her new husband to his house. But, in Lia's case, she was already there and they would live with Josef's family until they could save enough to rent a flat or buy a house of their own—a dream almost beyond comprehension.

Yet, even limited by their means, old protocols were observed. Many of the married neighborhood women came to the house to give Lia small gifts. Still sleepy and exhausted by the wedding party, the newlyweds laughed and blushed as the women joked and sang: *Well, well, well. Josef is a man, and Lia is his wife. And they will have a blanket in bed to cover them both.*

Finally, as was her role in this small performance, Janicka appeared in the doorway and let a broom fall to the ground. Lia picked it up immediately, asking her new mother-in-law where to put it. With this single, symbolic act, those gathered were satisfied that the bride would forever be polite and industrious.

CHAPTER 17

Learning every job there was to learn, Ondrej labored in the grim, stinking killing pens for the better part of seven years, alternating between the hog factory and the beef house, wherever another man had quit or turned up too sick or drunk to work.

He became miserly with money, and with Janicka's help and encouragement, he'd saved as much of his weekly pay as he could, rarely stopping off to have a drink with anyone after the long day was done. As his savings steadily increased, Ondrej anticipated the day when he'd have enough saved to approach his uncle for a loan against whatever additional funds might be needed to strike out for the farmlands of the west.

Although Max Stroh thought highly of him and Ondrej had come to like the rough company of his Irish and Polish coworkers, more and more he began to dislike the knives and hammers, the blood and stink of the butcher's trade. But as hard as he looked, he could find nothing else that would pay as well.

Josef too, was restless in his work. His job on the section crew had been fine when he was a single man, but now it kept him away from home too much—often requiring travel far from Chicago when extra hands were needed on a distant section. The pay was doubled and Josef never turned it down, but now that Lia was pregnant for the second time, she wanted him home at night.

"I am not suited for it, Josef," Ondrej advised him one night as they sat on the porch, drinking wine and smoking cigarettes. "But if I were you, I would try to own a *hospoda*."

"A saloon?"

Ondrej nodded. "From what I have seen, it is a fine and easy way to make money in this city—and the city is where you wish to stay, is it not?"

"Yes, of course, but why a saloon?"

"It is a place men will always go," Ondrej said. "With the Irish and Poles I work with—it is always the saloon. Morning or night, Roman Krutzel thinks of his 'shot and beer.' The Irishmen are the same. Josef, the saloonkeeper gets money from their pay before the wives do."

Ondrej was right. In Chicago, the neighborhood saloon was an institution second only in importance to the family and the church. Every corner had at least two, usually four, with a daily routine keyed to the rhythms of the neighborhood. Workers stopped in as early as five in the morning for an eye-opener, and at the noon whistle, men rushed out of mills, foundries and factories to the corner saloons for nickel drafts, ten-cent shots of whiskey, and often free lunches of cold meats, sausage, cheese, pickles and rye bread.

Those too lazy to fight the lunchtime crowds would pay boys at the factory gates a penny to race to the nearest saloon and have their lunch pails filled with beer.

The tavern business slowed after lunch, but the places began to fill again when the factories let out and stayed busy until far into the night.

"These are not bad men," Ondrej told his brother. "They work very hard and take most of their money home. But they drink hard, too, and many cannot read or write. To them, the saloon is like the daily newspaper. From the owner and others at the bar, they learn of what is going on in the city and the neighborhoods, where jobs are, who had a baby, who is sick, and who has died.

"When Matek first came here," Ondrej went on. "He did not have Drago Kosek to find him work or a place to stay. For that he relied on the saloon-keeper."

"I didn't know that," Josef said.

"He told me, himself," Ondrej replied, stubbing out the butt of his cigarette and placing it in his pocket to avoid making a mess on the porch. "He said the saloonkeepers were like advisors to those just arrived in Chicago. They found them rooming houses and jobs, they cashed paychecks and loaned them money—all for a fee. But Matek said it was always a small fee."

Josef nodded, thinking of the three saloons on nearby Morgan and Cullerton Streets, and of five more near Cullerton and Racine. Svoboda's Tavern and most of the others let regular customers and their families use their telephones to call the hospital or the doctor in case of emergencies. On occasion, Oscar Svoboda also acted as the neighborhood pharmacist—dispensing a stein of stale beer for an upset stomach, or his own remedy of hard-boiled eggs, stewed tomatoes, and horseradish sauce for a hangover or a cold.

Josef recalled that on hot, humid summer nights in the closed-in neighborhoods of the west side, Svoboda's always offered those who lived in small rooms, flats, or basements some relief—with its cold draft beer, open doors and ceiling fans.

"Uncle Matek says that half the Democratic precinct captains were saloonkeepers," Ondrej added. "People in the neighborhoods trust them. They are respected. Running a saloon is a way to move up in the world."

A precinct captain, Josef thought, and why not? I am as good as anyone else, and if it would give Lia and the baby a better life? "What would one have to do to own a saloon?"

Ondrej drank his wine and shrugged. "That I don't know. Why not ask Oscar Svoboda?"

"It ain't too hard these days," Svoboda said, drying mugs and glasses. Josef sat at his bar and sipped a whiskey. Like their father, he and Ondrej despised American beer. None of them would drink it, but Josef had no quarrel with selling it to those who would.

A hot September had turned into a crisp, cool October, and the ceiling fans in Svoboda's Tavern were still for another year, not to be turned on again until summer, and even then, not till customers began to complain of the heat. Oscar Svoboda was a big man, with a ruddy complexion and a good word for everyone who patronized his corner establishment. He was almost fifty now, having come to America with his parents during the first great wave of Bohemian immigration—in July of 1856.

His father, Vaclav Svoboda had chosen the United States to be the family's new home, even though Oscar's mother had relatives who'd left Moravia and settled in Johannesburg, South Africa three years earlier.

"*Pah* on *Jižní Afrika*," Vaclav pronounced, becoming a patriot nearly a year before he'd even set foot on the soil of his adopted land. "The future is bright *only* in America."

He brought his small family to the growing Bohemian ghetto on Chicago's near north side. But within less than a year, Chicago Mayor Wentworth led what came to be called "The Battle of the Sands." It was a massive effort on the part of the city, using the Chicago Police Department, to push poor Bohemian families out of their north side neighborhoods, claiming the area had turned into a "den of vice." In April of 1857, the police rampaged through the streets—killing, beating and arresting dozens of people. In the end, Vaclav, his wife and son, along with many others, relocated to a rundown, neglected area farther south that would come to be called Little Pilsen. But Vaclav Svoboda remained a proud American and was still a patriot four years later, in April, 1861, when Beauregard's Confederate batteries opened fire on Fort Sumter in Charleston Harbor.

Vaclav Svoboda joined up as quickly as he could—in the 24th Illinois Infantry out of Chicago. He was killed two years later, by a rebel ball at Missionary Ridge in Tennessee—leaving young Oscar and his mother alone and poor in a city that offered little charity to those in such unfortunate circumstance.

Marie Svoboda was uneducated, but she could sew a fine seam and took in alterations and repair as well as laundry. Oscar stopped going to school and found a job sweeping floors in a neighborhood tavern to help his mother pay their rent.

Marie and her ambitious son survived poverty, illness, and the great Chicago Fire—and by the time he reached thirty, Oscar had saved enough money to get married and buy his own saloon, and he'd never wanted for money since.

"These days, the breweries will put a young fella like you into business, Joe," Svoboda said. When he arrived in America, Oscar had been far too young to remember the old country, and although coarse, his English was more accomplished than his Czech. Over the years, more than one thirsty immigrant laborer had learned his English talking to Oscar Svoboda.

"You won't own the place yourself," Svoboda went on. "But you'll still make a decent living."

"I don't own?"

"*Naw*, not at first. But if you work hard and save your money, you can quit and buy your own place. You'll know the business by then, and if your joint is profitable—hell, the sky's the limit."

"But I don't own?" Josef was confused.

"It's like I said, the breweries in town have been followin' the system they use in England," Oscar explained. "It's called a "tied-house" system. You're *tied* in with the brewery, see? You only sell *their* beer. For two hundred bucks the brewer sets you up—he pays the rent and the license fee, along with supplyin' the beer and bar fixtures."

"Two hundred—"

"Yeah, you got that much?"

"I got some," Josef said with a shrug, trying his best to speak to Svoboda in English. "The rest I borrow, maybe."

"Well, hell—then why not take over this place?"

Josef was suddenly confused. He thought Oscar Svoboda and his tavern to be a part of the neighborhood—like the butcher shops, the bakeries, and the grocery stores—they went on forever, these places, and under the same names.

"But Oscar, this your saloon."

"Sure, but nuthin' stays the same forever," Svoboda said as he poured Josef another glass of rye, then one for himself. "My old lady's got the consumption, Joe. Doc Malek says I need to take her west—Arizona maybe, someplace it's dry.

"The Siebens Brewery is after me to sell out," Oscar went on. "Maybe it's time I did. This is a good neighborhood to peddle beer and they want this place bad. One word from me, and they'd let you run the joint."

"You would do this for me, Oscar?" Josef asked. "You would speak for me?"

Svoboda nodded. "If you can get two hundred bucks and work for me for three months—sure, why not?"

"I work for you?"

"Goddamned right," Svoboda said. "This ain't a business any greenhorn farmer off the boat can run. You need to learn the tavern trade, Joe."

That Saturday morning, when Josef returned to the house, he could barely wait to tell both Lia and his parents the news of Oscar Svoboda's offer—but his wife and little Michael were nowhere to be found and his mother was gone as well.

A minute later he heard some commotion and a sharp cry from the second floor—where the Staneks lived. Josef hurried out to the back porch and called upstairs. "*Paní* Stanek—is anything wrong? Is everything all right up there?"

"She is having her baby," Janicka called down. "Lia is helping me with her. "Go, run for Rudi Stanek's work and tell him to come home quick—he's going to be a father."

Rudi Stanek worked as a wheelwright for the Sturvitch Wagon and Buggy Repair Company at 16th and Ashland. As Janicka had instructed, Josef ran the entire way, excited and out of breath when he finally reached the large, cluttered shop.

He entered through the wide doorway and saw a heavyset man smoking a cigar. "Where is Rudi Stanek?" Josef asked him, trying to catch his breath.

"I'm shop foreman here," the man said. "Who wants him?"

"I am Josef—Josef Novak. I am neighbor."

"Back in the wheel shop," the big man said, pointing over his shoulder.

Josef found Rudi Stanek carefully turning a hub on his lathe. The wheelwright's shop was cramped. A large hub reamer took up one corner, while another held stacked rows of damaged wheels of various sizes. In addition, Rudi was surrounded by the tools of his trade. He looked up when Josef barged in.

"Josef—is anything wrong?"

"Marika—she is having the baby. You must come."

"The baby," Rudi said excitedly, peeling off his apron.

"What the hell's going on?" the cigar-smoking foreman asked. He'd followed Josef into the shop.

"His wife is having baby—he must come."

"He ain't going nowheres," the man growled. "He's got orders to fill—his old lady don't need Rudi to have her kid. He's already done *his* job."

"I must stay?" Rudi asked.

"Goddamn right," the foreman said. "We pay you wages for a ten-hour day. This ain't no nursery school."

Rudi Stanek turned to face Josef and shrugged, ashamed and already tying his apron back on. "You heard *Předák* Stryszyki—I cannot go. Tell Marika, Josef. She will understand."

It was at that moment that Josef—if he'd harbored any doubts at all about taking Oscar Svoboda's offer—swore that one day he'd be his own boss, and unlike poor Rudi Stanek, never let himself be intimidated by a superior, or take orders from another man again.

"Sure, I will tell her," Josef said, but as he turned to leave, the foreman blocked his path. "Don't come around here no more," the big man growled. "I don't want you goddamned bohunk anarchists and freethinkers meddling in my shop."

Josef faced Foreman Stryszyki, his fists balled in anger. "Rudi needs job," Josef said in the best English he could command. "He cannot say himself, so I say for him—you are big polack asshole."

Rudi Stanek was horrified. Nobody spoke to Otto Stryszyki in such a manner. "No, no," Rudi stammered, trying to wedge himself between the two men. "He is hothead, he don't mean it."

But it was too little, too late. Without taking the cigar from his mouth, Otto Stryszyki grunted, stepped back and set his right foot hard, then smashed a ham-sized fist into Josef's face. The powerful blow was so solid that Rudi Stanek saw his friend and neighbor go weak in the knees and drop to the floor like a bag of rocks.

That night, still tired from helping Marika Stanek through her labor, Lia found herself nursing a husband with one eye swollen shut and a broken nose.

Above them, on the second floor, Rudi Stanek was clutching a half-full bottle of slivovitz in hand. Leaning out the parlor window, Rudi was drunk and celebrating the birth of his first child.

"I have a son," he cried out to anyone on the street who cared to listen. "Thanks be to the little Infant of Prague." Rudi paused for a moment, then quickly added: "And thanks to Josef Novak—who tried to help me today—as fine a fighter as John L. Sullivan, and as much a hero as our good king Wenceslas."

"Some hero," Lia laughed, shaking her head and staring at her husband's battered, flattened nose.

"I never hit Stryszyki once," Josef mumbled. "If Rudi hadn't stopped it, that big polack might have killed me."

Tired and sore, he decided that tomorrow would be quite soon enough to tell his wife he planned to quit the railroad and put them into the saloon business.

Giving his notice a week later, Josef shook Pavel Barshukov's hand and bid farewell to the rest of his CB&Q section crew. Then he went to work for Oscar Svoboda at a dollar a day, considered by the tavernkeeper to be a fair enough wage for an apprentice—and Josef's education in the saloon business began.

While Janicka took care of the children, Lia found a job as a sales clerk for a women's clothing store on 26th Street. Her salary was small, barely enough to cover their expenses until Josef took over the management of Svoboda's saloon.

"Michael and little Matthew will have as much as they need," Lia made Josef promise. "You and I can go without things until you are bringing home more money—but not our children."

"I promise it," Josef told his wife, grateful for her help. "And one day, we will not have to worry about money again."

"Oh? I will believe that when I see it," Lia said, laughing.

"Oscar Svoboda told me so," Josef insisted. "Why would the man lie?"

Josef was in his second month of helping Oscar Svoboda run his tavern, when Matek and Anna Holub decided to have the entire family for a traditional Christmas Eve dinner. Both Josef and Lia were relieved, for they themselves faced a Christmas with too little money to buy the necessary items for a fine holiday meal.

In Matek and Janicka's family, it had been the custom to fast the entire day of Christmas Eve, but when they were living back in Třeboň, the Novaks had never done this. Valentyn was convinced that putting enough food on the table each day was risky enough, without tempting fate by voluntarily going hungry.

"I doubt the fasting will be difficult," Josef commented, as he ate a piece of stale bread and drank a cup of reheated coffee before leaving for the tavern—his impatience too strong to keep hidden from his wife. "We should be used to it by now."

"Only another month, Josef," Lia reminded him. "Then you will start earning better money."

On the morning of Christmas Eve, the Holub's Christmas tree was already decorated—mostly with red paper ornaments, walnuts, gingerbread, and sweet sugar candies. Margie Holub had stood on a chair to place the Star of Bethlehem at the top of the tree.

That evening, as soon as the first star could be seen, the whole family sat down to dinner. Anna Holub put out a feast—a meal that was as fine as any the Novaks had ever seen.

Matek said a short prayer before pouring glasses of wine. On the table, Anna had put out a loaf of bread and dinner started when Matek cut it into slices. Each slice was smeared with honey and passed, first to Valentyn who was the oldest, and then to everyone else by age.

"Back home in Třeboň," Valentyn offered, staring in wonder at the mountain of food on the table. "Only Jakub Schwarzenberk could enjoy such a meal as this."

"Forget about Třeboň," Matek said, raising his glass in a toast to the season. "America is our home now, brother-in-law, and in America we feast—*na zdraví!*"

Then, the many courses followed. First were steaming bowls of mushroom soup, followed by *kuba*—a traditional baked dish of mushrooms, barley, onion and garlic.

Along with a large, baked carp were platters of rabbit in sour creamed gravy, fat, garlicky sausages, and crisp roast duck. Anna had put out great bowls of sauerkraut, potato dumplings, and sweet peas prepared in the old way—sprinkled with brown sugar and gingerbread. At the end of the meal, strudels were passed around, made with nuts and dried apples and plums, along with *vanocka* that Lia had baked—a special Christmas bread.

After finishing dinner, Ondrej tapped his glass with the edge of a knife and stood to speak. He looked first to Matek, who gave a small, almost impreceptible nod, and then to his parents. "I have good news," he said quietly, with a marked measure of excitement. "A surprise for everyone. Uncle Matek has agreed to lend me money. With that, and with what I have saved, I will be leaving for Montana this spring."

"Montana," Janicka exclaimed. "Where is this Montana?"

"West, *Matka*," Ondrej told her. "West across the prairies."

"Is it farther than Minnesota?" Josef asked.

"Yes, much farther."

"Why must you go so far away?" Janicka groaned, glancing at her husband for support, but Valentyn merely grunted and helped himself to another piece of strudel.

"Land, *Matka*, cheap land—and lots of it." Ondrej reached into his coat pocket and handed her a single-page pamphlet printed by the Great Northern Railroad. It was printed in Czech, showed a farmer pushing his plow through a great pile of shiny, gold coins, and promised every homesteader three hundred and twenty acres of land and three years to irrigate it.

"Three hundred and twenty acres, *Matka*," Ondrej said. "Just think of it—the four of us lived on two hectares back in Třeboň. But three hundred and twenty acres—that is almost as much land as Jakub Schwarzenberk had."

"That old German owned fine shotguns," Valentyn offered. "I saw them when I called on him. He was fondling one as if it were a beautiful woman."

"Be still, you old fool," Janicka said. "What would you know about beautiful women?"

"I married one," Valentyn said with a shrug, lightly pinching her cheek as everyone around the table laughed and clapped.

Ondrej could barely contain his excitement at the prospect of homesteading. More than thirty years earlier, Congress had passed the Homestead Act, which gave three hundred and twenty acres to any claimant who irrigated the land within three years of filing a claim. By law, he would have to pay twenty-five cents per acre up front, then only an additional dollar per acre after the irrigation was finished. After dreaming of it for so long a time, Ondrej would finally have his farm.

Christmas Eve ended with Midnight Mass, with Father Hruska looking out over the pews to see who'd stayed awake late enough to attend. Among others, he noted, were the Holubs and Novaks—and if he wasn't mistaken, young Lia Novak looked as if she might be expecting another child.

PART III

NEXT YEAR COUNTRY

CHAPTER 18

In May of 1905, Carrying only a cheap valise, Ondrej stood on the steam-filled Chicago, Milwaukee and St. Paul railroad platform shaking his father's hand first, then his brother's. He embraced them both, then turned to Matek and hugged him, too.

"*Děkujeme vám,* Uncle Matek," Ondrej said quietly. He was wearing his only suit, the same one he'd bought for Josef and Lia's wedding, "Thank you for all you have done for me—for all of us."

"Yes, yes," Matek said, somewhat embarrassed. "Go find your farm, nephew, and make your parents proud."

Finally, he gave a gentler embrace to the women. Janicka and Lia had tears in their eyes, while Aunt Anna was smiling broadly. Cousin Margie kissed him on the cheek and Cousin Eddie warned him of the Indian dangers in far off Montana, especially from the Blackfeet and the Sioux. "They'll take your hair off if you aren't careful, Andy—they told us about that in school."

Ondrej boarded and found a seat on the coach that was to take him north to St. Paul. Once there, he would transfer to a westbound Great Northern train that would carry him, his saved and borrowed money, and his battered valise, as far as Great Falls—one of the largest towns in Montana.

Ondrej quickly took a window seat and studied the country as the train jerked and rattled north. The journey to St. Paul was long and uneventful. The train had a fine dining car with white linen tablecloths, and he heard one man comment that the dinner menu boasted fresh oysters and rack of lamb. Such delicacies weren't part of Ondrej's budget. Instead, Janicka had sent him off with a lunchbox of pumpernickel bread, sliced thick, with a block of soft cheese, a six-inch length of garlicky *prasky* sausage, and a paring knife with which to slice it.

By the time he'd eaten a sandwich for supper, twilight was already beginning to fall on the Illinois countryside. Once they'd left Chicago, heading north, the land became rural again, regularly spotted with prosperous looking farms, most all of them planted in corn. Night fell as they passed through Waukegan, and once it was dark outside the coach's window, Ondrej rested his head against the seat and closed his eyes, but he was much too excited to sleep.

Hours later, they slowly screeched to a stop at the Milwaukee train station. It was much smaller than the one in Chicago, and as Ondrej watched people gather their luggage and step off the coach, he thought briefly about Josef and Lia—and of his parents. Janicka and Valentyn were growing older. Would he ever see them again? He decided that being apart from his family would be a hard thing to bear, but there had been little choice. Somewhere to the west, in this new land of America, was *his own farm*—the dream he'd held for most of his life.

He would come back to Chicago when he was wealthy, he told himself, to visit and to make them proud. When that might happen he had no idea, but when it did, he hoped the old folks would still be there to make a fuss over him.

After pulling out of the Milwaukee station, the coach was even less crowded. Those passengers that remained consisted mostly of businessmen of one sort or another, as well as a few well-dressed women and sleepy children. All through the Wisconsin night, the swaying coach passed through towns with Indian-sounding names—Kenosha and Waukesha, Tomah and Menomonie—reminding Ondrej of the family's first journey by rail in America, from New York City to Chicago along the bottom of the Great Lakes.

Despite his excitement, Ondrej finally slept. But his sleep was light and fitful. Along the way, he awoke each time they came to a stop in some small station, then he'd drift off again as they pressed northwest through the rolling dairy farm country of Wisconsin.

Finally, as dawn broke behind them, the train was still eighty miles outside of St. Paul. At a stop in Eau Claire, Ondrej bought coffee from a vendor at the station, then ate some bread and cheese for breakfast. They crossed the Mississippi River two hours later and soon arrived in St. Paul, where he gathered up his valise and changed trains.

Even though it was still early in the day, as Ondrej boarded the Great Northern coach, he had to look hard to find an empty seat. The coach was crowded and filled with a blue haze of smoke and the sweet smell of tobacco—mostly pipes and cigars. Unlike the first leg of his journey, this train was empty of women or children, and most of the men were roughly dressed.

Ondrej stuffed his valise into the overhead bin and quickly sat down on one of the few empty seats. He was opposite a wiry little man wearing a striped shirt, suspenders, bow tie, and bowler hat. Next to them, by the windows, slouched two other fellows wearing soft caps and overalls, both fast asleep and snoring loudly.

"Luther Platt," the man wearing the derby said, putting out his hand, obviously hopeful of some conversation.

"Ondrej—Andy Novak," Ondrej replied, correcting himself as he shook the man's hand, determined to use his American name in this new place he was headed for. "I go to Great Falls in Montana."

"What's takin' you there?"

"I homestead farm," Ondrej replied. "Make my fortune."

"I figured as much," Luther Platt chuckled. "You *honyockers* is all of a piece—thinkin' Montana land is just milk and honey, just waitin' to push cash money right up out'n the ground."

"What is—honyocker?" Ondrej asked, puzzled.

"Well, I sure hope you farm better'n you talk English," Platt said, shaking his head and lighting his pipe.

"A honyocker is you," Platt went on. "And all you emigrants comin' out here to homestead. It's the ranchers and sheepmen that give you folks the name—once they was all through fightin' with one another.

"If it ain't the Chinamen or the niggers," Platt added. "There's always somebody that gets the short end of the horn for a time—and in Montana, you homesteaders is it."

"It is bad name?" Ondrej pressed.

"Well, these days it's more or less just a name," Platt told him. "The winter of '86–'87 took most of the starch out of the big cattle outfits. In January of '87, there was a blizzard and the temperatures dropped to almost seventy below. Their beeves was fenced up and couldn't drift before the storm. They bunched up in the ravines and along the fence lines and died by the tens of thousands."

Luther Platt shivered just recalling it. "That storm pretty much knocked the slats out of the big ranchers, but in the old days they was a damned hard bunch. They might cut your fences and drive their animals through your gardens and crops, or poison your hogs and your milch cow, hopin' to break you and run you off. There was even a few squatters hung. Yessir, them big cattle and sheep outfits wanted the grass all to themselves. But things have changed since then. The ranchers learned that Montana has her own way of cullin' out the weak—some of theyselves included."

Ondrej shook his head and filled his pipe. "In Chicago, I am called dumb bohunk, and in Montana I am honyocker. I think that Americans do not like strangers."

"Well, we ain't all such hardcases," Platt said, handing Ondrej a white business card. "I own the biggest mercantile in Great Falls, where you're bound for. We stock most everything from chewing gum to threshing machines. I wish you luck, Mr. Novak, and if you're needing anything, I'm the man to see."

Ondrej studied Luther Platt's engraved card, and even though he couldn't read it, he carefully placed it in the breast pocket of his coat pocket where it would be safe.

Platt was an affable and talkative man. "Most of the good land close to town has been settled on," he told Ondrej. "You'll have to range out aways to find anything worth your trouble. And the job'll be easier if you hire a locator."

"What is—*locator?*" Ondrej asked—another new word.

"A fellow that knows the land," Platt answered. "What's still available and what ain't. He'll usually charge a fee of thirty-five or forty dollars to take you around in his buggy and find you a plot, hopefully with access to water."

"Do you know such a man, Mr. Platt?"

"I know a few," Platt said. "Some is better than others. Was I you, I'd hook up with Adolphus Sweeney. He's got a small office in Great Falls. Dolph likes his whiskey, and talks sort of flowery—but he's as honest as the day is long, and that's most all you need to know about dealin' with anybody out here."

Great Falls, when they finally reached it, seemed to Ondrej to be a settled and pleasant enough community. It was located in the very heart of Montana, nestled on farmland, and only miles away from the majestic Rocky Mountains to its west and the Little Belt Mountains to the east.

As they were approaching the station, Platt explained that the town had been settled around the Missouri River, which provided Great Falls with its name.

"As the river cuts through town," Platt said. "It drops near five hundred feet in a series of rapids and waterfalls—they call 'em the Great Falls of the Missouri.

"The injuns knew of 'em," Platt went on. "But it weren't till 1805 that the explorers Lewis and Clark first caught sight of them falls. They said they heard the roar of that water over seven miles off."

Ondrej had never seen a waterfall and listened with interest as Platt went on to tell him that that the town itself was the brainchild of a fellow named Paris Gibson, who'd come west in May of 1882. As he listened, Ondrej marveled at how young everything seemed to be in America. He knew that many cities in Europe went back a thousand years or more, while the bustling, prosperous community of Great Falls was less than thirty years old.

"Old Man Gibson had it in his mind to build a town," Luther Platt went on. "He had a plan but no money, so he hooked up with Big Jim Hill. Hill was a big muckety-muck in the railroad business and smart enough to know that a town smack dab in the middle of Montana would make a fine connection for the railroads. So Hill put up the money, and Great Falls got itself built."

Once they were off the train, Ondrej could see that Great Falls had been planned by a practical, thoughtful man. While organizing the town, Gibson made sure the streets were laid out in a precise, arrow straight pattern. He set aside almost a thousand acres to be used as city parks, and believing that beauty was important to any place humans lived, Paris Gibson saw that elm, ash, and fir trees were planted on every street and boulevard.

"I think I shall enjoy living nearby such a place," Ondrej told Luther Platt.

"Shitfire," Platt exclaimed with a snort. "You ain't goin' to be anywheres near Great Falls. All the close in land has been settled up for years. My bet is that Dolph Sweeney'll have you lookin' at empty scrub up near the Marias, or somewheres down around the Little Belts. Them places is more'n fifty miles away, but that's the only land still left."

After thanking the storekeeper for his company and his advice, Ondrej found a small room in an inexpensive, run-down hotel near the railroad station. For supper, he finished the rest of his sausage and bread, slept soundly, and was awake and dressed at first light. After a donut and a cup of strong coffee at a small café down the street, Ondrej began asking directions to the office of the man named Adolphus Sweeney.

Sweeney's small office was located on Sixth Street. In the window was a handmade sign that stated: *Adolphus Sweeney, Site Location, Claims Assistance, Real Estate and Legal Services—a square deal to all who enter these premises.*

When Ondrej took off his cap, opened the door and stepped into the office, he found Adolphus Sweeney playing solitaire and whacking flies with a flyswatter. "It's not yet eight o'clock in the morning," Sweeney complained. "And these vile, bloodsucking insects have already become annoying."

"I am Ondrej—Andy Novak," Ondrej said, putting out his big hand. "I look for farmland in Montana."

"Mr. Luther Platt send me to see you," Ondrej added.

"Well, he steered you straight, my friend," Sweeney said as he came out from behind his desk to shake hands. "Might I inquire as to your place of residence before coming west?"

Ondrej grinned and shook his head. "I am sorry—my English is not so good yet."

Sweeney smiled. "Where did you live, sir?

"We live in Chicago—in Illinois."

"No," Sweeney said. "Before that. Your accent marks you as Eastern European, if my ears do not mislead me."

"Before Chicago—in Třeboň. That is in Bohemia."

"Ah yes, Bohemian," Sweeney said approvingly. "There are many of your brethren already here. Fine people. Hardworking and steady, for the most part."

"I look for farmland," Ondrej repeated.

"Yes, of course. Do you have funds to pay for my services?"

"I have forty dollars—yes."

"Excellent," Sweeney said, nodding. "Give me a few moments to prepare my rig and we'll venture into the wilderness."

Although there were a growing number of automobiles among the more well to do citizens of Great Falls, Adolphus Sweeney drove a Texas buckboard—old, but in fine repair—a serviceable vehicle built to withstand the punishment of frontier roads. He was short and stout, an avid student of Gibbons' *Decline and Fall of the Roman Empire,* and fond of quoting Shakespeare as well as passages from the Old and New Testaments.

"I do enjoy my Bible," Sweeney confessed as they drove north from town. "Although I believe very little of what is written in that book, the words are fine. They roll off a man's tongue like honey from a spoon. Don't you think so, Mr. Novak?"

Ondrej could only smile and nod. Most of the time he couldn't understand what Adolphus Sweeney was talking about, but didn't wish to insult the man by letting him know it.

Even though they left early and the roads were good, it took them most of a day to reach the tiny community of New Edom, twenty miles distant from the banks of the Marias River. Sweeney pulled his buckboard up in front of a paint-peeling frame building boasting a simple sign that read *Hotel & Meals.*

"We'll retire for the night," Sweeney said. "And proceed on to examine available properties in the morning. The room rates are three dollars per night, and are not included in my fee."

The following morning, after a hurried breakfast of biscuits, bacon and coffee, Sweeney readied his rig and they were off again, making their way across the small streams and around the breaks surrounding the few stores and houses that made up New Edom, then striking north into open country.

Ondrej had never seen so much open land in his life. His eyes would wander from the ground passing beneath the wheels of the bouncing buckboard to the low, sandstone cliffs and beyond to the emptiness of the far horizon. Back in Chicago, there was no land to look at—only buildings, one next to the other as far as a man could see. And in Bohemia, most all the land was settled, and had been for many centuries—small, scattered towns, neat farms, and tidy stands of timber with all fallen deadwood and branches regularly removed. Remembering it now, Ondrej couldn't help but marvel at the softness of his homeland, compared to the remote wilderness of central Montana.

"Just set your gaze upon this paradise, Mr. Novak," Adolphus Sweeney said, with a dramatic sweep of his chubby arm. "As yet untouched by plow and unleached by rain, the land holds fast the accumulated fertility of the ages. It awaits only the trickling, quickening kiss of canal-borne water to yield abundant harvests, as well as to provide a splendid home for your wife and children."

"I am bachelor farmer," Ondrej said. "I have no wife."

"Oh, but soon you will," the little man assured him. "Usually a man is able to endure his first Montana winter alone, but rarely his second. Rest assured, Mr. Novak, two years from now you will be a happily married man."

After another hour, Adolphus Sweeney brought the buckboard to a halt. Ondrej turned in his seat, staring in all directions. They'd come to a stop two hundred yards from a thin line of cottonwoods and the near bank of the slow-moving Marias River.

Sweeney patiently waited until Ondrej finally looked back at him. "This is one of the few decent parcels left, Mr. Novak," the locator announced. "So far, not too many others have come out this far from Great Falls—at least not yet."

Ondrej looked around again. The land itself was dry and flat, sloping slightly toward the river. He would have to compensate for it by digging his irrigation ditches to overcome that slope—just a simple matter of gravity, not difficult to accomplish.

"Of course, you'll need to dig a well, too," Adolphus Sweeney offered. "The river water is fine for irrigation, but drinking it often results in nausea and fractious bowels."

Ondrej grunted. He hadn't paid the little man forty dollars to settle on the first plot he saw. "Maybe we look some more? Maybe find someplace better."

Sweeney lit a cigar. "I assure you, sir, this is as fine a claim as you'll find. If you wish, I can take you bouncing and clattering all over the countryside, but you'll not discover anything better. Were I you, Mr. Novak, I would not hesitate an instant—this piece of land will not remain available for long."

"There are others who want it?" Ondrej asked.

Sweeney grunted. "I suspect the Janda brothers have their eyes on it," he stated. "They'd be your closest neighbors to the west—fine, hardworking boys and ambitious, too. They've been claiming plots as fast as they can put the irrigation in, and this one's close to being next on their list."

Sweeney told Ondrej that four years earlier, along with two friends, Frank Janda first arrived in Montana. They'd come west from Fargo, North Dakota, bringing a team of horses. All three were broke. One of them soon decided he'd had enough of living poor and went back to Fargo, but Frank and Karl Kovarik managed to find enough work in Great Falls to survive their first few weeks.

"Frank and Karl moved on to set up a homestead," Sweeney said. "There was no lumber to put up a shack, and they had to haul planks all the way from a sawmill in Shelby—about ninety miles."

"They get married after first winter?" Ondrej asked. He rarely thought much about his own matrimonial prospects until Adolphus Sweeney mentioned it.

"Of course," Sweeney said. "Frank did, anyway. Love worked her charms on him the following summer, and he was betrothed to a lovely girl named Majka Simek. Her parents kept a small butcher shop in Coffee Creek, and Frank fancied their sausage. He'd drive a team seventy miles for a few pounds of it. One July afternoon he and the young Simek girl married and she went back north along with ten pounds of sausage—*debrecinky* I believe he called it. I've had the good fortune of tasting it, and it *is* delicious."

"What about other fella?" Ondrej asked. "He marry, too?"

Sweeney shook his head sadly. "No, I'm afraid Karl Kovarik was not so fortunate. The young man was kicked in the head by an ill-tempered mule a week or so after Christmas and never regained consciousness. When he passed on, the ground was frozen too hard to dig a proper grave, so Frank took coal oil and cremated the body behind his barn."

"But you say brothers," Ondrej pressed.

"Yessir, aside from the regrettable fact that Frank was forced to burn his partner, he was greatly encouraged by his prospects. Soon after, he invited his two brothers, Ladik and Emil, to come out and join him. A sister named Irena made the journey as well—fleeing a broken heart, some say."

Across the river, the land was broken by arroyos and closely rimmed by sandstone cliffs, with little or no level land for planting crops. "It's why I brought you here first," Sweeney said. "Flat land and easy access to water."

Ondrej slowly nodded, seeing the sense of it. "Luther Platt say you are trustworthy man. Maybe I must trust you now."

Sweeney drew deeply on his cigar. "*Ye shall not steal, neither deal falsely, neither lie to one another,*" he intoned, quoting from Leviticus. "I make a point of being honest in my dealings, sir."

"Then I claim this land," Ondrej said decisively. "What about other neighbors?"

"German folks to the east," Sweeney told him. "A family by the name of Koeller, from someplace in Wisconsin. Ernst Koeller and his wife are good people—but they have a fifteen-year old boy born peculiar. The poor lad drools and speaks gibberish most of the time. He's a halfwit, I fear, and Ernst only has him do the simplest of chores.

"And to the south," Sweeney went on. "Are the Cervenkas—another Czech family. Martin and his wife, Helen, came west two years ago. From Chicago—just like you. He was diagnosed with the consumption and told to move to someplace dry.

"They had an arduous first year," Sweeney said. "Dwelling in an old Sibley tent like savages as they built their shack. Martin dug a well sixty feet deep only to strike water so alkaline that the well was scrapped and the hole filled in again."

Ondrej nodded and climbed down from the buckboard. While Dolph Sweeney finished his cigar, Ondrej paced a hundred yards in each direction, turning over clods of dirt with the toe of his boot; squatting down and breaking it apart, then letting it sift through his fingers.

His heart raced and his head ached with the realization that he finally had the land that would be his farm. Now, it was truly his to walk upon—three hundred and twenty acres of Montana badlands, mostly dry, with scattered fields of wild buffalo grass—as distant from their poor two hectares in Bohemia, Ondrej mused, as the earth was from the moon.

Two days later, with Adolphus Sweeney's help, Ondrej filed his "rights." Later that morning, he went to Platt's Mercantile to busy himself with buying the necessities of homesteading—a plow and harness, seed, metal cups and plates, pots and pans, shovels, saw, hammer and nails, an inexpensive old single-barrel shotgun, a box of shells, and finally bacon, coffee, salt, sugar, and flour.

Listening to Sweeney's advice, and Luther Platt's, too, Ondrej began to realize that the first few years of his homestead would be mainly concerned with survival. A profitable farm, if such a thing ever came at all, would only be far in the future.

"Grow just what you need to eat," Platt advised him. "There's more than enough game out there that you can shoot your meat. Along with that old smoothbore, you ought to buy a rifle, too."

Ondrej had left his boots, heavy coat and winter clothing back in Chicago and would make arrangements to have them shipped to Luther Platt's store. When he thought he had everything he needed, he inquired into lumber for a shack and basic furniture, as well as a used wagon and team to haul it all back to the Marias.

By nightfall, Ondrej was back in New Edom. The settlement was quiet and seemingly empty of people as he tied his horses to a hitch post in front of the one small restaurant and saloon. His team, made up of two aging mares, pulled an old, but sturdy Studebaker wagon. Piled up high over the sideboards and lashed down with rope, rode everything that was to make up Ondrej's new home.

He drank a whiskey and wolfed down a supper of biscuits and beans in the restaurant before paying his bill, stepping back outside and climbing up onto the wagon.

The restaurant was part and parcel of New Edom's only hotel, and the proprietor, a little man named Nestor French, followed him out into the street. "Why not stay the night?" French asked. "Our rates ain't all that costly."

"No, I go home," Ondrej answered. "I spend first night on new land."

"Well, good luck to you, Mr. Novak," the hotel man called out as Ondrej turned his rig and drove north out of town. "Stop by now and then, and wet your whistle."

Ondrej spent that night wrapped in a woolen blanket, watching the full moon cast its pale light on the river, and finally fell asleep sitting hunched over on the wagon seat.

CHAPTER 19

The next morning, as the sun broke over his land, Ondrej woke to find a coyote sitting on its haunches and watching him. He'd never seen a coyote and thought it was a dog.

Feeling totally alone for the first time, he quickly decided that a dog might be fine company far out here in the scrub. *"Zde, pes,"* he whispered softly, snapping his fingers. "Come here, dog."

But the coyote just stood and loped off, turning once to watch him for a moment, before finally disappearing over a low bluff on the river's edge.

Along with the blanket, Ondrej shook off sleep and climbed down from the wagon. He urinated, then made his way to the river where he found the ground covered with stones and broken limbs of bleached driftwood that had been washed down by a flood from somewhere upstream, then deposited here on the edge of his land. Useless for anything but kindling, the wood was light and dry, and he spent the next hour gathering it into a large pile near the wagon.

Even though Adolphus Sweeney had cautioned against it, once Ondrej had a decent fire going, he used river water to make a pot of strong, dark coffee. If *průjem*—diarrhea—were the result, he'd have to endure it at least until a well was dug. A man could last a long time hungry, Ondrej knew, but not long without water.

Lighting his pipe, he sipped from his cup and fried up a bit of bacon. The smell of it soon brought the coyote back. It sat, curious, about sixty yards off, watching him. Ondrej was tempted to throw it a piece of bacon, but decided against the idea. Good company or not, he couldn't yet afford to share food with an animal.

The day dawned clear, and there was much to be done. When he'd filed his claim, they'd given him a copy of the Homestead Act and Adolphus Sweeney helped him read it. His holding was three hundred and twenty acres, a quarter of which fronted the river, and he had three years to "prove up"—to irrigate and build a dwelling.

Shelter would be his first priority. There were no shade trees in sight, so Ondrej located his temporary homesite close enough to the river to haul water, yet far enough away to avoid the possibility of flooding in case of storms.

He first unhitched his team and led them down to water before hobbling them and letting them graze. Satisfied that the two mares were taken care of, Ondrej then began to unload his lumber and tools from the wagon, and with crude drawings and a set of simple directions sketched by Luther Platt on a piece of foolscap, set about building a claim shack.

Well before noon, he had the two by four foundation framing square and securely nailed together, and was about to start framing the walls when he heard the two mares whinny, and some distance off, a man's voice calling in German: *"Grüsse ans Haus, dürfen wir uns nähern?* Hello the house, may we approach?"

"Yes, come ahead," Ondrej answered, wiping the sweat from his forehead with a bandanna.

"I am your neighbor, Ernst Koeller," the man said, reigning up his team and reaching down to shake Ondrej's hand. "And this is my son, Kurt. The lad is slow—not right in his head, I'm afraid, but he is a good boy. Welcome to Montana."

Ondrej introduced himself and shook hands, offering each of them coffee. With a drool of saliva on his chin, the boy stood off to one side, staring and silent, as Ondrej and his father sat on a pile of one by twelve boards. They smoked their pipes and tried to speak mostly in English, with just a spattering of German.

"Is your son a soldier?" Ondrej asked. He'd noticed that young Kurt wore a faded blue army tunic over his bib overalls, with the chevrons of a corporal sewn to its sleeves.

"*Nein, nein,*" Ernst Koeller laughed. "That is my old uniform. I was corporal in army once, when I was young man. *Ja,* I fight the Apache *Indisch* then—in the New Mexico and Arizona territories. Our Kurt wears that coat all the time. My wife thinks it is the brass buttons he favors so much.

"We are from Milwaukee," Koeller went on. "Nestor French, at the hotel, says you are from Chicago—not so far from where we lived."

Ondrej nodded. "My family is still back there. We came from Bohemia almost ten years, now."

"And now you are here—on the prairie."

"*Ja*, to homestead—as you did."

Koeller chuckled and shook his head. "*Ja*, goddamn, you have chosen a difficult life, *Herr* Novak. My wife calls this Montana the Next Year Country."

"Next Year Country? I do not understand."

Koeller laughed. "Because I must always tell the poor woman that next year, things will be better."

The German stood and nodded to his son. "We will help you build your shack, *Herr* Novak. I have tools in my wagon."

"That is kind of you," Ondrej said. "But you must have your own work—"

"*Ja*, there is always some work to do, *mein Nachbar*," Koeller agreed. "But in this country, neighbors must also be helped."

"*Danke*. I will not forget your good will."

With the Koeller boy handing them the lumber, the three went about the business of finishing the shack. According to Luther Platt's plan, it was only a twelve by fourteen-foot room, built of rough lumber, with black tar paper for an outer covering and a slightly arched roof. The pages of old newspapers would serve as its only insulation. Having lived in one himself, Koeller knew that such a poor shack was frigid in the winter and stifling hot in the summer.

Yet, even with all their drawbacks, there were proven, sensible reasons to erect such a shelter in just such a way. First, they were cheap to build and all the materials could be hauled in one load.

Second, by using twelve and fourteen foot lengths of lumber, there was practically no waste and no sawing. One man skilled with a hammer and nails could reasonably build his house and be living in it within two days, depending on his determination. But, with the help of Ernst and Kurt Koeller, Ondrej would have it built by nightfall.

They took a short break for the noon meal, and as Ondrej fried up bacon and potatoes, Koeller explained more about the merits of such a shack. "It takes some skill to frame rafters," he pointed out. "But almost anyone can nail a two by six board, placed on edge for a stringer down the centerline, lay a few two by fours in the same way and then bend roof boards over them to nail to the plate."

As they ate lunch, Koeller chuckled and shook his head again. "Once we have it up, *Herr* Novak, and covered with tarpaper, you will soon see that you will be living in as depressing a structure as humans ever contrived."

Working through the afternoon, Koeller was careful to do the best work he could, often doubling the amount of nails in areas he thought necessary, reinforcing joints with whatever scrap lumber was left over, and making sure the tarpaper was put on with a generous overlap—so that no bare wood would be exposed to the weather.

Just a little better than it needed to be—it was the German way of building anything. Ondrej still remembered German efficiency from the old country, and rightly considered himself fortunate to have Ernst Koeller for a neighbor.

"This summer, when you have time," Koeller advised. "Pack sod along the sides to help keep the house warmer in winter. If you build it strong, you can someday use it as a shed, or perhaps a henhouse—even as a spare room to the proper house that you will someday build."

Late that afternoon, as they were almost done, Koeller brought out a double-barreled shotgun and a half dozen shells from beneath an oilcloth in the bed of his wagon.

"Kurt—*Hasen*," he instructed his son, handing him the gun and the shells. "Shoot two jackrabbits for our supper."

"The lad is—skilled in hunting?" Ondrej asked, as young Kurt broke the shotgun, dropped two shells in the breech, and walked off into the scrub.

Koeller nodded slowly and when he spoke, there was sadness in his voice. "*Ja*, the boy is skilled in some things but not others. It is very strange. He can take direction in English or in *Deutsch*, but can only babble nonsense. Drool runs from his mouth like a baby and he sometimes soils himself. On the other hand, he has a sixth sense about game. He is a fine hunter and a dead shot, and has only to hear my wife play a piece on the piano once, before he can sit down and duplicate it. He plays Mozart. It is a mystery to me."

"Have the doctors seen him?"

The German fired his pipe. "*Ja*, back in Milwaukee, when he was younger." Koeller shrugged and sighed. "There is no medical explanation for it and no hope for the boy. When my wife and I are gone, Kurt will go into asylum, I'm afraid."

They had the shack finished before the boy returned with two skinned jackrabbits strung on his belt, as well as the bloody carcass of Ondrej's curious coyote slung over his shoulder.

"He shot the dog?" Ondrej wondered aloud.

"No, that is a coyote," Koeller said proudly. "You will lose no hens to that one, and the pelt might bring ten dollars in Great Falls. We will share it equally, *Herr* Novak, as the animal was taken on your land."

"No, you must let my share go to your boy," Ondrej insisted, embarrassed by his ignorance—mistaking a coyote for a dog.

Young Kurt had already dressed the rabbits and washed them in the river. Once they were cut into pieces and salted, Ondrej fried them in a skillet of bacon grease—along with more potatoes.

After supper, the Koellers were anxious to get home. Ondrej reached up to shake hands as his neighbors climbed up into their wagon. "I must thank you for all your kindness," he said. "I'll hope I can repay it one day."

"*Ja,* maybe so," Ernst said. "Our farm is just two miles away. You come and visit sometime. My wife makes good strudel, and you are always welcome."

By week's end, with the days growing warmer, Ondrej had broken ground next to the shack for a small first-year garden. He'd also dug a narrow irrigation ditch running from the garden plot to a small creek branching off the river.

Having worked all week, he decided to take Sunday off from hard labor and just concentrate on tidying up a few things around the shack. Wearing only his long drawers, Ondrej was seated on a ten-pound lard pail, sewing a ragged tear in his trousers when the horses whinnied. He looked up to find Indians watching him.

At least Ondrej thought them to be Indians. More than a week before, Adolphus Sweeney had pointed out a few on the street in New Edom, and these visitors appeared to be similar.

Ondrej put aside his sewing and stood up. "Hello, I am Ondrej Novak," he said.

"You maybe got whiskey?" one asked, as the other two busied themselves poking around the shack.

"No, no whiskey," Ondrej said nervously. He had no idea how to behave around Indians. His cousin, Eddie, had studied Indians in school and warned him of being scalped or worse, but these three looked more tired and hungry than bent on scalping and torture.

"I have pancakes," Ondrej offered. "Are you hungry?"

"Not hungry—want whiskey."

"I'm sorry, I have none to give you."

"Maybe give money—for whiskey?"

As Ondrej shook his head no, one of them stumbled from the shack holding an open jug of molasses. Disappointed that it wasn't whiskey, the Indian was still laughing as he poured it into his open hand and licked the syrup from his palm. Ondrej saw that much of the molasses was wasted, running through the Indian's fingers and dripping to the ground.

Made angry by such foolishness, Ondrej made a move to take back the stolen jug, but just as he did, a rifle shot rang out, causing a covey of sharptail grouse to burst from their cover, shattering the morning quiet with their wingbeats and startled *chuk-chuk-chuk.*

Both Ondrej and the Indians stopped and stared as three white men slowly rode in from the west. They were on horseback rather than driving a wagon, and one had just fired a Winchester repeater into the air and was jacking another shell into the chamber.

"You fellas go away now," the man with the rifle called. "You got no business here. Go back to your homes."

Sullen and grumbling, the Indians moved off and disappeared over the riverbank—making their way northeast. Ondrej picked up the molasses jug, re-corked it and set it down in the shade of the little shack's doorway.

"*Jak se máte, Pan* Novak," the lead horsemen said in Czech. Sliding the rifle into its saddle scabbard, he reached down to grasp Ondrej's hand. "I am your neighbor, Frank Janda, and these are my brothers, Emil and Ladik. We are Bohemian people—like you."

"The *Indický* are like gypsies—thieves and scoundrels," Emil Janda said. "Do you have a weapon of your own?"

"Yes," Ondrej said. "A shotgun and a rifle."

"Then keep them close at hand," Emil said. "The Indians will not cause mischief if they know that you are armed."

The three dismounted and tied their horses to Ondrej's wagon. All three were big men, dressed in work clothing and wearing wide brimmed hats, unlike the flat cap Ondrej favored. Frank Janda had deep set eyes and a thick, curved mustache that drooped down past the corners of his mouth. He wore a set of wire-rim spectacles and looked to be the oldest.

Emil Janda sported a full beard and carried a belly that pushed out over his belt. Ondrej noticed that only Emil wore high leather boots, while the others made do with heavy brogans.

The third Janda brother, Ladik, made himself busy inspecting Ondrej's shack. He stepped back to check the level, then observed the smooth curve of the roof and the careful pattern of tarpaper.

"Not bad," Ladik said, voicing his approval. "You have built houses before, *Pan* Novak?"

"No," Ondrej admitted. "I had help. Ernst Koeller came by last week with his son. They helped me build my house."

"*Ah,* the Dutchman," Ladik said. "Koeller is a good man with a hammer and saw."

Ondrej offered them coffee, and for fifteen minutes or so they made small talk about the old country, winter weather, last year's crops, and their families.

"We've had our eyes on this claim," Frank Janda told Ondrej. "But were not yet able to prove up on it. It is a decent piece of land—you were lucky to deal with Adolphus Sweeney. Not so many are as honest as him."

"Work hard, Ondrej," Emil Janda laughed, slapping Ondrej on the back. "If you starve out, the Jandas will come for this land."

"But today, we came out here to invite you to a picnic," Frank Janda finally got around to saying. "It is a birthday celebration for my daughter—next Saturday. The Koellers will be there, and the Cervenkas, too. You will meet everyone."

"*Děkujeme vám,*" Ondrej said. "Thank you. I would be happy to attend your daughter's party."

Before the brothers could mount up again to leave, Ondrej was curious about the Indians who'd come to call. "I know little about *Indický,*" he admitted. "Can you tell me something of them?"

"Those were Gros Ventre," Frank Janda explained. "From the agency at Fort Belknap. In French, their name means "big bellies"—just like *bratr* Emil—he is a Gros Ventre, too."

All three brothers, including Emil, thought it a fine joke. They guffawed and punched each other on the arm. Ondrej laughed, too. He'd taken an immediate liking to the Janda brothers—they were an amiable, friendly lot—jocular and easygoing with strangers and among themselves as well.

CHAPTER 20

Unlike Ondrej's shanty, the Jandas had built a group of sod houses within easy shouting distance of the other, and convenient to them all was a small, natural spring, around which grew a number of tall cottonwood trees.

Aside from those growing along the riverbank, these spring-fed cottonwoods afforded the only shade in nearly a thousand acres of Montana land that comprised the Janda brother's holdings. And it was beneath these trees the picnic was held.

"One day, perhaps we will put a bit more distance between the houses," Frank told Ondrej, as he poured him a glass of rye. "But for now, the women and children enjoy each other's company."

At his wife's urging, Ernst Koeller and his son had wrestled her piano out of their house and into the yard early that morning, then loaded it onto their wagon for the short trip to the Janda's.

Along with studying her German Bible daily, Martha Koeller diligently practiced the keyboard for an hour every day and never passed an opportunity to show off her talents to any listeners other than her husband and her son. Her walnut-cased Gebauer upright had been carefully leveled and placed in the shade of a tree. While the Janda women busied themselves with setting food on the long table, Martha sat on her stool and played "Beautiful Dreamer."

The picnic had been planned to celebrate Marceline Janda's sixteenth birthday. Marcy, as most everyone called her, was pretty, smart, and ambitious—the apple of her father's eye.

Marcy thought herself special as well. Two years before, when her cousin Maureen had died suddenly from a burst appendix, Her Uncle Ladik and Aunt

Nora had seen fit to lay out their daughter in a beautiful white dress. Marcy was only fourteen, but was more interested in the dress than in the corpse.

"She must go away to find husband," Marceline's mother was convinced. "Out here she can only marry a boy cousin or that poor, weak-minded Koeller boy."

"I don't want her marry dirt farmer," Frank Janda often said. "Our Marcy is special—she must go off, get fine education."

Frank and Majka Janda had two boys as well, Joe and Emmett, who enjoyed none of their sister's status. Their father figured that his sons would inherit the land, and that was to be the extent of his obligation to them. Joe and Emmett worked long and hard around the place, but were treated more or less like hired hands.

During the course of the picnic, Ondrej was fussed over by the women, as any newcomer might expect, and sipping whiskey with the men, he listened to stories of windstorms, floods, and blizzards; illness, accidents, and death. But the day proved most valuable by teaching him much about his neighbors.

Majka Janda, he learned, was born in Kralovice, Bohemia. Her brother, Joe Simek, was the first to leave the old country in search of adventure and a better life. He first settled in Iowa, and after his parents and his siblings joined him, they moved to Grand Island, Nebraska. But Joe was always restless, and eventually talked the family into trying their luck even further west—in Montana.

Nora Janda was from Rice Lake, Wisconsin. After her mother died, her father sold his hardware store and brought the family as far west as Kolin, Montana to homestead.

Teresa Janda journeyed to Montana with her parents from Red Wing, Minnesota. The family homesteaded just outside of Coffee Creek where her wedding to Emil took place.

All three Janda families continued to homestead, with the men working almost communally, helping each other in the fields and with most of the tasks—threshing grain, building corrals, barns and sheds, sharing the rental costs of large equipment.

"Between the three of them," Nora Janda joked. "We got three strong backs and maybe one whole brain."

The wives raised hens for meat and eggs—which they usually sold in New Edom. With whatever cash they earned, they bought what they couldn't grow or make themselves. Irrigated, carefully tended gardens supplied their families with fresh vegetables, and adding to these, they picked berries and wild mushrooms, canning most of what they picked for each year's long, harsh winter.

The Cervenkas, Martin and Helen, were the oldest in the small group of neighbors. They'd been on the land five years, and were making a second try at homesteading.

Helen Cervenka had been born in a small village near Prague. After her mother died, she and her younger brother immigrated to America to live with an uncle and aunt. Her uncle operated a small boarding house on Chicago's north side, catering mostly to newly arrived Bohemian, Polish, and German immigrants. There, Helen met Martin Cervenka, who'd left the old country less than a month before.

They courted and were married six months later. Martin made his living as a bricklayer, but soon after the wedding he developed a rasping cough and was diagnosed with tuberculosis.

"Move to a dry place," the doctor advised, and so they chose South Dakota, where land was available and the climate was dry.

But things did not go well. Helen told Ondrej how their small crops were threatened or destroyed by dust storms, cyclones and *kobylka*—locusts. "There was so little we could do," she said with a shrug "Just spread poison and pray. Sometime it work good, but usually not, and we were ruined."

After three years of struggle and the deaths of two children to cholera, the Cervenkas admitted defeat. After a last failed harvest, they sadly forfeited their claim and went back to Chicago. "Martin go to work for big steel factory in Gary," Helen went on. "But two years later he get cyanide poisoning. So we decide to try farming again—and come here to Montana." She laughed lightly and shook her head. "Second try is not much easier."

Martin Cervenka was gaunt and hollow-eyed. Though all his days were spent working in the sun, he had a gray complexion and the look of a man with few years left to live. But Martin's sense of humor was intact. "I want enjoy just one profitable year," he told everyone at the table. "Then goddamnit, I take rest and maybe kick the bucket."

"You don't fear the hereafter, Martin?" Nora Janda asked. She had never made much of religion.

Martin Cervenka took another bite of chicken and shook his head. "I am afraid of wind and lighting, that is all."

"And of me," his wife added, laughing. "He is afraid of me."

Ondrej couldn't remember eating so well since Uncle Matek brought the family together the preceding Christmas.

The Jandas had butchered almost a dozen chickens, and these had been coated and fried golden brown. Roast venison, dumplings and mashed potatoes, along with a large bowl of mushroom gravy was on the table, too. The meat was from a whitetail buck that Joe Janda had killed two weeks earlier.

With the five or six platters of fried chicken and venison, the long table was slightly bowed under the added weight of plates of hot, buttery biscuits, bowls of different vegetables, and servings of pudding, cookies, and cake.

Once the meal was finished, the men brought out their pipes or fired their cigars while the women made themselves busy tidying up and cleaning the table. Running all about the yard, laughing and chasing, were a dozen or more Janda children of various ages, as well as an equal number of excited dogs.

As young Joe and Emmett watched, they laughed and shook their heads. Two of Emil Janda's little boys were riding tandem on Kurt Koeller's back, whacking the dull-witted boy with a stick as if he were a reluctant pony. Kurt only grinned and drooled, dutifully toting his little riders about the dusty yard on his hands and knees.

Ondrej smoked his pipe and talked with the other men, yet all through dinner and before, he'd found his gaze directed at Frank Janda's younger sister. Ondrej was certain that Adolphus Sweeney had mentioned her, and if memory served him right, Sweeney had said her name was Irena.

Irena Janda was tall and what some described as "big-boned." Her features were plain, but not unattractive—more of a handsome woman than beautiful. Had Irena been a horse, Ondrej mused, she would have been more valued for work than for speed.

Irena had followed her brothers west to Montana after the boy she'd fallen in love with back in Fargo took sick and died of blood poisoning after accidentally cutting his leg with an axe. The death of her first and only beau had been such a heartbreaking event to Irena that she'd soon convinced herself only a complete life change might offset it—and this had been the promise of Montana.

Living with her oldest brother, Frank and his family, and more educated than any of her three sisters-in-law, Irena spent much of her time schooling the younger Janda children.

Although rarely talked about, the consensus of the family was that Aunt Irena might live out her years a spinster, so it was with a great deal of interest among the Janda women that Ondrej Novak, a single man, had now become their neighbor.

"He is not bad looking," Teresa Janda observed. "A little too skinny for my liking, but Irena could fatten him up."

"Did you see him looking at her?" Nora asked. "Ondrej must be interested, all right."

"Why wouldn't he look?" Majka Janda laughed. "Our Irena is maybe only single woman between here and Great Falls."

Of course, Irena herself was privy to none of this speculation, but she, too, had been aware of Ondrej's attentions. Once or twice their eyes had met, held for a moment, then quickly moved away, more awkward than embarrassed.

After a while, Martha Koeller decided the party needed another sampling of her talents. Adjusting her long skirt on the piano stool, she started off with a rendition of "The Sidewalks of New York," then went on to play "Let Me Call You Sweetheart," "Down By the Old Mill Stream," and "Goodnight Ladies."

"Play the music, Mama," Ernst Koeller called out, laughing. "Play so that our good neighbors can dance."

"Good," Emil Janda said. He'd always been a fair hand on the button box and had enough whiskey in him to offer Martha Koeller some accompaniment.

A few days earlier, with the help of his sons, Frank Janda had nailed planks together to make a crude, but serviceable dance floor. Once built, they hitched it to two mules and had the animals drag it from the barn to the small grove of cottonwoods.

With Martha Koeller sipping a tall glass of lemonade and Emil Janda drinking rye, her piano and his accordion blended to play a spirited version of the "Chimney Sweep Polka."

Now the prairie afternoon was filled with the sounds of heavy boots and brogans as the men clomped and stomped their partners about the plank dance floor.

Ondrej had never fancied himself a skilled dancer, but as a shy bachelor he suddenly found himself in great demand. To be polite, he danced with Majka Janda first, then both her sisters-in-law, and with Helen Cervenka whose tubercular husband, Martin, could not polka long without having to rest.

Finally, between tunes, Ondrej felt a tap on his shoulder and turned to see Irena Janda. "It seems every woman here has danced with you, Ondrej Novak," she observed. "I would be remiss in my manners if I didn't do so as well."

"Of course, Slečna Janda," Ondrej stammered nervously. "It would be my honor."

Martha Koeller and Emil Janda launched into the traditional and popular "Bird in a Bush Polka" as Ondrej and Irena began to whirl about the floor.

Although Irena wasn't a small woman, she moved lightly and with an effortless grace that made Ondrej feel as if he were cursed with two clubbed feet. When the tune was ended, Irena laughed. "I do not wish to seem rude, Ondrej, but I hope you farm better than you dance."

"Oh, I do, I do," Ondrej answered earnestly. "And it is for this reason I do not understand why all the ladies wished to dance with me. I am as clumsy as an ox."

"Because you are someone new," Irena told him, smoothing her hair against a little breeze that came out of the west. "We don't see very many new people out here, and when we do, everyone is anxious to know them."

Now that the ice was broken, they sat on a wooden bench and sipped lemonade. It had become late afternoon and Martha Koeller was supervising her husband and Emil Janda as they loaded her upright back into the wagon. Martin and Helen Cervenka too, were shaking hands all around and getting ready to go home. When they finally reached Ondrej and Irene, Helen Cervenka leaned forward and whispered: "You two make good looking couple—maybe next time we have wedding party—*kdo může říct?*"

As the woman chuckled and walked away, Ondrej felt his face grow hot and red. What could Irena Janda be thinking?

But Irena, too, was laughing lightly. She looked at Ondrej and saw his embarrassment. "*Paní* Cervenka is never shy about saying things," Irena quickly said, hoping to allay his discomfort. "And I suppose it is true that a single woman like myself, living the life of a spinster out here on the prairies, thinks often of marriage."

"For myself, I have not thought of it much," Ondrej admitted.

"Well, you should be careful Ondrej Novak," Irena said coyly. "I too, am frank in my speech. In Montana we do not stand much on niceties or courtship—and most men don't travel far from their homes. They tend to marry whoever is handy."

Riding back to his shack that night, Ondrej couldn't get Irena Janda out of his thoughts. He was positive something unusual had passed between them, something that had left Irena satisfied and happy—yet as far as he could see, Ondrej had no clear notion as to what their conversation had implied.

CHAPTER 21

By mid-June, Ondrej had most of his irrigation ditches dug, and a small vegetable garden laid out behind the homestead shack. There were few trees any distance from the river so he was able to put his garden almost anywhere and be guaranteed of steady sun. He ran his rows north and south, exposing both sides of the rows to sunlight, fertilized with the dung of his mares, and kept it watered from a single narrow ditch that stretched out to one of the river's small backwater creeks. He'd planted beans and cabbage, carrots, and onions, and one entire corner of the plot was given over to redskin potatoes. For the first month or so, Ondrej shot most of the fresh meat he ate—venison, rabbits, and the occasional grouse.

When he finally tired of toting water from the river, Ondrej hitched the team and drove into New Edom, asking the hotel man, Nestor French, about the availability of a dowser.

"You'll want to see old Charlie Coffee," Nestor French said. "I guess he's about the best damn water witch in the county—lives in a shack south of town about three miles."

If there was a poorer dwelling than his own, Ondrej found it in the small, meager shanty that Charlie Coffee occupied. As Ondrej drove up, the white-haired old man was outside his door, seated on a rusty kerosene can, skinning a coyote he'd shot. Three skinny cur dogs were lazily sprawled in the warm sun, completely unmindful of Ondrej's approach, and a slit-eyed, blue-nosed mule was hitched to a nearby post.

"Watch that goddamned mule," Charlie Coffee said, as Ondrej climbed down from the wagon and tied his team. "He's a biter."

The men shook hands, and Ondrej nodded toward the bloody, half-skinned coyote. "You will sell hide?" he asked.

"Yessir," Charlie Coffee said, spitting tobacco on the ground. "I'll sell the hide, and the rest of him goes in the stewpot."

Ondrej was surprised. "You would eat coyote?"

"Damn right, me'n the dogs. Who the hell are you?"

"I am Ondrej—Andrew Novak," Ondrej said. "I have claim on Marias. I am looking for man to find water, and Nestor French sent me see you."

Charlie Coffee spit tobacco again. "Sure, I can find you water. It'll cost you twenty dollars—you got that much?"

Ondrej nodded. "Yes, I have."

"You pay when I find it, not when you strike it," Coffee said. "If it ain't where I say it is, you get your money back. I don't never cheat nobody."

As Ondrej waited patiently, the old man finished skinning the coyote, salted the hide, rolled it up, and put it on a high shelf inside the shack. With a heavy cleaver and a sharp knife, he reduced the coyote's carcass to small pieces, placed them in a burlap bag and lowered the bundle of meat down into the cool darkness of his own well. The innards he tossed to the dogs.

Wiping his bloody hands on his pants, Coffee nodded toward the mule. "I'll tie Jupiter to the back of the wagon, and ride up with you on the seat."

Once they reached Ondrej's claim, Charlie Coffee wasted little time. He took a metal spring from his overalls and walked toward the shack. "If we're lucky," he told Ondrej. "We'll find your water close by the house."

Starting at the steps to Ondrej's door, and holding the dowsing spring in front of his chest, the old man began to walk in widening circles from the house. He walked slowly and would stop every few minutes to spit a stream of tobacco, or to just stand and stare at the lightly held spring. Finally, forty feet from the shack, Charlie Coffee stopped and nodded as the metal spring began to tremble and vibrate.

"You got water right here," Coffee said, calling for Ondrej to put a stake in the ground. "Eighteen feet down or so, if you care to dig for it."

Having little else to lose but his small garden, Ondrej was the least hurt among his neighbors when the grasshoppers came during the first hot days of July.

He'd gone into Great Falls to pick up the boots and the heavy winter coat that Janicka sent him, but he was buying a cane pole, a few cork bobbers and a dozen fishhooks when a rider galloped into town and banged through the weathered door of Platt's Mercantile. The fellow was wide-eyed and covered with dust.

"Hoppers," the rider said excitedly as Luther Platt poured him a whiskey. "They was seen yesterday over Hardy—millions of 'em heading northeast. I was sent to bring the word."

"That'll put them in Great Falls by suppertime," Luther said. "Where's your claim, Andy?"

"On Marias," Ondrej said.

"Best you get home then. I expect you and your neighbors will be a mite busy this time tomorrow."

Ondrej doubted that any swarm of locusts would bother with his little garden, but the mid-summer fields of his neighbors would be tempting targets. He thought first of helping the Jandas, hoping to see Irena again, but then changed his mind. Among them all, in numbers alone, the Jandas were the most able to help themselves.

Ernst Koeller had his son. Even though simpleminded, the boy was strong and willing. It was the Cervenkas who would welcome help the most. Martin Cervenka was the oldest homesteader on the Marias, and suffering ill health as well. The Cervenkas would need all the help they could get.

After deciding where he'd be most useful, Ondrej pushed his team hard through the night and reined up in front of Frank Janda's house two hours before dawn. He got down from the wagon and banged on Janda's door.

"Kobylka," he told Frank, who had opened the door still half-asleep and holding his pistol—a Colt revolver. "Locusts. They are coming our way. I have driven all night from Great Falls."

"Goddamnit," Janda swore, looking up at the sky. "We break our asses all year and then these cursed insects come."

"I am going on to warn the Koellers," Ondrej explained. "And then to help Martin Cervenka."

"Dobrý," Frank Janda nodded. "That is good. As proud as he is, old Martin has become too frail to do without some help."

Stepping off the porch to return to his wagon, Ondrej turned to Frank. "When your sister—when Irena awakens, please give her my regards."

Ondrej made a quick stop at his own place to feed and water the tired team. He threw a light canvas tarp over his vegetables and then thought better of it. Who knew how long he would be at the Cervenkas? One day, maybe two—perhaps even a week? If so, his covered garden would be wilted and dead by the time he returned home. It would be better to let the plants have the sun and hope the locusts passed him by.

Ondrej carefully lifted the tarp away, folded it and put it under the shack, then got back in the wagon, took one last look around, and drove off again, striking east toward the Koeller farm.

It was past dawn as he reined up in Ernst Koeller's yard. Ernst was milking the cow, his wife was busy washing clothes, and Kurt Koeller was sitting in Martha Koeller's own garden, happily eating onion tops.

"*Guten morgen, Herr* Novak," Ernst called, leaving off from the cow's teat. He wiped his hands on his pants and approached the wagon. "You are out and about so early."

"I have driven out here to tell you," Ondrej said, speaking in German as they shook hands. "Grasshoppers were seen over Hardy yesterday morning, and the man said they were coming this way."

"*Ach, Scheisse,*" Koeller swore. "If they come down, we lose a year's work. "*Mutter,* we must fill the oil drums."

"I cannot stay to help you, Ernst," Ondrej apologized. "I am going on to help Cervenka."

"*Ja,* go on. I have our Kurt to help. Go to Cervenka, he is an old man. Good luck to you."

Ondrej pushed his weary team south toward the smaller farm of Martin and Helen Cervenka. Much of Cervenka's claim still lay fallow. With his worsening consumption and various weaknesses brought on by cyanide poisoning in the mills, Martin was able to farm only a portion of his holdings—just enough to let himself and his wife break even.

It had been only weeks since Ondrej had last seen Martin and Helen at the birthday party—but even in that short time the old man looked as if he'd grown weaker. His face was more ashen and his eyes seemed tired.

At the news of the oncoming locusts, Helen Cervenka buried her face in her hands and began to sob. Martin made no move to comfort her and when he spoke, his voice was cold and measured.

"Your tears will not chase away the *kobylka,* woman. Instead, we must put out the smudge pots and foul our own air. Perhaps the goddamned pests will choose to find their dinner somewhere else."

"I have come to help," Ondrej said.

"You have your own claim," Cervenka pointed out.

Ondrej shrugged. "As of yet, I have little at risk. Only a small garden, nothing more."

"Stay then," the old man said. "We are grateful for your help."

They spent the next few hours filling oil drums with rags, old hay, horse dung, clumps of sage, and pieces of an old mattress that Helen still kept squirreled away in the barn. All these were mixed and pressed tightly together, then soaked in coal oil. When this was done, they loaded the five drums onto the wagon and positioned them around Martin's fields of wheat and corn.

In his worst nightmare, Ondrej had never imagined anything like it. When the locusts finally arrived over the Marias, they came in swarms so large they dimmed the afternoon sun and sounded like a hailstorm.

Although neither Ondrej nor the Cervenkas heard of it until a month later, outside of Great Falls the evening before, the hoppers had been several inches deep on the ground and the Great Northern locomotives couldn't get traction because the crushed bodies of the insects made the rails greasy and slick.

In Great Falls that evening, an arthritic old-timer named Dad Pickles had settled into a rocking chair on the porch of his rooming house, watching a dozen or so of his younger neighbors in their futile efforts to eradicate the pests. When he had a few drinks of whiskey under his belt, Pickles liked to tell folks that he'd come into the country back in '68 with nothing but a Colt Dragoon pistol and a hard-on—and that he still had the pistol.

But old Dad Pickles could remember the spring of 1874, when millions of grasshoppers had suddenly materialized over the Great Plains from Manitoba to Texas and from the high Rockies east to the Mississippi River. "They come ever' summer for four years after that," he told a traveling drummer who'd rented a room. "And et ever' goddamned thing they could—includin' the wool right off the backs of my sheep. Then they jus' disappeared like smoke, and we ain't been pestered much since—at least not more'n ever' few years. This batch is the biggest I seen in a while, though."

On the Marias, Ondrej, Martin, and Helen Cervenka did their best to stop the hoppers by raking them into piles, like leaves, and burning them with kerosene. Because of the sheer numbers of the ravenous little creatures, these efforts proved a waste.

"Mama," Martin told his wife around noon. "Cut some bread and fry up bacon. We might as well eat lunch ourselves."

Angry but calm, Cervenka knew from past experience that the hoppers might stay for two days to a week and then leave as they'd come, on the wind. The best the three of them could do, he knew, was to save a little of what they'd grown for themselves—and even that was chancy. There was no use hoping for any better outcome, and as far as old Martin was concerned, no profit in being hungry while they raked, and smashed, and burned the pests.

As they sat in the Cervenka's small kitchen, Martin took a bite of his sandwich and grinned at Ondrej. "We've fought against the little bastards before," he shrugged flicking a hopper off his bread. "Each time we lose our crops, it is true, but what else is there to do but kill as many as you can?"

"They are a strange sight," Ondrej offered. "Almost beautiful if you can forget the destruction they bring."

Martin Cervenka laughed and glanced at his wife. "This young fellow is a *filozof*, Mama—a philosopher. Listen to him. Beautiful, indeed—locusts!"

"Or an artist," Helen Cervenka teased; her eyes still red from weeping. "Perhaps he is an artist."

Yet it was true, Ondrej thought, flicking locusts off his own sandwich. Even as they ate their lunch, twelve or twenty feet above the ground, the sky was filled with the insects, reddish brown, with bright, gauze-like wings. When the sun's rays caught them it was like sea foam reflecting sunlight, and when you saw them against a cloud, they resembled the dense flakes of a driving blizzard.

Raking and piling and burning the pests all morning, Ondrej felt he'd never before realized immensity in number. Everything else was nothing compared to the millions of insects that darkened the sun above and covered the ground beneath their feet. The hosts of locusts came in clouds and settled on the crops like there could be no end to the ruin—and yet, Ondrej thought, each by itself was a small, harmless creature easily picked up and cradled in the palm of a hand, then casually crushed at whim. Yet, in their immense numbers and appalling hunger, their power of collective damage was not to be believed.

As they finished their lunch and went back outside, the fields were covered black with locusts. On they came like an unstoppable flood. With Helen Cervenka doing as much as any man, Martin and Ondrej dug trenches and kindled fires, beat and burnt to death heaps upon heaps, but still the effort would prove utterly useless. The insects rolled across the surrounding prairie and poured over rocks and walls, ditches and hedges, those behind covering up and passing over the masses already killed.

On the Marias that summer, the grasshoppers took three days to pass. The noise made by their foraging was like a heavy shower of rain upon a distant forest. The few cleared roads that existed were covered with them, all marching and in regular lines, like armies of relentless little soldiers, with their leaders in front; and all the opposition of man to resist their progress was in vain.

They seemed the incarnation of hunger, and Ondrej had never witnessed a hunger anything like it. To millions upon millions of separate appetites, nothing was too minute to escape. He watched them first devour ripening plants and foliage, grass and leaves, everything that was green and juicy—then attack the young branches of trees, and finally the hard bark of the trunks, leaving the remaining trees like skeletons with bare branches.

For as far as sight could reach, the prairie grasses had been devoured, so that the ground itself looked scorched. Even homes and barns and storage sheds were vulnerable. The fields finished, the hoppers made their way through the smallest chink or opening in search of food; hay, straw, even linen and woolen clothes.

When it was over, the Cervenkas as well as many others, were ruined—at least for that season.

"We can replant our kitchen garden," Helen said with a weary resignation. "And Martin can still shoot meat for the supper table. I expect we can survive until next year."

"Yes," Martin agreed, slamming his big fist down on the table. "We survive till next year—so that the drought can ruin us then, or hail, or something else. Just one profitable year in this goddamned country before I die—is all I ask."

CHAPTER 22

All that was left of Ondrej's own little garden was a bare patch of ground that had that same scorched, burnt over appearance, and the cottonwoods along the river were stripped bare. When he returned home, weary and needing sleep, he saw the locusts had even gotten under the shack and eaten a small portion of the canvas tarp before quitting his place. Pulling off his brogans and laying down to rest, Ondrej suspected the damage was the same with the Jandas and the Koellers and other more distant families, those he hadn't met yet, who had homesteads on the Marias.

At first his sleep was fitful, muscles cramped and aching from the three days of grueling toil, then exhaustion set in and he began to dream of home—not his Uncle Matek's two-flat in Chicago, but their little farmhouse in Třeboň, surrounded by meadows, forests, and fields, as well as by tiny lakes and ponds and the slow-flowing River Lužnice—all of it small, tidy and ordered, compared to the vastness, loneliness, and heartbreaking wilderness that was central Montana.

Ondrej slept all that day and most of the following night. He finally woke before dawn, feeling refreshed. He made coffee and ate a few biscuits that Helen Cervenka had given him, then decided to finally start work on his well, and when he tired of that—to re-till his garden and begin to replant his beans and spuds.

With no large crop to concern him, Ondrej had studied out a plan for the rest of the summer. He'd work on the well during the cool, early morning hours, then tend to whatever needed to be done in the garden, and finally spend late afternoon hunting for meat. At night after supper, he resolved to start keeping a diary and to write home to his family once a week. His mother would be concerned with the state of his health and well being, and Uncle Matek would want reports on his investment.

Ondrej expected digging the well would be difficult work. The first few feet would be relatively easy, the loose dirt and rocks easily dug and thrown aside, but he knew once the hole grew deep it would be a two-man job. He would need a person on top to raise and lower the dirt bucket as he stood below—working with pick, shovel, and rod. For this, he'd decided to hire Kurt Koeller, if the boy's father would allow it.

But Ondrej calculated the need for help was still weeks away. In the meantime, he would get started and do all that could be done working alone.

To the north, Irena Janda was almost sick to her stomach with the stink of burnt and rotting locusts. The Janda's chickens, ducks, and turkeys had gorged themselves on so many of the little insects they could barely strut.

She'd been pleased Ondrej had left his well wishes for her the morning he'd stopped to warn her brother of the locusts. She'd been thinking of him for the past three days—all the while she was helping kill, rake, and cremate the pests. She hadn't been afraid for his safety, but rather for the state of his resolve.

"Now he's seen what the hoppers can do," she confided to her sister-in-law. "And God knows, he's not even spent a winter here. I fear by next spring, my Ondrej may be back in Chicago."

"*Your* Ondrej?" Majka Janda asked, surprised. "Since when?"

Irena quickly glanced up at her. "We have an—*understanding*. At least I think we do."

Majka shook her head. "*Švagrová*, this country is a hard place for spinsters, and you are no longer a young girl to have your heart broken. You may know *your* feelings, but you should be certain of his as well."

Irena exaggerated. "We talked a bit at Marcy's birthday party. He didn't seem terribly put off by the notion."

Majka just grunted. She was busy making potato dumplings to go with the roast duck she planned to serve for supper. "Well, that still doesn't sound like a marriage proposal to me."

"Invite him for supper, then," Irena suggested.

"It is better that the invitation come from you," Majka pointed out. "As well as the cooking."

"Very well," Irena said. "Next Saturday evening. I will send one of the younger boys to invite him."

"Go yourself," Majka suggested.

"Never," Irena protested. "I may be a spinster with uncertain prospects, but I still have my pride."

But a personal invitation to Ondrej would prove unnecessary. That night, after supper, Frank Janda drank too much. Seeing a season's work destroyed by the locusts, neither he nor his brothers were in any mood to stay sober.

"Goddamnit, I want to have another picnic," Frank announced, swallowing his third glass of rye whiskey. "A Fourth of July party—with all the neighbors."

"The Fourth of July was two days ago," Majka reminded him. "We had the grasshoppers as our guests."

"To hell with grasshoppers, this is no time to cry in our beer. I want to make a party."

Everyone finally agreed. The next day, both Emil and Ladik Janda rode out in different directions to look over the damage their neighbors suffered, and to invite them to forget their troubles at the Janda farm the following weekend.

For her part, Irena was relieved. In truth, she wasn't as certain as she'd pretended to be about Ondrej's feelings, and another party would be a good way to bring them together a second time without seeming overly personal.

Swinging a heavy pick, and nearly up to his waist in a hole, Ondrej was surprised the next day when Ladik Janda called out his name and rode up on a tall bay mare.

"*Dobré ráno,* Ondrej," Ladik said, casting an interested glance at the beginning efforts of the well. "Are you digging to China?"

"See for yourself," Ondrej laughed, stopping his work. "This is my second day digging—and this is as far as I've gotten."

"Digging a well is not easy work," Ladik agreed, getting down from his horse, and then adding: "It would be easier if you had a wife to help you."

"I will hire Kurt Koeller to help," Ondrej laughed again. "And save myself the expense of a wedding."

Ladik reached down and picked up a shovel. "Here, see, I will help you a little for free."

They dug together for an hour and then stopped to smoke and drink coffee. Ondrej was amazed at how much more could be done with two men working. In the space of an hour, they had deepened the well another two feet.

"How was it with the locusts?" he asked Ladik, as the two of them lit their pipes. "The Cervenkas were almost wiped out."

Ladik nodded. "With us, too, it was bad. It will be a difficult winter, but my brother is not discouraged—he sent me to tell you to come to a Fourth of July party this Saturday."

"Another party, so soon?" Ondrej asked, surprised and pleased at the prospect of seeing Irena again. "But, when do the Jandas get any work done?"

"There is little enough to do now," Ladik pointed out. "Except to rake and burn dead grasshoppers."

The three Janda women had put on their best dresses and took a wagon into New Edom. Along with canned goods, sugar and salt, they returned to the farm with rolled yards of festive and patriotic bunting. On Saturday morning, their yard was brightly draped and decorated in red, white, and blue. The day before, Frank Janda had butchered a young pig, and for most of the morning, guests were recruited to keep it slowly turning on a metal spit.

Ondrej wasted no time seeking out Irena. He found her in the kitchen, busily baking loaves of *houska*. Taking off his cap as he approached her, he lightly clicked his heels and made a slight bow as she looked up.

"I am pleased to see you again, *Slečna* Janda," he said, unsure of whether or not to address her by her given name.

"There is no need for such formality, Ondrej," she whispered, glancing about the kitchen to make sure no one else had heard him. "You may call me Irena—I'd prefer it if you did."

"Of course," Ondrej said, slightly embarrassed by his mistake.

She wiped her hands on her apron, and took his hand in hers, shaking it firmly. "I am glad to see you again, Ondrej. My brother said you left a greeting for me on your way to the Cervenkas."

"It was kind of you to help them as you did," she added.

Ondrej shrugged. "As of yet, I have little enough of my own to protect. I thought I might be more useful helping them."

Just as he was running out of things to say, Majka Janda came up and shooed him out of the kitchen. She had a crowd to feed and a minimum amount of patience for casual conversation in her busy kitchen. "Out," she ordered, good-naturedly. "Go outside and talk to the men, Ondrej—Irena won't run away."

In the yard, Martha Koeller had again transported her piano to the party, and was playing "The Battle Hymn of the Republic," in keeping with the patriotic nature of the occasion.

There were at least six families in the yard that Ondrej hadn't met before—most had driven down from the northwest, where they lived on claims near Galata and Shelby. Frank Janda took Ondrej around and introduced him to the men, while among the gathered women, the word quickly spread that Ondrej was a bachelor.

"Not bad looking," one of them observed. "But those jug ears ruin him."

"We have cows with smaller ears than that," another agreed.

Ondrej learned that the farms near Shelby had seen no locusts. Guided and driven by the vagaries of wind, the hordes of hungry insects never reached that far north. Yet, it was just the opposite five years before, when the Jandas were untouched and Shelby was decimated by a hopper plague that lasted nearly a week.

Once again, Majka Janda and her sisters-in-law put out a feast of generous proportions. Along with platters of roast pig, the long, sagging tables were loaded with at least three hams, fried chicken, dumplings and sauerkraut, mashed potatoes, biscuits, canned beans and peas, and finally an assortment of cookies, cakes, and pastries.

Once the food was finished, the tables were cleared and taken away, to be quickly replaced by the makeshift planked dance floor. After running up and down the scale a few times, Martha Koeller launched into her bag of polkas and waltzes.

As the music played, once again to Irena's annoyance, Ondrej was a novelty, pestered by all the married women who wanted to dance with someone new—a partner offering something different—the opportunity to dance with a man who was neither their husband nor a well-worn, boring neighbor.

When they became tired of dancing, Ondrej and Irena sat off by themselves and sipped lemonade. It was all Ondrej could do to make interesting conversation. When he made an attempt to be witty, he fell on his face, and when he tried to be serious, it was as if a shroud hung itself over their discourse. For her part, Irena was amused. It had been quite some time since a man had courted her, and even though he didn't realize it, courting was what Ondrej was about this July day. Sensing his discomfort, Irena finally took reins in hand and steered their talk into areas in which she thought he might be more comfortable.

"How did you make your living in Chicago, Ondrej?"

"I was butcher," he told her, trying to speak English as much as he could. "In the packinghouses."

"Did you like it?"

Ondrej shook his head. "No, not so much. It was bloody work, but good pay."

"But a farmer must often be a butcher, too," Irena pointed out. "How else could we have eaten *vepřová pečené* today?"

"To kill one hog is nothing," Ondrej told her, lapsing back into Czech. "But to kill and butcher thousands each day is quite another matter."

"Yes, I suppose so," Irena said, deciding to change the subject. "But what of your family? You have met all the Jandas, and yet, I know nothing of your people."

As they sat in the shade of the leafy cottonwoods, Ondrej told her of his mother, father and brother, and the family's poor farm in Třeboň, and of their long, cold journey to America aboard the *Graf Waldersee*.

He recalled the fear and apprehension they felt on Ellis Island, the long train trip west from New York, and he described Matek's crowded two-flat, and their lives in Chicago.

"Now, it is ten years since we arrive in America," Ondrej said, shaking his head. "But it seems like a hundred."

"Your family was very brave," Irena told him. "To make such a journey takes great courage. Along with my parents, my brothers immigrated to North Dakota when they were small boys, but I was born in Fargo, and know nothing else but America."

Ondrej nodded, remembering that Irena had chosen to come to Montana with her brothers, and Adolphus Sweeney had mentioned that she might have had her heart broken back in Fargo. Afraid of what she might answer, but determined to know, he strengthened his resolve and asked if she had a *milenec*—a sweetheart.

Irena smiled sadly and shook her head. "I was betrothed once, to a young man who died. I've had no one since."

Ondrej took a deep breath, relieved at what she'd told him, but still unsure of his feelings, and confused. Unlike his brother, Josef, who'd always had an eye for the ladies, Ondrej himself, had little experience with women.

"I am not skilled with words," he admitted nervously. "Even when I speak in Czech. But would it be—too bold of me to speak to your brother, and ask for his leave to call on you?"

"You would ask permission of Frank?" she asked, laughing. "I am a grown woman, Ondrej. I don't need my brother's permission for anything, and I would be pleased to have you call on me."

Once she'd said this, they both relaxed and laughed. Now it is fine, Irena told herself happily. Now we *do* have an understanding.

Although none at the party knew of it, something occurred that hot July afternoon that would twist the last waning days of summer and turn them as dark as anyone could imagine.

As the day wore on, young Marcy Janda grew bored with the party and wandered off behind her father's barn where two of her little boy cousins had Kurt Koeller treed at the top of a rickety old ladder. Kurt was grinning foolishly as the mischievous boys took turns hurling horse turds up at him.

"Now you two leave off and git!" Marcy scolded. "And let the poor thing down off that ladder."

The boys ran off, and when Kurt finally climbed down, Marcy took a broom to him. It was annoying, she'd often thought, that the only boy within miles near her age was Kurt Koeller—with drool on his chin and the brain of a child. As she brushed Kurt off, she noticed the growing presence of a bulge in front of his bib overalls.

When her male cousins were just babies, Marcy had helped her aunts bathe enough of them to know about boys' *willies.* And once, a year or so earlier, she'd even walked in on her own brother, jerking at his in the tool shed.

"Oh, did I make yours do that?" she asked Kurt, surprised and amused, as he grinned and obediently stood still. Looking around to make sure they weren't being watched, Marcy took off Kurt's jacket, unfastened the bib of the boy's coveralls and peeled it down past his waist. She'd turned sixteen less than three months earlier and was suddenly convinced that if she were ever going to get a close look at a grown boy's willy, there might never be a better chance. What she was doing was wicked, and her ma would tan her hide if she ever found out, but Marcy told herself that Kurt could never tell anyone—and that was the beauty of it.

"Now you just hold still and let me see it," she said, furtively reaching into the front of Kurt's drawers. Once his member was out, Marcy was surprised at its size—and by the fact that it was growing even bigger. As her warm hand gripped his swelling flesh, Kurt Koeller opened his eyes wide, gave a surprised grunt, and promptly spent himself—soiling her white cotton dress.

"Oh, now see what you've done," Marcy blurted, even more surprised than Kurt. "You disgusting halfwit, look at how you've ruined my dress."

The boy was suddenly confused. He sensed she was angry and suspected he must have done something terribly wrong. Marcy had just made him feel wonderful, but now she was angry and he didn't understand why.

Marcy quickly buttoned him up and shooed him away, then sneaked back to the house and changed her dress. When she came back into the yard, Kurt was near the pens, playing a game of tag with her cousins. The poor thing has already forgotten about it, Marcy told herself, so it would be all right. She'd had her look and no one the wiser.

CHAPTER 23

When it was finished, the well would be a luxury, Ondrej thought, hacking into the hard ground with pick and shovel. Without it, he was required to haul water in the wagon, usually every day.

With each swing of the pick he hoped to see a quick flood of water gathering around his boots.

In addition to giving him easy access to water, a well could even double as cold storage of sorts, keeping milk, cream, butter, and even meat passably cold when lowered down into the coolness of the shaft.

In Great Falls, Luther Platt had told him the job of digging a well might take weeks, and if there were layers of rock—it could easily stretch into months. He'd struck rocks at a few levels, but never enough to seriously slow the work.

He had Kurt Koeller helping every day. Kurt's job was to raise the heavy bucket filled with stones and dirt, empty it into Ondrej's wagon, then lower it back down into the well. Kurt not only hauled up the earth, but also lowered the curbing boards. After every two feet of digging, Ondrej would put his pick and shovel aside, pick up hammer and nails, and using the boards, carefully box the walls to prevent a cave-in. Until he struck the water table, this procedure would be necessary throughout the entire length of the shaft.

Once he struck water, Ondrej knew there would still be much work to do to get it from the well. Knowing this, he'd made a point of asking questions and observing the methods his neighbors had put into place.

The Jandas had built a windmill that drove a pump, dumping fresh water into a trough, while Martin and Helen Cervenka used a simple bucket on the end of a rope. Ernst Koeller had engineered a heavy wooden beam over the top of his well, with steel cable going from the bucket through a pulley on the beam, where it could then be hooked to the harness of his mule, using the animal's strength to pull water up in a very large bucket.

The family had drawn their water from a well on the farm near Třeboň, Ondrej remembered. It was a very old well that had been dug by his grandfather, and the job of cleaning it was given over to Josef and himself. At least once a year, he or his brother had to go down into the well and clean it. Along with drowned rats and mice that fell down the shaft looking for water, the wind blew leaves, insects, and everything imaginable down into it.

The yearly cleanup had been a dirty job. The curbing timbers near the water were covered with slick moss and algae. Working in the stink, they'd scrape the foul coating off the best they could, sending up buckets of slime and mud to be carried off and dumped in the fields. And once every five years, they'd have to replace the rotting wood, which not only formed tannic acid and turned their water undrinkable, but could completely rot away, causing a cave-in and the necessity of re-digging the well.

By late August, Ondrej was down eighteen feet and still hadn't struck water as old Charlie Coffee had predicted. The morning was cloudy and cool, and he hoped to dig at least three feet deeper if he had to. But shortly after breakfast, it was Ernst Koeller, rather than Kurt, who showed up in his yard.

"I help dig today," Koeller said amiably. "We send the boy out to hunt. My Martha wants venison in the smokehouse."

Later that morning, they struck water at twenty feet down, and Ondrej had his well.

Marcy Janda was happy to be taking her pa's wagon into New Edom. A trip into town always meant a frolic. Her mother might buy her a bottle of root beer, or even vanilla ice cream if Nestor French had some in his icebox.

But this time, for the first time, Marcy was making the trip by herself. They'd needed sugar and coffee, as well as canned goods, a few boxes of shotgun shells and a dozen other various items, and Majka had been feeling too poorly to go.

"I'll send list with her," she told Frank. "Marcy is old enough now to run errands into town."

"Oh, Pa—why can't I?" Marcy squealed when she saw a look of reluctance on her father's face. "Please let me go."

"Dobře," Frank Janda finally relented. "Go then, but do your business and come right back home."

He'd hitched Butter to the wagon. The old dun mare had made the trip many times and knew the way between New Edom and the Janda farm as well as she knew her own corral.

"Don't forget to ask Mr. Vondrak if we have any mail," Majka instructed. Rural Free Delivery hadn't yet been put into effect, and running the general store in New Edom, Victor Vondrak was the town's postmaster as well—and Majka was hoping to receive the latest catalogue from Sears Roebuck.

It was dark and overcast, and as she traveled south on the New Edom road, Marcy feared rain. At her father's stubborn insistence, she'd brought along a stiff, oilcloth slicker—rolled up and stuffed beneath the seat, but she was just as stubbornly determined not to put it on unless a storm broke.

If that happened, and it rained hard enough to turn the roads to heavy mud, she might even have to spend the night at Mr. French's small hotel. Mr. French knew her pa well enough to take her in on credit, as well as serve her supper in the hotel's small restaurant.

Marcy knew that French's hotel, its restaurant, and the town of New Edom itself weren't too much to brag about, but they were far more interesting that daily life on the farm.

The past two or three years, Marcy had taken to daydreaming more and more about her future. She poured over the periodicals to which her Aunt Irena subscribed: *Scribner's, Vanity Fair* and the *Ladies Home Journal*—imagining herself as one of the lovely and elegant women adorning their pages.

Marcy Janda thought more of her mirror than almost anything else. Once, when a traveling salesman stopped to call, the man was so stout that his chair collapsed beneath him. Struggling to his feet, coughing and wheezing, he looked at Marcy with such surprise and confusion that she briefly wondered: *is it my fatal beauty?*

Her thoughts of late had been of marrying a young lawyer or a wealthy banker and someday living in San Francisco, surrounded by her children, housemaids, and a Japanese gardener or two. It is never too early to plan ahead, her mother often told her, and Marcy was taking that advice as she absentmindedly let her eyes wander over the dun's ears—toward New Edom.

Riding easy on his father's sorrel mare, Kurt Koeller disliked the darkening weather as well. Although he enjoyed hunting for his parents, he missed helping the man who was digging the well, whom he now thought of as his friend. Ondrej Novak made him work hard, but was always kind to him and never raised his voice, as other people often did.

In his head, Kurt knew the word for *rain* although he couldn't say it. It was the same with most words. He knew their sound and what they meant, but when he tried to say them, other sounds and words came out—sounds and words that no one else could seem to understand. To Kurt, it had always been a puzzle.

Yet, he'd never been puzzled by the behavior of animals. He knew that if the weather turned bad, any deer would be reluctant to move about until after the storm passed. But the animals could also sense when the rain would stop and would slip out of heavy cover the moment it began to let up.

Urging the placid mare on, Kurt reached into his father's army coat and brought out one of the biscuits his mother had given him. If it did start a downpour and if he could hunker down near thick cover—a stand of timber or a thicket of heavy brush—he might get a fine shot at a restless buck or a careless doe.

It wasn't until the age of four, when most infants start using words and short sentences that Ernst and Martha Koeller gradually began to suspect something wrong with Kurt. He'd been their only child, and their joy. Born late in the marriage, the baby came as a blessed surprise. Ernst Koeller doted on his little son shamelessly, causing Martha to tell people that "Because he came so late, Kurt's a spoiled little egg."

But at five years old, the child still drooled and his speech was no more than a baby's gibberish.

At the age of seven, when most other children were in school, Kurt Koeller was kept home, an embarrassment to his heartbroken father.

"Our poor boy is not right in his head, Mama," Ernst had said one night in bed, tears in his eyes. "What can we do?"

"Never mind," Martha told her husband. "He is our son."

"But he is not right," Ernst insisted.

"So what should I tell you, *mein Mann*—to put the child in a sack and drown him in the river? He is the son God gave to us. He is the son God asks us to love."

"*Gott helfe mir,* I cannot," Ernst sobbed, his big shoulders shaking as he wept into his hands. "I am ashamed, but I cannot."

Yet, as time passed, Kurt grew into such a kind, sweet natured, obedient boy, that his father's heart was softened. All the years of shame and embarrassment gradually turned to acceptance, and Ernst Koeller's only concern became what would someday happen to his son when he and his wife were gone.

As it began to thunder, with flashes of lightning to the north, Kurt was puzzled to see a wagon approaching on the New Edom road, just thirty minutes after he'd tied the mare and found a place to wait out the coming storm. He was in one of the scattered stands of ponderosa pine that rimmed the wheat fields and grazing land southwest of the Marias.

As the wagon grew closer, Kurt recognized its horse as Butter, the dun mare that belonged to Mr. Janda. He suddenly felt surprise and excitement, seeing it was Marcy Janda driving the wagon.

He thought Marcy to be close to his own age and the prettiest girl he'd ever seen, not that he'd seen that many. Kurt remembered that she'd done something a few weeks earlier that had given him a sudden, brief pleasure. But then she grew angry with him afterward—and he still didn't understand why.

Watching her approach, Kurt wondered if she would be happy to see him again, and then he wondered if she was frightened of the rolling thunder and the lightning.

If Marcy Janda was afraid, would she want his help, or would she still be cross with him? Surprised and confused at seeing her, young Kurt was unsure of what to do.

Suddenly, the threatening storm arrived, and wind-driven, the rain sliced across the land in howling sheets. Nearby, a loud clap of thunder crashed and the stand of pines was enveloped in a brilliant flash as a bolt of lightning hissed and crackled, shattering a nearby tree and striking the earth with a deafening *boom.*

His eyes searching through the slashing rain, Kurt saw Butter rear in fright. As Marcy kept the terrified dray tightly reined and fought to keep her from bolting, Kurt Koeller was already mounted and galloping toward them.

Along with being frightened, Marcy Janda was annoyed with herself for underestimating the approach of the storm. She'd fully expected to be in Vondrak's store—warm, dry, and comfortable—by the time it hit. Instead, she was still on the prairie, cold, soaked to the skin, and dealing with a fractious horse. Rather than being a lark, Marcy thought angrily, her first trip into town by herself was fast becoming a disaster. Struggling to steady the dray, she caught a bit of motion in the corner of her eye. Squinting through sheets of rain, she made out a rider racing toward her at a gallop.

Just before the horseman reached her, Marcy recognized him as Kurt Koeller, who looked to be just as soaked as she was after riding the seventy-five yard distance from the trees. Kurt reined up short and was off his horse, grasping Butter's headstall, mumbling softly into the frightened animal's ear.

When the mare was finally calmed, Kurt led both horses back toward the trees and tied them to a deadfall. Grinning foolishly, he glanced up at Marcy and motioned her to step down. His plan was for them to hide beneath the wagon until the rain stopped.

Marcy was certain that she'd never been more miserable in her life. What had earlier started as a frolic was now a disappointment, and here she was—cold and muddy—hunkered beneath her wagon with an imbecile for a companion.

For his part, young Kurt was happy. They were safe under the wagon bed and just being in her company, the discomfort of their surroundings didn't bother him. Kurt was thrilled to be alone again with Marcy Janda. Maybe they could play like last time, when her soft touching had sent the rush of good feeling through him and out of him—just thinking of it caused Kurt to grin at her and drool.

"Oh, you're so disgusting," Marcy said, lifting the hem of her muddy skirt to wipe saliva from his chin. As she did, Kurt grabbed her by the wrist and forced her hand down to his crotch—the place he remembered feeling pleasure.

"No, you dirty boy," Marcy screamed, jerking her hand away. "Go home and do it with your pa's sheep if you care to—but you better let me be—do you understand?"

Kurt didn't understand. He wanted her to play like before, but realized she was becoming angry with him again—just like before. He didn't want her to be angry and shouting like she was, and he began to shake his head and cry.

"No, no," he managed to say, the first words of his that Marcy had ever understood. He took her shoulders and gently shook her, hoping to calm her as he'd done the horse.

But that only seemed to make matters worse. Marcy began to scream, pushing him away and striking at him with her fists. "No, no," Kurt said again, tears running down his face. She was hitting and clawing at him now. He pushed her to the ground and wrapped his strong arms around her to keep from being struck. He was hurt, frightened, and confused as she went on struggling and screaming. But he found the tighter he squeezed, the less she fought. Soon, her screams became slowly weaker, then petered out altogether as she fought for breath. Marcy was calmer now, Kurt thought, and that was good. If he squeezed her just a little tighter, she might get over being angry and they could once again be friends.

Moments later, Kurt felt her relax and go limp beneath him. At first, he thought the girl was asleep, but how could she sleep with her eyes still open? Maybe she slept differently than he did. Maybe when she woke they could play again. He decided to sit and watch over her while she slept, certain that Marcy wouldn't be angry with him for doing that.

Three hours later, the storm had passed on to the south as Kurt still sat hunched beneath the wagon, holding Marcy Janda's hand. He would mumble and gently shake her from time to time, hoping she'd wake up.

But she didn't. All this time, Marcy's eyes had remained wide open, but their bright blue was gone and her pretty face had turned an ashen gray. He could barely move her fingers and her hand had become cold. It was only then that Kurt recalled the many deer and rabbits he'd hunted and killed, and how those animals had grown cold and stiff as well.

Staring down at Marcy, he suddenly became frightened. Kurt had no idea what to do, but suspected he'd already done something very bad. He knew he had to run away, had to run home, where his mama and his papa would take care of him.

He slowly crawled out from underneath the wagon and untied both his own horse and Butter. If the dray mare became hungry, he didn't want to leave her tied and unable to graze.

Mounting up, he took one last look at Marcy, and with tears in his eyes, turned his horse and struck for home.

CHAPTER 24

For another hour, Butter grazed in a slowly widening circle around Marcy's body, but once her hunger was satisfied and she received no guidance from a driver, the mare soon grew restless and made off in the direction of home.

Later that day, when the horse and wagon returned without his daughter, Frank Janda was alarmed. The wagon bed was empty, so he assumed that, for whatever reason, she had never made it into New Edom. Although it was long before his time in Montana, just twenty years earlier, Janda's first fear would have been the Sioux, Crow, or Northern Cheyenne, but those grim days were long gone, and aside from a few drunken bucks now and then, homesteaders on the Marias had few problems with Indians.

Could the horse have shied and thrown her from the wagon? If that happened, Frank was certain, Butter would have stood and not abandoned her. Unless a bear spooked the mare and she bolted. A grizzly would put terror into any horse. If it was a grizzly, Frank knew, and Marcy was left on foot—God help his daughter.

"Butter is home without our Marcy," he told Majka. "I will go find Emil and Ladik. We will search for the girl."

"Ó, můj Bůh!" Majka said, putting a fist to her mouth. "What could have happened?"

Frank shrugged and kissed her lightly on the forehead. "I don't know. Most likely she lost control of the horse, tumbled from the wagon, and is walking back."

"Lost control of Butter?" Majka questioned. "Butter is as well-mannered as a nun."

"Perhaps in the storm," Frank reasoned. "Who can know? We will find her."

Mounted, with each man carrying a carbine in his saddle boot, the Jandas rode south along the New Edom Road. The storm had passed and left the land bathed in the golden light of late afternoon.

As they rode, Ladik and Emil tried to assure their brother that Marcy would be found safe and sound. The weather was warm and fair, they pointed out, and becoming lost was out of the question as long as she didn't stray from the road.

"Maybe she fell from the seat and broke a leg," Frank offered, then, as an afterthought—"Or struck her head."

"Then she would not be far from the road," Emil insisted. "We have only to stay on it and we will find her."

They followed the familiar rode over each rise of rolling land, all three squinting into the distance, hoping to see the small figure of Marcy Janda coming toward them, trudging her way home.

It was nearing dusk when Emil Janda suddenly reined up his horse and stood high in the stirrups. "Buzzards," he said hoarsely, pointing toward a distant stand of trees.

In wide, spiraling circles, the dark, silent birds soared high in the sky, broad wings outstretched, bodies gently rocking on rising pockets of warm air. Although long aware of the three approaching riders, their hunting senses of smell and sight were focused on the still form below. The dozen buzzards already on the ground were slowly, warily approaching downwind of the body.

Frank dug his heels into his mount's flanks, quickly drawing the carbine from its scabbard as the startled horse lurched forward. Quickly narrowing the distance, he made out a rounded figure on the ground—a figure with honey blonde hair, wearing a light blue dress. With Emil and Ladik following close behind, Frank cursed as he raced across the slippery mud, firing his rifle over the horse's flattened ears—bullets slapping into the wet earth, splattering mud and small stones, scattering the startled carrion birds.

They found Marcy just as young Kurt had left her, laying on her back, eyes fixed and staring at the darkening sky. If it was any comfort, her father and uncles had arrived before the buzzards had begun their grisly work.

Frank Janda knelt in the mud and gathered up his daughter. He buried his face in her hair, weeping as his brothers stood by with their hats in their hands.

They'd left in a hurry and hadn't thought to bring a packhorse, so Emil and Ladik decided to ride double on Ladik's big chestnut, while they carried Marcy's body home on Emil's smaller mare.

As Frank gently lifted his daughter from the ground, her right arm fell limply, and something bright dropped from her hand. Emil stooped over and picked it up, wiping it clean of mud.

"See here, a button," Emil observed, turning the small object over in his hands. "A brass button—with an eagle on it."

Stamped into the button was the heraldic image of an eagle, its wings outspread, on its breast a shield, emblazoned with the letter *C*—for cavalry.

"God help us," Ladik said, shaking his head. "I have seen such a button before. It is the same as those on Ernst Koeller's old army coat. The one his son is fond of wearing."

Frank Janda looked at each of his brothers. "Kurt Koeller," he whispered in rage. "That drooling, half-wit boy killed my Marcy."

CHAPTER 25

Ondrej awoke to a hard pounding on his door, annoyed by the fact that it was the middle of the night and someone had ridden up as he was fast asleep and snoring. Not that he feared danger, but it spoke poorly of his vigilance, and as he pulled his trousers on, he vowed on his next trip into town he would get a dog.

He opened the door to see a wagon outside, and Frank Janda standing in his yard. Janda's face showed pallid in the moonlight, and in the wagon sat all four Janda women—Majka at the reins, along with Teresa, Nora, and Irena. Emil and Ladik were both mounted and Emil held Frank's horse.

"Do you have weapon?" was all Frank Janda said.

Ondrej nodded, unsure of what was happening. In addition to his shotgun, he'd purchased a used .38-40 Colt Lightning rifle for hunting deer or antelope. "Yes," he told Frank. "I have a rifle."

"Good. Get dressed and bring it."

"Co dĕláte?" Ondrej asked, confused. "What is going on? Bring the gun where?"

"We go to the see the German."

"Ernst Koeller?"

"Yes."

"Is there some trouble?" Ondrej asked, buttoning his coat.

"His son has killed our Marcy."

Having no saddle, Ondrej rode in the wagon with the women. The August moon was risen high and full, and washed the prairie a pale, ghostly white. No one spoke, and when Ondrej glanced up at Irena, sitting across from him, she lowered her eyes.

They stopped at the Cervenka farm, where Frank dismounted and knocked at the door. In a moment, a yellow light flared inside the house and Helen opened the door. She was in a nightdress and held a lantern.

"Frank Janda," she said. "Do you know what time it is?"

"We need Martin to come with us."

"Martin is feeling poorly," Helen said. "He has had bad cough for two days now—I want him in bed. What has happened?"

"Our Marcy is dead," Frank told her. "She was murdered by the Koeller boy."

Now old Martin was at the door, too. In the moonlight his face looked drawn and pale—even more so than usual. Coughing into a handkerchief, he shook his head sadly.

"Kurt is an unfortunate halfwit," Martin offered. "But the boy has never been violent—how can you be certain?"

"We have proof."

Helen Cervenka looked at the wagon in her yard. "I am sorry for you, Frank, but you have both your brothers and Ondrej Novak. You don't need my Martin to help take the boy in."

"We do not go there to take him in," Janda said.

"What, then?" Helen exclaimed. "In the middle of the night?"

"I am going to hang him."

"Hang him?" Martin snorted. "Shame on you. I could never be part of such a thing—never!"

Janda stepped back from the door. "If it was your daughter, Cervenka, you would knot the rope yourself."

"I would take the boy in for trial," Martin argued. "Just as you should do." Somewhere off on the prairie, a coyote barked.

Frank Janda turned abruptly and walked to his horse, leaving the Cervenkas framed in their doorway. It was the first time Ondrej had heard anyone talk of *hanging,* and like old Martin, he wanted no part of it. At first, he was going to tell the Jandas that, and stay behind if necessary. Then, thinking he might be of more help once they reached Ernst Koeller's farm, Ondrej decided to stay where he was and say nothing until the time was right.

For a moment, he looked at Irena. If her eyes showed sadness, they revealed little else. Marcy had been her niece, and yet Ondrej found himself unable to judge the depth of her grief, or her appetite for revenge.

Frank Janda mounted his horse, tipped his cap and apologized for disturbing his neighbors at such an hour. "I hope you will take care of your cough, *Pan* Cervenka. I bear no ill will toward you for not coming with us."

In the darkness, the coyote yipped again—a strange sound, Ondrej thought, almost the sound of madness. He felt a shiver pass down his spine as Majka turned the team and followed her husband and her brothers-in-law out of Helen and Martin's yard.

Dawn was just breaking when they arrived at the Koeller farm. As Majka brought the wagon to a stop next to Ernst Koeller's well, Ondrej noticed the light of a lamp still burning in the kitchen and a grayish curl of smoke coming from the chimney. He suspected the Koellers were just finishing breakfast.

All three Janda brothers had their Winchesters out and resting across the pommels of their saddles. "Hello, Ernst Koeller," Frank called out in German. "*Kommen sie mal raus?* Will you come out of the house?"

Not expecting company at such an hour, Ernst Koeller came into the yard ready to offer his visitors some coffee and strudel that Martha had baked the night before. Then he saw the rifles.

"*Mein Gott,*" Koeller said in amazement. "What is the trouble that our neighbors visit us with weapons?"

"Where is your boy?" Frank Janda shot back.

"Kurt? He is helping Martha in the kitchen."

"Bring him out."

Ernst Koeller stiffened his back, suddenly sensing a threat. "I ask you again, *Herr* Janda, is there some trouble between us?"

"The boy is guilty of murder," Janda said.

"Murder? Who has been murdered?"

"He killed our daughter, Marcy. We found her late yesterday afternoon, on the New Edom road."

Koeller shook his head, his eyes wide with fear. "*Nein, nein*—not my Kurt—he is not murderer."

"We have the proof," Emil Janda said.

Ernst Koeller's fear was turning to anger. His face was flushed and his hands trembled. "Where is proof? Show me proof."

Emil Janda reached into his pocket and brought out the button he'd found, then tossed it to the ground at Ernst Koeller's feet. The German farmer bent to pick it up, slowly turned it over in his hand, rubbing off the dust with his thumb. "Where did you get this?"

"It was in my little girl's hand," Frank Janda said. "When we found her."

"Mama," Ernst Koeller called, turning toward the door. "Keep Kurt inside, but bring out his coat."

Martha Koeller had heard everything taking place in her yard. When she first heard his name mentioned, she'd made Kurt hide in their bedroom. Now, she wept as she came out carrying the faded, blue army tunic, handing it to her husband with one of the sleeves up, showing a nub of thread where a button had been torn away.

"I did not see it until now," she whispered to Ernst.

Holding the coat, his face now turned pale, Koeller looked up at Frank Janda. "We will not run away," he said. "I will bring Kurt into Great Falls and give him over to the sheriff. It must have been some sort of accident. I will hire a lawyer for my son."

"No!" Janda suddenly shouted. "No accident. No lawyer. No goddamned trial." He suspected that any judge and jury that heard the case might take into account Kurt Koeller's mental weakness and let themselves be swayed by a skillful attorney, ruling in favor of accidental death—at best, committing the boy to some asylum, at worst letting him go free. Frank Janda wouldn't let that happen. He'd already tried the boy and found him guilty—all that was left was to carry out the sentence.

"Bring the boy out, Ernst," Janda ordered.

"For what purpose?" Koeller asked angrily, straightening and throwing back his shoulders.

"So that I can hang him."

Hearing these words spoken, Martha Koeller gave a low moan and slumped to the ground. Ernst kneeled down to tend to her and once satisfied that his wife had only fainted, he stood again to face the Jandas.

"I am unarmed, *Herr* Janda," Koeller said. "But you will have to kill me first—I will not let you hang my boy."

As he sat in the wagon, Ondrej felt sick and ashamed. Koeller had been the first neighbor he'd met—and the man who'd helped him to build a proper shack. For weeks, young Kurt had dutifully worked with Ondrej on his well, hauling heavy buckets of dirt out of the hole, and stopping to rest only when Ondrej did.

Irena or no Irena, Ondrej told himself, it would not be right to just sit on his ass and let such a thing happen. He had no idea as to whether the Koeller boy was guilty of murder or not, although the torn brass button seemed to be damning evidence. Even though, he reached over and tugged at Irena's gray, cotton skirt, whispering: "I have no stomach for this business."

Irena just closed her eyes and shook her head slowly, sadly, as if to say: *Nor do I.*

Having no clear notion of what he should do, Ondrej slipped off the wagon and positioned himself to the right of Ladik Janda's restlessly pawing horse.

"I got right to hang him," Frank shouted, and to Ondrej it was as if he were making his case to everyone there. "As father, I have right to avenge my daughter."

"Hurry Frank, we are wasting time," Emil Janda whispered.

"You men must kill me first," Ernst Koeller repeated, solidly blocking the door.

Just as Frank levered a shell into the chamber and pointed his rifle at the distraught German, Ondrej stepped forward and spoke. "I think this new country is land of laws," he said. "With laws and courts, there is no room for revenge. *Pan* Janda, you must take this boy in to have trial. I will not help you hang him."

As Ondrej was looking toward Frank, Ladik Janda stretched in his stirrups and brought the butt of his rifle around in a swinging arc, smashing Ondrej Novak in the side of his head and knocking him cold. Ladik dismounted and picked up Ondrej's rifle.

Seeing Ondrej fall, Ernst Koeller seemed to lose all resolve. He sagged to his knees on the ground and began to beg: "I cannot stop all of you," he told them, kneeling next to his weeping wife. "If I could, I would—but if the boy must hang, give Martha and I five minutes with him—just to say goodbye. It is so little to ask."

"*Bratr,* we are wasting time," Emil said again.

"Shut your goddamned mouth," Frank Janda cursed in Czech. "My little girl is dead. I would have given anything for five more minutes with her before she died."

Ondrej was beginning to come around. Irena had jumped from the wagon and was wiping blood from a purplish lump on the side of his head.

The fact that he'd spoken up for the Koellers impressed her. Irena had been fond of her niece, but unlike Frank and Majka, not so fond that she was unaware of Marcy's vanity and selfish nature. But, rage and revenge was consuming her brother, and whether the boy was simpleminded or not, she suspected that Frank wouldn't rest until Kurt Koeller was punished.

"Five minutes," Frank Janda said. "To pray with him—but no more. I am not so unreasonable as to deny a father's request."

The Koellers turned and went back into the house. Martha was sobbing as her husband put his arm around her shoulders.

Inside, Kurt was still in his parent's bedroom, frightened and confused. He knew the people outside were angry with him, and he was certain it had to do with Marcy and the fact that he'd run away when he couldn't wake her up. His parents had just assumed he'd come home because the storm had spoiled his hunting, and he lacked the ability to tell them what had happened beneath the wagon.

Martha and Ernst sat on the bed beside him. Martha gently stroked his hair and wiped his mouth as Ernst spoke slowly and softly in German: "*Sohn,* did you see the Janda girl yesterday?"

Kurt grinned and nodded.

"Did you hurt her?"

"Play—" the boy managed to say.

"Yes, play," Ernst Koeller said, his heart sinking. "But did you hurt her?"

Kurt nodded again and began to cry.

Ernst Koeller buried his face in his hands. When he looked up again, his wife had left the room. He found her seated at the supper table, sobbing quietly.

"Mama," Ernst said, trying to console her. "Our Kurt does not lie, and there are too many outside to stop them. But I swear to you that I will not let Frank Janda hang our son."

Ernst Koeller held his wife close and finally kissed her lightly on the forehead, then turned away, went back into the bedroom and shut the door.

Ondrej was just struggling to his feet, when the gunshot ripped the quiet morning—quickly followed by another. At the same time, Martha Koeller reeled from the doorway in tears, pressing a fist to each side of her head and wailing like a madwoman.

"Ernst could never let you hang the boy," Martha cried, finally collapsing to the ground, her shoulders heaving as she poured out her shock and anguish into the grass.

Cursing under his breath, Frank Janda was off his horse and into the house first, followed by his brothers. They found both Kurt and his father dead in the bedroom. The boy had been shot once in the back of the head and was lying on the floor. Then, it looked as if his father had placed the old .44 Navy revolver in his own mouth and pulled the trigger. Sprawled backward on the blood-soaked bed, most of the top of Ernst Koeller's head was gone.

"God in Heaven, I did not want this," Frank Janda howled. "I wanted only justice for Marcy."

His head aching, Ondrej finally stood and walked slowly toward the open door, following the others into the house. Outside in the yard, Irena was kneeling next to Martha Koeller, hoping to be of some small comfort. Still in the wagon, the other three Janda women sat stiff and stone-faced.

"There is no justice here," Ondrej said. He was leaning against the bedroom's doorframe, with blood still running from his head. It was nothing compared to the amount of blood in the room.

Ondrej glanced at Frank Janda and their eyes met. "Now there are *three* graves to dig," Ondrej said. "Is your poor daughter's soul happier for that?"

The day after he helped Martha Koeller bury her husband and her son, the widow offered Ondrej her three hundred and twenty acres as well as the house and barn for thirty cents on the dollar.

"Janda would pay more than that," Ondrej said, stunned at her offer. "Even Martin Cervenka—"

"Martin and Helen are too old," Martha interrupted. "They can barely farm their own place—and I could not sell to the Jandas, no matter how much they offered."

"Then I would like to buy at that price," Ondrej said excitedly.

"I cannot stay another winter here," Martha told him tearfully. "And I cannot work the farm alone, so I am willing to sell the land at a loss and go back east to live with my sister in Milwaukee."

She shook her head sadly. "I hope I shall never see this terrible country again. It has brought me only heartbreak, and taken away my family."

"I am sorry for what has happened," Ondrej offered.

Martha nodded. "It was not your fault, you tried to help."

Then she added, with a sad smile: "Now at least, my Kurt will never have to go into an asylum as we once feared."

Driving Ernst Koeller's wagon and team, Ondrej drove Martha into Great Falls two days later. As she bought a train ticket east and booked a hotel room near the station, Ondrej visited the bank and made arrangements for a loan using his own improved claim, as well as almost everything else he had as collateral. As character references on the application, he listed Luther Platt, Adolphus Sweeney, and Victor Vondrak.

An hour later, after shaking hands with the banker, Ondrej was standing on Central Avenue, watching the city traffic and carefully pocketing a Wells Fargo bank check made out to Martha Koeller.

Ondrej Novak marveled at the power of established credit and bank loans. In the short time it took the loan officer and himself to sign the papers, he'd changed from a *honyocker* homesteader to an established farmer—a man of some property.

Events had almost occurred too fast for him to comprehend.

In addition to the water well and his own poor shack, Ondrej now owned six hundred and forty acres along the Marias River, half of which was already under cultivation.

With the new property came a milk cow, a six year-old mule, three horses and two saddles, seven fat hogs and two dozen laying hens, a spare Studebaker wagon and harness, corrals, a small barn and tool shed, a smokehouse, and a two-bedroom house built with Ernst Koeller's German attention to quality and strength.

CHAPTER 26

Even though he now lived in a proper dwelling, Ondrej had never known the twin threats of fear and loneliness as much as he did during his first winter on the Marias.

In October, as the skies went slate gray and the weather began to turn cold, he butchered one of the older hogs, remembering back to that long-ago Christmas in Třeboň, when he and Josef had been so bold as to poach one of Herr Schwarzenberk's prized boars.

Almost every day, from their first storm in November, through a bleak, lonely Christmas, and on into what seemed a never-ending April of wind and swirling snow, Ondrej found himself thinking of Irena and the prospect of marriage.

"Dolph Sweeney say I would marry," he'd mutter, thoughts of Irena haunting him during the long days and even longer nights. Another winter alone, he thought, and I might put gun in my mouth just like Ernst Koeller."

He couldn't remember when he first started talking to himself. He only knew that a man could not stay sane just hearing the howl of wind or staring out the door and suffering the unbearable silence of a vast white prairie covered by four feet of snow. He had meant to get a dog for companionship, but none were to be found in New Edom the October day he came in to stock up for the winter.

"That's unfortunate," Victor Vondrak stated, helping Ondrej pick out canned goods from the shelves. "A wife is best, but short of that, a mindful dog would do. Hell, I'd sleep with a goddamned skunk before I'd winter on them baldies all alone."

With his parents, Vondrak had left Bohemia as an infant. The family settled in Lincoln, Nebraska and coming of age in America, Victor had no European accent. Ondrej envied the storekeeper's skill with English.

"I have understanding with Irena Janda," Ondrej told him with a shrug. "Maybe next year we marry—who knows?"

"I've met Irena once or twice," Vondrak offered. "She seems a nice enough young woman. A man could do worse."

And by mid-December, with the wind howling, sheets of sleet hammering the house, and drifts of snow nearly to the roof, Ondrej was convinced that the storekeeper was right.

That first winter, after the daily chore of feeding and watering his animals, there was little else for Ondrej to do except stay warm and hunt for meat. Even the Koeller's wood stove quickly proved inadequate for the Montana winter. Keeping it stoked and burning all night, he was still forced to sleep fully dressed and wearing his winter coat, covered by wool blankets, tarps, and anything else that might help keep him warm.

Most mornings, it was so frigid he had to break a layer of ice in Koeller's well by dropping a heavy rock tied to a rope.

In early November, Ondrej had taken the Colt Lightning rifle and saddled his new sorrel mare, managing to shoot a fat doe. He'd eaten some of it fresh in a rich venison stew, and then smoked the rest. The smoked pork and venison, with an occasional rabbit, and his store of canned vegetables had been enough to keep him going.

Even though he was now deeply in debt, both to Uncle Matek and the Wells Fargo Bank, the most frightening aspect of Ondrej's life was the grim, unending winter, the loneliness that threatened to drive him mad—the long months of brooding, impenetrable silence that hung over the still, barren land like a pale white shroud.

In mid-May, blessed spring finally returned to the Marias. The crocuses were in bloom and the meadowlarks sang. Each day, the sky was filled with long skeins of Canada geese flying north, while on the river Ondrej could see mallards rafting on the water.

Along with making the ground ready for planting, he was busy clearing and cleaning his irrigation ditches, putting in his vegetable garden, and then breaking his first furrow in the moist, softening earth. His heart raced as he saw those first strips of sod curl back from the blade of his plow.

The grass that covered the ground was called *niggerwool*. He once heard Frank Janda call it that and never heard another name for it. It was short, curly and highly nutritious—a fine grass for the soil. The roots were tight, matted together, causing the sod to turn in long strips before breaking. Beneath the short grass was a black half-inch thick layer of fine, rich soil. As the furrows were turned, fat grubworms appeared and the crows and blackbirds followed the plow, feasting on them.

By the beginning of June he had his fields done and his wheat planted. This first year, he planned to farm only the land that Ernst Koeller had cultivated. To do any more would require machinery and help, and Ondrej could afford neither.

The moon had shown pale the night before, and his father had always maintained that a pale moon would bring rain. It was one of many weather proverbs they'd held in the old country, and if it was true in Třeboň, it might also hold true in Montana. Irrigation could do only so much, and the newly sown fields would welcome a fine, soaking rain.

On a pretty June morning, his chores done, Ondrej decided to saddle his sorrel mare and pay the Jandas a visit. He wasn't certain how he might be received; not having seen them since the grim, bloody morning that Ernst Koeller shot his only son and then killed himself.

But throughout all the long days of grueling work, Ondrej's thoughts had remained fixed on Irena. As Adolphus Sweeney had predicted a year before, a man with any sense at all might be able to endure his first Montana winter alone, but never a second.

Sitting easy on the mare, a gentle horse named Sunny; Ondrej took in deep breaths of air, savoring the land through which he rode—much of it his own. The meadowlarks had company now—curlews and bluebirds—and along with them, the first flowers of the season. Weeks before, stubborn snowbanks had finally yielded to the sun and the hillsides were vivid with color. The soft, early summer air carried the fresh feel of a changing of the seasons and as he rode, Ondrej could only think: *I wish so much that my father and mother were here to see this wonderful country.*

Two hours later, his reception at the Janda farm was cordial. Met by Majka and Irena, Ondrej was invited inside for coffee and strudel. Frank and his brothers were already out working. They'd rented a huge "Big 4" tractor, and with three drills attached in tandem, were busy harrowing and sowing the last of their wheat. As he dismounted and tied his horse, Ondrej squinted through the dust, marveling at the steam tractor's awesome size—built by the Gas Traction Company in Minneapolis twelve years earlier—he'd never seen anything like it, not in Montana and certainly not in the old country.

"With such a machine as that," Ondrej told Irena. "I could have finished my fields and come calling two weeks ago."

"Someday, with luck, you'll grow enough wheat to rent one as well," Irena said with a slight smile. "You must be patient, Ondrej, to farm this country requires patience as much as sun and rain."

"Come inside and eat," Majka insisted. "Frank and the others will soon be quit for lunch."

"We hold no ill will toward you, Ondrej," Frank Janda said, as he, Ondrej, Emil and Ladik smoked their pipes on the back porch. Ondrej was feeling sleepy—with his belly full of strudel, coffee, pea soup and a large ham sandwich. At Irena's urging, he'd joined the brothers on the porch after lunch to talk and smoke.

"The business with Ernst Koeller was bad," Frank went on. "I was only seeking justice for my daughter as any father would. Why the German did what he did, I do not understand."

"To kill one's own son is something most men could not live with," Ondrej offered, drawing deeply on his pipe. "Even to keep him from hanging. Ernst did what he thought was best for the boy—then punished himself for having done it. He could not bear to go on living after such a terrible deed."

Janda sighed and shrugged his shoulders. "You may have an understanding of the man that I do not—I only know that I wished Kurt to be punished, not his father as well."

"How could you live as neighbors to the Koellers after you'd hung their son?" Ondrej asked.

Frank Janda tamped his pipe and stared off into the distance. "Never again as friends, perhaps," he said, nodding his head. "But as neighbors—yes, I think so."

He patted Ondrej on the knee. "You will learn that out here, neighbors are a practical matter, that people need not be friends to be good neighbors. As long as they are willing to help—"

"The boy was guilty," Frank went on. "And his parents knew it to be true. Had I hung him, Ernst and Martha would have cursed my name until the day they died."

Janda looked down at the porch floor and nodded. Ondrej had never heard him talk this much. "But if the locusts came again next year, or the year after, or maybe drought, windstorms, blizzards—if illness or accident came to Koeller's house or ours—neither they nor us would have hesitated to help the other in time of need."

"You truly believe that?" Ondrej asked, incredulous.

"I do," Janda said firmly. "It is how we survive out here."

"**Y**our brother is an interesting man," Ondrej told Irena as they strolled near the river. "He has an unusual way of seeing things."

"What was all that serious talk on the porch?" she asked.

When Ondrej finished relating what Frank had told him, Irena nodded in agreement. "My brother is right. After what happened, the Koeller's may have held ill will against us, but refusing to help a neighbor would have made them outcasts up and down the river—and it would have been the same with us.

"Next to family," Irena went on. "Good neighbors are valuable as money. It is why my brother holds no grudge against you—even though you spoke against him that morning."

"I would have tried to keep that boy from being hung."

"He knows that, too," Irena said.

By this time, it was late in the afternoon—quiet and still along the Marias. The loud, rhythmic clanking of the huge steam tractor had stopped. The Janda brothers were done for the day and in from the fields, washing for supper—a meal to which Ondrej had been invited. The sun, low in the western sky, cast lengthening shadows behind the river cottonwoods and showed off the land in a golden orange light. As Ondrej looked across the water, wider here than near his own farm, he watched a great blue heron wading near the far shore. In the middle of the stream's easy current, a small raft of mallards settled in.

Ondrej and Irena had fallen into a long silence as they walked, as if the quiet beauty of the river would be shattered by voices. He had just ridden out to visit her today, but the setting seemed to call for something more.

Marshaling his courage, Ondrej paused in mid-stride and took Irena's arm, gently turning her to face him. "I do not yet have what your brother has," he said nervously. "But Martha Koeller has sold me her land and her house at a very good price. With it came some stock and harness, pigs and two dozen laying hens."

Irena smiled and nodded.

"It is a fine house with a sound roof," Ondrej went on. "But it needs a—it should have—the winter was so—"

"*Osamělý?*" Irena asked. "Lonely?"

"Oh yes," Ondrej said. "I was alone, and thought of you every moment. I could not stop thinking of you."

Irena nodded and lightly brushed his cheek with her fingers. "I know what it is to be alone," she whispered. "I was thinking of you as well, Ondrej—wondering about us—and if you would still wish to see me after what happened."

Ondrej could feel sweat beading on his forehead. "I am not the most handsome of men," he mumbled, fidgeting with his cap.

"Nor am I the most comely of women," Irena answered with a light laugh. She looked into his eyes and saw uncertainty there. He was no longer uncertain of marriage, her intuition told her, just the means of getting there.

"Can you say it, Ondrej?" she whispered. "Can you ask me?"

"I—I am not so good at—"

"Oh, please, *můj miláček,*" Irena whispered. "I would like so much for you to ask me."

Swallowing hard, Ondrej wiped a sleeve across his forehead, put his cap back on his head, and took both her hands in his. "Irena Janda," he managed to say. "Will you become my wife?"

"Yes, of course I will," Irena answered, feeling happiness and comfort in the strength of his hard, callused hands.

PART IV

GENERATIONS

CHAPTER 27

"Lia, we should not have closed the tavern," Josef grumbled. They were scheduled to meet his parents at the Chicago River dock near the Clark Street Bridge at seven o'clock that morning. "It will be a hot day, and the neighborhood will be thirsty."

"One Saturday off in a year won't hurt us, Josef," Lia insisted, turning to smile at her three children crowded in the back seat of the Ford. "Your parents have been excited about this outing for a long while, and it was kind of them to invite us along."

Even early that morning, it already felt muggy, the air heavy and humid. Josef and Lia had been up before dawn, urging the youngsters to get dressed and be ready for the automobile ride downtown and then the steamship trip across the southern tip of the lake to Michigan City, Indiana.

They were joining Valentyn and Janicka that summer morning for the annual Western Electric summer picnic. Four years earlier, Josef's father had taken a job as a watchman at Western Electric's Hawthorne plant just outside Chicago in Cicero. A week before, seven thousand tickets had been distributed to company workers and their families. The tickets for himself, Janicka, Josef, and Lia cost Valentyn seventy-five cents each, but the younger members of the family would be admitted free.

For the pleasant cruise across the lake, the Novaks planned to board the steamer *Eastland,* now moored from its starboard side to docks on the south side of the Chicago River.

"None of us have set foot on a ship since we came to America on the *Graf Waldersee,*" Lia mused. The intrepid Jewish peddlers, already busy stocking their stands, hardly glanced up as the Ford Model T rattled through the intersection of Halsted and Maxwell Streets. "Do you still remember it, Josef?"

"Why wouldn't I?" he asked, reaching over to touch his wife's knee. "It was on that leaky tub that I met the most beautiful woman I'd ever seen."

The *Graf Waldersee,* Lia thought. It seemed so long ago—a lifetime ago—although it had been only eighteen years. So much had happened since they'd left Europe. Josef and Lia's family had prospered and grown with fifteen year-old Michael, another son, Matthew, who was five years younger, and their daughter, Julia, who'd just turned seven, but it had also been split by the loss of Ondrej—now a married man and living happily on his farm somewhere in far-off Montana. Lia laughed lightly and touched Josef's shoulder. "Let's say a prayer that none of us gets seasick this time."

Josef drove the Ford north on Halsted Street until he reached Jackson Boulevard, then took Jackson to Michigan Avenue where he turned north again. Saying nothing, Lia looked at the big estates that lined both sides of the wide, tree-lined thoroughfare—homes she'd once cleaned. So very long ago, she thought, looking back at her daughter and her sons, it has been a good life and Josef and I are still young enough to enjoy it.

Alongside the Clark Street dock lay the two hundred seventy-five foot *Eastland.* To Janicka, the twin-screw passenger steamer looked handsome and sleek in her white paint. She leaned over the railing on the bridge, noticing that the five other excursion ships; *Theodore Roosevelt, Petoskey, Maywood, Racine,* and *Rochester,* all of which had been chartered for the picnic, were moored on the river close by the *Eastland.*

Josef's parents had been there for twenty minutes, waiting for them and impatient to board. "Everyone says the *Eastland* and the *Theodore Roosevelt* are the newest," Valentyn said. "I want to take one of them across."

"Like everyone else," Janicka said, glancing at the crowds on the dock. She had brought a picnic basket along, filled with potato salad and smoked beef tongue, cabbage rolls, and *koblihy*—jelly donuts that were Valentyn's favorite.

At half past six, the *Eastland* began to take on her passengers. The river was calm and empty of traffic, the skies were beginning to show clouds but there was little wind and the morning promised an easy trip across—a welcome escape from the summer heat that would cover the city like a heavy blanket.

The *Eastland* was scheduled to depart at seven-thirty sharp. Her captain, Norwegian-born Harry Pederson, watched from the bridge, noting the size of the growing crowds with a slight twinge of apprehension, suspecting his vessel might become overloaded.

Fifty-five years of age and experienced on the lakes, Captain Pederson was aware of the *Eastland's* shortcomings. The ship had been designed and built for speed—narrow, with a shallow draft—causing it to be somewhat unstable in the water. In fact, Pederson knew the *Eastland* had a history of near accidents and was known as a top-heavy ship. He was also aware that once built and put into service, numerous changes and modifications had been made to the steamer, each of which had added to the top-heaviness of the ship and made it an even less stable vessel.

Ten minutes after the Novaks and the other passengers started boarding the ship, the *Eastland* began a slight list to starboard.

"*Můj dobrota*," Janicka exclaimed in Czech. "My goodness, what is happening?"

"Is the boat sinking, Pa?" Matthew asked.

"It's nothing to be afraid of," Josef assured them. "It's just that we are all still crowded on one side of the ship, and it makes us tilt a little."

The list affected smooth loading of passengers, however, and the *Eastland's* Chief Engineer, Joseph Erickson, ordered the port ballast tanks to be filled enough to help steady the ship. Within ten minutes, the vessel was once again at an even keel in the river.

Now the tug *Kenosha* slowly maneuvered into place alongside the *Eastland's* bow, but a few moments later, as her grandchildren wandered off to explore the decks, Janicka felt the ship begin to list again—this time to port.

"Josef," she whispered. "Call Michael and the other children back. I think something is wrong."

Now Josef was becoming concerned. It didn't seem normal for a ship of any size to be so poorly balanced, especially one secured to a dock in calm water with no wind or waves. He left Lia with his parents and set off to round up his sons and his daughter.

A minute later, as the list to port reached ten degrees, Erickson ordered the starboard ballast tanks partially filled. The stubborn list was straightened temporarily, but he and Captain Pederson were still watching passengers boarding at the rate of almost fifty per minute—and both men knew they'd reached capacity.

"Stay here and watch your brother and sister," Josef ordered Michael, herding the three of them toward Lia. "I don't want them wandering around by themselves."

Janicka and Valentyn were annoyed with being jostled by the mass of other picnickers on deck. They could hear shouting on the docks as the latecomers still lining up to board were being directed by a Western Electric security man. He was using a bullhorn to tell them to board the *Theodore Roosevelt* on the east side of the Clark Street Bridge.

Over the next ten minutes, even as the gangplank was closed and drawn up, the *Eastland* continued to slowly list more and more to port—until she finally began to take on water through scuppers on her lower deck.

The Novaks were apprehensive, but as Josef and Lia glanced about, they saw that no great panic was occurring among the other passengers—most of them young and single, and excited about the day's outing. Lia even heard one group begin to make jokes about how the ship was swaying and leaning.

Adding to the air of fun and excitement, Bradfield's Orchestra, hired by Western Electric for the round-trip cruise, started playing on the promenade deck, attracting many of the young passengers who were eager to dance. With the easy sounds of "You Made Me Love You" floating over the *Eastland,* Captain Pedersen began to make preparations for immediate departure.

"Josef, I'm frightened," Lia said, taking her husband by the arm. "Maybe we should get on one of the other ships."

"We can't," Josef told her. "They have already brought up the gangplank. We'll be all right, Lia, I'm sure the captain knows what he is doing."

Lia wasn't so certain. Usually she trusted Josef's judgment, but her husband was a tavern keeper, not a sailor. Although neither she nor anyone else crowded on deck knew it, water had begun to enter the *Eastland* through the port gangways.

Determined to be underway, Captain Pedersen called out for the opening of the Clark Street bridge, but the harbormaster, Adam Weckler, refused: "She's listing too much," he shouted. "He's got to trim his vessel before I open that bridge."

Pederson had already rung a "stand by" to his chief engineer in the engine room and Charlie Lasser, a baggage man for the Chicago & South Haven Line had just cast off the stern line.

"No more lines, goddammit," Weckler shouted again. "I want that ship kept moored until she's trimmed."

But with a worsening list of nearly twenty-five degrees and her stern line loosed, the *Eastland* swung out stern first into the river.

At almost the same time, the Novaks were pushed and shoved along as the upper deck passengers crossed from the starboard rail to port, waving to a Chicago fire boat that was sounding its whistle as it passed. In the course of two minutes, the list had become so severe that members of the crew were among the crowd, frantically ordering passengers to hurry back to starboard.

At that moment, Janicka and Lia became terrified. "My God, I think this ship is going to capsize," Janicka told her daughter-in-law. "Keep the young ones close to you."

The musicians in Bradfield's Orchestra were busy struggling for balance, attempting to play their instruments while at the same time bracing themselves against the increasing list. The promenade deck had become far too crowded for dancing so the orchestra had switched to playing ragtime to entertain the passengers.

Suddenly the list reached an angle of thirty degrees. Near the waterline, more water began to rush into the ship from openings in the port side, while heavy wooden deckchairs, picnic baskets, and bottles were starting to slide across the decks.

"Josef!" Lia cried, reaching for her children as she braced to compensate for the roll of the deck. "Josef—watch them! Do not let them get separated from us."

Older and not as steady, Janicka and Valentyn were suddenly down on the deck, struggling to regain their feet. The increased list had reached nearly forty-five degrees.

"Goddamnit," Josef cursed, trying to steady his wife and reach out to help his parents at the same time. What was happening here? The question raced through his head. This goddamned fool of a captain was actually letting his ship capsize next to her dock in the Chicago River!

The *Eastland's* furnishings now began to topple over with loud crashes, sliding across the decks. Below, in the galley, dishes were sliding off shelves in the pantry, and in the elegant dining room, Chief Steward Albert Wycoff watched in horror as his dinnerware slid out of their racks and were shattered to pieces.

The piano on the promenade deck lost its hold and started to slide across to the port side, almost crushing two young women in its way. Alarmed, Bradfield's Orchestra stopped playing and put down their instruments in the middle of "12th Street Rag."

"Oh God, my God!" Lia was crying. "The ship is tipping over. We're going to drown."

"No!" Josef screamed at her, above the panicked howl of the crowd. "We may get wet, but we'll not drown. All of us can swim if it comes to that."

Dirty river water was pouring in through the aft port gangway and the portholes on the main deck. Passengers began to rush to the staircases leading up to the 'tween deck, which would prove to be a death trap for those passengers who'd already gone below.

Now the *Eastland* was doomed. Captain Pedersen realized the situation had become hopeless. "For God's sake, open up your gangway!" he shouted to men on the wharf. They tried, but it was already too late.

As Josef and Lia watched in horror, many of the passengers and crewmembers began to jump off the ship to starboard, either landing on the wharf or in the river.

"We must jump, too," Lia insisted.

"No," said Josef. "Any of us could break our neck in a jump like that—or be caught and crushed between the hull and dock. Be ready to swim—we'll take our chances with the river."

Valentyn and Janicka had made it to their feet, when they fell again and began to slide across the deck—down toward the black water. At almost exactly seven-thirty that morning, the exact time that they'd earlier been scheduled to depart for a day of fun on the dunes and beaches of the Indiana lakeshore, the *Eastland* finally rolled over into the water. Her three forward lines were still in place. The spring line and the headline soon snapped, but the breast line held, pulling over the spile to which it was tied.

In front of the shocked and horrified crowds still on the docks, the *Eastland* came to rest in the sucking mud of the Chicago River, her stricken hull submerged in twenty feet of water—her bow less than twenty feet from the wharf, and her stern only seventeen feet farther.

Floating among the screaming passengers in the roiled water, one of the *Eastland's* lifeboats had broken free from its davits and seven-year-old Julia Novak, calling for her mother and choking from the water she'd swallowed, struggled to climb aboard it.

After coughing up water, little Julia peered over the lifeboat's gunwale. For a long moment, the young girl was shocked at what she saw. Thick masses of people were in the river, fighting to survive, and clustered so tightly that they literally covered the surface of the dark water. A few were swimming around the *Eastland's* sunken hull—attempting to reach the docks. The rest were just floundering about—some lunging toward the lifeboat Julia was in. Others were clutching at anything within reach—floating furniture, picnic baskets, and pieces of wood. Many were grabbing each other, pulling each other down and screaming in terror. Julia had never heard such screaming.

At first, she was at a loss to find her parents or siblings among the screaming, flailing mass of people in the dark water. Then she heard her father's voice—calling her name.

Some passengers had already pulled themselves to safety and were standing on the starboard hull of the ship. Many others, not so fortunate, had been trapped inside or beneath the Eastland's steel hull. But most were trying to stay afloat in the currents of the river, and Josef Novak was one of those.

They'd all gone into the water together, and Josef knew that if everyone kept their wits and surfaced as quickly as possible—they would still be near each other. He was right. He found Lia almost at once, coughing and choking, but determined to stay above the surface. Close by, Michael and Matthew came up next, but along with Janicka and Valentyn, Julia was nowhere to be seen.

"*Dcera*," Josef cried out, fighting to catch his breath. "Julia, Julia—where are you? Can you hear me?"

"Over here, Papa—in the boat."

Josef heard her and thought, thank God, the youngest is safe. I have Lia, and the two boys are strong swimmers, but where are my mother and father?

His parents were poor swimmers, Josef knew, and the thought of it made his stomach turn. Holding onto Lia all the while, he turned this way and that as they all struggled to stay afloat, hoping against hope to spot either Janicka or Valentyn on the surface.

"Julia is safe," he shouted to Lia, trying to be heard over the screaming confusion. "You and the boys must swim for the dock—people will help you there."

"What of you?" Lia asked, gasping to catch her breath.

"I will be fine. I must try to find mother and father."

With that he was gone, confident in Lia's ability to get herself, Michael, and Matthew the short distance to safety. Josef fought his way through the flailing passengers in the river's cold and currents, calling out his parents' names over and over—without result.

Other vessels in the area, their crews, and shocked bystanders began helping with rescue operations. Some kicked off their shoes and dove into the river, or jumped onto the boat itself to help those struggling to safety. Others, frightened of the river, threw wooden planks and crates into the roiled waters to help desperate survivors stay afloat.

Exhausted after another ten minutes in the water, Josef finally gave up and swam to the nearby tugboat *Indiana,* still moored on the opposite bank of the river. He was promptly offered a hand and pulled aboard. After drinking a cup of hot coffee, he left that ship and made his way up the stairway to Clark Street. As he crossed the bridge to the other side, he glanced over the railing and stared down at the river—now filled with floating corpses.

Along with his daughter, Julia, Josef found Lia and the boys safe on the opposite dock, all wrapped in woolen blankets—yet still shivering in the summer heat.

He wanted to take them all home—to someplace safe and dry, but he couldn't leave until he'd found his parents. Josef reached into his pocket and gave Lia money—bills crumbled and soaked with water.

"Here," he said, handing them to her. "All of you go home on the streetcar. I'll stay for awhile."

"No," Lia said quietly. "We will stay till they're found."

"It may be hours," Josef protested.

"We are fine. We will all stay and wait."

As the Novaks watched, ashes from the fireboxes of nearby tugs were being spread over the *Eastland's* hull so rescue workers had dry footing on the wet, slippery surface. Men were beginning to cut holes in the side of the hull, hoping to take out survivors as well as the dead.

Earlier, the muffled screams coming from those trapped inside the ship were too horrible for many to bear and curious onlookers began to drift away from the docks. By the time holes were cut in the hull, many of those who'd been alive when the *Eastland* rolled over, had since drowned and remained trapped below.

A team of salvage divers was called in to remove victims from inside the ship. One of them surfaced sick and too shaken to go on. He had seen, sunk in the black mud of the river's bottom, a number of baby buggies—all with the infants still in them.

Although it seemed like days to the Novaks, within less than an hour, all survivors had been pulled from the river—still with no sign of Janicka or Valentyn.

"They are dead," Josef whispered to Lia. "They must be dead, and there is no use pretending otherwise."

"Hush," Lia told him. "We must pray and hope for the best."

Josef shook his head, there were tears rolling down his cheeks. "The best is that they died right away—not like those poor souls trapped in the hull of that ship."

The Western Electric picnickers hadn't been assigned to ships, so there were no passenger lists, and none were written while the vessels were being boarded. Later that afternoon, the great amount of bodies that had to be identified lay in rows, covered by sheets, in the Second Regiment Armory on Washington Boulevard.

Although Josef tried to find his parents among the bodies that were being taken to the armory, the police and firemen were strict in keeping friends and relatives away.

By suppertime, her sons and daughter exhausted and hungry, Lia finally agreed to take them home. By this time, she suspected that Josef was right. Her in-laws, as close to her as her own parents had ever been, were most certainly among the dead.

"How much longer will you stay?" she asked him.

"Until they let us in the armory."

Lia nodded, reached up and rubbed her husband's neck. "We will pray for them," was all that she could say.

It wasn't until midnight that those who believed their relatives had perished were finally admitted into the makeshift morgue. As he slowly walked the rows of bodies, Josef saw the dead had been numbered, their papers, valuables and identification placed in large envelopes with numbers that corresponded to the bodies.

Along with grieving relatives, friends, and Red Cross workers, the armory was crowded with policemen, priests and officials from the Chicago Board of Health.

It took nearly an hour for Josef to find his parents. Janicka and Valentyn lay side-by-side, faces ashen but serene—as if death had been a peaceful thing.

"They your relations?" asked the fireman standing watch.

Josef nodded. "Yes—my parents."

The fireman grunted. "Don't know if it'll be a comfort to you or not, but we kept these two together for a reason." The fireman pulled back the wide sheet covering Janicka and Valentyn Novak, then nodded at the mud-covered bodies.

"When the divers found them, the poor souls was still holding hands—just like you see there."

CHAPTER 28

With a line stretching far into the street, the visitation of Valentyn and Janicka was attended by more people than the couple had ever known in life. Josef and Lia were surprised and touched by the number of mourners filing through Hajek's Funeral Home on 26th Street—most of them regular customers of the tavern.

"They come out of respect for you," Lia whispered to Josef as they greeted people and accepted condolences.

Josef nodded. "Yet, I wish my brother was here."

"Ondrej and Irena are more than a thousand miles away," Lia pointed out. "And in the middle of the growing season. Your father and mother were farmers—they would understand."

Neither Josef nor Lia were aware of it, but nervously pacing the linoleum floor of his house on the Marias River, Ondrej Novak felt almost overwhelmed by both grief and worry.

He'd received Josef's hurried telegram telling him of the death of their parents three days before, but this warm summer morning, Ondrej was forced to be concerned with more than family tragedy or this year's crops of durum and red spring wheat.

Inside the bedroom, with Majka Janda serving as midwife, his Irena screamed and struggled to give birth to their fourth child. Up till now, all her births had been easy and the other three children huddled near the door, frightened and confused.

"What's the matter with Mommy?" little Sarah asked, crying. "Why is she screaming like that?"

The two older boys, Tom and Charley, were no less concerned—especially after seeing how upset their father seemed to be.

"Will our ma be all right?" Tom finally asked.

"I think so," Ondrej said, gathering them up and moving to the covered porch. "You have all seen calves born—pigs and puppies, too. Usually they come easy, no? But sometimes it is hard."

"Is it hard for Ma?" Charley asked. He was slight, tow-headed and full of freckles.

"Yes," Ondrej told them. "The three of you came easy, but she is having trouble with this baby."

"Can't you help her, Pa?"

"Aunt Majka is helping her," Ondrej explained.

"Auntie Majka smells like sauerkraut," Sarah offered.

Valentyn and Janicka Novak were laid to rest side by side in a wide single grave in the Bohemian National Cemetery on the city's far north side—in a specially prepared section for victims of what Chicago's newspapers were now calling the "Eastland Disaster."

In his tavern the following day, every first drink was served free of charge in memory of Josef's parents, and the day after that, life simply went on and their lives returned to normal.

A year earlier, Josef and Lia had taken a mortgage on a newly built two-flat on Harding Avenue and 31st Street—in the settled Bohemian neighborhood of South Lawndale. In style, their house was similar to Uncle Matek's on Cullerton Avenue, although theirs was built of red brick. Josef and Lia offered the lower flat to his parents, but Janicka and Valentyn had chosen to stay in Pilsen with her brother.

"Old people belong with old people," Lia remembered Janicka saying. "You and Josef have your lives to live."

Josef now spoke and read English passably well, having long since graduated from the *Denni Hlasatel* Bohemian newspaper, he now received his news in the pages of the *Chicago Tribune* and the *Police Gazette*—old copies of which were always neatly stacked on one end of the saloon's mahogany bar.

Each day, the *Tribune* carried news of the world and Josef had become fascinated by foreign affairs—especially those articles that concerned the war in Europe.

Off the coast of Ireland earlier that spring, the huge passenger ship *S.S. Lusitania* was torpedoed by a German submarine. The ill-fated Cunard liner sunk in eighteen minutes, taking almost twelve hundred souls down with her—over a hundred of them American citizens.

Three days after the *Lusitania* vanished beneath the waves, the newspapers carried Woodrow Wilson's solemn words: "There is such a thing as a man being too proud to fight," the president said. "There is such a thing as a nation being so right that it does not need to convince others by force that it is right."

"*Kecy!*" Josef stormed. "That is bullshit. Always the Germans are eager for war—the president should teach them a lesson. I will put on a uniform myself."

"Yes, you would make a fine soldier," Lia joked. "An old fart like you would terrify the Kaiser."

"I would punch the fat bastard in the nose," Josef laughed. But deep inside were memories of the *Graf Waldersee* and their voyage across the Atlantic fifteen years earlier. In those days, no one knew much about torpedoes and undersea boats, yet even after all those years he could easily recall the windswept, endless Atlantic, and he shuddered to think of the *Lusitania's* victims—perishing beneath those cold, gray waves. Yet, neither he nor Lia had suspected then that Valentyn and Janicka were destined to meet a similar end in the dark, roiled waters of the Chicago River.

Ondrej Novak became a father for the fourth and last time at three o'clock in the morning on July 27th, 1915—on the same day the baby's grandparents were buried in Chicago.

After a long and difficult labor, Irena gave birth to a baby girl whom they would name Maria. Thinking of his brother's telegram, Ondrej could not help but ponder the irony of life—one generation of Novaks taken out of the world, while in just a matter of three days, a new addition to their family was brought into it.

"Another girl," Irena whispered as Majka brought Ondrej and the other three children into the room. "Are you disappointed?"

"Of course not," Ondrej said truthfully, kissing his wife on the cheek. She felt warm and her forehead was moist. "A baby girl will do just fine—how do you feel?"

"Very tired," Irena said, smiling weakly. "Perhaps our family has grown as large as it should be, Ondrej. I'm not certain I have the strength for another one."

He caressed her face and then the baby's. "You must rest now, and sleep—the children have promised to be quiet."

"It was a difficult birth," Majka told him as they sipped coffee in the kitchen. "The child was a breech. Irena will need a great deal of rest—she is no more a young woman."

Once she was certain that her sister-in-law and the new baby were resting comfortably and out of danger, Majka drove off in her small buggy, leaving Ondrej alone on the porch.

Lighting his pipe, he thought back on their years of marriage. Over that time, they'd built a second story addition onto the house, increased their amount of stock, and expanded their cultivated fields to the point where they'd become prosperous enough to rent mechanized equipment each year just as the Jandas always did.

After each harvest, even poor ones, he sent as much money as they were able to Uncle Matek in Chicago. In addition, a mutually agreed upon percentage of the farm's earnings went to the Wells Fargo Bank in Great Falls.

In the early years, Irena was constantly preoccupied with debt and doggedly insisted they live as frugally as monks. She'd spend on betterments to the farm and their growing children—but little else. Ondrej wore out clothing, gave it over to Irena to patch, and then wore out the patches. The first suit he'd ever had was still the only suit he owned. Her only exceptions in allowing him luxuries were tobacco and whiskey—two expenses on which she'd relented only after a heated quarrel and the realization that this was the hill on which her responsible, ordinarily even-tempered husband chose to make a stand.

"Tobacco and spirits are the same as food and drink," Ondrej argued, slamming a big hand down on the table. "*Můj* Irena, so far and no farther—I will not have them taken from me."

"We must pay off our loans," Irena shot back.

"We will," Ondrej told her firmly. "But I will not be deprived of the few goddamned pleasures left to a farmer."

"Such language," Irena clucked. "Your pleasures will not ease our debt, Ondrej, they will only—"

"Woman, enough!" Annoyed and angry, he'd mashed his cap on his head and made for the door. "I will listen to no more of this nonsense. We will talk no more of it."

Thinking back over the years, Ondrej grinned, remembering it as one of the few times they'd ever quarreled, and perhaps the only time he'd ever won.

On the weekends, Josef rarely opened the tavern before noon, and late one Saturday morning, three months after his parents were buried, a short, stout man rang the Novak's doorbell. He carried a thick leather briefcase and introduced himself as Karl Cizek—an attorney with offices on 26th Street.

"You have inherited a sum of money, *pani*," he told Lia. "Not a fortune, I'm sorry to say—but a substantial amount."

"Money?" Lia asked. "From whom?"

"You had an aunt—Emilka Kovar?"

"*Teta* Emilka?"

"Yes," Karl Cizek said pleasantly, drawing papers out of his briefcase. "I'm sorry to tell you that she passed away three weeks ago—of pneumonia, at Cook County Hospital."

"Good riddance to bad rubbish," Josef mumbled, lighting his cigar.

Lawyer Cizek glanced at him and then at Lia. "I'm afraid that I'm ignorant of your personal relationship to your aunt," he said. "But she named you as her only relative in America, and the sole beneficiary in her will."

Lia sighed and shook her had. "We had a falling out years ago. It was—unpleasant."

"Nevertheless," the lawyer said with a shrug. "The woman left you her entire estate—some jewelry and a bit over eight thousand dollars."

"Eight thousand dollars?"

"Yes, all the savings she had."

After signing all the necessary papers, lawyer Cizek gave Lia a brown envelope that contained a few pairs of earrings, a number of rings, and three pearl necklaces—along with a bank check in her name, for the sum of eight thousand forty seven dollars.

After Cizek bid them good day and left, Irena held the check up in front of her, looking first at it, then at her husband. "Eight thousand dollars, Josef, what will we do with this?"

"Burn it, maybe?" Josef suggested. "You know how your aunt made her living."

Lia looked at him and shook her head. "I am not a fool, Josef. We are saloonkeepers—we are not the Rockefellers to throw away money. What Emilka did to me in life was horrid and unspeakable—what she's done in death may be her way of asking forgiveness."

Josef drew on his cigar. "How could I forgive such a woman?"

"You don't have to," Lia told him firmly. "And if *I* do, it will be *my* business, and not yours. In the meantime, the money will go into the bank. We'll let it make interest for us against a time when we may really need it."

"Do whatever you wish, then," Josef said. He knew better than to argue with Lia when her mind was set. Their years together had been good ones. The children were healthy, and the tavern brought them a comfortable living—enough to afford them one of the few automobiles in the neighborhood.

They rarely spoke of Lia's ordeal at the New Century Club. It was a subject, Lia knew, that after all these years could still tear at her husband's heart. With a woman's practical perspective on such things, she had accepted it from the beginning. It had been rape—and nothing more. Through no fault of her own, she had lost her virginity, but never her dignity and certainly not her soul.

As Lia made herself busy in the kitchen, Josef looked at his pocket watch, quickly stubbed out his cigar, and kissed his wife on the cheek. "I'm off to work," he told her cheerily. "Even with your great inheritance, we still must make a living."

"Yes, that's true," Lia shot back, grinning slightly. "And even so, my proud, foolish husband—you were ready to burn it."

"Dirty money is what it is," Josef answered stubbornly, being careful to say it under his breath.

CHAPTER 29

In 1917, after a growing number of German provocations, and to Josef's satisfaction, President Woodrow Wilson finally committed the United States to the war in Europe. Soon after Wilson's speech to a joint session of Congress, the *Chicago Tribune* began to write about an American general named John J. Pershing.

"The papers call him 'Blackjack,'" Josef told Lia one evening after supper.

"What does it mean—this 'Blackjack'?"

Josef shook his head. "I don't know."

"It's just a nickname, Pa," offered their oldest son, Michael. "I don't how he got it, but they say Blackjack Pershing is tough, and that President Wilson wants him to build an American army to go up against the Hun."

"What do you know of such things?" Josef asked.

"I read the papers, too, Pa,"

"An American army," Lia said, teasing her husband. "Here is your chance, Josef, to punch the Kaiser's nose."

"Well, pa might be too old to go," Michael said. "But I ain't."

"Better you stay home," Lia told him. "And help your papa in the tavern."

"Ma," Michael objected. "Congress passed a Selective Service Act. I'll be eighteen soon, and they'll be drafting fellows my age."

"I will say prayers to the Infant of Prague that they don't," was all Lia could say.

Along with Secretary of War Newton Baker, President Wilson gave Blackjack Pershing wide latitude in their instructions for the course he was to pursue in France. Wilson stressed in writing that the entire effort would need to be made with a view of an eventual separate and distinct American army.

On May 28th, 1917, General Pershing and a small, handpicked staff sailed secretly from New York on the liner *Baltic* and arrived in Liverpool, England eleven days later. Pershing enjoyed a cordial British reception and was promptly received by King George at Buckingham Palace.

The American general now faced the most difficult task of his career. Both he and his staff knew it would take months, possibly a year or more to put an American army in the field. It would be the general's task to convince the Allies to wait for that army, but he quickly learned that the desperate British and French did not want an American army—rather they just wanted replacements.

This made Pershing's task doubly difficult. He had to deny the Allies the men they wanted and yet depend on them for supplies. For months he struggled with building supply depots and lines of communication, complicated by differences with the French about problems of supply, and with the British about shipping.

One by one the problems were solved and American troops slowly began to arrive overseas. The first American divisions were trained by French officers, who expected this to be a permanent arrangement, thinking that the American troops would be brigaded with their troops and would be commanded by French divisional headquarters, but Pershing would not permit this.

His efforts to build a distinct American army clashed with the allied military and political leaders, and so strong was resentment against Pershing's stubborn resolve, efforts were soon being made by allied leaders to have him removed.

To Lia's dismay, soon after his eighteenth birthday, Michael received his induction notice just as he'd predicted, and was ordered to Camp Grant in Rockford, Illinois, for basic training.

After living at home all his life and working behind the bar or in the store-room of his father's saloon six days a week, the thought of army life and being on his own appealed to Michael Novak.

"Give those Heinies a kick in the behind," his younger brother Matthew instructed as Michael waited to board a train for the short trip to Rockford. "I sure wish I was going with you, Mike."

"One is enough," Lia said, aware of all the other young men waiting nervously on the platform. The whole family had come out to see Michael off—even Uncle Matek, who now walked with a cane, and Aunt Anna, still plump and good-natured.

Finally, decorated with bunting, the special troop train arrived and came to a stop with a grinding screech of brakes. A Negro conductor called for all to board, and there was a sudden, rushed churn of activity as recruits and their families said their goodbyes.

"Well, I guess this is it," Michael said.

"Be a good soldier," Josef Novak told his son. "But be careful and come back home."

"I will, Pa," Michael said, shaking his father's hand. Then he turned to embrace Lia. "Goodbye, Mama."

"Be a good boy," Lia told him with tears in her eyes. "Promise me you will stay safe and write us when you can."

Michael nodded, and as the engineer's whistle blew he said his goodbyes to his aunt and uncle, shook young Matthew's hand and hugged his sister, Julia.

"God bless you, *syn*," Lia called out as Michael swung up into the doorway of the coach. As the train gathered speed and pulled away, his parents were lost to sight on the crowded platform.

The train was full—mostly with men of Michael's age. Some looked older and some younger, but in all their faces was a look of apprehension—the look of young men embarked on an adventure they couldn't yet understand.

Michael found a seat on the aisle, next to a tall, blond-haired fellow who was nervously smoking a cigarette.

"Mike Novak," Michael said, offering his hand.

"Homer—Homer Stump," his seatmate said, shaking hands. "I guess you're a Chicago boy. I'm from further west—a little bit of a town called Seneca, on the Illinois River."

"Never been there," Michael told him. "Never been out of the city before, now that I think of it."

"Well, you ain't missed nothing if you missed Seneca. It ain't much of a place—my pa's got a farm down near there."

"A farm—my old man owns a saloon. I helped him run it."

Homer Stump nodded and stubbed out his smoke. "Guess I'd rather spend my time in a saloon than growing corn and slopping a bunch of durned hogs."

"My Uncle Andy's got a farm," Michael told him, as the troop train rattled and the countryside slipped past. "Somewhere way out west—Montana, I think."

Homer whistled low and shook his head. "I heard that's some coun-try—that you can just about see forever."

"I ain't been there," Michael said. "Maybe someday—"

It was mostly small talk, the talk of men who didn't yet know each other well, young men attempting to get over their anxiety and evaluate each other as possible friends and comrades.

Less than two hours later, Michael, Homer Stump, and almost two hundred other recruits got off the crowded train in Rockford and boarded one of five army trucks bound for Camp Grant. Most of the men on Michael's bus were from Chicago, but like Homer, many were from smaller towns outside the city.

As they neared camp, Michael could see rows of long, low, freshly painted buildings. He remembered reading in the paper that the government had built thirty-eight of these new cantonments throughout the country. In a short period of five months, the corn fields, pastures, and orchards of northern Illinois had been razed, and Camp Grant had been built, consisting of camp headquarters, officer's quarters, mess hall, supply depot, post hospital, canteen, and enough two-story barracks to house forty thousand men.

As the recruits jumped from the trucks, a tall sergeant ordered them into formation and they were marched to the post hospital for physical examinations. This meant shuffling barefoot and naked from room to room, being poked, jabbed, and injected by a battery of bored medics.

Once their physicals were over, the barbershop came next and a head shaving was in order. When he was finished, Michael stood up, rubbed his naked head and stared at the pile of his brown hair littering the floor. "Ain't much left," he said to the grinning barber, a private first class from Peoria, Illinois.

"Keeps them lice from takin' hold," the barber offered.

Next, they were double-timed to the quartermaster's sheds—drawing mess kits, blankets, a bed sack that would be stuffed with straw, and finally, their army uniforms.

The doughboy's dull, olive-drab consisted of a tight-fitting blouse of rough, scratchy wool, and trousers cut like riding britches—roomy in the seat, and tapered towards the knees. Their leg wraps were six-foot lengths of woolen bandage wound around each leg from the ankle to the knee.

Michael went through four pairs of boots before finding a pair that fit. A sergeant watched them carefully. "You boys kin fight in coats and britches that don't fit like tailored suits," he said. "But you won't be much good if your feet is ruined."

Their uniforms were topped by a tan, high-peaked, army issue campaign hat with a wide brim to keep off sun and rain—the same hats issued to the cavalry nearly twenty years before.

Regulated by the bugle, their days began at half past five in the morning. The recruits found themselves hurrying to meals, then waiting outside the mess hall in the rain—or holding towels and soap, taking their place in the shower line, and waiting until just before their turn, when the hot water might run out.

Their first days of basic training were given over to the first rudiments of soldiering—a proper salute and housekeeping.

To their company first sergeant, a stocky red-haired Irishman from Bridgeport named Sweeney, tightly made beds were critical to America's successful war effort. If Sergeant Sweeney couldn't bounce a coin off a recruit's bed, that man got hours at attention, wearing full field pack and shouldering a Springfield rifle. Other punishments included cleaning latrines, or picking up cigarette butts and candy wrappers in the company streets.

When basic training turned to learning combat skills, Michael and Homer perked up. This, at last, was the business of soldiering. But weapons were in short supply throughout the camps. At Camp Grant, like most others, artillery practice consisted of loading and aiming with cannon cut from telegraph poles, and the meager supply of rifles forced most recruits to drill with wooden guns.

Despite shortages, Pershing's training camps kept the draftees busy from dawn to dusk. By the time taps floated over the camp at night, Michael was too tired to write home, and too sleepy to pay much attention to his lumpy mattress, or to even hear the snoring of sixty other men.

In spite of diplomatic pressure, General Pershing managed to assemble an American Army of half a million men. A truce came in his controversy with the French and British military in March 1918, when German forces overwhelmed the British Fifth Army and threatened to cut through the Allied lines, with a possibility of the long war finally ending in victory for Germany.

In light of these events, General Pershing performed one of the most dramatic acts of his entire career. Temporarily laying aside his efforts to build a separate American force, he went to Marshal Ferdinand Foch's headquarters and put at the French commander's disposal, the entire American command in France, to be utilized as Foch saw fit.

"I have come to tell you," Pershing said. "That the American people would consider it a great honor for our troops to be engaged in the present battle. I ask you for this in their name and my own."

"We have so many differences, *mon général,*" Foch replied.

Pershing shook his head. "At this moment, there are no other questions but of fighting—infantry, artillery, aviation, all that we have are yours. Use them as you wish. More will come, in numbers equal to your requirements."

Foch grunted, still undecided.

Pershing went on. "I have come especially to tell you that the American people will be proud to take part in the greatest battle of history." He handed Foch a letter to that effect.

"Very well," the French commander said. "The Americans, French and British will engage the enemy as one."

When basic training was ended, the recruits were anxious to be shipped overseas. Michael had never felt in better shape. He was wiry and strong, he knew how to march and obey orders, how to fire a Browning water-cooled machine gun, treat trenchfoot or a wound, wear a gas mask, and use a bayonet.

Toward the end of training, all of them began to talk about the ocean voyage ahead, and few had ever seen an ocean. For his part, Michael was nervous about boarding a ship—his thoughts always returning to that tragic morning on the Chicago River.

When the time came, they were again loaded aboard a train at the Rockford station, traveling back south to Chicago where they boarded troop trains bound for the east coast. With few exceptions, the trains all converged on New York Harbor, the Hoboken docks, or Brooklyn—and then a short ferry ride across the bay, where the troopships waited.

Neither Michael nor Homer had ever seen an ocean-going ship before, and both were amazed at their size.

"Never seen nothing like it in my life," Homer stated. "These durned boats are ten times the size of my whole town."

The troop transports were converted ocean liners that had been hurriedly pressed into service, and in these years of war in Europe, the U-Boat haunted Atlantic was no longer safe for civilian cruise ships. The *Lusitania* had taught the country that.

No longer proud queens of the sea, the converted liners now left port "dazzle-painted" in squares and stripes of black, white and gray—designed to break up their silhouettes to confuse German submarines. The liners' amenities vanished along with peacetime colors. Their gilded, baroque ballrooms, elegant dining rooms, and elaborate parlors had become bare-bones dormitories—with bunks stacked four high. Some men were jammed ten to a room in cabins on the passenger decks.

One by one, the transport ships hoisted anchor, made way out of New York Harbor and through the Verrazano Narrows—with the soot-gray skyline of Brooklyn on one side and Staten Island on the other. They sailed past Coney Island and Brighton Beach, and on deck, feeling the cold salt spray on his face, Michael was lost in thought.

"My folks sailed into this harbor more than twenty years ago," he mused. "With my grandparents—all the way from Europe."

"My people come from England," Homer said. "A long time ago, I guess. They settled in West Virginia first—then some lit out for Illinois. I still got relations back in them West Virginia hills."

Already waiting for them out at sea were escort cruisers, and a few battleships—riding shotgun for the convoy, ready to attack any German submariner that might break through the blockade.

Michael and Homer's unit, the 341st Infantry Regiment had been assigned to the six thousand-ton *Koenig Wilhelm*, a German Hamburg-American liner seized shortly after America entered the war, then repainted in black and gray camouflage and renamed the *Madawaska*.

As the skyline of New York City faded in the fog-shrouded distance, everyone aboard came under the iron law of the convoy. The transports formed groups of six, following behind each other in long parallel lines. Five hundred yards separated each troopship, with a mile or more between each line. On the convoy's flanks and rear, the fast cruisers patrolled.

It wasn't long before men became sick and every gangway on the *Madawaska* stunk from vomit. "When you boys write home to yer folks," Sergeant Sweeney said. "You kin tell 'em you get six meals a day—three down and three up."

Throughout the convoy, regimen was tightly controlled and nothing was left to chance. No detail or inattention, however small, was overlooked if it might alert German warships or submarines to the troopship's course and location. Normally thrown overboard to string out behind each ship, garbage was sunk in weighted sacks, while tin cans were flattened, or had holes punched in them so they would fill with water and sink. Portholes were screwed shut and painted over.

Aboard the troopships, the night was an edgy, nervous time. If the weather was mild it could be quiet and beautiful, yet everyone understood that the darkness concealed danger and sudden death.

The convoys moved in total blackout. The tiniest light might attract U-boats, and they were all warned of the harsh penalties that would fall upon a man thoughtless enough to smoke a cigarette on deck at night.

Yet, it wasn't until they finally neared the coast of France that the most dangerous part of their long journey began. These were waters the German wolf packs prowled—the U-boat's killing grounds. Security aboard ship tightened even more. Everyone on board was called out for lifeboat drills day and night, and kapok preservers were worn constantly, even as they slept.

As they moved even closer to the coast, the lead vessels ran up a signal flag and the convoy began to zigzag as one—executing a series of sharp turns to starboard and port, in hopes of spoiling a submarine commander's aim.

One morning as the sun rose, Michael and a group of others smoked their cigarettes on deck and suddenly noticed that the big cruisers and battleships were gone.

"Gone back home," a corporal named Charlie Dornback said. "If we'd been smarter and joined the navy, we'd be ten days away from shore leave now."

"Guess they went back to bring another bunch across," Homer speculated. "We're on our own now."

"No," Michael said, pointing off to starboard. "No we ain't—look out there."

Through the thick fog, crashing through the swells, they could see small, fast destroyers and subchasers to escort them the rest of the way to the French coast. Like frisky dogs, these ships plunged through the waves, weaving in and out among the slow, lumbering troopships.

"They're lookin' for pigboats," Sergeant Sweeney told them. "As long as they're with us, the Hun ain't going to take the chance of getting his ass blown out of the water. You boys better go below and start studyin' them French dictionaries."

When the *Madawaska* landed in the port city of Cherbourg, there were five American divisions in France. Pershing considered his army fit for battle, yet Foch distrusted their dependability and didn't employ them against the German drive, but rather left them in quiet sectors, where they relieved French divisions.

Not until late in July, as these scattered American units were helping push the Germans back, did Marshal Foch finally agree that the time had come to assemble all the doughboys serving with the Allies into a single American army under General Pershing's command. Plans and preparations began for the first American offensive, to be carried out early in September and to consist of the reduction of the St. Mihiel salient.

Michael and the rest of the 341st disembarked at Cherbourg carrying over-loaded backpacks that contained everything the War Department thought essential for an American soldier in France. Along with his woolen blanket, extra boots, clothing and personal hygiene kit, he and the others in his regiment were loaded down with more than fifty pounds of various items.

Each carried a canteen and waterproof groundsheet, bandages, gas mask, a .30-06 Springfield rifle, bayonet, .45 Colt revolver, two hundred rounds of ammunition, six hand grenades, and an entrenching tool. A two-pound British-style steel helmet rested heavy on their heads.

Immediately upon arrival in France, Michael's division, along with the 343rd, was ordered to reinforce Pershing's newly formed American army in the St. Mihiel sector. They traveled by truck and horse-drawn wagon through the mud and pouring rain toward the Western Front. Near St. Mihiel, elaborate movements of men and supplies were already under way, and the date of attack had been set for September 12th.

But once again, the issue of the independence of the American army flared up. On the day Pershing took command, Foch traveled to the general's head-quarters, proposing a change of plan involving limiting the St. Mihiel operation along with withdrawing several American divisions and incorporating them in the French Army in the Meuse-Argonne.

Frustrated and angry, Pershing refused to entertain the idea of splitting up his forces.

Equally annoyed at the American general's inflexibility, Foch listened to Pershing's arguments and then asked: "*Mon général*, do you wish be a part of this battle?"

"Most assuredly," Pershing told him forcefully. "But only as an American Army and in no other way. If you assign me a sector I will secure it at once."

"Perhaps," Foch said with a shrug, smoothing his mustache. "But neverthe-less, my authority is such that I must once again ask you to put your forces under French and British control."

Leaning over the table, Pershing declared: "Marshal Foch, you have no authority as Allied Commander in Chief, to call upon me to turn over command of my American army, to have it scattered among Allied forces, where it will cease to be an American army at all."

Foch sniffed. "*Général* Pershing, I'm afraid I must insist upon these arrangements."

"You may insist all you please," Pershing said coldly. "But I decline absolutely to agree to your plan. While our army will fight wherever you decide, it will not fight except as an independent American army."

The next day, Pershing stated his argument in writing, telling Foch of the difficulties that American troops had had under French and British command. He wrote that he'd delayed the formation of an independent army only in deference to urgent Allied demands for replacements, and declared that he could no longer agree to any plan that involved a dispersal of American units.

They finally settled the matter by agreeing that the American operation would be limited to the actual pinching out of the salient, and beginning another attack, as soon as possible after St. Mihiel, in the Muese-Argonne.

CHAPTER 30

Waking from fitful sleep in the middle of the night, Michael was shivering. He could never recall being so cold, miserable, and frightened in his life—even three years before, as he and his family struggled for their lives in the murky waters of the Chicago River.

The slippery, sucking bottom of his muddy trench was filled with eight inches of pale gray water that had soaked his boots and socks, his leg wraps, and his britches up to the crotch. In the filthy moonlit water he saw all manner of refuse—cigarette butts, soiled bandages, rainbow-hued slicks of oil, dead rats, and floating half-submerged—human turds.

"Whether it was Fritz or one of our boys," Homer Stump said in disgust. "I believe I'd shoot any sonofabitch that would shit in a durned trench."

Like some muted, far-off storm, the low rumble of cannon was constant, along with frequent, withering flashes of light along the horizon—artillery batteries in a distant salient. Michael was only a veteran of three weeks in the trenches, yet he could already tell the difference between the sounds of the cannon—the dull *crump* of the trench mortars, the sharper *crack* of the French 75s, and the ground-shaking *boom* of the German heavy guns.

For both the Allies and the Germans, the long stalemate of the Western Front had created its own world, a strange, surreal world of trenches—front-line trenches, support trenches, reserve trenches and connecting trenches that stretched from the Channel Coast to Switzerland.

Any amount of rain turned the trench networks into a thick sea of grayish, sucking mud. The prospect of death by enemy shelling or sniper fire was always real, as was the constant sense of fear and confusion—it was life in a dreadful, filthy, stinking maze.

In the trenches on both sides of the line, there was the never-ending scourge of lice. And, out of a hideous nightmare, millions of large, bold trench rats—vicious creatures with pointed noses and evil eyes. Almost like familiar pets, they lived side by side with the troops, stealing stores and rations, growing fat on garbage and the rotting flesh of the unburied dead. Utterly fearless, their screeching and chattering was as unnerving as the guns, adding to the terror of the troubled night. They scrambled over the faces of sleeping men, or burrowed into their packs and haversacks for food.

Their first night on the line, Michael recalled the grim advice they'd received from Sergeant Sweeney. "If any of you men is hit and wounded, make damned sure you keep it clean and covered. A sojer with an open wound has got more to fear from the goddamn rats than anything else."

In the trenches and underground dugouts were hungry cats and dogs as well, along with coiled strands of barbed wire, exploding shells and bombs, blood and stink, corpses in all stages of decay, filth, bullets, and disease.

Trench warfare meant living with the dead, or at least the sight and smell of them. In the eerie moonlight, directly in front of their position, Michael and Homer Stump could see a dead soldier. The corpse was sitting up, his back against a tree stump, so filthy and decomposed that only the familiar coal-scuttle helmet next to him identified the dead man as a German. They didn't know how long the body had been there, but its face was nearly a skull, the teeth exposed in a gruesome smile.

"I swear the sonofabitch is grinnin' at us," Homer said, as they hunkered down and shared a cigarette. "I don't care much to look at him."

"Me neither," Michael agreed, chunking an empty ammunition box at a curious, advancing rat. "I wish he'd just topple over so we wouldn't have to see him any more."

Even in quiet times, men saw things that people shouldn't see; bodies stacked like rows of firewood, others no more than bits of human beings, scattered in the most unlikely places. The land they fought over was dead as well—just a bomb-blasted waste of shell craters filled with stagnant water. Low forests of broken, shattered trees shared the violated ground with corpses, garbage, and the broken machinery of war.

The drive on St. Mihiel was carried out on schedule, and under Pershing's direction it was a success, winning commendation as a perfect piece of planning and execution.

Michael and Homer Stump had gone through the fighting side-by-side, yet neither had the slightest idea of whether or not what they'd been through was a success or a failure.

As best they could remember, the battle of St. Mihiel had just been days and nights of noise, confusion, and the hard, exhausting effort of advancing through mud.

Neither of them had seen a German soldier—at least none that were still alive. Scattered and clumped together, corpses had been plentiful throughout their advance. German corpses mostly, often in the odd, twisted poses of sudden death.

The battle had lasted four days, with the Germans in constant retreat. After the fighting was ended, Pershing immediately turned his attention to the Argonne.

Pershing suspected that this would be the greatest battle in which American troops would be engaged, and the general kept in close touch with it, visiting commanders close to the line to confer on strategy and to encourage them. The drive was directed at the enemy's most sensitive point, his main line of communication, through Carignan, Sedan, and Mezieres.

Each day, it was slow, dogged slogging through a hard region of muddy, heavily forested hills behind which the line was being desperately defended by the Germans.

At night, both armies would rest, finding brief opportunities to sleep or eat whatever rations they had.

An hour before dawn, gunflashes lit the sky.

"Barrage!" Sergeant Sweeney shouted. Doughboys hunkered even farther in their trenches as German high explosives began to pound them. The shells fell in the pattern of a square, advancing slowly forward until they were exploding all around the troops.

Although no thunderstorm could have compared to it, flashes of man made lightning lit the sky. The noise of the shells could be felt as well as heard, the wind made by their passing overhead felt to Michael like a strange, solid ceiling of sound.

As the bombardment reached its peak, heavy shells landed in their position at the rate of fifteen or twenty a minute. Tall trees broke like twigs, crashing down as if felled by an ax. Great bulging domes of earth rose and fell with a force that shook the ground. Small, jagged chunks of shrapnel whistled overhead, while slivers of rock or stones cut through the air at the speed of bullets.

Michael and Homer huddled in their small section of trench, helpless against the force falling around them. Nothing they did, or neglected to do, both knew, made any difference in whether they might survive. Chance alone decided life and death.

Some soldiers just vanished in a crimson spray, while others merely shook their ringing heads and stumbled back into their hole after being thrown a dozen yards by a shell's concussion.

After a while, low moaning and cries came from the trenches. Some men whimpered like children, while others screamed at the top of their lungs to drown out the terrible din of exploding shells.

Suddenly the shell bursts ended. The unexpected silence made Michael wonder for a moment if he'd gone deaf.

"It's over," Homer Stump shouted, laughing. He stood up and began to dance a little jig. "Fritzie's done with us!"

Get down you damned fool, Michael thought, but in the split second before he could shout it, there was a flash and a concussion that struck him like a fist—driving him backward into the mud and causing blood to run from his left ear.

It had been a trench mortar, and when the smoke cleared, all that was left of Homer Stump were his legs and his waist just above the belt. The rest of him, the upper half, had disappeared.

Homer never saw a live German, Michael told himself, except for a few prisoners. But they killed him anyway.

Now it was Homer, yet they'd seen so many dead in the last few weeks. The night before, near Clermont, Michael's squad went down flights of plank steps into captured German dugouts. The doughboys were astonished by their depth and strength. The Allies didn't build like this, they all agreed, pawing through the refuse for souvenirs. German industry was impressive, yet they'd overrun the German works and the dead bodies of German soldiers lay in those grim, dark rooms, slaughtered by French and British airmen who'd dropped hand-grenades on them.

Sick at the sight, Michael and Homer had drawn back from the fat, swelling corpses. They looked monstrous, lying there crumpled among a foul litter of clothes, stick-bombs, old boots, and bottles. Other groups of German dead lay in trenches. Some had been shot, and some bayoneted. One of them, a man who looked too old to be a soldier, sat with his back to a bit of earth—his hands half raised. He had a slight, satisfied smile on his gray face, though he'd been stabbed in the belly and was stone dead.

Some of the German dead were young boys, Michael saw, too young to die for old men's politics. Others might have been old or young. It was difficult to tell, because they had no heads or faces—just masses of red meat in bloody uniforms. Often, legs and arms were strewn about, with no bodies near to claim them.

So now, Homer Stump was dead, too, and Sergeant Sweeney's voice could be heard above the smoke and confusion: "Here comes Fritz, boys, look lively!"

There was no time for Michael to mourn the loss of his friend. There would be time later, he thought, although he remembered the reaction of a corporal in B Company, whose entire squad had been taken out by a German shell—leaving him the only one alive.

It was a fluke of luck, and it left the corporal with a giggling excitement. "I'm still here," the man laughed, unbelieving. "God in Heaven, I'm still here and all of them are gone—what luck!"

The death of other men could not grieve him, Michael vowed in sudden realization. Homer Stump was dead and he was not. He could not afford to waste the precious, threatened moments of his own life in pity for someone killed. The momentary possession of life had suddenly become a glorious thing. Michael Novak still lived and Homer Stump was dead—what luck!

Off to his left, where C Company was dug in, he heard flares whistling up, along with the clatter of the Vickers guns. Once the heavy smoke was blown away, the green light of the bursting star shells showed German troops, hunched over, with blackened faces, advancing on the American positions.

Sergeant Sweeney, waving his .45, went up and down the line, shouting encouragement. "Aim and fire, boys—don't let Fritzie overrun us!"

But the Germans came on, cursing, stumbling over their dead and ignoring the cries of their wounded. As they counter-attacked the American-held trenches, machineguns poured fire along the trench line. As each weapon spit out five hundred rounds a minute, the attackers went down in neat, even rows.

Stubbornly, the German troops reached the waist-high coils of barbed wire. Some entanglements were already torn apart or blown away by the shelling, so they passed through easily.

At other places along the line, German engineers cleared paths with banga-lore torpedos—lengths of steel pipe tightly packed with dynamite—while Michael and the rest of the Americans fired at them as fast as they could load their weapons.

Trying to remain calm, Michael aimed and squeezed off shots in the flare-lit night. But the ebb and flow of actual battle was so confusing, he wasn't completely sure he hit anything he aimed at.

The German soldiers who survived the advance began to drop into the American trenches. The battle became hand-to-hand, with soldiers fighting singly or in small groups. In such close quarters, Michael discarded his Springfield, drew his pistol, and began firing at anything not wearing khaki. Each sap, each firebay, became a small, isolated battleground with pistols, bayonets, and grenades as the chief weapons.

In the confusion of battle, Michael suddenly turned to face a young enemy soldier. The German wasn't much more than a boy. His helmet was gone, and his eyes were wide with fear. As their eyes met in a knowing stare, the frightened young German brought up his Mauser rifle.

Instinctively, Michael aimed his Colt into the boy's face and heard the hammer fall on an empty chamber. Cursing his stupidity, Michael felt something smash into his chest. When he opened his eyes, there was a strange taste in his mouth and he was face down in the mud. Suddenly, he was cold and began to shake—but he felt no pain and could see the leggings and boots of the men fighting around him.

I've been hit, Michael thought, *now I'll be going home.* As the noise and confusion of battle seemed to recede, he could see Lia's face. *Yes son, come home,* she was saying, with a mother's warm smile. *It's time to come home.*

He rolled slowly over on his side, as his mother's face faded in the darkness—a darkness that edged closer and finally covered him gently, as if it were a warm, comforting blanket.

CHAPTER 31

Our Michael is buried in France, Lia wrote.

Ondrej took off his spectacles, rubbed his eyes and shook his head. "Michael was a little boy when I left," he told Irena. "About as old as Charley is now. Such a sad thing for Josef and Lia."

Putting away dishes, Irena nodded in agreement. "Thank God that horrible war is ended. I was afraid the fighting might last long enough to take our boys, too."

"I had the same fear," Ondrej admitted.

"How are they otherwise?" Irena had never met her in-laws in Chicago, but Ondrej talked of them often and she had even written Lia Novak once or twice.

"Lia says they are fine, but that others in the neighborhood are ill—some sort of pneumonia, she thinks."

In that crisp autumn of 1918, barely two months since Michael Novak had finished his training and sailed for France to be killed, Camp Grant had more than a hundred soldiers sicken and die in a twenty four-hour hour period—all from a raging illness that had the military doctors baffled.

On the east coast more than two months earlier, during the last sweltering, humid days of summer, a naval physician stationed at Chelsea Naval Hospital overlooking Boston Bay, got word of an unusual illness just across the water at Commonwealth Pier.

Dr. Colgan was expecting a routine month, but as he heard of the strange sickness sweeping through the sailor's barracks known as the Receiving Ship, Colgan wondered if the weeks ahead might no longer be routine.

Curious, Colgan and a few other navy doctors climbed aboard a launch and crossed the bay to visit the Receiving Ship infirmary. When the physicians examined those who'd taken sick, they were unaware that the illness they were seeing was making its second appearance in America. They were ignorant of the fact that it had originated at Fort Riley, Kansas the previous spring, and then accompanied troops across the Atlantic to Europe.

The men they examined were suffering from no influenza that Colgan had ever seen. In his experience, the flu was usually just a nuisance ailment resulting in aches, a low fever, and a few days of bed rest. But most of the patients they examined showed a cyanotic complexion with purple blisters. They'd been brought down by hoarse, dry coughs and extreme difficulty breathing—the efforts of many barely supplying enough oxygen to keep them alive.

Less than two weeks later, two thousand officers and men of the First Naval District had come down with this strange, deadly influenza. Yet, as startling as these numbers were, more shocking was what was found within the bodies of those who'd died: lungs soaked and sodden with a bloody, foamy fluid that seeped out from beneath the medical examiner's scalpel.

In the weeks to come, the disease would begin its rapid march from the eastern seaboard west across the continent. Four thousand people were to die in Philadelphia, over three thousand in Chicago.

Some called it the "Spanish Flu"—while in other parts of the country, it was known as *La Grippe*. By whatever name it took, the disease moved across America as the early settlers had—following the same traces and trails, now become roads or lengths of steel track and ties.

In the east, it raged on an axis from Massachusetts to Virginia, at first ignoring such isolated, sparsely populated backwaters as the deep woods settlements of northern Maine.

It crossed the rolling Appalachians, and did its deadly work on the great inland river systems. Along with Chicago, it devastated Buffalo, Cleveland, and Detroit on the Great Lakes watershed, Minneapolis, Louisville, Little Rock, Greenville, and New Orleans along the Mississippi.

In that grim fall and winter of 1918, the pandemic would draw its shroud westward—leaping clear across the waving plains of grass, over the high Rockies to finally end in the far western cities of Los Angeles, San Francisco and Seattle.

Soon after, with grip and foothold on both coasts as well as the interior, the killer took its time to creep into every niche and corner of America.

A week before Thanksgiving, Lia fell ill. She'd been doing an inventory of the tavern's supplies when she began feeling flushed and lightheaded. By suppertime, she was burning with fever, every muscle in her body ached, and she couldn't stop coughing.

Seeing his wife helpless in bed and fighting to breathe, Josef was frightened. All around them in Lawndale, neighbors were sick, and for a month the saloon had been losing its customers. Until Lia became ill, they'd been lucky—but now the dreaded influenza was in their home, too.

A pall was over the city. Over the past few weeks, social clubs cancelled meetings, even political campaigns were put on hold. In Lawndale, and other surrounding neighborhoods, city streets were hosed down each morning, and the papers were reporting that city health officials would soon be meeting to discuss the possibility of closing schools, poolrooms, saloons, cabarets, ice cream parlors, and motion picture theaters.

All night, Josef sat in the bedroom by Lia's side, bathing her face and chest with cool water when she was hot, and covering her with the goosedown *periňa* when she felt chilled.

By morning, little had changed. She was too weak to take any food, and could barely sip water. Just before noon, the doctor was at their door. Josef had sent Matthew to fetch him.

Dr. Zavertnik tied a mask on his face and examined Lia. When he was done, he patted her shoulder and joined Josef in the kitchen. Zavertnik looked worn out and tired. He was usually well dressed and well groomed, but this afternoon his suit looked rumpled and his face showed a shadow of beard. "Lia has a high fever and fluid in her lungs, probably pneumonia. No different than ninety percent of those I've been seeing for the past two months."

"What can be done?" Josef asked, afraid of the answer.

"Not much, I'm afraid," the doctor told him. "I've given her a medicine called Dover's Powder, as well as aspirin to bring down her fever."

"Is there anything I can do?" Josef asked.

Zavertnik shrugged. "Just keep her comfortable. It's important that she cough up sputum to clear her lungs. Place hot, wet towels over her throat, chest, and back to open the pores. Rub VapoRub on those parts until the skin is red. Spread it on thickly and cover it with hot flannel cloths."

"What are her chances, *doktor?*"

Zavertnik shook his head. "It is difficult to say, *Pan* Novak. I can tell you that many recover completely—"

"Be frank with me, please."

"Your wife will either recover or succumb," Zavertnik said with a weary sigh. He'd given this stark prognosis to so many over the past few weeks. "If it is the latter, it will be the pneumonia that takes her, not the influenza. So it is important that you try to keep her coughing."

God, let her live, Josef prayed after the doctor had left. *You must let her live.* He did just as Zavertnik told him to do, following the doctor's instructions for the next forty-eight hours—and yet, no matter what was done, Lia seemed no better.

On the morning of the third day, she looked up at him through red-rimmed eyes. Then she reached for his hand and held it tightly. "I fear I am dying, *můj láska.*"

"No, no," Josef insisted, shaking his head. He had hardly slept over the last two days and was feeling exhausted himself. "You are strong. You will get well. You must get well."

"Bring in Matthew and Julia," Lia said in a dry whisper. She was shivering, but her forehead was soaked in sweat and she gave off heat like the wood stove in their kitchen.

When her son and daughter entered the darkened bedroom she motioned them to come toward her. Taking both their hands, she smiled weakly. "You must promise me that you'll not be sad," she whispered. "And that you'll always listen to what your father tells you."

"Ma," Matthew said, his voice choking. "Don't talk like that. I know you'll be better soon."

"Yes mother, please," Julia added. "You'll be fine."

Lia squeezed their hands and smiled once more. "Just promise, and then tell your father to come back in and stay with me."

It was nearing three o'clock the next morning when Josef felt Lia's fingers lightly caressing his hair. He'd been sleeping in a chair next to her bed and woke with a start. "Is something wrong?"

Lia was awake and looking at him. "I think the fever may have broken," she whispered. "I'm feeling better—hungry."

"*Děkuji Bůh*—thank God," Josef said, shaking off sleep. He felt her forehead and it was cool and dry. Her breathing was easier as well. "You must stay still—I will bring you soup."

Trembling in the kitchen, Josef fell to his knees, tears flowing from his eyes like a fountain. He shook his head and looked up at the ceiling. "Oh God, thank you, God. Thank you, thank you."

The Spanish Influenza didn't reach the Marias River Valley of Montana until shortly after Christmas. Yet, by a week into the New Year, people were beginning to sicken and die. As more and more were stricken the schools began to close.

That winter, bundled in two layers of long drawers and an old buffalo robe, Luther Platt, the storekeeper, went everywhere in his buggy, delivering medicine or groceries to those unfortunate souls who were sick or bedridden. Luther Platt maintained that his ever-present cigar, along with liberal doses of rye whiskey, were all the insurance he needed against the disease. For more than a month he went through the epidemic without sleep or rest, carrying hopeless accounts, acting as a doctor and often arranging burials.

One morning, searching for a lost heifer, Ondrej noticed that his nearest neighbors to the north—the Axelrods—hadn't started their fire that day. When he stopped to check on them, he found the entire family bedridden—all were fevered, gasping for breath, and too weak to help each other. Bundled up on one of the beds, a child was already dead, and another so ill she would die that night.

Ondrej's own daughter, Maria, took sick four days later. In the morning, she was helping her mother bake bread, and by the time supper was finished, with the wind howling outside, the little girl was burning with fever.

"Ride for New Edom," Irena told Ondrej. "See if you can find Dr. Smett and bring him here."

Just before midnight, bundled warmly in woolen gloves, plaid mackinaw and fur hat with earmuffs, Ondrej rigged the wagon and set out south in the darkness and swirling snow. He knew he might travel faster on horseback if the roads stayed clear, but if it came a blizzard, Ondrej reckoned to wrap himself in the wagon's tarp and wait things out in the wagon bed.

The wind blew snow all night, but not enough to drift and the ride to New Edom was slow, but uneventful. When he arrived, two hours before daybreak, Ondrej found Dr. Smett laid up himself—a victim of the influenza.

"My little girl is bad sick," Ondrej told him.

"God help her, then," Dr. Smett wheezed, fighting for his own breath. "I was never much of a doctor anyway, and now I can't get up and I doubt I'll leave this bed alive."

Ondrej stayed in New Edom only long enough to gulp down a cup of hot coffee and eat a few doughnuts at Nestor French's small restaurant. "The family sick?" French asked.

"My Maria—the youngest."

Nestor French shook his head. "It's hard times—I lost a niece and a nephew a week ago. They lived in Fargo."

With the roads still clear, Ondrej pushed the horse hard all the way home. When he tied up in the yard, a thin curl of white smoke rose from the chimney, but the house was shut up tight against the wind and blowing snow. Only the dogs, shaking off sleep, came out from under the porch to smell and greet him.

When he came through the door, Irena was nowhere to be seen but Charley was in the kitchen heating pails of water on the stove. "It's for the steam," Charley told his father. "Ma says it's good for breathing."

"How is she?" Ondrej asked. "How is your sister?"

"Maria is better," Charley said. "Her fever broke and Sarah is with her—keeping her in bed. But Tom's sick now. He's real bad. Ma's in with him."

Ondrej found Irena at Tom's bedside. She was gently bathing their oldest son's fevered forehead with cool water and singing an old Bohemian lullaby, "Hush and Sleep, My Little Son."

In troubling contrast with the peace and security of the lullaby, Tom was unconscious and labored. His breath came in harsh rasps, and his bed sheets were soiled, wet, and twisted. Irena looked up and stopped her lullaby. "Thank God you are back—is the doctor here?"

Ondrej sighed and shook his head. "Dr. Smett is sick himself. He could not come."

Exhausted, Irena sagged in her chair. "Then I fear we may lose our son, Ondrej. I've sat here all day watching this illness suck the life from him. He is burning with fever and can't breathe."

"But Maria has gotten better," Ondrej pointed out.

"Maria was not as sick as Thomas," Irena said. As he listened to her, Ondrej decided he'd never before heard such an absence of hope in his wife's voice.

He took her arm and helped her up from the chair. "Charley is heating water for steam. Go to bed now and sleep for awhile. I will tend to Thomas."

Ondrej sat with the boy until the small hours of the morning. In the house, the rest of the family was sleeping soundly. Ondrej too, fell in and out of sleep—just little catnaps, uncomfortable and restless in the wooden chair. Near daybreak, he was brought fully awake by the howling of a wolf, answered by one of his own dogs, Sunny, a shepherd-bluetick cross.

He blinked and rubbed his eyes. There was an eerie stillness in the room. Ondrej looked at the bed. Young Thomas was still now, cool to the touch. He lay on his back with his eyes half open in the breaking light, finally at rest and no longer fighting to breathe.

When it was over along the Marias, Thomas Novak had been taken, both Martin and Helen Cervenka were dead—found in their bed, covered with quilts and holding each other. Ladik Janda was dead as well. In addition to her own son and a brother, Irena lost a niece and two nephews—all children of Frank and Majka.

CHAPTER 32

Now we have both lost sons, Ondrej wrote three weeks later. *How strange fate can be.* It had been many years since he'd written his brother. After he married, the chore of letter writing fell to Irena. She seemed to enjoy it, had a fine hand, and was better with the language than he was. Letters also served to build a bond between Irena and her sister-in-law. Although they'd never met, Irena and Lia grew close through this correspondence, trading news of the families, photographs, and small gifts.

"Perhaps we should pay Josef and Lia a visit," Irena suggested after supper one evening in July. "It would be a welcome change of scene and I have never seen a city like Chicago."

"You're no poorer for it," Ondrej told her. "It is just a big city. Crowded, dirty, and full of noise."

"Nevertheless, I would like to finally meet Josef and Lia."

Ondrej grunted and fired his pipe, reaching down to rub a knee increasingly troubled by arthritis. "Maybe next year we can go and I will see if my brother is feeling as old as I am."

Ondrej went out onto the porch to smoke his pipe. Sitting in a rocker, he gazed out past the barn to the low hills beyond. There was a slight westerly breeze crossing the porch, but it was a warm breeze—nothing that would cool down the heat of the night. June and July had been hot. During these last two months, there seemed to be heat everywhere: heat lightning, heat mirages, panting dogs, tin roofs that cracked and banged.

Such weather, Ondrej thought. Spring is too short and so is the autumn. We freeze in the winter and boil in summer.

After Thomas died, Ondrej was forced to build a fire on the snow-covered hill behind the house—just to thaw it enough to dig his son's grave. One buried in France, Ondrej reflected, thinking of Josef's boy, Michael, another in the frozen ground of Montana—and both taken too young.

He sat and smoked his pipe, feeling tired. Inside the house he could hear Irena straightening up in the kitchen. Maybe he *should* take his wife and children back east to visit, Ondrej thought. Yet, the farm came first—and there was always so much to do.

The screen door banged shut as Irena joined him on the porch. Still in her apron, she settled down on the steps, shooing away the dogs that gathered around her, sniffing and nosing for any scraps they hoped might come their way.

"I miss our Thomas," she said with a sigh.

"Yes," Ondrej said softly. "But try not to think about it."

"Why would God take him from us?"

"Who knows why God does what he does?" Ondrej answered, tamping out his pipe. "Why does God give us locusts, hailstorms, drought, and wheat scab—or blackleg and hoof and mouth in the cattle? Why is Nestor French's little girl born with a clubbed foot? All day, the sky looked like a sheet of brass. Why does God bring down heat such as this—or such cold and snow in winter to freeze our cow's teats? Who knows about God, *vážení* Irena? Try not to think about it."

They sat without talking for a while. Little Maria had already been tucked into bed, while Charley and Sarah were in the parlor playing checkers. To the north, heat lightning flickered, and down by the riverbank, they could hear bullfrogs croaking and the never-ending chatter of cicadas in the cottonwoods.

"Are you happy, Ondrej?" Irena asked unexpectedly.

"Happy?" The question caught him by surprise.

"With me, and the children—with the farm?"

Ondrej shrugged. He'd never given it much thought. "Yes, of course I am happy. Why do you ask such a thing?" Suddenly, these questions about God and happiness—Irena was acting strangely.

"I don't know," his wife said, sighing again. She smoothed her apron and stared out at the lengthening shadows in the yard. To the west, the sun showed as a great, yellow ball, slowly sinking behind the hills. Smiling, she reached over and patted Ondrej's knee. "I'm just feeling restless, I guess—and old."

Feeling old was something Ondrej knew about, but the *restless* part was new to him. He'd never given that much thought, either. All Ondrej knew was there was no other place he'd rather be than on this porch, of this hot summer evening, with this woman, living on their six hundred and forty acres of fertile, irrigated ground. He may have had his share of other problems—but feeling restless wasn't one of them.

Ondrej looked at his wife and shrugged. "Restless—*restless*, what does that mean?"

Irena smiled again. "Husband, I'm nearly forty, and I've never been anywhere but the Marias Valley and Fargo, North Dakota. I might like to see some things before I die."

"But there is the farm," Ondrej argued.

"Yes, yes," Irena said sadly. "There is always the farm."

Ondrej felt he was on shaky ground. He called to mind the last strong-willed, restless woman he'd had dealings with—*his mother*—and her restless behavior had brought them to America.

"All right, all right," Ondrej said. "If you are restless, we will make a trip to Chicago to see Josef and his family."

"When?" Irena asked.

"Soon," Ondrej assured her.

CHAPTER 33

Less than a year after losing his son, Josef Novak was facing the loss of his livelihood as well.

The 18th Amendment to the Constitution of the United States, ratified in January 1919, now prohibited the "manufacture, sale, or transportation of intoxicating liquors." Prohibition, as it soon came to be called, was enforced and defined by Congress in the Volstead Act, which was passed over President Wilson's veto.

"That goddamned flu killed half our customers," Josef swore one evening at supper, pushing away a half-eaten plate of meatloaf and mashed potatoes. "Now the goddamned congressmen want to take away the rest."

"Josef, hush," Lia scolded. "I don't like Matthew and Julia to hear such language in the house."

"Ma," Matthew laughed. "We hear worse than that in school."

"I don't care," Lia argued. "I will not have it around the dinner table and that is that—we are not coarse people."

"Lia, what can we do?" Josef asked her later in bed. "We have hardly any customers left—and in a year, Siebens will no longer be able to ship us beer. It is the same with the whiskey."

"I'm not certain, Josef," Lia said. "We'll have to do something different, I suppose."

"Something different?" Josef asked, astonished that Lia would say such a thing. For years, the tavern had been all he knew—and it had given them a good living. They owned their own home and drove one of the few automobiles to be seen on the block. "Maybe I'll just go back to Pavel Barshukov's section crew," Josef huffed. "Mending track for the CB&Q."

"Don't be silly," Lia said.

"What then?"

"Go to sleep. We will think of something."

That Sunday after Mass, Lia served a fine meal of roast pork, sauerkraut and dumplings, topped off with warm slices of freshly-baked strudel—a wonderful dinner prepared in hopes of lightening her husband's disheartened mood. After the meal, Josef went out on the porch, lit a cigar, and gave his attention to the Sunday paper. Matthew joined his friends for a game of softball in the street, and Julia offered to help her mother with the dishes.

"Where'd you learn to cook, Mama?" Julia asked, drying a dinner plate.

"Mostly from *Babi* Janicka," Lia said. "Grandma was the real cook—she could feed the King of England with a few potatoes and a cabbage. She knew what your father liked, and taught me to cook most of it."

"Would you teach me?"

"I guess I can," Lia said, pleased and surprised. Her daughter had never shown much interest in the mysteries of the kitchen. "All of a sudden you want to be a cook, eh?"

"Well, I have a boyfriend now," Julia announced proudly. "And someday I might get married. What if that happened and I didn't know how to cook him a meal?"

"Marry a rich boy," Lia laughed. "And let him take you out to fine restaurants every night."

Julia giggled. "Why do we never go to restaurants? Are we poor? I've never even been inside one."

Lia just shrugged. "Papa and I go out to dinner once a year, on our wedding anniversary, but your father says he can't get as good a meal in any restaurant as those he gets at home."

"Well, I'll bet he's right about that."

Suddenly, Lia stopped what she was doing and turned to look at Josef sitting out on the porch. *Restaurants,* she thought, why did I never think of that?

"A restaurant?" Josef snorted. "This is a crazy idea. We own a saloon."

"The two are not so different," Lia argued forcefully. "What is the difference between serving people beer and whiskey or serving them chicken soup and pork chops?"

"I can draw a beer," Josef protested. "I cannot cook a chop."

Holding back her laughter, Lia told herself that if her husband were not so stubborn and shortsighted, he would be a very amusing man. She could not believe he actually thought she expected him to do the cooking in such an enterprise.

"I will cook the food," she stated. "And keep the books."

"And myself?" Josef asked. "What part shall I have in such a boneheaded scheme?"

"You can bargain with the butchers for meat, and the peddlers for everything else. And wait on our customers."

"I'm to be a waiter, then?" Josef asked, incredulous. What was this foolishness that had gotten into his wife's head? "And bargain for cabbages with the sheenies and dagoes in the alley?"

"Yes, and we will have another business of our own," Lia told him. "So you won't have to go back to the section gang."

Josef threw up his hands and shook his head. "You are mad."

"Listen to me," Lia said, with a purpose in her voice that Josef hadn't heard before. "We must do something very soon. Another year and the saloon will be no more. I can cook good food, and you are accustomed to dealing with customers. A restaurant will be not so different than a tavern, and the government is not trying to take food away from the people—at least not yet."

Josef was reluctant to admit it, but what his wife was saying seemed to make sense. A restaurant was something that had never entered his mind, yet he was certain that anyone would pay two or three dollars for one of her meals.

"Aside from the whiskey," he pointed out. "The tavern has no assets. We don't own the building; Siebens will just stop delivering beer and probably take back the taps and fixtures. So where do you think we will get capital to open a restaurant?"

"From *Teta* Emilka's inheritance money," Lia said. "And with a little credit from the bank."

Josef sighed. He'd forgotten about Emilka's money and now he'd run out of arguments as well.

Eight months later, with Lia's inheritance and a loan from the bank, they went down to City Hall and paid a hundred dollars for a restaurant license. After a few weeks of searching, they rented a vacant corner storefront on 26th and California. The store had both a showroom that would be the dining portion of the restaurant, and a large storeroom that would serve as a kitchen. Shopping carefully on Maxwell Street, they bought two used stoves and ovens, along with inexpensive silverware and eight sets of tables and chairs. But their biggest expense was a large Kelvinator refrigerator, bought brand new and set off in one corner of the kitchen. Lia made up her menus and had them printed, and in each window of the restaurant was a small jungle of potted plants and ferns, and freshly painted on the glass, in curving gold letters, were the words:

LIA & JOE'S
Delicious Home Cooking

Their menu was simple, featuring six standard items, plus one or two specials every day; depending on what kind of deals Josef was able to make each morning.

Dealing with the local butchers came easy for him. Most were Bohemians who'd been patrons of Josef's saloon at one time or another. But doing business with the peddlers was another matter. These men, who still plied their trade by horse and wagon, were either Jews or Italians, two groups of people with whom Josef had had few dealings in the past.

With the tavern, he'd done business in a straightforward way. The men at the bar knew that a stein of beer would cost them so much, and the same with a whiskey. Aside from the small yearly increases in liquor costs, which he could pass on to his customers, there were few surprises in the saloon business.

With the peddlers, business was different—all street talk and bargaining. The Italian peddlers loved to talk and the Jews loved their bargaining, but Josef soon learned their trade.

"Hey Joe, how you do?"

"My back hurts, Cosimo. How is the lettuce?"

"*Bella*, Joe. You never seen such lettuce. How the missus?"

"Fine, fine, show me the lettuce."

"Ten cents for the cabbage, Mr. Restaurant Man."

"Ten cents? Ike, they smell like shit."

"Then you can have for seven."

"Give me the fresh—for six."

"*Oi vai iz mir!* Okay, okay—for you I give them away."

While Josef was on the street early, buying meat and produce, Lia was already in the kitchen, preparing meals for the day. Later in the morning the deliveryman would bring bakery and bread—hearty loaves of fresh-baked rye, with *houska,* pie, and *koláčky* for those customers with a taste for desert.

Each day, by noon, they were open for business, attracting the hungry shoppers on 26th Street. In Lia's kitchen were huge pots of steamed dumplings, sauerkraut, beets, green beans and carrots. In her ovens sat slowly roasting loins of pork, chickens, and cutlets of veal. On top of each stove simmered pots of liver dumpling soup and a vat of thick beef stew with potatoes, carrots and onions. The radiators banged and clanked, and the windows steamed up in the winter months. But when Lia was at work in the kitchen, the entire corner was filled with the smells of Czech cooking.

CHAPTER 34

It wasn't till nine years later that Ondrej kept his promise to Irena. In mid-November, after they'd finished with harvest, the family traveled to Great Falls and boarded the eastbound train—bound for Milwaukee, and then south to Chicago to spend Thanksgiving with Josef and Lia.

"You will not like the city," Ondrej grumbled, as they picked their seats and settled in. He'd been grumbling about it ever since they'd decided to go.

"Let me be the judge of that," his wife told him. "Aren't you happy to be seeing your brother again?"

"I will be happy to see Josef, yes."

"Then why such a long face about going?"

Ondrej grunted and stared out the Pullman's window. "When I left Chicago," he told her. "I promised myself I would only return after becoming rich."

"So, you think you are poor?" Irena asked, raising an eyebrow. "Ondrej, think of what little you had when you left Europe—now you own a house and a farm, and our family drove to Great Falls in a new Ford automobile."

In all the years he'd loved her, Ondrej thought, Irena remained constant—she always managed to see the best in everything.

That summer preceding the journey, there had been a flurry of correspondence between Irena and Lia. Both women were excited about finally meeting each other. Although the winter months were their busiest time, Lia decided to keep the restaurant closed for the week that Ondrej and his family would be visiting.

"We'll take a vacation ourselves," Lia told Josef. "And show them the town—we were all too poor to do it when Ondrej left."

Ondrej was astounded at how railroads had progressed since the last time he'd been on one—more than twenty years earlier. They were smoother and faster, he thought, the Pullman cars were longer and their seats much more comfortable.

"Pa, this thing's going faster than the Ford," Charley said, his eyes glued to the window. He'd never been aboard a train.

"We are riding on steel rails," Irena pointed out. "There are no ruts in this road." This was her first time aboard a railroad as well. When she'd first come west from Fargo, she'd made the trip in her brother Emil's old Studebaker wagon.

"How fast *are* we going, Ondrej?" Irena asked.

"I don't know," Ondrej admitted. "But the ticket man said it is only two days and a half from Great Falls to Chicago—when I first come out here, it was almost four days to make the trip."

"Our teacher says airplanes are even faster," Charley offered. "And someday people will travel across the country on them just like they do on trains." He'd seen stunt flying at the Montana State Fair and was fascinated by the marvelous and exciting things that a Curtiss JN-6H "Jenny" could do.

Now, young Maria was curious. "How many times have you ridden on trains, Papa?"

"Three—no, four times," Ondrej told her proudly. "This time now, and when I first come to Montana. Before that, we take the train from New York City to Chicago—and the first time was from Třeboň to Hamburg."

"Třeboň? Where's that?"

"In Bohemia," Ondrej explained. "They call it Czechoslovakia now, since the war. It is in Europe, far away—"

"—and long time ago," he added.

The railroad hadn't been the only change, Ondrej noticed. The towns they passed through going east—the same communities he'd seen twenty years earlier—all seemed bigger, more developed. On the farms and in the fields, the sight of mechanized equipment was common, and when there were no automobiles back then, now they often saw three or four waiting at a crossing for the train to pass.

When he mentioned it to Irena, she questioned his surprise. In Great Falls, too, there has been growth, she pointed out. "It's just that we travel there more often. The growth is slow, and we don't notice it as much."

"What must Chicago be like, then?" Ondrej wondered.

"I can hardly wait to see," Irena said, reaching over to take his hand. "Thank you, *milovaný,* for taking us."

Two and a half days later, after changing trains in Milwaukee, they arrived at Chicago's old Union Station on Canal Street.

"You come back an' visit again next year," a Negro porter told Irena. "Your train be comin' into the big, new station—they almost done buildin' it—between Adams and Jackson."

Union station was crowded, with more people scurrying back and forth than Irena had ever seen. Suddenly becoming nervous, she told her son and daughters to hold hands and stay close to her as she followed Ondrej through the crowds.

Finally, they heard a woman's voice calling: "Ondrej—Ondrej Novak—is that you?"

Ondrej quickly turned and recognized his sister-in-law. "Lia," he called out, waving. She looked older, he thought briefly, but just as pretty as the day he'd left. A young man and woman, both well dressed and attractive, stood by Lia's side, but as hard as Ondrej searched, his brother was nowhere to be seen.

He quickly brought his family toward Lia and the two of them embraced. "You have not changed," Ondrej told her.

"Neither have you, *švagr,*" Lia said, laughing.

"Lia, this is Irena—my wife."

"Oh, Irena," Lia said, her eyes welling with tears.

Irena could only nod, holding back tears herself, and the two women hugged and held each other tightly.

When Lia introduced his niece and his nephew, Ondrej could hardly believe his eyes.

"Welcome back, Uncle Andrew," Matthew and Julia said, holding out their hands.

"No, no," Ondrej said, laughing. "You two were babies when I left—and look at you now, all grown up."

"They are in college," Lia announced proudly. "And home for the holidays."

After everyone was introduced, Ondrej finally asked, "Where is Josef? Lia, is my brother all right?"

"Josef is fine. He went off to buy cigars."

Lia had no sooner said it than Ondrej heard the sound of his brother's old familiar voice. "*Bratr*—you are finally here."

Ondrej turned and there stood Josef—just as he'd remembered him. His brother's hair and mustache were turning gray and Josef had put on a little weight around the middle, but the same grin and sparkle in his eyes were there.

"Josef, Josef," Ondrej mumbled as the two men embraced. "It has been too long."

"Much too long, brother—half a lifetime."

"Are you well?"

"Yes, yes, all of us are fine," Josef said. "But now you must introduce me to your wife and family."

More hugs and handshakes, and when that was done Josef told them that there were too many to fit in the Ford. "I hope you won't mind riding the streetcar to our home."

"Just like the old days," Ondrej laughed, remembering back to the time they'd first met Uncle Matek and Aunt Anna at the train station so many years ago—greenhorns, right off the boat.

"Yes, just like the old days," Lia agreed. "Except that now, we are the old folks."

CHAPTER 35

"**W**ell, brother, you are finally the farmer you've always wanted to be," Josef said. "How does it suit you?"

He and Ondrej were sitting in the parlor smoking cigars, while Lia and Irena sipped coffee at the kitchen table, busily planning the week's activities. Matthew and Julia had taken their cousins to the popular Atlantic Theater on 26th Street. No one in Ondrej and Lia's family had ever seen a moving picture, and the theater was featuring *The Thief of Baghdad* with Douglas Fairbanks.

"Irena and I are happy with the life," Ondrej said. "Some years are better than others. Last year was very good, but three summers earlier, we lost more than half our wheat to the locusts."

Josef shook his head. "Locusts, *pah*—here there are only the mosquitoes and fireflies in summer—but in the alleys there are rats bigger than cats."

The small talk went on through most of the evening—brothers who hadn't seen each other in twenty years busily reminiscing.

In the kitchen, Irena and Lia chatted, happy to be away from the smoke of their husband's cigars. "We were so sorry to learn of Michael's death," Irena said. "That horrible war."

"And you had to lose your Thomas," Lia said sadly. "I was ill with the influenza myself. I was certain I'd die."

"And that terrible accident aboard the steamer," Irena went on, as if recounting the family's tragedies would somehow bring them both even closer. "We read all about it in the *Great Falls Tribune*, but never thought you and Josef might have been aboard until we received your letter. Poor Janicka and Valentyn—I often feel as if I really knew them."

They waited for the children to return from the movies before going to bed, and as Irena slid her bare feet down beneath the thick goosedown *periňa,* she could barely contain her excitement.

"Tomorrow we are going *downtown,* Ondrej," she whispered. "To ride on the elevated train and shop at Marshall Field's and The Fair store—can you believe it?"

The next morning, after a hurried breakfast of bacon and eggs that Irena helped make, both families boarded a streetcar that took them north on Crawford Avenue as far as 22nd Street, where they climbed the black, iron stairs that led to the boarding platform of the Douglas Park elevated train.

Charley Novak could barely believe his good fortune—not only another train ride, but aboard a remarkable transport that rode on elevated rails *above* the city's streets. To him, it was the next best thing to flying in an airplane, which he'd resolved to someday accomplish.

"You can look right in people's windows," Charley marveled.

"Well, keep your eyes to yourself," Irena admonished. "It's bad manners to snoop on other people." But she too, was amazed at such a marvelous conveyance. Ever since they'd left Great Falls, the trip had been one of wonder and discovery for Irena. She had always thought she was happy and satisfied with her life in remote Montana, and felt that way still. Yet, she couldn't help but wonder if a life of more convenience, enjoying the comfort and excitement of a great city like Chicago, might not be an equally satisfying way to live. Catching herself, she quickly put such thoughts out of her head. No matter how inviting they might seem, she knew, Ondrej would never consider trading their farm for life in the big city.

"Are you enjoying it?" Ondrej asked, taking her hand in his.

"Oh yes, it's all so wonderful."

"As wonderful as dawn—over the Marias?"

Resolved not to worry or disappoint him, Irena smiled. "Not so wonderful as that, *manžel,* but a close second, I think."

Excited at the day's promise, they got off the elevated train at Adams & Wabash streets, in the heart of The Loop, close to The Fair, Marshal Field's, and all the other big department stores where Irena, Lia, and the three girls could shop to their heart's content. In the meantime, Josef, Ondrej, and the boys made their way south by streetcar toward the imposing concrete steps and Greco-Roman columns that constituted the entrance to the famed Field Museum of Natural History.

Just before they went through its great doors, Charley Novak got a good look at Lake Michigan and his jaw dropped. "Is that the ocean, Pa?"

"No, not the ocean," Ondrej said, rubbing the boy's hair. "It is one of the Great Lakes—Lake Michigan. One of the biggest bodies of fresh water you'll ever see."

"I never seen no lake that big," Charley whistled.

"You mean: you never *saw* a lake that big," Matthew Novak corrected. He was hoping to be a schoolteacher some day.

Charley was somewhat embarrassed at his poor grammar, but he liked his older cousin, Matt. "Sorry," he said cheerfully, before repeating the offending sentence. "I never saw no lake that big."

They spent more than four hours in the vast museum, viewing each exhibit and room upon room of expertly stuffed animals. The Montana Novaks had all spotted grizzlies at one time or another, but never as close as the one shown in the museum, standing on its hind legs, with four-inch front claws spread wide.

"This fellow looks bigger than the one that killed our yearling calf," said Ondrej, calculating the stuffed grizzly's size.

Now it was his brother's turn to be impressed. "You have such fearsome beasts in Montana?" Josef asked.

"Oh yes," Ondrej told him. "But I'm afraid the locusts cause far more mischief than the bears."

North of the museum and in the middle of Chicago's bustling downtown, was the area people called the Loop because of the horse-drawn cable-car routes that once used the district's streets to loop back toward their points of origin. But the cable cars were long gone now, replaced by electric streetcars.

Irena commented on how dark the city seemed. They were on State Street, strolling toward The Fair Store. The streets were full of crowds and noise, with horns honking in the heavy traffic.

"It is because of the buildings," Lia explained over the noise. "The skyscrapers are so high that they block out the light."

Irena laughed and shook her head. "It is so different from our farm—so different, even, from where you and Josef live."

"Different, yes," Lia agreed. "The neighborhood is home and it seems safe and comfortable. We still have the old customs. We speak the Czech language and eat the old foods, and we know so many people—it is almost like still being in the old country. But even though, Julia and I like to come downtown once or twice a year. It is exciting."

Irena nodded. "I was born in North Dakota. I never knew the old country, but Ondrej sometimes speaks of it—was it pleasant?"

"If you had money," Lia said, shrugging. "And power. But for most people it was merely hard."

Irena wondered if life was just naturally hard. Whether it was across the ocean in far off Europe, or in Fargo, North Dakota, or on a drought-ravaged, locust-infested farm on the Marias River. It had always seemed as if things were hard—even though Lia and Josef didn't seem strapped for cash.

"Your little restaurant," Irena asked. "Is it doing well?"

"We work hard—long hours," Lia sighed. "But we are making some money now, and even though Josef feels safer with the bank, I put some of it into the stock market each week. Soon the stocks will be making more than the restaurant."

"The stock market," Irena said with a little laugh. "Ondrej and I know nothing about the stock market—only wheat futures, but we never have enough money to gamble on those."

They spent an hour shopping at The Fair, where Lia and Irena bought new hats, Julia a silk scarf, and both Sarah and Maria got silver charm bracelets with a small casting of Chicago's old Water Tower attached to the chain.

At noon, holding their bags and bundles, they made their way to the Berghoff Restaurant on Adams Street for lunch, where Josef and Ondrej were waiting for them in the men's bar. The Berghoff had opened in 1898, as a saloon—serving Dortmunder-style beer for a nickel and offering sandwiches for free.

"Now, with Prohibition and the police watching, they can only sell this goddamned near beer," Josef grumbled, raising a glass to his lips. "But they do serve a fine meal—mostly German food."

"They did what you did, then," Ondrej observed. "From beer and whiskey to a restaurant."

Josef nodded. "Goddamned Prohibition," he swore. "I miss the saloon, Ondrej. It is harder to make money in the restaurant trade."

As they talked, a small boy came through the door and called out for "Joe Novak."

"That's me," Josef said, turning.

Although the Berghoff's restaurant was open to everyone, the stand-up bar had traditionally been closed to women. "Your wife's waitin' outside," the scruffy little fellow said. "She give me a dime to come and tell you."

Irena thought it was the most beautiful restaurant she'd ever seen. As a dour waiter hurriedly seated them, she admired the rich woodwork throughout the room, the elegant stained glass windows and brass light fixtures, and the hand-painted murals on the walls.

"This is wonderful," she whispered to Lia.

"It is just a noisy place for lunch," Lia said. "And the waiters all are rude, but Josef likes the food here. Tonight, after the movie, we'll have dinner at Henrici's on Randolph Street—there is where you'll find elegant dining."

"We are seeing a moving picture, too?" Irena asked. "How wonderful—neither Ondrej nor I have ever seen one."

Lia laughed. "Well, it's 1927 and about time you did. *Wings* is showing at the Chicago Theater, with Clara Bow and Gary Cooper—and it's a matinee."

The week went by quickly and when the time came to leave, Lia and Irena were in tears. Sarah and Maria had met a few other neighborhood girls their age, and Charley had come to admire his older cousin, Matthew—while at the same time developing a huge crush on his other cousin, Julia.

"Soon there will be airplanes crossing the country," Irena told her sister-in-law. "You must come west and visit us."

"We will try," Lia promised. "And we must keep writing one another. The men will never take the time to do it."

At the railroad station, Josef took his brother by the sleeve and spoke to him softly, so the women would not hear. "None of us are getting any younger, Ondrej. Montana is so far off, and who knows what the years have in store? This may be the last time we see each other."

"Yes, *bratr*," Ondrej mumbled sadly. "I've had such thoughts myself."

Looking into each other's eyes, they shook hands firmly and then embraced. "Be happy in your life, older brother," Josef said. "And live to be a hundred."

"I will try," Ondrej assured his brother. "And I hope that you and Lia will be there to bury me."

PART V

YEARS OF DARKNESS

Ondrej had no trouble sailing right back into the routine of work around the farm, but Irena missed the excitement of Chicago and was blue for weeks after coming home.

Once again, the year ahead held the promise of hard work and generous profits. The past few years had been good for wheat. The world was in need of it and the market was paying a good price.

Throughout Montana, the Dakotas, and the plains states to the south, farmers with shiny new tractors and combines purchased after the phenomenal crop of 1926, plowed and planted wheat with a resolve rarely seen before. The lands were being planted to wheat year after year without a thought as to the damage that might be being done, and grasslands that should have stayed grasslands were being plowed and broken up.

"This is the time we make up for the bad years," Ondrej told Irena with excitement in his voice. "These are the crops that will put our Charley through college."

"Oh, and what about the girls?" Irena asked, still missing the excitement of Chicago, and somewhat annoyed by her husband's narrow view of things. "Maybe our Sarah and Maria will want an education, too."

Ondrej shrugged. "To be farmwives, they don't need books."

Irena was washing dishes and slammed a plate down so hard it cracked into three pieces. "Sometimes you are a very foolish man, Ondrej," she said heatedly. "Just because I've let *myself* grow old working night and day on this farm does not mean our daughters need do the same."

Ondrej looked at his wife in surprise. He was always surprised at how easily a simple conversation with Irena could suddenly turn into a troublesome quarrel. "What would you have them be?" He asked. "Doctors or lawyers, maybe? Why not moving picture stars or even senators?"

"I'd settle for seeing them become teachers or nurses," Irena told him. "Or anything else they want to be—but I won't see them married to some farmer and locked into the same life as ours, just because you think that's the way it has to be."

"I got work to do," Ondrej said irritably, slapping on his cap and heading toward the door. "Quarreling won't get it done."

In 1929, near the end of March and shortly after the first small market crash, Lia became edgy. She'd been introduced to the stock market by the Czech-Slovak Protective Society insurance man, Drago Kosek, who held their insurance policies and who'd helped them greatly in the past.

Kosek stopped into the restaurant a week after the market's brief plunge and quick comeback. He was eating alone, so Lia sat down and their conversation drifted to stocks. "I am a conservative man," Kosek admitted. "And my company is conservative as well. This boom we've enjoyed can't last forever. We are both watching the market very carefully."

"Can you advise me, Mr. Kosek?" Lia asked.

"Of course," Kosek told her. "You and all the others who have placed their trust in me. If everyone lost their shirts, where would the money come from to pay their insurance premiums?"

Even a year earlier, only a few on Wall Street took any heed of warnings that predicted a coming economic disaster. It seemed clear to everyone involved in the speculative boom of the late twenties that stocks would eventually drop, but most people didn't worry that much. They were making money and letting the good times roll.

The post-war world was rebuilding and many of those with spare cash were caught up in the stock market. It was almost a craze to play the market. Little people like Josef and Lia could speculate with the same chance of profit as the Astors and Vanderbilts on Wall Street.

The only difference between Lia Novak and so many others was common sense. Agreeing with Drago Kosek's philosophy of refusing to gamble with money he didn't have in hand, Lia only bought what she could pay for, while throughout the country, others bought stock with cash down and the rest on credit. Not a bad deal, most thought, especially when the collateral was your ownership of the stock. The first small crashes and fast recoveries began on

Monday, March 25, 1929, and for the next six months, the market was nervous.

"Don't be frightened yet," Drago Kosek advised his worried insurance holders. "There are still a few dollars to be made."

The hot, humid summer of 1929 saw rallies, hearkening back to the good old days of optimism. And even though there still was an air of nervousness, Wall Street seemed to be stable.

But during the first week in October, Lia received an evening telephone call from Kosek. With no clue as to the reason for such advice, the insurance man suggested she sell all of her holdings. "It is just a feeling, Mrs. Novak, based on some experience."

"I urge you to take my suggestion," he added.

Lia trusted him—she had no reason not to. The next morning, to Josef's great relief, she sold all their holdings at a decent profit. When the check arrived from the broker, Lia quickly deposited it into the Lawndale National Bank on 26th Street.

Then she began to faithfully buy the morning *Chicago Tribune*, following news of the market each day.

The news turned dark on Thursday, October 24, 1929. A record number of shares changed hands on the New York Stock Exchange—nearly thirteen million in a single trading day.

In the restaurant's kitchen, Lia was listening to the radio when this news was broadcast. Wall Street was a very, very busy place, the announcer said, as were the markets worldwide.

"What is going on?" Josef asked as Lia sat glued to the small Philco table radio she'd bought to listen to Amos 'n' Andy, Rudy Vallee, and Fred Waring and the Pennsylvanians. She was falling behind on orders.

"It's the stock market," Lia said, preoccupied. "I'm not sure."

"Well, this is a restaurant," Josef scolded. "And there are at least six hungry customers out front, wondering about their food."

Even at telegraphic speed, the ticker tape machines weren't able to keep up. The volume was having an effect on time. Issues were behind as much as one hour to an hour and a half on the tape. Phones were just busy signals on hooks. The radio was reporting masses of angry investors gathering outside the New York Stock Exchange.

Lunch and the noon hour eased the panic somewhat and New York paused to take a breath. The radio reported bargain hunting in the afternoon, and by the end of trading, the market came back to regain much of its losses.

Early the next morning, Lia opened the newspaper to read that Montgomery Ward, a stock she had owned and sold, had opened at eighty-three and dropped to fifty before recovering to seventy-four. That Friday, as Lia was serving a special of fresh lake perch, the mixture of margin call bargains combined with sells waiting from the late tickers on Thursday led to a small gain. The trading was about six million shares, and there was a short session on Saturday that brought everything back to the level of two days before.

Drago Kosek came in for a fish dinner that evening. "Watch out for next week," he warned.

That weekend, Lia and Josef went to the movies on Saturday night. On 26th Street, the Atlantic was showing *The Blue Angel* with Marlene Dietrich. After losing a son in France, Josef harbored no affection toward Germans, but he reluctantly agreed to go.

On Sunday, the *Tribune* editorial page predicted a strong rally in the market and another long run of profitable investing.

"Maybe Kosek was wrong," Lia speculated. "Maybe we should have stayed in."

"The insurance man gave you good advice," Josef argued. "Our money is safe in the savings and loan."

On Monday, the trading volume was huge—over nine million shares bought and sold. The losses were great as well, but unlike the week before, there was no dramatic recovery.

Drago Kosek left the office early that day. He went home and poured himself a glass of wine.

"Are you all right?" his wife asked. Drago and Erma Kosek had been married over thirty years and she wasn't accustomed to seeing her husband home so early in the day—and drinking wine at that. "Is anything wrong?"

"I'm fine, *mila*," Drago said. "But yes, something is wrong."

Drago Kosek was a well-read man, a student of history and a man fond of observing the follies of mankind. There is a reckoning that occurs every so often in history, he mused. A time when debts are paid, when wars are fought, or when disease ravages the land, when crops don't grow, or when nature brings earthquakes, floods, and tornadoes.

The next morning, a day the papers would begin calling *Black Tuesday*, the reckoning of years of boom, based in large part on credit, came due. There were over sixteen million shares traded on that day, with stock prices collapsing. In order to get out of the market, investors had to sell at market value, and all those who'd bought stock on margin, on credit, were forced to put up the cash to cover their losses. All over the country, brokers were asking for cash to cover investments, and when investors failed to pay, the banks took what was left of those investments and went after the shareholders for the rest of the bill.

People were dumping their securities and causing even more downward pressure on the market. Despondent stockbrokers, some in tears, were hopelessly trying to get in touch with customers for margin. This time, the panic selling made certain, once and for all, that there would be no quick fix, that the recovery would be slow and painful.

By the time the final bell rang on that long and terrible day, the market had crashed through the basement floor and Drago Kosek went to bed that night a little drunk and somewhat uncertain of what the days ahead might have in store for the country. "We are fine," Drago assured his wife before drifting off into a deep and untroubled sleep. "Our money is safe."

CHAPTER 37

The next two years were dry, dryer than usual along the Marias, and yet, each year, most of Ondrej's neighbors made a wheat crop. Then, in 1931, the country had good rainfall and the nation's wheat was considered a bumper crop with over twelve million bushels produced. Wheat was everywhere—in the elevators, on the ground, and along the roads. But the supply forced prices down from sixty-eight cents a bushel in 1930 to twenty-five cents in July of 1931.

Misreading the market, both Ondrej Novak and his inlaws, the Jandas, almost went broke that year—while others up and down the river lost everything and were forced to abandon their fields.

"The Koellers used to call it the Next Year Country," Ondrej said over supper one evening in June.

"I remember," Irena replied, spooning more mashed potatoes onto her husband's plate. Recalling memories of Ernst and Martha Koeller always caused Irena sadness and a certain amount of guilt. Both were fine people, she remembered, who worked hard to make a home for themselves and their simpleminded son. But when Kurt Koeller killed young Marcy Janda that summer so many years ago, it had brought tragedy upon them all.

"Those times seem so long ago," Irena mused.

"More than twenty-five years," Ondrej tallied. "Novaks have been on this land more than a quarter of a century now—and your family even longer."

"Yes," Irena asked, sighing. "And what do we have to show for it—any of us? Half the time, weather or insects ruin our crops, and when the wheat *does* grow, the market falls through the floor."

"This is our home," Ondrej said softly, patting her hand. "This is our life. Are you thinking of Chicago again?"

"Perhaps I am."

"Times are not easy there, either," Ondrej pointed out. "I have read Lia's letters to you."

Irena began to cry. "Lia is not affected by the price of wheat."

"Things will get better," Ondrej assured her.

"When, Ondrej? When will things get any better? We've only ourselves to think of now," Irena said, making a case for a different sort of life—one that even she was unsure of.

And it was true—they had only themselves. Two years earlier, Charley forgot about the crush he had on his cousin, Julia, and decided to marry instead of going to college—a girl named Ann Thurston, from Helena, whom Charley had met at a dance in New Edom, where Ann was visiting relatives. Ann was pregnant for the second time and they were trying to sharecrop a two hundred acre spread near the little town of Floweree.

Sarah had married as well—a young dentist named Norman Cobb from Great Falls whom she'd met at a dance—while their youngest daughter, Maria, was in her last year of teacher's college at Albion State Normal School across the border in Idaho.

From all they could see, Charley was hardworking and happy. As far as her daughters were concerned—both girls had escaped what Irena had come to consider the doleful fate of becoming farm wives, and for that she was thankful and relieved.

Even while the east and Midwest were being ravaged by the Depression, in the west that year and the year before, the decade opened with prosperity and growth. A national magazine went so far as to label the panhandles of Oklahoma and Texas as the most prosperous regions in the country—a marked contrast to the apple sellers and long soup lines back east.

With the price of wheat bottomed, and the constant possibility of dry years ahead, Ondrej and most of his neighbors made ready to weather the storms. The nearly forgotten survival methods of pioneering were brought out from collective memory, dusted off and put into practice. Both Ondrej and the Jandas increased their herd of dairy cattle. The cream from the cows was sold and the skimmed milk was fed to chickens and pigs.

When wheat crops failed, corn was relied upon, and when the corn came up shriveled and stunted, thistles were harvested. When even thistles failed, some dug up soapweed, which was chopped in a feed mill or by hand and fed to stock.

And each New Year's Eve, when the growing family gathered at Ondrej and Irena's house, Ondrej would raise his glass. "We are still here, goddamnit. We are still on this land."

In September of the year before, they'd read about the torrents of rain that fell in the Oklahoma Panhandle—over five inches in a few hours. With the flooding came a dirt storm the papers said had damaged several small buildings and granaries. Later in that year, both the southern and northern plains were whipped by another strong dirt storm from the southwest until the winds gave way to a blizzard from the north.

The winters of 1930 and 1931 brought blizzards to the plains, and after them, the drought began. First the northern plains felt the dry spell, but by July the southern plains were suffering, too.

It wasn't until early autumn that the ground had enough water to justify planting. Because of the late planting and early frost, much of Montana's wheat was stunted and weak when the spring winds of 1932 began to blow. The crops were also beaten down by blowing dirt from abandoned fields. That March, there had been twenty-two days of dirt storms and drifts began to build in the fencerows.

By 1934, the dirt storms were fewer, but it was the year that brought national attention to what was now being called the Dust Bowl. In May, Ondrej could only shake his head after the *Great Falls Tribune* reported the latest severe storm had blown dust and dirt from Texas, Oklahoma, and Kansas as far east as New York City and Washington D.C.

Drought first hit the eastern part of the country in 1930. In 1931, it moved toward the west, and by 1934 it had turned the southern Great Plains into a desert. The blizzards of dust were not as severe along the Marias as they were further south, but Ondrej and the Jandas often spent long days doing what work they could in scorching heat and blowing clouds of dirt.

In early April of 1935, Irena sat down at her kitchen table and penned a short letter to Lia in Chicago.

Dearest Lia,

As I write to you this afternoon, our kitchen as well as the entire house is covered by a fine film of grit—no amount of cleaning can keep it out for long. I can look out the window and see Ondrej in the corn, wearing a wide-brimmed straw shade hat and a handkerchief over his face. When the dust blows hard, we must put Vaseline in our nostrils. Even our early spring weather has been extremely hot and both our wheat and corn are suffering because of it. These are hard times for certain.

Charley and Ann are struggling as well, while Sarah and Norman are living fairly comfortably in Great Falls—thank God for that. Our Maria has taken a teaching position in a small Oklahoma town, where the drought and dust are even worse than we have here. We miss her very much, but are grateful that her livelihood does not depend on bringing in a crop.

Although eight years have passed since we've seen each other, I think about our days in Chicago often. How wonderful they were! Please give our love to Josef and the children. I remain—

Your loving sister-in-law,

Irena

Less than two weeks later, Maria Novak hitched a ride from Keyes, Oklahoma—the little town in which she was living—into Boise City with an old fellow named John Ledbetter, who almost everyone in town called Uncle Johnny. The old man and his wife owned the boarding house where Maria lived. They'd been happy to rent to a young schoolteacher. She had her own furnished room as well as full kitchen privileges.

Three miles out of Keyes, Uncle Johnny mumbled something that Maria wasn't able to understand. She glanced at him behind the steering wheel and saw that his false teeth were missing.

"Where are your teeth, Mr. Ledbetter?" Maria asked.

"It's the wife's fault," Uncle Johnny explained. "She don't let me go nowheres with them teeth in."

"Why is that?"

"Oh, it goes back aways—it's a long story, miss."

"Well, it's a long drive in this flivver," Maria pointed out.

"OK then, here goes," said Uncle Johnny, grateful for a little chat. His wife was stingy with conversation while Uncle Johnny considered himself skilled at it.

"Back when we was farming," the old man began. "Before she made me sell the place, move to town and take up the hotel trade—I was out on the John Deere. I turned my head sharp for one reason or another—and lost my glasses.

"I clumb down," Uncle Johnny went on. "And begun to root around in the dirt like a old boar hog, lookin' for them specs—and while I was at it, damned if I didn't lose my teeth."

"You lost your teeth," Maria repeated, holding back laughter.

"Yes'm, I sure did," Uncle Johnny admitted. "Both my glasses and my teeth. I was down there on all fours now, annoyed by the whole situation, just diggin' and scratchin' the ground—and then the strap broke and I lost my watch."

Maria howled in laughter. Her sides ached from holding it in. When she was finished, she apologized. "I'm sorry, Uncle Johnny, but that's an awfully amusing story."

"You might think so, Miss Novak, but my old woman weren't amused. These days, she don't allow me to go nowheres without leavin' them choppers safe at home."

Maria planned to attend Sunday Mass and then do her grocery shopping for the week ahead. As Uncle Johnny's old Ford bounced along on a broken leaf spring, the day was already warm and pleasant, with a gentle breeze out of the southwest. After weeks of wind and dust storms—one near the end of March that destroyed nearly five million acres of wheat, Oklahomans grateful for the fair weather went out to do their chores, go to church, or to picnic and just be lazy underneath the bright, blue skies.

"Folks is right glad to see the sun again, it looks like," Uncle Johnny commented, spitting out the window as they drove through town.

"Yes, and who wouldn't be?" Maria said. "It's a blessing after all our terrible weather."

After Mass an hour later, Maria made her way toward Yupp's Café on First Street. Uncle Johnny was off running errands for his wife—she'd sent him for laundry detergent, dish soap, a slab of bacon, and a fresh bottle of Jayne's Laxative Pills.

"Why didn't Hester come with us?" Maria had asked. "We could have shopped together."

"She don't care to be seen with me when my teeth ain't in, is why," Uncle Johnny explained. "Plus, I know where to buy a little busthead whiskey in this town—an' she takes a dim view of that."

"So will I," Maria told him. "If you show up pie-eyed later."

Before she headed off to church, they'd agreed to meet at two o'clock that afternoon, back where the Ford was parked. She knew that if Uncle Johnny showed up drunk, she'd have to drive home—and driving wasn't one of Maria's strongest skills.

She bought a Sunday copy of the *Daily Oklahoman* and settled into a booth at Yupp's. When the blonde, heavyset waitress came over to take her order, Maria asked for a hamburger with french fries, and a chocolate milkshake. People were always telling her how thin she was—so she was bound and determined to put on a few pounds before seeing her folks on the Fourth of July.

"You want that shake thick, hon?" the blonde waitress asked. "Or super thick? We put more ice cream in it that way—you gotta eat it with a spoon."

"Super thick," Maria said, before opening her newspaper and turning to the funnies.

After lunch, she made her way to the grocery store. Strolling the sidewalk on First Street, Maria felt a little puff of breeze and glanced at the sky, which looked to be growing overcast. *Rain,* she wondered hopefully, we sure could use it.

By mid-afternoon, as she finished shopping, the temperature had dropped and outside the store, birds were chattering nervously. She grew impatient with the young checkout girl who was slowly counting out her change. If it were to come a downpour, Maria told herself, they'd best hurry back to Keyes before the roads became a sticky mess of mud.

When she stepped out onto the sidewalk, she was surprised to see a crowd standing in the street. One of them was a man holding a baby, and pointing toward the southwest.

"Who-ee," the man said with a whistle. "Will you look at that black sonofabitch."

A thin, young woman who looked to be the fellow's wife tore the sleeping infant from his arms and began to run. "It's the end of the world," she was screaming.

Maria stepped into the darkening street; stared in the direction the man had been pointing, and could barely believe what she saw. With a thunderous roar, an enormous black cloud—a hundred foot solid wall of dirt and dust was blotting out the sky, rolling down on Boise City at sixty miles an hour.

"Oh, my God," Maria gasped, turning and bolting for the open door of the grocery store.

By the time the storm hit, there were more than thirty terrified people huddled in the grocery. The girl at the checkout counter was a teenager who only worked Sundays so the store's owner could go catfishing on the Beaver River. She'd never seen so many folks in the store on a Sunday before.

They huddled in the dark for the better part of four hours as the monstrous cloud passed over town, blotting out the sun and turning day into black night.

Those in the store choked and fought for breath. The store's windows were shattered by the wind and the impact of the dirt blowing in was like large shovelfuls of fine sand thrown into their faces. Outside, people that were caught in their own backyards had to grope for the doorstep, while automobiles lurched to a standstill, their headlights useless against the darkness of the swirling dust.

When the night finally passed and gave back the evening light, Maria and the others emerged to find a town that looked as if it had been scoured by sandpaper.

Stray dogs and cats that had no place for refuge lay dead in the streets and alleys. In the fields outside of town, cattle had become blinded during the storm, running in circles and inhaling dust until they fell and died, lungs caked with dirt and mud. Newborn calves suffocated. Carcasses of jackrabbits, small birds, and field mice lay by the hundreds in ditches and along the roads.

Maria picked up her two bags of groceries and made her way back toward the old Ford. Halfway there, she came upon another crowd. Elbowing her way through, she saw a body on the street. It was Uncle Johnny Ledbetter.

"My God, what happened?" she asked, kneeling to help him.

"Dunno miss," a man said. "We just found the old gent laying here. Don' know if he suffocated or took a heart attack—poor fella was dead when we found him."

Maria stood up and straightened her dress. "This man is Mr. John Ledbetter of Keyes," she said. "He was my landlord. Is there a reliable undertaker in town?"

"Why, sure there is," a woman said. "We got a number of 'em. Percy Purcell over on Second Street—he does a first rate job."

Maria sighed. "I'd appreciate it if some of you men would be kind enough to carry Mr. Ledbetter over there. I'll have to drive his car home and break the news to his wife."

CHAPTER 38

President Herbert Hoover, underestimating the seriousness of the crisis, had dismissed the Depression as "a passing incident in our national lives," assuring Americans it would be over in sixty days. A strong believer in rugged individualism, Hoover did not believe that the government should offer any relief to the poverty-stricken population. Focusing instead, on a trickle-down economic policy to help finance businesses and banks, President Hoover met stubborn resistance from businessmen who found it much easier to just lay off workers.

"Hoover doesn't know his ass from a *knedlík*," Josef and most of his neighbors maintained as the 1932 elections had loomed. Blamed by many for the Great Depression, Hoover was widely ridiculed: an empty pocket turned inside out was called a "Hoover flag" and the shantytowns appearing around the country took the name "Hoovervilles."

Franklin Delano Roosevelt, the governor from New York, was offering beaten-down Americans a New Deal, and was elected in a landslide victory. He took quick action to attack the Depression, declaring a four-day bank holiday, during which Congress passed the Emergency Banking Relief Act to stabilize the banking system. During the first hundred days of his administration, Roosevelt laid the groundwork for his New Deal remedies designed to rescue the country from the depths of despair.

Lia didn't know what they would have done if Drago Kosak hadn't given her the good advice to sell off their stock before the market crashed. Stock prices eventually bottomed out in November and recovered by the end of the year, but the damage had already been done. Soon after that, even the banks were in trouble—over a thousand of them failed and closed in 1930 alone. Lia and

Josef were frightened as they read the *Chicago Tribune* each morning—rumors of impending bank closings usually brought out mobs of depositors determined to withdraw their savings before the doors closed and left them broke.

"Maybe we should take ours out, too," Josef suggested. "And hide the money somewhere in the house. These days, those with cash are king."

But when they questioned Mr. Novotny, president of the bank, he assured them their savings were safe. "We've never missed a dividend payment, Mrs. Novak, and we don't intend to start now. If you and your husband are truly worried, you're able to draw out a fixed percentage of your savings each week—then there is no run on the bank, and no depositor looses a penny."

After discussing their options over a cup of coffee at Sedlak's Bakery, they went back and told the banker to hold their money.

"I trusted Drago Kosak," Lia told him. "And we will trust you, too, *Pan* Novotny."

But even with few debts and a small amount of savings, times proved hard. Lia and Josef's restaurant was suddenly hurting for business—down more than fifty percent since the market crashed.

They were forced to close during the afternoon—few people ate lunch in restaurants these days, and even fewer shopped along 26th Street. But they opened each evening for supper, holding on stubbornly, cutting costs, varying the menu and hoping to keep the restaurant a profitable enterprise—even with fewer customers.

It was finally Utah's deciding vote, in December 1933, for the Twenty-first Amendment and the repeal of Prohibition that saved them, and Josef was quick to take advantage of it. "We are slowly going broke," he told Lia, while at the same time admitting that the restaurant had been a fine idea and had gotten them through fifteen years of Prohibition. "But these times cannot support a restaurant, *miláček,* I am tired of seeing only four or five people come in each night, tired of watching you work so hard for nickels and dimes—and I am very, very tired of waiting tables. People will be drinking again, and I want to be back in the saloon business."

Lia couldn't argue, in fact she had no intention of doing so. It was true; the restaurant had been a good idea and had given them a living for many years. But now, things had changed once more—things always seemed to be changing. She too, was becoming tired of the hot kitchen, of preparing food when no one came through the door to eat it. Josef had been a good provider when he owned the tavern—and now it was time to let him have his way again.

"Yes Joe, this time you are right," Lia said with a sigh. "We won't renew the lease, and we'll sell all the kitchen equipment to a second hand supplier. You can go back to the tavern trade."

With all the problems the Depression brought, Lia and Josef were grateful the children were doing well. Both had graduated from Blackburn College in Carlinville, Illinois. Matt was living back in the neighborhood with his wife, Ida, teaching Freshman English at Farragut High School, while Julia, had gone on to nursing school, and was working in the crowded surgical ward at Cook County Hospital. She was about to be married to a Chicago policeman named Milton Terhune.

When Julia became engaged, Josef had misgivings about his daughter's choice of a husband. "*Irský*," he grumbled. "The girl is marrying a damned Irishman."

"Be still," Lia told her husband. "Our daughter loves him, and after all, the young fellow *is* a policeman."

Josef was unimpressed. He could still remember the stout Irish copper that Pavel Barshukov clubbed the night that he, Ondrej, and the Russian had rescued Lia from Sol Levine's whorehouse. But he didn't mention it to Lia.

"That is a profession *almost* as respected as a saloonkeeper," she added, with good-natured sarcasm.

"It was respected in the old days," Josef shot back.

"Yes, well," Lia said with a grin. "I'm still patiently waiting to see my husband become Josef Novak—the alderman."

By May of 1935, on both the southern and northern plains, it seemed as if the wind and dust had been blowing for as long as anyone could remember.

"These winds and duststorms have us just trading farms, Pa," Charley said, shaking his head. "Swapping land with the farmers in Idaho, Wyoming and North Dakota."

In Montana, as elsewhere, rain had become an event occurring mostly in dreams. "Annie got hit in the head with a drop of rain yesterday," Charley joked at Sunday dinner. "It knocked her cold. I had to throw a bucket of sand in her face to wake her up."

Even with a sense of humor, the days and months and years brought a slow, grinding, spirit-destroying misery; thick clouds of brown, gritty dust sweeping down, howling across the countryside and carrying with it topsoil, seed, and the fading hopes of the Great Plains farmers.

—I remember our first bad dust storm, Irena wrote Lia in the autumn of 1936. *The meadowlarks and other birds fluttered, the jackrabbits ran, and the sky turned black. Ondrej and I thought it was a twister, and we took to the root cellar and stayed for about an hour. When we came back into the house, the dust was so thick in our bedroom that we just moved the mattress into the parlor so we could sleep.*

Yet most years, dear sister-in-law, our prayers are answered and we seem to make a crop—

It was a hellish, inescapable heat in mid-summer—along with parching drought and furnace-like winds. The storms came with regularity, and Irena often thought she might go mad. She recalled reading of the many old-time pioneer women who'd lost their minds to loneliness and the constant, howling winds of the prairies, and she worried that she'd fall victim to a similar fate. If it hadn't been for the company and support of her husband, her son, and the Jandas, Irena was certain she'd be in a crazyhouse.

When the dirt wasn't blowing in clouds, it settled down as fine silt, constantly seeping under doors, between window ledges, and easily finding its way through any opening in the house. No matter how much sweeping, mopping, beating of carpets, and vacuuming Irena did, there was always grit in the air, settling on her as well as on the furniture.

Even though Prohibition had been repealed, as the Depression worsened, even the tavern business wasn't what it had been. It was a hot, humid Saturday afternoon in July, and Josef's saloon had only four or five patrons sitting on stools at the bar, sipping their beers and complaining of the heat. In the old days, when he'd first started out in the saloon business, Josef might have been serving twenty or thirty customers on a hot afternoon, but now only air conditioning could bring in a crowd like that.

"These days, not many can afford to drink, Joe," Bill Kalivoda offered. Bill had been a regular ever since Josef had gotten into the saloon business. He was a veteran Chicago fireman—a tiller driver on a ladder truck out of Engine Company 99 on 30th and Kedvale.

"You come in regular enough," Josef pointed out.

"That's because I ain't out of work," Kalivoda said. "There's always fires to fight. Hell, some guys torch their own houses just to collect the goddamn insurance. Times ain't easy."

Bill Kalivoda was right. All over the city, weary, hollow-eyed men patiently stood in employment agency lines that stretched for blocks—only to be told at the end that there was no work.

Many men were forced to ask for lines of credit at the local grocery store, and even when their wives bought on credit, beans replaced meat on the supper table.

People began to pawn valuables, to sell apples on the street, as well as resort to outright begging. Some men put all their cash into the gas tanks of their automobiles, packed up the family, and began to search from state to state for work.

Things changed for the Novaks, too. The tavern was providing a living, but not an overly comfortable one. There were no more fancy dinners on Sunday. Most Sunday afternoons, Matt and his growing family would come to visit after Mass at Blessed Agnes, as would Julia and Milton, if neither happened to be working that day. But Lia's Sunday fare now usually consisted of casseroles rather than roast pork or chicken.

"Joe, I almost had to shoot a guy last week," Milt Terhune told Josef one Sunday evening. Dinner was over, and along with Matt, they were in the parlor listening to the radio. Julia, was pregnant, and the women were fussing over her in the kitchen.

"What happened?" Josef asked, lighting his cigar. Although he'd come to like Milt Terhune, he'd never been very happy with the fact that his only daughter's husband was a cop—and an Irish one at that.

"About midnight, me and my partner was patrolling near the White Castle hamburger joint," Milt related. "We seen a bunch of guys in back of the place—maybe twenty—fightin' over a bin of garbage. I tried to break it up, an' a guy came at me with a razor—he was a nigger. I had my revolver pointin' right at his goddamned forehead when my partner knocked him cold with a sap. The rest o' those lads took off runnin'—I ain't told Julia about it."

Josef nodded. "No need," he said. "She would just worry."

"But things are bad on the streets," Milt went on, shaking his head. "Robberies are up, and suicides, too. We're always getting a call about some poor stiff turned on the gas, or hung himself in the damn closet."

"Maybe you should think about a different line of work," Matt suggested, but Milt disagreed.

"Nothin' doin'," he said, snubbing out a cigarette. "They ain't layin' cops off yet, and it's steady pay—we'll be needin' it when the baby comes."

"Well, Roosevelt's doing his best," Josef maintained, although he wasn't so sure he believed that himself, but he didn't care to see his son-in-law get down in the dumps. Josef had been in the saloon business long enough to know there were few things worse that a gloomy Irishman. "Things'll get better—you'll see."

In August, Charley was helping Ondrej mend a fence that had been torn up by the windstorms. Charley's older son, Harland, had come along to help. The boy had just celebrated his ninth birthday and had been allowed to hunt with his father for the first time. "We went out looking for quail," Charley told Ondrej. "I let him tote the little 20-gauge—the one you got for me when I was small."

"Yes, I remember," Ondrej said. "We bought it for you when you were only ten, for *your* birthday—from the Montgomery Ward catalogue. You were so excited you almost peed your pants."

"I got to shoot it, Grandpa," young Harland said. "But I didn't hit nuthin.'"

"Well, quail's a small target," Charley told his son. "And they fly swift, too."

"Maybe start him off on something bigger," Ondrej suggested. "A jackrabbit or two."

"Hell," Charley said, grunting as he sunk a post. "I ain't seen a jackrabbit around here for years—ever since these winds started to blow. I believe they just dried up and blew away—like ever'thing else."

Two hours later, just as they'd sunk their last post and were fixing to string wire, the winds picked up from the southwest and they could see a duster coming at them in the distance.

Ondrej cursed and tied his bandanna over his nose and mouth. "It looks like we'll be working in a blow," he said, disgustedly.

Suddenly, young Harland was doubled up on the ground. He was sweating, groaning and clutching his side.

"What's wrong, boy?" Charley shouted over the wind.

"My side, Pa—it hurts."

Harland's pain had begun an hour or so earlier, but he hadn't said anything for fear that his father or grandfather might think him lazy and trying to avoid work.

His hurting became steadily more severe, sending sharp knives through the boy's stomach with any movement he made. Now, he could only stand the increasing pressure in his belly by lying on the ground and pulling his knees up tight to his chest.

Charley tried to pick him up, but the boy screamed. "No, Papa, please—don't move me."

"Son, are you snake bit or what?" Charley asked, looking for any sign of a puncture wound. Harland's forehead had become wet with sweat.

"It's my stomach, Pa—it hurts so bad."

"I think it's his appendix," Ondrej offered. "Your brother Tom had it when he was little."

It was blowing hard now. Ondrej took a large piece of canvas out of the bed of his pickup truck and covered the boy to protect him from the wind and dust.

"I'll stay here with him," Ondrej told Charley. "You drive into New Edom and get Dr. Smett out here fast."

The trip to New Edom was short, but with the heavy wind and blowing dirt, the loose soil was being pushed into drifts and across the roads so that Charley could barely see where the road was.

Despite his grim prediction of twenty years earlier, Dr. Walter Smett had survived his battle with influenza, and spry for his age, still kept a small office in New Edom, even though he was nearing eighty. When Charley Novak showed up at his door, Dr. Smett was busy shaving a corn on his left foot.

"It sounds like an appendix," Doc Smett said. "Did the boy's belly feel hard?"

"Yessir—and real sore."

"We'd best get going," the doctor said, pulling on his sock and tying his shoe. "Time's not on our side."

All the way back to the farm, Doc Smett questioned Charley about little Harland's condition: Was the boy sick to his stomach and vomiting? Did he have any constipation or diarrhea? Fever?

Harland was crying and biting his lip when his father returned with the doctor. As soon as Dr. Smett got out of the truck, the wind took his hat and sent it bouncing down the fence line.

"How far to your house?" Dr. Smett asked Ondrej.

"A half-mile."

Smett shook his head. "Goddamnit, that's too far," he shouted over the wind. "I don't want to move him that far. I wish the boy was back there, though—it'd make things easier." He took a bottle of antiseptic, a scalpel, tape, and a length of rubber tubing out of his black leather bag.

"You men will need to hold the little fellow down," Dr. Smett ordered. "I suspect his appendix has ruptured, but I can't open him up with all this god-damned dirt blowing."

"Then what will you do?" Ondrej asked.

"I'll have to put a hole in him," the doctor said, applying some antiseptic to the right side of Harland's abdomen. "Then I'll put in this rubber tube to let the pus and corruption drain out. He should feel better after that, and as soon as he does you need to get him to the hospital in Great Falls—they'll take out the infected organ and clean out any infection that didn't drain."

"Hold him still now," Dr. Smett said, drawing out the scalpel.

Throughout the hurried procedure, as the wind and dust blew across the Novak farm, and as his father and grandfather held him down, Harland kept his eyes shut tight, and never made a sound.

CHAPTER 39

Teaching her rural school in Keyes, Oklahoma, Maria Novak often had to light gas lanterns in her classroom so the children could see to recite. On two or three occasions, she and her pupils were forced to stay in the schoolhouse all night to keep out of the dust blizzard winds raging outside.

Each day, she watched the schoolchildren carefully, knowing the hardships they and their families endured. The children rarely complained, but their eyes told of broken dreams and frustrations, of families haunted by hunger and deprivation, their thin bodies recalled months of subsisting on turnips or potatoes. She could see their torn and worn-out shoes, often resoled with old automobile tires, and children's clothing made of curtains when there were no more garments left in the house to cut down.

Maria would never forget a day in September when one of her students—a pale little girl named Pearl McCanna—kept falling asleep at her desk.

"Why don't you go home, honey," Maria told her during the morning recess. "Have a bite to eat and take a nap."

"Oh, I can't, Miss Novak," the girl said earnestly. "Today is my baby sister's turn to eat."

One Sunday, Charley made an announcement after his mother cleared the dinner table. Sunday dinner had been two tired old hens that were no longer giving Irena eggs.

"I'll be leaving for a while, folks," Charley said quietly, as his wife began to cry. "I was hoping Ann and the boys could stay here with you."

"Leaving?" Ondrej asked. "Where are you going?"

"East, Pa—over near Glasgow." Charley held out a newspaper article he'd torn from the *Great Falls Tribune.* "That big dam the government's building on the Missouri—seems like they're hiring workers."

"What do you know about building a dam, son?" Ondrej asked calmly. It was unsettling to hear his daughter-in-law cry.

"Well, not much," Charley had to admit. "But the article says no experience necessary, and they're paying fifty cents an hour. I guess I know a lot about farming corn and wheat, but I can't make no damned living at it. These Sundays are the best my family eats all week."

"I got to make money somehow," he quickly added.

Less than a week later, as another windstorm was threatening, Charley kissed Ann and and his mother goodbye in the yard, then shook hands with his sons, making Harland and Walter promise to be good boys and to help their mother.

"Don't be pesty to your ma and grandma," he told them.

Before getting into his father's truck, he squeezed his wife's hand once more. She had tears in her eyes again.

"It ain't for all that long, hon," Charley told her. "I'll be back as soon as I figure we're ahead."

Then he and Ondrej drove to Fort Benton, where Charley was planning to catch the regular scheduled bus to Havre, and then east to Glasgow. He was edgy and nervous but tried hard not to show it. The day before, he'd looked at a highway map and figured he'd be nearly two hundred miles away from the farm on the Marias, and Charley had never been that far from his family before.

"Save your wages," Ondrej told him sternly. "I've heard of the towns around that dam—they are hard towns, with a lot of ways to steal a man's money."

"Don't worry, Pa, I'll send the money home to Annie."

Charley rode a Greyhound bus as far as Glasgow, then hitched a ride south from there on a flatbed truck hauling alfalfa. The truck driver was a tall, sallow fellow from Spokane, Washington, named Earl Popper. Earl Popper was missing an ear.

"Shrapnel took it," the driver explained. He'd noticed Charley taking a furtive glance at the pale, rubbery ridges of scar tissue that had once been his right ear. "At St. Mihiel, in 1918—you was way too young to remember that."

"I was nine," Charley told him. "But my old man says I lost an older cousin in the war. His name was Mike."

"Lots was lost over there," Earl Popper agreed. "And for what, I wonder. The country's gone to hell—hardly no jobs around, folks beggin' in the streets, and that fellow Hitler runnin' Germany."

"Don't make no damned sense," the driver added.

"No, it sure don't," Charley said. "I was raised to be a farmer, but I can't support my family at it."

"You lookin' for work on the dam?" Earl Popper asked.

"Yessir."

"Well, the work's there, I guess," Popper said, gearing down for a low hill. "If you ain't scairt of snakes, skeeters and scorpions—and I hope that valise of yours is packed with warm duds, 'cause you'll freeze your balls off in the winter, and pant like a damned dog all summer long."

Charley nodded and lit a smoke. "Montana weather's harsh," he said, wondering if it ever got cold or hot in Spokane, where Earl Popper came from.

"I'm goin' right through Fort Peck," Earl said. "I can drop you off right in front of the hirin' office."

"I'm obliged," Charley said, as the big Kenworth diesel rolled south along Montana 24. They were only a few miles out of Fort Peck when a scattering of shacks and stores and saloons came into view on either side of the road.

"We here?" Charley asked.

"Not yet," Earl Popper said, spitting tobacco out the window. "Fort Peck's just ahead. This town's called Wheeler—it ain't good for much besides gettin' drunk or havin' your cob oiled."

Charley whistled as they passed through Wheeler. It was about the closest thing he'd ever seen to the store-fronted old west towns portrayed in Tom Mix movies.

Wheeler was just a slopover from the government-built town at Fort Peck Dam, Earl Popper explained. "It ain't on gover'ment property, so it's free to go its own way—mostly saloons, dry goods stores and whorehouses."

Ten minutes later, Popper stopped his Kenworth in front of the Fort Peck hiring office and wished Charley good luck. "You take care of yourself, sonny," the truck driver said. "There's been some killed on this dam, and a lot more got themselves hurt."

Just before he opened the door, Charley glanced up at the sign hanging above it: *Army Corps of Engineers,* it said in block letters. *Fort Peck Hydraulic Dam Project—Employment Office.*

"Any skills, son?" The man asking was a balding little fellow with thick glasses low on his nose. He was wearing a gray vest and a polka dotted bow tie. The sign on his desk said *Porter Lennox, Employment Supervisor.*

Nervous, Charley set down his valise and cleared his throat. "I can grow wheat," he told Mr. Lennox. "Or corn, beans and most anything else—if there's enough rain and sunshine."

"Hell, my old lady can do that," Lennox said. "And so far, we ain't found cause to hire her. The Corps of Engineers don't need farmers, young fellow. What else can you do?"

"I can fix things," Charley said. "Cars, trucks and tractors, and such as that."

"A mechanic, eh? Well, we can always use mechanics." Porter Lennox was about to push a job application across the desk when he stopped and asked: "Can you read and write?"

"Why, sure I can," Charley answered, annoyed at what he felt to be a dis-courteous question. "I ain't stupid—I been to school."

"Good," Lennox said. "Then fill out that form. I'll hire you as a mechanic at a half dollar an hour. If I get a good report from your foreman a month from now, I'll change your employment status to that of a skilled worker—that pays a dollar-twenty an hour—fair enough?"

"Yes sir," Charley said enthusiastically. He knew that a dollar and twenty cents an hour was a top wage, and he was grateful for a chance at it.

"Fine," Lennox grunted, standing and offering his hand. "Be here at six o'clock tomorrow morning. Anything else you need?"

"Yessir, a place to stay."

The supervisor shook his head. "Fort Peck's all filled up, son. I expect you'll need to find someplace in Wheeler or Square Deal. You know where they're at?"

"Yessir, I come through Wheeler on my way here."

"I'd try there if I was you. But you'll have to hoof it. We ain't got any vehicles going that way."

CHAPTER 40

"Ten bucks a week," the fat woman said, looking Charley over as if he were a piece of trash that had blown up onto her porch. "An extra two bucks'll get you supper six nights—I don't do no cookin' on Sundays."

Pleased at having been hired so quickly, Charley had walked the three miles back to Wheeler and stopped at the first boarding house he saw. The faded wooden sign outside didn't say rooms for rent—just *Bed & Food*.

The landlady's name was Mae Grinder. She'd come west with her husband fifteen years earlier, from Muncie, Indiana, and tried to homestead a worthless piece of land two miles out of town.

"Elmer wanted his own land real bad," Mae Grinder often told people. "And he had it, too, poor as it was, until the fool got hisself stung by a hornet. Poor Elmer swelled up like a big old melon and died. He stayed swelled, too—we barely got him in the box."

"Ten bucks for a bed seems steep," Charley protested. "That's more'n two day's wages."

"Well, it ain't exactly a bed," Mae admitted. "It'd be more like just a mattress on the floor."

"Hell, that's got even less appeal," Charley grumbled.

Mae Grinder shrugged and began to close the door. "This ain't the Waldorf, bud, and you don't look like no high hat, neither. But if my place ain't to your taste, just head on down the road—this is Wheeler, and I don't expect you'll find much better."

From the little he'd seen, Charley believed her.

"OK, I'll take it," he said.

In Chicago that warm spring of 1937, things finally seemed to be getting better. In the evenings and on weekends, Josef counted more and more men coming into the saloon—most of them were old, steady customers whom he hadn't seen for a long time.

"A lot of them laugh and tell jokes," Josef told Lia over supper one night. "They don't look so sad any more."

"If those men have money to buy whiskey, they're probably working again," Lia suggested. "Having a job is reason enough to laugh these days."

As she cleared dishes from the table, Lia reflected on the eight long years that had passed since their insurance man, Drago Kosek had advised her to take their money out of the stock market and put it in the bank—just before the market crashed.

It was Drago that had saved them, Lia knew, not her own good judgment or common sense. She'd been overly ambitious, reluctant to take her husband's advice when Josef tried to persuade her to take a more conservative course with the restaurant's profits. She'd been greedy, Lia admonished herself, greedy for more of the remarkable returns her investments were bringing. And because of her greed, they'd almost lost it all.

Only now, after almost a decade of uncertainty and fear, was Lia beginning to feel secure again. They had their savings in Mr. Novotny's Lawndale National Bank and the saloon was bringing in a modest living, as it always had, even through the hard times.

Lia briefly remembered back ten years, when Ondrej and Irena and their children had taken the train east from Montana to visit. Recalling that week, it seemed as if that had been the last time any of them had been without worries and fears.

"Charley has gone away to work on a big construction project now," she told Josef as he was reading an article in the newspaper. They'd received a letter from Irena just that morning. "Irena says they are building a dam on the Missouri River."

"How old is Charley?" Josef asked, looking up.

"Twenty-six or twenty-seven I think, why?"

Josef shook his head. "That won't keep him out."

"Keep him out of what?"

Josef slowly folded the paper and took off his glasses. "A war, if it comes. The *Tribune* is already beginning to talk about another war in Europe—a war with Hitler."

"*Pah*," Lia said, dismissing the possibility of war with a wave of her hand. "The newspapers always write about Hitler these days. There will be no war—President Roosevelt doesn't want war."

Ondrej shrugged and lit his cigar. "The president might not be able to stop it—and a war could take our Matt as well."

"No!" Lia shouted, "Not Matthew!" Her mind had leaped back almost twenty years; to the dark winter afternoon they'd received the telegram about Michael. Now Lia was trembling and her legs felt rubbery and weak. She found herself forced to lean on the back of a chair to keep steady.

"You must not say such a thing," she shouted at Josef. "Never, never! The *posraný* Germans took our firstborn son—they will not have Matthew, too."

Rarely did Lia use such vulgar language. Surprised by such an outburst, Josef quickly stood and took his wife in his arms, trying to calm her fears. He could feel her body pressing against him, still as slender now as she'd been forty years before, when they'd first met on the voyage to America.

"It was foolish of me to talk that way," Josef whispered as he gently stroked her hair and tried to calm her. "Of course there will be no war—there is no need for you to worry."

Lia nodded. She had buried her face in his chest and Josef felt her moist tears soaking into the fabric of his shirt.

The Novaks were planning to attend a Memorial Day picnic at Pilsen Park on 26th Street that spring. At the last minute, Julia called to tell them that her husband, Milt, was being called in to work that day and that she and the baby would have to come alone.

"On the police force," Julia told her mother. "When they tell you to work, you don't argue."

"It is the same with any job these days," Lia agreed. "And if a man is sensible he'll go along with it."

Milt Terhune knew the value of his job. When Captain Boyle tapped him for Memorial Day crowd control duty at the Republic Steel plant on the city's far southeast side, Milt had little choice in the matter, even though he'd been looking forward to the picnic in Pilsen Park. If there was one thing his wife's people knew how to do, Milt often told other cops in his precinct, it was how to eat and drink. "Jesus," he'd laugh. "Them goddamned bohunk relatives of mine'll feed ya till ya can't barely walk—then drag ya to your feet to dance a polka."

That Memorial Day in 1937 was hot, humid, and sunny—the perfect day for both picnics and parades. Red, white, and blue bunting decorated streets in many of the city's neighborhoods, high school bands teamed with Salvation Army members and aging war veterans outfitted in outdated, ill-fitting khaki uniforms from both the Spanish-American War and the mud-filled trenches of France. A few parades even boasted ancient, arthritic old men who needed canes or even wheelchairs to get around, but nevertheless proudly wore faded blue uniforms of Illinois regiments tested in Civil War battles—nearly seventy-five years before.

"There ain't many of those old boys left," remarked a parade marshal. "But we put them first in line."

For Chicagoans on the south and west sides, Memorial Day was a day for boating in Jackson Park, for soaking up the sun on 12th Street Beach, or for taking a long ride into the country.

It was a day when all the waving flags and patriotic sentiments could be washed down with Coca-Cola, lemonade, beer, or an ice-filled Tom Collins.

"I guess them goddamn Communist strikers at Republic Steel might be in a holiday mood, too," Captain Boyle told Milt Terhune and the small company of Chicago policemen that his precinct was sending to join a much larger force scheduled to be stationed near Republic Steel's Chicago plant that day. "Your job is to keep 'em nice and peaceful. Them orders come down from the mayor."

Republic Steel had been using espionage to discourage the possibility of a strike. Management had been firing union men and hiring strikebreakers, as well as building up a supply of weapons—including guns, tear gas, and clubs—placed in the various plants of Republic in preparation for any strike that might occur.

When the strike finally began, late in May, most smaller steel companies quickly shut down operations. Both Inland Steel and Youngstown Sheet and Tube closed their plants and prepared to wait out the strike, expecting that because of meager union strike benefits, things would quickly turn hard for the steelworkers.

Mass picket lines were set up by the Steel Workers Organizing Committee at every plant that closed, the pickets put in place to stop any attempts to reopen them. Some of the Republic Steel plants were completely closed, but a few remained open, and one of these was Republic's South Chicago plant.

When the walkout started at South Chicago, half of Republic's two thousand workers joined it—and the company protected those who didn't. To keep production going, Republic brought in food and cots and housed the scabs in the plant, hoping to reduce any effect picket lines would have on the move-ment of strike breakers through the gates. Plant management had also been in close contact with Chicago's mayor and police officials in an effort to insure uninterrupted production.

When the walkout began, Chicago police quickly entered the South Chicago plant—clearing out the union men and preventing them from encouraging other workers to join. The strikers gathered on Burley Avenue outside the plant gate, and once the organizers arrived, they formed a picket line.

Under the orders of Captain James Mooney, the police moved into the street and forcefully broke up the line. They pushed it two blocks from the plant gate, arresting anyone who refused to move.

Working a beat in Lawndale, Milt Terhune hadn't been a part of this action, and when he read about it in the *Tribune* the next morning, he shook his head. "Jesus Christ, it ain't a crime to strike—is the department working for Repub-lic Steel now?"

Julia shrugged. The baby hadn't slept well and was crying as she tried to feed him. "That's happening way over on the east side, Milt, it's not your concern."

"I'm a cop, honey. They send you where they want you."

That day, an attempt was made to reinforce the pickets. In the late after-noon, three to four hundred strikers and members of the women's auxiliary began another march to the gate. They ran into a few policemen on 117th Street, but the march continued when the police gave way.

When reinforcements arrived, the police line stiffened around Buffalo Ave-nue. The marchers came on and fighting broke out. The police used their nightsticks and drove the marchers back with a few bloody heads. Before the fight ended, a few policemen drew their revolvers and fired into the air.

On Saturday, things were quiet at the plant, with only limited picketing, but in protest against the actions of the police, the Union District Director called for another march and a mass meeting at headquarters on Memorial Day.

That same afternoon, Captain Mooney received an anonymous report that the next day an attempt would be made to invade the plant and drive out the non-union workers. Without checking the rumor with any union officials, he ordered almost three hundred policemen to be on duty at Republic Steel on Memorial Day.

Milt Terhune was one of them.

At the South Chicago plant, almost twenty-five hundred men were on strike for a raise in wages. Over the past few days, dozens of the strikers had been arrested and beaten. Their automobiles had been smashed and destroyed. Even some of the men's wives and girlfriends had been beaten and hauled off to jail, where a few maintained they'd been treated obscenely.

"The National Labor Relations Act guarantees us our rights," an organizer shouted through a megaphone. "And today we're here to demonstrate in support of them rights."

Although the strikers felt good about their enterprise, Republic Steel president, Tom Girdler, had told the newspapers that he'd go back to hoeing potatoes before he met the strikers' demands.

"That high-hat sonofabitch could do worse than earn an honest living hoeing spuds," someone pointed out, and soon the sentiment made its way through the rank and file. The strike was less than a week old that Memorial Day, and both strikers and their families hadn't yet felt the pinch of no wages coming home.

That morning, when the bus unloaded Milt and twenty other officers near the plant, they could sense a strong bond of solidarity among the striking men.

Because it promised to be such a fine spring day, many of the strikers brought their children out onto the prairie to attend the first big mass meeting; and wherever the police looked, they saw two year-olds and three year-olds riding piggyback on the shoulders of laughing steelworkers—and because it was such a special occasion as well as being a patriotic holiday, their women had come out in their best and brightest summer clothes.

Along with a large company of other policemen gathered on 117th Street, Sergeant Ahern lined up his officers. "If it comes to trouble, Captain Boyle says for us to bust a few heads. That'll calm things down."

From the start, Milt Terhune didn't like the look and feel of it, and began to wish he were back in Lawndale, getting ready to take Julia and their little boy to the Pilsen Park picnic. These strikers were just working stiffs looking for better pay, Milt thought, the same as anybody else. He didn't like it at all.

A strike headquarters had been established in Sam's Place, an abandoned tavern and dance hall, at 113th and Green Bay Avenue, about six blocks northeast of the plant gate. In small groups, the strikers and their families began to drift toward Sam's. Once a ten-cent-a-dance joint, the old saloon was now the center of the strike. It was where the women had set up their soup kitchen, and where the Union Strategy Board planned the day-to-day work. Food was collected at Sam's Place, and the tired picket marchers used it as their barracks.

"This duty ain't worth a shit," Milt whispered to the officer on his right, another Irishman named Tommy Walsh. He and Tommy had often worked beats together.

"Don't be gettin' nervous, now," Walsh grunted. "We bust a few of their goddamn skulls and we'll all go home early."

As the lines of uniformed officers watched, several thousand people were slowly gathering around a platform set up in front of the saloon. It was a serious occasion, but something in the day, the holiday, the sunshine and the warm spring morning kept the festive air alive. Vendors wheeled wagons of cold pop through the crowd, and Neapolitan ice cream, three flavors in one, was being sold for a nickel a brick.

A group of girls began to sing, hesitantly at first, and then with more vigor, strengthened by the deeper voices of the men. Their voices rising, the crowd sang the stirring tale of Joe Hill, the union organizer whom police had killed in Utah years before.

I dreamed I saw Joe Hill last night
Alive as you and me
Says I, "But Joe, you're ten years dead"
"I never died," says he
"I never died," says he

Once the singing petered out, the meeting was called to order. The chairman was Joe Weber, who represented the Steel Workers' Organizing Committee. Speaking through microphones set up on a quickly constructed platform, Weber said a few words of welcome, then introduced Leo Krzycki, an Amalgamated Clothing Workers organizer on loan to the SWOC. Krzycki's remarks concerned the national labor picture, the crowd applauding loudly at the mention of President Roosevelt and John L. Lewis. Krzycki told the crowd a few jokes and concluded on an upbeat note, urging his audience to support the right to organize. As soon as the meeting finished the strikers and their families began to form their picketline and the whole thing took on a parade air. The strikers began to sing again:

"In Salt Lake, Joe," says I to him
Him standing by my bed
"They framed you on a murder charge"
Says Joe, "But I ain't dead"
Says Joe, "But I ain't dead"

Some of them had made their own placards and a whole forest of other signs came out of headquarters. The slogans were simple and direct: "REPUBLIC STEEL VIOLATES LABOR DISPUTES ACT."—"WIN WITH THE C.I.O."—"NO FASCISM IN AMERICA." The signs were handed out, many of them to boys and girls who carried them proudly. At the head of the column that was forming, two men took their place with American flags

> *"The Copper Bosses killed you, Joe*
> *They shot you, Joe," says I*
> *"Takes more than guns to kill a man"*
> *Says Joe, "I didn't die"*
> *Says Joe, "I didn't die"*

News reporters, who'd driven south from their downtown offices a short while earlier, were all over now, taking photos of everything going on. There was a quite a bit of good-natured give and take between the strikers and the newsmen. When the column began to march, down the road from Sam's Place and then across the prairie toward the Republic Steel plant, the news photographers moved right with it, some walking and some in their cars.

The Republic Steel Plant rose harsh and abruptly from the flat, empty prairie surrounding it. The marching line of pickets slowly crossed the meadow, still singing. Suddenly the voices wavered and the sunny day seemed to turn ominous. Ahead, five hundred policemen had taken up stations between the strikers and the plant. Both the singing and the line of march slowed for a moment, and then someone shouted: "Don't stop—we got our rights!"

The voices rose again and the strikers came on, as the police ranks closed and tightened.

> *"Joe Hill ain't dead," he says to me*
> *"Joe Hill ain't never dead*
> *When workers strike and organize*
> *Joe Hill is by their side*
> *Joe Hill is by their side"*

About two hundred and fifty yards from the plant, the police and the strikers met on the flat ground of the prairie.

A police captain named Mooney stepped forward and spat on the ground. "This is it," Mooney shouted. "This is as far as you go, you Red bastards." Billies and clubs had already been drawn and the police moved forward—prodding, nightsticks edging into the women's breasts and the groins of the men.

"Stand fast! Stand fast! What the hell's the idea?" the strike leaders protested. "We got our rights."

Captain Mooney spat again. "You got no fucking rights, you sonsabitches—no rights at all."

"Say, that's bullshit," one of the strikers, a big, burly fellow, stepped forward and shouted. "It's you cops that ain't got the right to stop us from marchin' on that plant."

"OK, take him down," Mooney ordered, as three policeman clubbed the big steelworker to his knees. From somewhere in the crowd a woman started screaming and someone threw a rock.

"Draw your weapons," Mooney shouted. For a moment, Milt Terhune could barely believe such an order. These poor stiffs ain't even armed, he thought. But he drew his revolver anyway.

Tear gas grenades began to be thrown, the gas settling among the crowds like an ugly cloud. Children suddenly cried with panic, and the whole picket line collapsed, with men stumbling, cursing, and gasping for breath.

Here and there, Milt could hear revolvers being fired. It was *pop, pop, pop,* at first, like capguns or tiny firecrackers. Then, as the steelworkers and their families broke under the gunfire and began to run, the police began to shoot in volleys. Milt watched in stunned disbelief as many of his fellow cops ran after fleeing men and women, pressed revolvers to their backs and shot them down—then continued firing as victims sprawled on the ground, coughing up blood. When a heavyset woman tripped and fell, four cops gathered above her, smashing her with clubs.

For his part, all Milt Terhune did was wave his billy in the air and urge the frightened strikers to run. "Get the hell out of here," he shouted at them. "Beat it if you don't want to get hurt—"

In the brief time it went on, the fight left ten strikers dead or dying on the field, and over a hundred more wounded. One of the older, veteran reporters could only stare and shake his head. He'd stopped making notes. "Jesus Christ," he mumbled to Milt, who'd holstered his pistol and put his nightstick away. Milt was kneeling and trying to attend to an injured woman. "I was in France during the war," the reporter stammered. "And I never seen nuthin' as bad as this over there."

I dreamed I saw Joe Hill last night
Alive as you and me
Says I, "But Joe, you're ten years dead"
"I never died," says he
"I never died," says he

CHAPTER 41

Charley Novak missed his home, but the paycheck he banked each week was near sixty dollars, more money per week that he'd ever earned in his life.

The food Mae Grinder cooked and served was poor. Charley wrote home that he'd lost nearly twelve pounds in two months. In addition to inferior provisions, he shared a room with twenty other men, each sleeping on a mattress on the floor.

"Hell, it don't make no difference," most of them were fond of saying. "We got jobs, ain't we? We're better off than most."

When the project got underway, the two existing small towns of Glasgow and Nashua could offer just a fraction of the needed housing, warehouse space, and services that were required.

It didn't take long for local landowners with property near the dam site to realize they'd struck it rich—leasing out their mostly worthless acres for the construction of boomtowns with saloons, stores, and countless tarpaper shacks where workers could live. Joe Wheeler, a local barber, founded the town of Wheeler on a quarter section of land that he owned near the dam.

An old fellow named Orly Grubb lived with Mae Grinder in an upstairs room. Orly took most of his meals with Mae's boarders and was fond of conversation. If you needed to know anything at all about Wheeler, Orly Grubb was the man to ask.

Charley soon learned that it had become the largest and most well known of the slapped-together settlements surrounding the dam. It was notorious for the "Wheeler Inn"—owned and operated by a woman named Ruby Smith, reputed to be from the Klondike.

"She's a real humdinger, that one," Orly cackled. "They say she fucked four Chinamen and a simple-minded nigger one night in Skagway, then made them all pay double for the favor—all except the coon."

"You fellas sure found the right place," Orly would say, when Mae took in new boarders. "All them other little towns around here is just shacktowns, made from boxes and tin cans, old boards and tar roofing. But Wheeler's a real town with real houses and stores—it's got damn near sixty-five businesses along both sides of main street, and close to a thousand houses scattered about."

Half a dozen all night saloons, too, Charley reminded himself, open from eight at night to six in the morning—not to mention the numerous whorehouses that never closed.

The saloons didn't offer floorshows; tired, lonely men just drank and danced, with the music playing all night until long after daylight. They didn't have to pay to dance, but the girls collected a nickel a glass for all the beer and whiskey they got the men to buy.

Behind the town was a separate settlement where the whores did business. Orly Grubb maintained that over a thousand women heard the call and drifted in to service the dam workers.

Wheeler was all wood. There wasn't a stone or steel building in town. It had no water system. One side of town had wells, and the other side didn't.

There was one small wooden church and two gospel missions, Orly told them. "Just in case you boys need to get some Jesus."

Most nights the streets of Wheeler were filled with drunken men and painted whores. Both gambling and liquor by the drink were illegal in Montana, but Wheeler paid no attention.

Charley knew you could sit in a stud game, and order glasses of "Forty Rod" whiskey from dark till dawn—a terrible homemade hooch that men swore could kill you at forty rods distance.

After two months away from home, Charley had lost whatever resistance he first might have had to the temptations of Wheeler. It took only a few whiskeys and one night of stud poker to convince Charley that what Ann didn't know wouldn't hurt her.

When the game broke up near dawn, he got up from the table a big winner, with a bundle of cash stuffed in his pocket that nearly equaled three week's salary. After work that day, he sent a letter to Ann containing a hundred dollars in cash money, and a short note explaining it away as a bonus.

Each week, Charley paid his rent and sent his wife twenty-five dollars. What money was left over he kept for himself—enough for smokes, a few drinks of whiskey on Saturday nights, and a Sunday meal of either pot roast, beefsteak and onions, or corned beef and cabbage at Moe's Diner on Main Street. Figuring too many choices just tended to confuse people, they were the only three dishes Moe put on his menu.

Charley became friends with a fellow boarder named Dermott Maguire, a big, amiable Irishman whom everyone just called Mott. Mott Maguire worked on a dredge barge and came from Portland, Oregon, where it rained most months of the year.

"We'll get rain, too," Orly Grubb told them during supper one night. "Not much, but when it comes you best hang on to your balls, 'cause them rains bring winds—sixty, seventy mile an hour winds. I was with the 3rd Cavalry in Cuba and we never even seen hurricanes as bad. And in the summer, when it don't rain, we sweat our balls off—why, last July, it got over a hunnert an' ten degrees one day."

"What's the winters like?" One of the newer men asked.

"Shitfire," Orly laughed. "Where you from, son?"

"Tampa," the young fellow said, lighting a smoke. He'd been in Wheeler only a month, and was one of the few CCC workers to survive the savage Labor Day Storm that hit the Florida Keys two years before. "I know what heat and hurricanes is like."

"Tampa!" Orly snorted. "Well, boy, you'd be damned smart to enjoy the autumn weather while we got it—when winter comes, all that's between you and the North Pole is a barbed wire fence. It's so goddamned cold, your balls will freeze and fall off."

"Sounds like Montana's harsh on a man's private parts," Mott Maguire offered. "I prefer to save mine for the whores."

The Fort Peck Dam Public Works Administration Project was drawing worldwide attention and was regularly written about in the *Great Falls Tribune*. Whenever Anna saw an article about the dam, she'd show it to her sons.

"That's where your pa works," she'd tell them proudly.

"When's Pa coming home?" young Harland would ask.

"I don't know, son. Soon, I hope."

Irena had begun to ask her daughter-in-law the same question. It wasn't as if she disliked Ann and the boys living with them. Ann was both a big help and female company, and while Walter was still too young, Harland was already doing more than a boy's share of work helping Ondrej.

Irena worried instead, that the separation—the longer it went—might harm Charley and Ann's marriage. Times were hard enough on young couples, she knew, and being apart for so long wouldn't make them any easier.

"When *is* he coming home, honey?" Irena asked one morning after breakfast. "Charley's been gone almost a year."

Suddenly, Ann started to weep. Her shoulders shook slightly and she had to sit down in a chair. "I don't know," Ann told Irena tearfully. "Charley writes and sends money every week—I've got nearly twelve hundred dollars saved—and you'd think that'd be enough. But he seldom mentions coming home, Ma. When I write him back and ask about it, he just says *soon*."

Irena gently stroked her daughter-in-law's hair. "Well, I guess Charley's intent on seeing you wealthy some day," she teased.

Although Ann paid for the food that she and the boys ate, she stubbornly saved every extra penny that Charley sent home. It wasn't only the money she valued, but rather the hope that each week her husband might say to himself *well, that's enough*, climb aboard a Greyhound bus and come home to them again.

"Ma, I don't need to be wealthy," Ann sniffed. "I just need to be married."

Irena nodded. "He'll be home soon, honey—don't you fret."

It was just two weeks later, that Irena's brother hung himself in his barn. Frank Janda was nearly seventy-five years old, and two months earlier; the doctors at the hospital in Great Falls told him he had cancer in his lungs.

"Can you cut it out?" Frank asked.

"We're sorry, Mr. Janda—if we did, you wouldn't have much of your lungs left."

Frank grunted, drove back home and began to paint the house and barn.

"Well, Lord knows, those buildings need it," Majka Janda told Irena. "But I'd rather see him stay in bed and rest."

Coughing up blood, Frank spent the next two months painting. The task went slowly as he began to tire easily. He concentrated on the painting and let his brother and a hired hand tend to most of the farm chores and fieldwork. When the job was done, he sat down to a fine chicken dinner, kissed his wife, and headed toward the barn, telling her that there was a bit more tidying up to do.

An hour later, with their dog howling and running around the yard in circles, Majka went out to find her husband hanging from a barn rafter. Frank had climbed up and balanced himself on a barrel, then kicked it out from under. She found a short note, written in Czech, pinned to his pant leg:

Můj drahá Majka—

My dear Majka—I am very ill and feeling much worse each day. I have enjoyed a good, long life and see little profit in being a burden to you or Emil. Both the house and barn are now painted as you have been after me to do. I wish our land and equipment to be passed to our sons, Joe and Emmett, in equal measure when the time comes. You have been a fine wife. Goodbye.

Majka buried her husband in a cemetery in Great Falls. "He's been on that farm long enough," she reasoned. "He doesn't need to spend eternity there."

A few of Frank's relatives from Fargo came to the funeral; kin that neither he nor Majka had seen in years.

"I'm glad that Lia and I write," Irena told Ondrej after they'd driven home from the cemetery. "It's not good for families to grow so far apart that they are almost strangers to each other."

Fort Peck Dam would be the largest earth fill dam in the world at a hundred and twenty million cubic yards. It would take five or more years for the fleet of pipeline dredges to place the hydraulic fill. The crest would span two miles across the Missouri plus another two miles of wing dam dike at the north end. When the project began, some ten thousand workmen were needed. First, to construct the dredges in a boatyard, then build miles of trestles, open a rock quarry a hundred miles distant, and bring in electric power almost three hundred miles from Rainbow Substation at Great Falls.

A hundred mile long lake would be created, the newspapers said, providing flood control protection, improved navigation and much needed hydroelectric power to Montana. President Roosevelt visited the dam site twice, as well as dozens of foreign dignitaries and university professors.

The cover of the first issue of *Life Magazine* featured a stark photograph of the dam's spillway by photojournalist Margaret Bourke-White, and inside the magazine's pages were photos of the surrounding boomtowns that housed the workers who drove the tunnels, manned dredges, operated the trains, and drove a fleet of several hundred trucks.

By late September 1938, work was still going at a rapid pace, and Charley had been called out in the middle of the night to repair a bulldozer that had broken down.

"Jesus," he grumbled, pulling on his overalls in the dark. "It's the middle of the night and it ain't my shift—don't anybody know that?"

"Well, Monty asked for you," said the fellow who'd come to roust him out—a rat-faced little man named Mort Crow. "I doubt I'd be fond of a dirty old pallet like that," Mort added, pointing at Charley's mattress. "I got me a proper bed in Fort Peck."

"Who gives a damn, anyway?" Charley said, lighting a smoke as he and Mort Crow climbed into the pickup truck parked in front of Mae Grinder's boarding house. "What's Monty want with me?"

Monty was Jim Montfort, the foreman of a night crew that was laying quarry stone near the east abutment of the dam. Charley and Mott Maguire had played poker with Montfort a few times and the three men liked each other.

"He's got him a busted Cat," Mort Crow said.

"Hell, ain't there a night guy to fix it?"

The little driver just shrugged. "He wanted you."

Arriving at the dam site, Charley stepped out of the truck and shook hands with Jim Montfort. "I'm glad my skills is so valued."

"There's the Cat," Montfort said, motioning toward the huge earthmover.

"What's wrong with it?" Charley asked.

"Won't run," Montfort said. "Early this shift, we was working off the mats, but when the weight of the machine was transferred to the gravel, the sonofabitch started to sink and quit runnin'—and there was water rushed up around the tracks.

"There's another thing," Montfort quickly added.

"What's that?"

"I think somethin's wrong with this dam."

"Wrong?"

"Yessir, that upstream pipeline shell is runnin' lower than it should, and there's a six-foot bow in the track."

"Jesus," Charley said, whistling when he saw it.

They poked around a little, finding water seeping through the gravel, and both could hear the sounds of water gurgling underfoot.

"I put the brakes on any more heavy work up here," Montfort said. "When that Cat's fixed, I'd be obliged if you'd hotfoot it into Fort Peck and wake up some engineers."

That afternoon, little more than an hour had passed since the day shifts quit for lunch. With Charley behind the wheel, District Engineer Major Clark Kittrell was eating a thick ham sandwich as he inspected the area from the Ford sedan's passenger seat.

"Montfort knows his business, Major," Charley offered. "And he's certain something's wrong."

Kittrell nodded. "Soon as I finish my lunch, son, we'll get out and have a look around."

Then it started—something strange and terrifying. Suddenly, the earth began to rumble and shake under the Ford. Dredge pipes and lengths of railroad track started to shift and sink as a massive section of dam slowly swung out into the upstream—as if it were a great earthen gate hinged on the abutment. Heavy machinery and helpless men were quickly swallowed by the moving, muddy hell as five million cubic yards of earth slid out into the Missouri River, where it formed its own island.

"Jesus Christ Almighty," Major Kittrell gasped, his mouth still full of ham.

Charley said nothing. He just slammed the car into reverse and floored it, spinning the rear wheels on gravel as they shot back and away from the disaster.

"The whole sonofabitch is going to go," Kittrell shouted. "Get this car back to Fort Peck."

Other men, those lucky enough to be out of harm's way, could only stare in horror. A worker named Henry Pitt was working as a striker on a booster pump station halfway down the face of the dam on the downstream tunnel side. After Pitt called in his hourly meter and gauge readings, he felt the earth begin to shake and glanced up toward the crest of the dam. Blinking in amazement, he saw whole sections of the dredge-fill line—those running parallel to the main axis—slowly disappearing, along with a Caterpillar tractor and a tall boom crane.

That night, it seemed to Charley that everyone in Wheeler had come to the saloons, and anyone he talked to had a story about the slide. "I guess old Harvey Fender's about as lucky as a pig in shit," Mott Maguire said as he sipped a whiskey. He'd been off shift and asleep when the dam went out.

"How so?" Charley asked.

"Harvey's a survey chief on the area that went out," Mott said. "After it happened, they sent in a crew to look everything over and see if there was clues as to what caused it to go. The crew passed the bed of a truck tore off its chassis, and a hundred feet further on they come upon a pair of trousers with the belt still attached and a leather billfold in the pocket. It had money and pictures in it, and an identification card that belonged to Harvey Fender."

"So far, that don't sound lucky to me," Charley said.

"Well, the thing is," Mott laughed. "Four hours later, Harvey walked into Porter Lennox's office and quit—he was naked as a baby, too. Harvey told Lennox that he'd gone down under the sand a few times while the earthfill was shifting and moving, and when he finally found himself on top of all that fill again, all his clothes was gone—just tore right off.

"Harvey's ears and eyes was all plugged full with sand," Mott went on. "He climbed up the west end of the slide and walked to the road. When traffic came by he thumbed a ride into Fort Peck and told Porter Lennox that the Corps of Engineers could shove the job up their arses—he was was done with buildin' dams."

On the farm the next day, Ann Novak saw the bold headlines and read about the slide, learning that eight men had been killed, and that six of the bodies hadn't yet been found. She started to cry and couldn't stop until the day after, when they received a telegram saying that Charley was all right.

CHAPTER 42

"How long since we were in New York?" Josef asked one Sunday evening in May. They'd finished supper and were relaxing in the living room, listening to Jack Benny on the radio.

"New York?" Lia asked. "Forty years ago, I think. Why?"

"I want to go back," Josef told her. "To see the World's Fair."

Six years before, they'd had the Chicago Century of Progress Exposition almost in their own back yard—but it had been the height of the Depression and they'd been too busy trying to eke out a poor living from the restaurant to think about amusements.

Even now, Lia was skeptical, and as always, had her eye fixed on their expenses. "Josef, it's only a carnival," she said. "Like the one St. Procopius sponsors each summer—just bigger."

"Yes," Josef laughed. "Bigger is right."

He stood and went out onto the porch, bringing back a folded section of newspaper and handing it to his wife. A week earlier, the *Chicago Tribune* had described the New York World's Fair as the largest, costliest, and most ambitious international exposition ever staged. The paper reported that the fair sprawled over more than a thousand acres in Flushing Meadow in Queens—made to order by filling in the entire Queens city dump and planting the site with ten thousand trees and a million Dutch tulips.

"A million tulips," Lia said, unable to imagine such a thing.

"The business is good, and getting better," Josef told her. "We should have a vacation—maybe take the whole family."

"But the money," Lia protested.

"To hell with the money," Josef said. "None of us are growing younger. We have it in Novotny's savings and loan, but what good is all the money unless we enjoy it?"

Lia shrugged. "All right, we'll go," she said with a grin. "Give me a date and I'll get the train tickets tomorrow."

But Josef shook his head. "I want to fly there," he said.

Two weeks later, driving separate automobiles, the family met in the busy parking lot of Chicago's Municipal Airport—just south of the Lawndale neighborhood on Cicero Avenue.

Lia was holding tickets for everyone, and both their children and grandchildren were so excited they could barely speak.

"Pa," Matthew stammered. "I can hardly believe we're doing this. Flying to New York City—only big-shots do that."

"We are big-shots," Josef laughed. "We are the Novaks."

"Yes, and your big-shot papa is going to put the Novaks in the poorhouse," Lia complained half-heartedly.

"Well, I'm scared silly," Julia offered.

Now Lia laughed. "Do you want to stay home?"

"Never," Julia said. "Wild horses couldn't keep me home."

On the tarmac with fellow passengers, they left their luggage with a uniformed attendant at the ladder leading up to the aircraft's door. They were boarding a Douglas DC-3 with American Airlines painted in red letters on its silver skin.

The DC-3 had twenty-one seats, cantilever wings, two cowled Wright SGR-1820 thousand horsepower radial engines, retractable landing gear, and trailing edge flaps. Up in the cockpit, the control panel included an automatic pilot and two sets of instruments.

"Will the Nazi pilots try to shoot us down?" asked ten year-old Donald—Julia and Milt's little boy.

The news of Germany's aggression in Europe was all over the radio these days. Hitler's army had taken over Bohemia, Moravia and Austria the year before. *Krystallnacht* had happened that past November. Julia often found herself thinking the world seemed to be hurtling toward madness. Japan had conquered Korea and Taiwan, and now Manchuria as well, while the Italian dictator Benito Mussolini occupied Albania and had invaded Ethiopia several years before.

"No, they sure won't, honey," Julia told her son. "The Nazis are far away from here."

Lia closed her eyes, squeezing them tight as the airliner roared and shuddered—then jerked forward and began to pick up speed as it rumbled down the runway. "Oh, my God, Josef, how fast are we going?" she asked above the roar of the engines.

"I don't know—fast," Josef told her as he stared out the little window next to him. Watching the airport buildings race past, he could feel Lia gripping his hand.

Suddenly, the frightening sense of speed was gone and the ride turned smooth. The DC-3 was airborne, and Josef stared down as the city quickly fell away beneath them.

"We are in the air," he said excitedly. "Lia, we are flying."

They climbed to altitude, then banked and turned east, flying high above the city. The grandchildren were crowded at a window, too, marveling at how small everything looked—especially the automobiles. Like toy cars, they all agreed.

Finally, the city passed from sight and there was only the deep blue expanse of Lake Michigan below. The two engines had been cut back from a howl to a steady drone.

Further on, as they passed over the farmland west of Toledo, Josef held his grandson, Johnny, up to the window. "Your grandpa and grandma came across there years ago—by train—can you see the tiny tracks?"

"Yes, Grandpa."

Josef could barely believe it himself. With all they owned in a few battered trunks, he and Lia, Ondrej, and his parents had rattled west on those same tracks more than forty years before, just as the last century was ending. How excited and frightened they'd been.

America was the dream, but America had proved uncaring and hard—offering only hope and the certainty of struggle. Yet now, it was their home—home to three generations of family—with all of them gathered in this wondrous machine that flew over the earth.

Lia squeezed his hand. "What are you thinking, Joe?"

"Nothing much," he told her, smiling. "Just how young we all were once. You and me and Ondrej—even my mother and father."

She nodded. "I wish we had those years back."

Hours later, Lia closed her eyes again as they banked on their final approach into La Guardia Airport. Once on the ground, two taxicabs took the entire family to a reasonably priced hotel near the fair grounds at Flushing Meadow, and that night they ate dinner in a Chinese restaurant.

"New York City," Josef said, trying to eat with chopsticks. "It was the doorway that let us into America."

"The same with my old granddad," Milt Terhune offered. "He came here with nothin'—just a dumb Mick willin' to work."

Constructed over a city dump, the World's Fair promoters had created three hundred futuristic buildings to house the exposition's fifteen hundred exhibitors. The printed program listed thirty-three states, fifty-eight foreign countries, and thirteen hundred business firms, ranging from Schlitz Beer to Ford Motor Company to Dr. Scholl's Footease, which conveniently maintained an emergency clinic to treat footsore fairgoers whose arches gave out along the Fair's sixty-five miles of paved streets and walkways.

Julia was stunned as she took it in. She couldn't help feeling that in some strange and unexplainable way, this fair in Flushing Meadow was an important moment in history—as if America and the world were pausing for a moment, looking backward over the scarred and battered landscape of the Depression, and forward to both the promise and uncertainty of bright tomorrows—darkened only by the ominous clouds gathering in Europe and the Far East.

"Look at all these modern things," Julia said. "Will it really be this way?"

"For you, maybe," Lia told her. "And for the grandchildren, I am sure. But Josef and I are too old to see such things come true."

Beneath the shadow of the Perisphere and Trylon, the World's Fair showed them the coming wonder of television, a nationwide interstate highway system, and perhaps the most dramatic exhibit of all, General Electric's animated "Futurama"—a scale-model designer's conception of America just twenty years into the future.

Josef and Lia's three grandsons—Donald, Johnny, and Carl—could barely believe what they were seeing. Each exhibit they saw was wondrous—as exciting as looking through the pages of a Buck Rogers comic book.

Throughout the Fair's labyrinth of streets, plazas and buildings stand operators sold hamburgers and hotdogs, along with Orange Crush, Coca-Cola, and root beer. Dairy stands offered ice cream, malted drinks, saltwater taffy, Cracker Jack, and popcorn.

Until the grandsons grew tired of science and technology, the family spent half of each day seeing the exhibits, then ate a lunch of hotdogs, and trudged over the Empire State Bridge so the boys could enjoy the Amusement Section—as joyous a carnival as any of them had ever seen.

Spaced around man-made Liberty Lake were more than eighty attractions—including thrill rides, the Aquacade, an archery range, Jungleland, Midget Town, a sideshow called "Nature's Mistakes," and two penny arcades.

The Amusement Section was a child's delight. While most of the family relaxed on benches and ate ice cream, Matthew and Milt took turns volunteering to watch the boys ride the Parachute Jump, the clattering, roaring Cyclone coaster, the Flying Scooters, and the Ferris Wheels.

As they sat on a wide bench shaded by trees, Matthew's wife, Ida, leaned over and whispered to her father-in-law. "Those three kids are just having the time of their lives, Pa—thank you so much for bringing us here."

Josef just shrugged. "It is for the grandparents to do if they can afford it—someday you and Matt will do it, too."

CHAPTER 43

"You've got yourself a dose of the clap, young fellow," Dr. Boone told the patient in his office.

"Jesus, I can't go back home like this," Charley groaned. "My wife'll kill me."

Dr. Boone just grunted and looked at Charley over his glasses. "Well son, you should of thought of that before you went waving your pecker at the whores—I swear, those ladies pretty much keep me in business."

"What can I do, Doc?"

"Fortunately, we live in modern times and penicillin will take care of it, but you'd best mend your ways."

Charley was nervous but relieved. He'd given the hiring office two weeks notice and had a Greyhound ticket back to Fort Benton where his father was to meet him. Almost another year had passed since the deadly landslide at the dam, giving months of extra work to anyone who wanted it.

But Ann had written what she called her final letter. She and the boys missed him, she wrote, pointing out that they had close to twenty five hundred dollars saved. As far as she was concerned, that was enough. If he didn't come home *now*, she'd take the boys *and* the money and go live in Helena with her relatives—a divorce would be part of her plan, as well.

Charley would be glad to see them all again, to be back home once more, yet he suspected there were things about the last two years in Wheeler that he'd miss.

Even though he'd sent the biggest part of his paycheck home to Ann each week, he'd still had almost two years of the single life again. Charley knew he was going to miss easy whiskey, the poker games, and the whores—even though one had given him the clap. Perhaps even more, he'd miss the company of men—rough-edged, hardworking men, all of them far from home. Friend-ships had been made, bonds between them formed. Charley wasn't altogether sure of how to explain it, but he recognized its presence, and knew that he'd miss it when it was gone.

"Well, boyo, I'll miss yer ugly gob," Mott Maguire said two weeks later, when Charley told him that he'd be leaving the next morning. "We need to cel-ebrate, then—one more good night at the Buckhorn—to fortify you for the long ride home."

"Sure, why not?" Charley agreed. He was stuffing clothes into his valise. "But no cards and no whores. I'm a family man again."

That evening, once their shifts ended and Charley had drawn his final pay, he and Mott had a supper of beefsteak and onions at Moe's Diner before mak-ing their way to the Buckhorn Saloon for a few glasses of whiskey.

It was a Friday night, and the Buckhorn had its usual crowd of workingmen, taxi dancers, and card sharps. On an ancient, battered piano a fat woman named Rose was playing "I'm in the Mood for Love," and the bar girls were pulling men out onto the floor.

"How long you staying on?" Charley asked, as they leaned on the bar, sip-ping glasses of rye.

Mott just shrugged. "As long as there's work, I suppose. The dam's to be fin-ished sometime next year, and once it's done, so is this town—Wheeler'll just dry up an' blow away."

"Back to Portland, then?"

"No, I reckon not," Mott said. "I got no family left back there. The old folks is all died off, and I ain't got a wife or kids like you. I been thinkin' of Alaska—maybe workin' the salmon boats."

Charley nodded and ordered another rye. "Well, I'm hoping to farm again. Me'n Ann got some dough put away now, and things seem to be getting bet-ter."

The bartender, a stout, bald-headed fellow named Jake Strong, shook his bald head and began to laugh. "Farmin' and fishin'—you boys is just pissin' in the wind, you ask me."

"Who asked you?" Mott Maguire said.

"Nobody, I guess," Jake said, pouring another drink. He had a lazy left eye-lid that drooped. "But I reckon both you fellas to be in the army soon enough."

"The army?"

"Yessir," the bartender said. "And a lot more'n you two'll get took. We're headin' for another war, sure as shit."

"How do *you* know so much?" Mott asked. "Even President Roosevelt ain't said we're goin' to war."

"Oh, it'll happen," Jake Strong predicted. "And when it does, you boys'll be bitchin' and wishin' you was back here in Wheeler, drinkin' rye whiskey and sparkin' the ladies."

Charley danced with a few of the girls he'd known for a while, letting them earn a little money, while turning down any offers of an hour or so back in the shacks.

Mott Maguire wasn't so inclined. He approached Charley with an auburn-haired whore named Red Molly on his arm. "Red talked me into takin' a ride," Mott said.

Charley nodded and laughed. "You Micks are suckers for red-headed gals—I guess I'll head on back to Mae's and get me a good night's sleep."

Mott Maguire stuck out his hand. "Luck to you, Charley. You been a damn fine friend."

"Same to you, Mott," Charley told him. "Get back in touch if you're ever near Great Falls."

The night had turned cool for June, and as Charley passed an alleyway on his way back to the boardinghouse, two men stepped out of the darkness and fell in behind him.

Not good, his instincts told him. Stopping in midstride to turn and confront his followers, Charley saw that one of them, a short, stocky fellow, had a dark, pockmarked face. He recognized him as somebody who'd been in the pay clerk's office earlier that day. In the moonlight, the other fellow looked to be an Indian.

"You boys are crowdin' too much," Charley told them, setting himself solid on both feet, ready for whatever might happen. He'd have felt a lot better if Mott Maguire were with him, but Mott was off somewhere with a red-headed whore.

"You follow any closer," Charley said. "You might just march right up my ass."

"You got a real smart mouth, bud," the stocky man said. "How about coughin' up them wages you drew this afternoon?"

That's about what Charley figured. The man had been in the pay clerk's office and watched him being paid. They'd probably followed him since then, and left the Buckhorn when he did. Most crimes in Wheeler were street robberies. Charley figured if these two had a car, they'd take his money and be long gone before he could even report the crime.

The town's law enforcement efforts were negligible. Wheeler was outside federal jurisdiction and too remote for county and state authority to have much weight. As far as Charley knew, the law in Wheeler was represented by a justice of the peace, a deputy sheriff and two constables.

It didn't make much difference, Charley thought. He'd always been a fighter and wasn't about to let himself be robbed.

"My dough stays with me," he told the stocky man. "You boys best go and find another sap."

"Hell, a tough monkey," the man hissed. "Let's see how tough he is."

Both men moved on Charley at the same time, but expecting it, Charley stepped back, set his right foot hard, and smashed a ham-like fist into the smaller man's pockmarked face. The blow landed so solidly that the thief grunted and dropped to the ground.

Now Charley and the Indian were warily circling each other. The other fellow was still down, resting on an elbow and holding a smashed nose. Charley marked him as a man without a lot of fight in him—someone who'd let the Indian do most of the work.

"Goddamn, coldcock the sonofabitch," the one on the ground called out. Before the Indian could respond, Charley closed and cut upward with a right hand—once, twice—short, powerful punches deep into the Indian's ribcage.

The fellow staggered backward, pain and surprise on his face. For a brief moment, he glanced down at his partner, still on the ground. "Damn you, Henry, get up and help me fight."

"I believe he busted my nose."

"That don't give you no leave to quit the fight—you're the one said he'd be easy."

Charley drove forward again, smashing the Indian twice more—and feeling a knuckle break against the side of the man's head. It would be the Indian that made the fight, Charley decided. The little fellow was still on the ground, his ruined nose smashed flat against his face—leaking long, ropy strings of blood and snot.

"Just give us your money," the Indian said, hanging back and breathing hard. Part of his ear looked torn and bloody. "We ain't going to ask again."

"I don't see why," Charley shot back. "Seems like you fellas is the one's doin' all the hurtin'."

The Indian cursed and came at him low. Charley tried to kick the fellow in the face, but missed. As the pockmarked one tried to struggle to his feet, the Indian's charge drove Charley back against the plank wall of a hardware store. He hit hard and before he could regain his balance, the Indian was on him, throwing punches into his stomach.

Suddenly, the Indian broke away and stepped back, looking at Charley queerly. Fighting to overcome it, Charley felt his knees go weak and buckle slightly. Surprised, he leaned against the wall and began to sag toward the ground.

"I guess he ain't so tough, now," the Indian said.

The smaller man's face was covered in blood. He squinted his eyes and wiped his nose with a sleeve. "Get his money—let's get the hell gone."

Charley was on his back in the alley. He wanted to get back up and finish the fight, but as hard as he tried, something was holding him down. He was feeling too weak to move, and his eyelids were heavy. When he forced them open and looked up, the Indian was going through his pockets.

"My money—" Charley whispered.

"Shut up, you should'a give us the damned money," the Indian said. "I wouldn't'a had to stick you."

"You ought to just cut his throat while you're down there," the stocky man said, still wiping his nose.

The Indian shook his head. "He ain't going to follow us."

The two men left, and Charley lay sprawled on his back in the alley, trying to keep his eyes open as he stared up at the clear, night sky. The stars were out, but their light seemed to shimmer—bright for a while, then dim and fuzzy before getting bright again.

For a moment, he thought he was dreaming.

In the moonlight, he saw Ann and the two boys standing over him, along with his mother and father, urging him to get up again, to get on the Greyhound bus and come home.

Charley was sure Ann would cry when he told her his money had been stolen.

But then, his family went away as he felt a sudden, sharp and tearing pain across his stomach. He touched himself there, feeling a warm wetness soaking his shirt and pants. When the sharp pain sliced across him again, he knew he wasn't dreaming—but he was so tired, it didn't seem to matter much. All he wanted was to close his eyes and let sleep come and take him.

Ondrej drove the two hundred miles to Wheeler and picked up Charley's body at the undertaker's parlor. At first Ann had insisted on going with him, but Irena had talked her out of it. "Ondrej can go alone—there's no purpose in upsetting yourself."

The drive across the prairies was long and lonely. Aside from their train trip to Chicago when Charley was just a boy, Ondrej had never traveled this far from the farm before.

As he drove through unfamiliar country, Ondrej couldn't help but wonder about his son—living and working this far from home, had Charley been lonely, too? He'd been good about writing. Ann got a letter from him every week, but aside from Christmas, he'd never wanted to spend money on bus fare to come home for a visit.

When he reached Fort Peck, Ondrej went to the employment office and collected Charley's things—which weren't much more than some work clothes, boots, and a wallet empty of cash.

"I'm real sorry about your son, Mr. Novak," Porter Lennox told him. "Charley was a fine young man—and a good worker."

"Where is my boy?" Ondrej asked, slowly turning the wallet in his hands.

"He's still in Wheeler," Lennox said. "His body was taken to Sweet's Funeral Parlor. Mr. Sweet is expecting you."

"I had to fix him up a little," the undertaker explained. He was a little man named Theo Sweet. "So there'll be a slight fee for that, plus the storage."

Ondrej nodded. "I'll need a coffin, too."

"Standard or deluxe?" Theo Sweet asked.

"Just a box to take him home in," Ondrej said.

CHAPTER 44

"You must look after your mother now," Ondrej told Harland and his younger brother, Walter. They'd buried Charley on the farm—next to his brother, on the little hill overlooking the river.

Sarah and Norman Cobb drove in from Great Falls, and Maria took the bus north from Lawton, Oklahoma, where she was now a high school teacher. Most of the Jandas came, as did many of the Novak's other neighbors along the Marias.

When Charley's services ended, everyone walked back to the house for refreshments and something to eat. It was in the kitchen, where Irena and Ann were preparing food, that Ondrej took his grandsons aside to explain that now they were to watch over their mother.

"Where is Pa now?" Walter asked.

"Your father's in Heaven with God and the angels," Irena told the boy. She was busy with a platter of sausage and cheese.

"He ain't either," Harland mumbled. "He's just in a damn box in the ground, like everybody else that's dead."

"You hush, Harland," Ann scolded. "Who told you to talk like that anyway?"

Two hours later, as the afternoon sun began to set and the last of their neighbors left, Irena found her husband in the barn alone. Ondrej was sitting on a small barrel, his shoulders hunched and shaking—the only time Irena could remember that she'd ever seen him weep. She came behind him and put her hand on his arm.

"Sarah and Norman are still here," she told him. "And Maria will need a ride to the bus tomorrow."

"Montana has not been kind to us, Irena," Ondrej said, shaking his head. "If you still wish to quit the farm and live somewhere easier, I will agree to it."

Irena looked down and smiled. She ran her fingers through his graying hair and caressed his neck. "No, we've buried two sons in this prairie, Ondrej," she said softly. "And my wish is for you and I to rest alongside them someday. We will stay on the Marias."

Two weeks later, Ann announced she was taking the boys and moving back to Helena to live with her own family. "With Charley gone," she told Irena, tearfully. "I've no real reason to stay here. It wouldn't be fair to you and Ondrej."

"Yes," Irena agreed. "You belong back with your own people, now—family is the most important thing. And you are still a young woman, with a long life ahead. Your prospects in Helena will be much greater than those along this river."

Young Harland heard them talking, and that evening at supper, Ann's oldest boy announced his own plans. "Ma, I don't want to go to Helena. I'd rather stay here with *babička* and *dědeček*—if they'll let me."

Ann Novak kept eating her supper. "Don't be silly, son. We're all going together."

Harland stood up defiantly. "No, Ma, I ain't going—you can whip me, but I'll run off if you make me go with you."

Ann put down her fork. "Right now, you go to your bedroom, and take your brother with you."

After the boys were gone, Ann first looked at Ondrej and then toward Irena. "What should I do with him? He's been disobedient and stubborn ever since we buried Charley."

Irena was about to say something, but Ondrej spoke first. "The boy's almost fifteen," he said. "When Charley was that age, he was almost doing a grown man's work—and so is Harland."

"What are you saying, Grandpa?" Ann asked.

Ondrej shrugged. "Let the boy stay if he wants to. He likes the farm and he's a big help to me."

"Grandma?"

"If you take him against his will," Irena pointed out. "He will do poorly and perhaps cause trouble. You've had enough trouble in your young life, Ann—why look for more?"

"Harland wouldn't be a bother?"

"Of course not, he's our grandson."

Ann was silent for a moment. Then she took a deep breath and looked at them both. "Let me talk to him first," she said.

"Harland," Ann said, after she'd stepped into the boys' room. "Grandma and Grandpa say you can stay here if you want to."

"Are you gonna let me?"

Ann nodded. "Yes, but I want to tell you something first."

She sat on Harland's bed and motioned him to come sit beside her. When he did, Ann tousled her son's brown hair and looked deeply into his eyes. There was a fire in them that reminded her of her dead husband.

"It's hard for a mama to leave her son," Ann began. "Almost unnatural. But I'm going to do it, because it's probably best for you. You like the farm, and that's your papa in you coming out. But if you're not a good boy here—"

"I'll be good, Ma," Harland interrupted.

Ann held up a hand. "If you're not a good boy here," she went on. "You'll have to come live in Helena with me and Walter. And if you ever have a change of mind about the farm, you know we'd want you with us—is that understood?"

"Yes, Ma."

"Then it's done," Ann said, wiping away a tear.

Off in a corner, little Walter was busy playing with a wooden tractor; he hadn't been paying much attention to what his mother and brother were talking about.

"How about you, Wally?" Ann said. "I suppose you want to stay here and be a farmer, too."

"Do they have picture shows in Helena?" Walter asked.

"Why, sure they do. It ain't like here."

"Then I want to go to Helena—and see Tom Mix."

CHAPTER 45

As the eyes of the world were focused on Europe, America slipped into the Christmas season of 1941 with the threat of world war on the horizon.

Early in the year, a revolution in Yugoslavia caught fire. With the support of the Croatians, German troops invaded the country in early April and hundreds of thousands of Serbians were killed by Croatian irregulars.

By early summer, German troops had invaded Soviet Russia, advancing rapidly against the Soviet army, and laying siege to the city of Leningrad.

On that first, crisp, cold Sunday afternoon in December, Lia was busy ironing clothes as Josef smoked a cigar and listened to a Chicago Bears football game on the radio. The Bears were playing Green Bay in a playoff game being broadcast from Wrigley Field, when the announcement came over the air: "*—we interrupt this broadcast to bring you an important bulletin from the United Press. Flash! Washington—the White House announces a Japanese attack on Pearl Harbor. Stay tuned for further developments as they are received—*"

"We've been attacked," Josef said, rushing into the kitchen. He looked shaken and angry. "At Pearl Harbor, by *Japonština*—the Japanese."

Lia put down her iron. "What does that mean, Joe? Where is Pearl Harbor?"

Josef shrugged and shook his head. "I don't know. We should call Matthew, he will know."

They found out that Pearl Harbor was on the island of Oahu in Hawaii, but it wouldn't be till much later that Josef and Lia, along with the rest of America became fully aware of the carnage that had occurred there. The early morning sneak attack had crippled the entire United States Pacific fleet. Five battleships, the *Arizona, Nevada, Oklahoma, West Virginia,* and *California* were sunk, while three others were badly damaged. Two hundred American aircraft were destroyed on the ground, and almost twenty-four hundred sailors and soldiers were killed.

The next day, Josef kept the saloon closed as he and Lia sat in their parlor glued to the radio—listening to President Roosevelt's declaration of war against Japan.

"What of Matthew?" Lia asked, frightened. "And Milton?"

Both had registered for the draft a year earlier. Josef shook his head. "I don't know. Neither one is that young and they both have children. We can only pray."

Two days later, Japanese forces landed on the island of Luzon in the Philippines, and took Guam in the Marianas a day after that.

Germany declared war on the United States four days after the attack at Pearl Harbor, allowing President Roosevelt to end United States neutrality in Europe. In Italy, Benito Mussolini echoed the German declaration, and Congress declared war on Germany and Italy—as well as Japan.

Life changed in Chicago, and throughout the rest of America. Meat and butter, sugar, shoes, and much more were soon rationed. In the groceries and butcher shops of Lawndale, the red and blue tokens were used like change. Lia and everyone she knew now had a ration book; if the item you purchased was less than the value of the ration stamp, you were given the tokens in change.

Within a year, every train station, bus depot, and airport in the country was overflowing with GIs traveling between training camps, military posts, and points of embarkation for overseas. The railroads carried ninety-seven per cent of the traffic, moving two million men a month. The *Chicago Tribune* reported that troop movements now required half of all Pullman space.

Josef and Lia had been considering a vacation trip out west to visit Ondrej and Irena, but to travel that distance by car would be impossible with gas rationing, airplanes were for soldiers now, and on the trains, civilian riders often endured cattle-car conditions—grateful for just standing room. A brisk black-market in Pullman reservations developed. In Chicago and throughout the country, scalpers sold tickets at markups of from ten to fifty dollars. Even legitimate travel agencies began tacking a twenty-dollar "service charge" on the price of a ticket.

"I'll be damned if I'll give those bastard scalpers our money," Josef grumbled. "Vacations can wait until after the war."

In addition to the discomforts of travel, people on the West Side of Chicago, and in other cities and small towns around the country were feeling the war.

During Chicago's cold, icy winter of 1942–43, fuel rationing was begun, and Lawndale residents had to make do with only two thirds of their 1941 consumption.

Everyday items of convenience or self-indulgence, long taken for granted, were suddenly hard to come by—liquor, laundry soap, facial tissue, cotton diapers, and hair curlers. Nylon had gone to war, too, and Lia reluctantly went back to wearing stockings of rayon and cotton.

The shortage that hurt most was meat. Beef supplies were way down. Housewives in Chicago and every other U.S. city had plenty of meat ration coupons to spare, but nothing to buy.

To Lia, the alternatives were the black-market butchers who received an estimated twenty percent of available beef—or to local substitutes. The Czech butchers along 26th and 31st Streets began to offer unrationed horsemeat at twenty cents a pound.

"I don't mind eating horsemeat," Josef said one night. "As long as we aren't buying it at beef prices."

"No," Lia assured him. "Frank Jedlicka is an honest butcher. He sells it as horsemeat, at horsemeat prices."

It was the rationing of gas that frustrated Josef. Like everyone else, he had a stamp placed on his car's windshield that determined how much he could purchase.

"If you need your car for business," he told Lia. "You are able to buy more gasoline."

"Do you need ours for the saloon?" Lia asked, annoyed by her own inability to buy various things.

"No, I walk to work."

"Then walk," she scolded. "And don't complain."

With butter in short supply, oleomargarine began to appear in the stores. It was a new product that came in a plastic bag and was the pure white color of lard.

"Josef, look," Lia told her husband, bringing a bag home from Otto's Royal Blue grocery on 31st and Harding. "The little bubble of yellow color on the side of the bag."

"What is it for?"

"Otto calls it food coloring," Lia explained. "You break it and knead it in with the oleo to make it look like butter."

Josef shook his head and laughed. "Now Ondrej and Irena are better off out there on the farm—they have cows to give them milk and real butter."

Most of the neighborhood people eagerly searched for things to do to help the growing war effort at home. Some served on draft boards and rationing boards, while others organized war bond drives and took part in scrap metal collections.

When they weren't in school, Julia and Matt's three boys scoured the neighborhood for scrap metal. They begged the local garages and auto repair shops, dug through people's sheds, and walked along the railroad tracks near 32nd Street. The spikes were valuable and often worked loose from the tracks.

On weekends, the boys would sit on their porches, listening to the radio and cutting the ends out of cans, then smashing them flat so that more would fit in boxes to be collected. They saved gum wrappers and scraped tin foil off cigarette packages, crushing it into metal balls. The foil was used, their teacher had told them, for electronic solder and wiring.

Lia dug up the entire back yard and planted a Victory Garden, giving them fresh vegetables in season—parsnips, turnips, carrots, cabbage, brussels sprouts, broccoli, cauliflower, peas, and beans.

Now, I am a farmer, too, Lia wrote Irena during the summer of 1942, *and we are all faring well and praying that the war will be over soon—*

Neither Matthew nor Milton had been drafted, but one wintry Saturday afternoon, the war in Europe came full-blown into Josef's tavern. There were ten or twelve men sitting on stools along the bar, drinking beer and whiskey, and listening to a football game on the radio. One of those drinking beer was an old, regular customer named Walter Becker. Josef knew Walter to be a widower who lived with a daughter and son-in-law on Komensky Avenue, five blocks away.

As he was wiping glasses and putting them away, Josef heard another customer—a fellow named Frank Sedlak—call him over to the far end of the bar. Sedlak had been drinking since Josef opened the place at ten o'clock that morning.

"Another one, Frank?" Josef joked. "You know, if I send you home pickled, your wife will come after me."

But Frank Sedlak ignored the joke, instead speaking under his breath. "Joe, how come you still let that old bastard drink in here?"

Josef looked at him quizzically. "Who are you talking about?"

Sedlak nodded his head toward the other side of the bar. "Old man Becker."

"Walter Becker? Walter's been coming in here to drink since I reopened the place in 1934."

"He's a goddamned German, Joe."

"So what, he's a good customer—the same as you."

"Joe, he's a kraut—a fucking Nazi—he could even be a spy."

Josef just shook his head. There were constant rumors of spies every-where—German spies trained to blend in and find out what the nation's defense plants were making. The Home Front was ripe with quickening fear and abuse against Japanese citizens and those with German surnames. The *Tribune* reported that a nationwide network of aircraft spotters had been carefully trained to identify the silhouettes of German and Japanese aircraft lurking in the skies over America, but as far as Josef knew, none had ever been seen.

"No more drinks for you, Frankie," Josef said. "You better just go home."

"Shit, maybe I'll just quit drinking here," Sedlak said, getting up from the barstool, annoyed by Josef's attitude. "Hell, you might want to start serving Japs, too. We could be drinking with Hitler and Tojo any minute now."

"Go home, Frankie."

"The hell I will," Sedlak shouted. "How about the rest of you? Are you men going to drink with a goddamned Nazi?" Sedlak was pointing his finger toward Walter Becker, who'd turned as white as a sheet.

"I am not Nazi," the old man stammered. "We are not Nazis—two of my sons are fighting the Germans in North Africa."

"That's right," a man sitting next to Becker said. "I've known Walt for years—he's a good guy."

"Yeah?" Sedlak said. "Well, maybe you're one, too."

"Fuck you, pal."

Sedlak took a few steps forward. "I ought to kick your ass."

The man who'd been drinking with Walter Becker got off his stool and faced Frank Sedlak. "C'mon then," he said, motioning to Sedlak to come at him. "You loudmouth sonofabitch."

Now Josef stepped from behind the bar, and moved between the two men. He was holding a police nightstick in his hand. Milt Terhune had given it to him one day, saying: "Here, Pa—in case you ever need to lay the knock on a drunk."

"Calm down, Frank," Josef quietly ordered. "I won't have no fighting in my place. You make more trouble, I'll bust your head."

"I ain't looking for trouble with you, Joe," Sedlak protested. "I just ain't about to drink with any Nazi bastard."

"Then go home, Frank," Josef said softly, trying not to further embarrass a steady customer. "Go home and cool off. You drank too much today—go home to your wife."

Frank Sedlak looked down at the floor for a moment. Then he nodded, grabbed his jacket, and walked shakily out the side door of the saloon. Josef was thankful it had gone no further.

"I am not Nazi, Joe," Walter Becker said again, as Josef filled his glass. Walter had tears in his eyes. "I am as good American as anybody else."

"I know, Walt," Josef told him, trying to reassure the old man. "It's not you, it's just this goddamned war."

CHAPTER 46

※

The army took Harland Novak in March 1943—a month after his eighteenth birthday.

"I'm sorry, Grandpa," he told Ondrej, as his grandfather drove him to the induction center in Great Falls. "If I could stay here and help you with the farm, I would."

"No," Ondrej said, sadly. "You must go off and fight, like the other men of your age. But you must be careful, Harland, and take care of yourself. You must not worry about the farm. I can hire any help that I need."

As he drove back to the farm alone, Ondrej stared at the bleak, wind-driven prairie on either side of the road and worried about his grandson. He couldn't help but wonder how much longer the war might last—and what the months ahead held in store for Harland.

Beginning to feel his age, and being a practical man, Ondrej knew he'd need to hire someone to do Harland's work on the farm. Before reaching home, he'd narrowed his limited prospects to a young fellow named Horace Pell, who was the eldest son in a poor family that lived in New Edom.

Horace had suffered with asthma for most of his life, and had been classified 4-F by the local draft board. He managed to earn a few dollars each week sweeping out old man Vondrak's store.

The young man can use more money, Ondrej told himself, and the war won't take him away.

After bidding farewell to his grandfather, Harland joined thirty other young recruits in Great Falls. They were loaded aboard buses and transported to Fort Douglas, Utah, where the army issued them uniforms, and brusque, impatient medical officers conducted quick physical examinations and administered immunization shots.

Two days later, they received their assignments and were put back aboard buses that brought them to the train station, and from there to their respective training camps.

Harland was sent to the Infantry School at Fort Leonard Wood in Missouri to receive thirteen weeks of basic infantry training. He was up at quarter to six each morning and had an hour to make his bed, shave, get dressed and be ready to stand reveille. At every morning formation, the instructors would announce what the day's training would consist of, and what equipment the recruits would need. Then, Harland and the others would fall out for that day's training, fully equipped with M1 Garand rifle, cartridge belt, field pack and raincoat.

After bad coffee and a hurried breakfast, they were marched to the parade ground or a separate training area, and taught close-order drill and military tactics, marksmanship, hand-to-hand combat and bayonet training, gas mask drill, and the operation of the Browning Automatic Rifle, the M1 Carbine, .30 and .50 caliber machine guns, mortars, rocket launchers, and hand grenades.

Early in July, after basic training ended, Harland was able to come home on a ten-day furlough before shipping out.

Irena invited everyone she could think of and threw a day long party in the yard. Harland's mother and younger brother took the bus in from Helena, Sarah and Norman drove to the farm with their two children, and the Jandas came as well. The last time the family had been together like this, Irena thought, was at Charley's funeral.

"Look at him," Ann Novak gushed, seeing her son in uniform for the first time. "I never saw a more handsome fella."

"I might be getting called, soon, too," Walter said hopefully. He and his brother were only two years apart. "I sure hope the war lasts long enough for me to shoot a Nazi or a Jap."

Seeing Harland in his uniform, even Horace Pell was envious. "I wish't I could go too," he told Harland. "But I got the asthma, so they won't have me."

"How did your army training go?" Ondrej asked, as he and his grandson took turns turning the suckling pig slowly being roasted on a spit.

Harland shrugged. "It was pretty tough at first," he admitted. "Then it either got easier, or I got used to it—don't know which."

Then Harland laughed and took a drink of beer. "We had to get up at quarter to six, Grandpa, so I got to stay in bed an hour longer than when I was here at home."

"When are they sending you overseas?"

"In another three weeks," Harland said. "Once my furlough's done, I got orders for Camp Shanks, in New Jersey."

"And from there?"

"They ain't told us yet," was all Harland could say.

Little more than a week later, he found himself on a crowded train filled with other soldiers; rattling east through the Minnesota darkness as it approached St. Paul and the Mississippi River.

At Camp Shanks, Harland was assigned to the 2nd Squad, 1st Platoon, "B" Company, 2nd Battalion, 36th Division, as a part of a Browning Automatic Rifle Team. As a gunner, he had an assistant and an ammo carrier. They, the squad leader, and two scouts made up half the squad, with five riflemen and the assistant squad leader making up the rest of it.

The battalion left Camp Shanks near the end of August, on a converted troopship named the *USS Mt. Vernon,* bound for Oran, in Algeria.

The *Mt. Vernon* sailed in convoy for twelve days, and on the thirteenth day, approached Oran. Throughout the entire voyage the days had been filled with discomfort and tedium, while the nights offered only fitful sleep, filled with dreams of home. Once or twice there had been alarms, but no submarine attacks occurred.

The battalion disembarked, off-loaded its trucks and jeeps, and rolled off into the low hills behind the city. The hills were as sun-baked and barren as any Harland had ever seen. "B" Company set up their tents in the hot sun and soon began to gripe about the lack of sea breezes.

"Shit," Sergeant Stolley said. "I never heard nobody bitch like you girls—you wasn't so keen on them sea breezes when you was bent over the rails, pukin' your breakfast."

Harland's unit was slated to be part of the first replacements to go in after the Salerno invasion of Italy in early September. But for now, there was nothing to do, nowhere to go, no escape from the boredom and heat.

"Get used to it," Stolley said, in a serious vein. "A month from now you boys might be wishin' you was back here, swattin' flies with the *Arabs.*"

Fifteen days later they were on the beach in Italy, reinforcing the 36th Division, Texas National Guard. The Texans had suffered heavy casualties, and reinforcements were welcome.

The storms and blowing dust had begun to peter out more than two years before the Japanese attack on Pearl Harbor. By that time, the southern plains had been so decimated by the weather that the country was crying for whatever wheat and corn did exist—mostly in Montana and the Dakotas.

With the United States at war in both Europe and the Pacific, Montana's economy suddenly found itself booming. The state's beef, pork, and grain were all in great demand, and its copper and other metals were vital to the war effort.

Ondrej was working too hard for a man his age. Even with the help of Horace Pell, who slept in one of the girl's old bedrooms, he'd often come in at the end of the day too tired to do much more than poke at his supper and fall into bed.

"*Manžel,* are you planning to let this damned farm make me a widow?" Irena inquired one evening, increasingly concerned with her husband's health. "You're working as hard as you did when we first were married."

"I am a farmer, Irena," Ondrej replied. "And this war, as bad as it is, is allowing farmers to earn good money for the first time in a long time."

Shaking his head and smiling at her, he quoted a Czech saying that he'd heard his mother say: "A full sack is heavy, but an empty sack even heavier."

"I know a few old proverbs, too," she answered. "A fast horse soon grows tired."

Ondrej laughed, and kissed Irena on the forehead. "Being tired has never killed anyone," he said. But his back ached so much that deep within himself, he could only hope that that was true.

Harland's first true taste of combat was on a mountain named Mt. Maggiore, north of Naples.

With a light snow falling on the second day of December, six hundred American and British guns began a synchronized artillery barrage on the mountain, in preparation for an attack by the 36th Division's 142nd Regiment.

During this action, Harland and his squad were under fire by German *nebelwerfers*—multiple rockets the GIs called "Screaming Meemies" because of the sound they made as they ripped through the tortured air.

Hunkered down in their holes, the squad watched an American B-17 flying at low altitude, limping back at half speed to its base in Foggia. Enemy antiaircraft fire hit the bomber and the GIs watched helplessly as the stricken plane came apart in the air and plunged to earth trailing a plume of thick black smoke.

"Those poor bastards," someone mumbled.

Harland was hit at San Pietro ten days before Christmas, a tiny chunk of shrapnel that tore through the muscle of his calf. He spent Christmas in a Naples hospital ward and New Year's Eve aboard a hospital ship headed back to Algiers in North Africa.

Once recuperated, he was sent back to his outfit at the end of February and promoted to squad leader with ten new replacements and an assistant squad leader who'd had combat experience with a different company.

Harland's unit pushed north from Anzio and were in Rome by the 6th of June. They learned a day later that it was the same day the invasion of Normandy began in France. The battalion had been short of ammunition and stores a few times in the past, but when D-day began, the supply lines to Rome grew even thinner.

He was wounded again near the end of June, north of Rome at a small town called Cervéteri—an artillery air burst sent another piece of shrapnel slicing down through his shoulder, lodging in his right arm just above the elbow.

Hospitalized in Naples again, Harland was still recuperating when his outfit made the southern France Invasion in the middle of August. Finally healed, he rejoined them in France a month later, and left Marseilles at the beginning of November for home.

When he was discharged in 1945, Harland Novak returned to his grandfather Ondrej's farm on the Marias River after two years and eight months in the army.

CHAPTER 47

"The doctors say a year, maybe two, before I'm strong enough to put in a full day's work around here," Harland told his grandfather. They were eating supper a month after he'd come home, and he'd just come back from his first monthly visit to the Great Falls VA clinic.

"You must listen to the doctors," Irena said. She was happy to see her grandson back home. His arm and shoulder were still weak from surgery and he admitted that pain was always there.

Ondrej nodded in agreement. "Then I'll keep Horace to help us—until you are fit again. He is an honest, hardworking boy."

Once home, and aside from his wounds, Harland put the war behind him. He shunned joining veteran's groups and rarely spoke of combat, or even thought of it—except to occasionally compare its miseries with the welcome comforts of civilian life.

And with the end of the war, life was indeed becoming more comfortable every day—not only for Harland, but also for people throughout America. The nation had struggled through a decade of depression only to face five more grim years of war and rationing. Now both were over, and the country was coming alive again.

As he drove his grandfather's car on the streets of Great Falls, Harland could see that the battered old Ford was a poor example of transportation compared to the much sleeker, more modern Buicks, Chevrolets, and Fords.

The stores in Great Falls were beginning to fill their windows again. Along with dealer showrooms displaying the newest model cars, trucks, and farm equipment, the Sears Roebuck store was full of new stoves and refrigerators, and a wide selection of food was abundant in the grocery stores.

America was standing tall in the postwar world. The industries that defeated Germany and Japan had now turned inward, building products and providing goods that Americans wanted. The nation was finally awakening from the devastation of Depression and its long nightmare of war.

Early one Friday morning, with Harland off to Great Falls for his monthly checkup at the VA, Ondrej and Horace Pell were busy cleaning out Irena's chickenhouse.

Once they had it emptied, they took the tractor and spreader to the ten acres that Ondrej had planted in corn. The spreader was heavy with a full load of nitrogen-rich chicken manure, but before starting work, Horace walked around to the back of the machine, and unbuttoned the fly of his overalls. Leaning up against the metal tines that shredded the manure, Horace began to urinate.

Already bone-tired and aching from the long morning's work, Ondrej was impatient to finish the job, but he also welcomed the short break. He leaned back and fumbled in his pocket for a stick match to light his pipe, and for some reason they were never able to determine, the tractor slipped into gear.

For a moment, Horace was the manure. He was pulled so far in that his wiry body locked the spreader's wheels. After stopping the tractor, Ondrej jumped down and ran back to him. Horace was hurt and screaming—with the tines digging into his flesh.

"Ah, God, get me out, Mr. Novak, don't let me die—"

Irena was fixing lunch, when Ondrej roared into the yard on the tractor, holding Horace over his legs. When she saw both men covered in blood she almost screamed.

"He is badly hurt," Ondrej said. "Help me put him in the car. We'll take him to Dr. Smett in New Edom."

"Christ Almighty," Dr. Smett exclaimed, eyes wide as he got a look at the bloody ruin that was Horace Pell. "This is no case for me, Ondrej. I'll call ahead to Dr. Vanneman in Great Falls and we can take him there."

With Dr. Smett tending to him in the back seat, Horace was bleeding badly and drifting in and out of consciousness as Ondrej drove as fast as he could toward Great Falls.

When they finally arrived, Horace was laid out on a table and Dr. Fred Vanneman, who'd been a field surgeon in France, quickly examined him.

"Quite a job of work you've brought me, Walter," Vanneman said, glancing up at Dr. Smett. "Then again, these farm accidents are usually grim."

The doctor looked over at Ondrej, who was standing to one side, his cap in his hands.

"You'd better leave, Mr. Novak," Vanneman said. "I can only care for one patient at a time."

"No, I will stay," Ondrej said. "It was my fault, I think."

"Please leave, sir," the doctor ordered bruskly. "You'll only be in my way."

Afterward, Dr. Vanneman came out of his office. "Well, I did the best I could," he told Ondrej. "And the boy's going to live, but I wouldn't give you a damned dime for him—he's just fortunate his guts weren't punctured."

Horace Pell was in the Great Falls hospital for more than three weeks. He'd been cut from hipbone to hipbone. Dr. Vanneman had even taken straw out of his wounds and the hospital nurses could feel the knots of catgut in his groin.

Smoking his pipe a week after the accident, Ondrej sat on the porch with Harland enjoying the cool of evening. His back ached, his knees ached, and he'd been having occasional dizzy spells that worried him. After a long moment recalling the accident and still blaming himself for Horace Pell's injuries, Ondrej looked up at his grandson.

"I'm over seventy," the old man said softly. "And I'm tired. I think I've farmed this land as long as I care to. It was supposed to go to your father, but he's gone—do you want this place?"

CHAPTER 48

It was Easter Sunday morning and Lia was in the middle of ironing one of Josef's better shirts for church when she felt what seemed to be a quick, bright flash behind her eye. For an instant, everything around her turned to black.

"Josef!" She cried out softly, feeling the strength go from her legs. She lost consciousness for just a moment and sagged slowly to the kitchen floor. When she opened her eyes again, her lungs fought for breath and she could no longer speak or move her legs.

Josef heard her fall. He dropped his newspaper and raced into the kitchen. Seeing Lia on the floor, his stomach churned with fear. He knelt, lifting her into a sitting position where her breath seemed to come a little easier, then moved her to the bedroom, where he propped her up with pillows.

"I will call the doctor," he whispered. "Don't worry."

By the time Dr. Zavertnik reached their home, Lia was already weaker. Even sitting up, her breath was coming hard.

"Rest," Josef told her quietly, gently wiping her forehead with a damp cloth. "The doctor is here."

Lia nodded and smiled weakly. She suspected that whatever had happened to her was very bad, and thought she might be dying. It mattered little, so long as Josef was with her—for he had been her life since they'd first met almost fifty years before, on the cold, wet deck of the *Graf Waldersee.*

It was dark and cool where Lia lay and if her breathing would come easier, she thought she could be comfortable. As the doctor examined her, Lia tried a time or two to tell Josef that she loved him, but she could no longer speak. Instead, she took his hand and squeezed it lightly, feeling it tremble slightly in her grasp.

My poor husband is frightened, she thought briefly, this old man who once left his country for a strange land, who put his own safety at risk to rescue me from Sol Levine—he is more frightened now than I am of what may be to come.

Dr. Zavertnik, now in his eighties, motioned Josef to follow him into the living room.

"She's had a bad stroke," the doctor said. "Perhaps a fatal one. Both her breathing and her heart are failing. All I can do is call the ambulance. They will have a pulmotor and if we can keep her alive until they reach the hospital—your wife may survive."

With the doctor on the telephone, Josef sat silently by Lia's side, feeling helpless and ignorant of what to say or do.

As they waited for the ambulance to arrive, Lia grew tired. For one strange moment, the cool darkness of the bedroom became the overcast day at sea when she'd first met Josef. For a moment, both of them were young and strong again. Her eyes filled with tears as she felt him squeezing her hand.

Then she saw a light that streamed in from somewhere outside the bedroom. It felt pleasantly warm and she forced herself to stand and leave her husband, to whisper a soft farewell to him and move her body toward that light.

With his own chest feeling as if it were about to break, Josef began to sob and shook his head, whispering softly in Czech: *"Můj milánka,* Lia"—as if his wife's name itself could somehow bring her back to him.

Lia Novak's funeral was a solemn, sad affair. Along with the immediate family, it seemed as if most of Lawndale was at Blessed Agnes Church for her Mass. Josef knew that a turnout as large as that was improbable, but he was amazed at how many *did* attend.

When Father Breska spoke—his words were not about Lia's death, but about her life. "Like most of us here, today," the priest intoned. "Lia Novak came to America with God in her heart and a dream in her head. Over the years, her dreams were fulfilled, and now she lives in God's heart forever."

We lived our dreams together, Josef thought, seated in the pew between his son and daughter, their spouses and children. And now those dreams are done.

He hadn't called or written Ondrej about Lia's passing. It was still too new, too hurtful. He couldn't yet share his grief with his brother or anyone else.

"Lia was a pious woman," the priest went on. "Who loved the church as well as her many friends and neighbors—a woman who made no enemies."

Joseph closed his eyes. Maybe not, priest, but you never knew her as I did—you never saw her angry. Then he told himself: Even angry, my Lia was life to me, everything to me.

That afternoon, Lia was buried beneath a large, shady elm tree in the Bohemian National Cemetery—close by to where Valentyn and Janicka had been laid to rest more than thirty years before.

After the funeral, Josef went back to his son's home, where his daughter-in-law had prepared a huge supper for everyone in the family.

"Mother would not want you to be sad," Julia told him. "She would tell you to live your life and to be happy that she's now with the angels in Heaven."

"Julia's right, Pa," Matthew added, putting his arm around his father's shoulders. "Life goes on and time is a great healer."

But Josef couldn't heal. He lived the next few months as if in a cheerless dream, sad and lonely in the tavern and at home, sick at heart and lost without his wife.

The family came together again on the Fourth of July—for a picnic at Pilsen Park. Frankie Yankovic, the Polka King, had come from Cleveland to play from the park's brightly bunted bandstand. The grownups drank beer and wine, while the children were happy with Coca-Cola and locally-made Canfield's root beer. More than a hundred families ate beef sandwiches, hot dogs, fried chicken, and potato salad, and the eager kids were soon organized into races and games, while young and middle-aged couples gathered into groups, drinking and eating, laughing and trading stories of the neighborhood, and plans for their lives and their family's futures.

Late in the evening, just before the fireworks show was about to begin, Josef called his own family together to make a surprising announcement.

"I am going to close the tavern for a month."

"The tavern?" Julia asked. "For a month?" She felt that with her mother gone, the tavern was all Josef had. "Why, Pa?"

"To go on a trip," Josef told them all. "I am going out west to Montana—to visit my brother and his wife."

A year before his wife's death, Josef and Lia had celebrated the end of the war by buying a brand new Buick Roadmaster—a long, streamlined beauty with a straight eight motor, power brakes and power steering, and low front fenders that swept back almost the entire length of the car. Josef had always driven Fords, but he'd spotted the Buick in the dealer's showroom on Ogden Avenue and fell in love with it immediately.

He'd made only two long trips in his entire life. The first, from Czechoslovakia to Chicago by ship and train, and the second, from Chicago to New York City just before the war—by airplane.

This time he would drive—taking the black Buick west across America. He wrote the American Automobile Association, asking for maps and studying them for hours on end, considering possible routes as he read the names of towns—Manitowoc, Waupaca, St. Cloud and Fargo, where he'd cross the Red River of the North, then on through Minot and finally into Fort Benton, where Ondrej had agreed to meet him for the short drive back to the farm.

Josef allowed himself a week for the trip, and two days before leaving he changed the Buick's oil, checked the brakes, and spent most of an entire day washing the car and waxing its black finish to a glistening Simoniz shine.

"It will be the most beautiful auto on the road," Josef assured his daughter. She and Milt had invited him for dinner the evening before he was to leave.

"Sure, Pa—until it rains," Julia pointed out. Ever since her father had announced his plans, she'd been uncomfortable with the idea of him making such a long journey alone.

"I don't know why you're driving," she maintained. "Why not just take the train if you're so set on going?"

"I have been in this country almost fifty years," Josef told her. "And in all that time I have barely seen any of it. Your mother and I had often talked of making such a trip—so now I will do it for the both of us."

"Can't you see the country from the train?"

"I am taking the Buick," Josef said stubbornly.

"Pa, you're over seventy," Julia argued. "You oughtn't to be driving such a long distance alone."

She knew almost anything could happen on a long motor trip. Bad weather, perhaps, or the Buick could easily break down and leave her father stranded somewhere. What if he had a flat tire and didn't have the strength or ability to change it?

"I won't be alone, *dcera*," Josef said softly. "I will have your mother with me."

Exasperated, Julia looked over to her husband, but Milt was smiling. "How can'ya argue against that, then?" Milt asked, with a shrug and his wide Irish grin. "Julia love, I guess your pa knows his own mind and you need to let him go."

The morning Josef set out was unseasonably cool. He stopped at Otto's Royal Blue for a box of donuts, and then at the Standard Oil station to fill up the Buick's tank.

The attendant, a young fellow named Eddie Vlcek, knew Josef and usually took care of him. "Check the oil, too?" Eddie asked.

"No, I've done that already," Josef told him.

Eddie nodded, pulled a squeegee from its bucket and began to clean the car's already clean windshield. "You're lookin' chipper this morning, Mr. Novak."

"Yes, I am going on a trip."

"A trip? Where to?"

"Montana," Josef replied proudly. "To visit my brother. I am driving all the way."

Impressed, Eddie whistled. "Montana—that's a long haul, Mr. Novak—you be careful now."

"Oh sure," Josef said, wheeling the big sedan out onto Pulaski Road, which he planned to take north to Cermak Road, then east to Lake Shore Drive and north along the lakeshore into Wisconsin.

He spent his first night on the road in a small motor court just outside Manitowoc. The manager in the office renting cabins was fat and amiable.

"I am heading west," Josef told him.

"Hell, I wish't I was goin' with you," the fellow said, taking a key down from a row of hooks on the wall. "I ain't been out of this town in ten years, although it ain't too bad this time of year—after the skeeters are gone."

Josef nodded. "I am going to Montana."

The man nodded and handed Josef the key. "Well, old timer, if you're headed for Montana, you got a damned long drive ahead of you. There's a little diner about a half-mile west of here that serves up a decent supper and a pretty fair breakfast. It don't do to be on the road and hungry."

If he wanted to see the country, Josef was seeing it now. The big, comfortable Buick ran like a train on rails. Built for just such a journey, it gobbled up miles with no effort at all. He tried to look at the land as Ondrej might have seen it almost a half century before—when both of them were young men just starting out. It was only now, when he could experience the vast distances of America, that Josef realized how courageous his brother had been.

To have left his whole family, Josef marveled, and traveled so far to make his dream of a farm come true.

Shaking his head, he turned to an imaginary Lia seated next to him. "Your brother-in-law had nerve," he said.

Josef often talked to the memory of his wife and saw nothing strange about it. She's with me still, he'd tell himself. She always will be. If my daughter believes her mother is up in Heaven with the angels, that's fine, but right now my Lia is right here in the car with me.

Since coming to America, Josef's thoughts had never ventured far from Chicago's urban sprawl. But now, driving west, he found himself fascinated by the changes in the land. Until he reached the western part of the state, Wisconsin had been mostly dairy farms, green and pleasant to look at. Then, the Wisconsin farmland added evergreens and hardwood forests. Josef began to see long skeins of geese in the sky, as well as an occasional deer along the roadside.

Minnesota had even more woodlands to offer, and bright, blue lakes that sparkled in the sun.

"This country is *so* big, *miláček* Lia," he told her, as he looked toward a horizon that now seemed to hold both a piece of his past and a part of his future. "Just look at it—it goes on forever."

Three days after leaving Chicago, Josef found himself driving along 1st Avenue in Fargo, North Dakota. He remembered, from Irena's letters, that she'd once lived in Fargo before leaving it with her brothers to homestead in Montana.

Josef had not yet told Ondrej and Irena of Lia's death. It was a thing he preferred to do in person and not through a letter. Ondrej would be saddened, he knew, but Josef feared Irena would take the news much harder. Although they'd met only once, the two women corresponded often and had grown close over the years.

The eastern portion of North Dakota was dull country, rolling and featureless, but as he drove west onto the Missouri Plateau and into the Great Plains, the land changed again—shaped by running water that often carved spectacular cliffs, buttes, and valleys.

Each time he stopped for gasoline, Josef had the tires and the oil checked. The Buick was running fine, but he suspected that if the automobile broke down anywhere along the road, his daughter might never let him hear the end of it. She'd been upset from the start, thinking he was too old to make such a long trip alone.

"Julia is stubborn, just like you," he playfully told Lia. "And she nags me just as you did—but I'm not so old that I can't drive a fine car across the country."

It was six days before Josef made the seventy miles southwest from the town of Havre and drove into Fort Benton, Montana—on the upper Missouri River.

He and his brother were to meet in the lobby of the old Grand Union Hotel—but Josef had reached Fort Benton a day earlier than he'd expected.

"The restaurant's real good," the bespectacled clerk was quick to assure him. "Best food in town—for my money."

The Grand Union Hotel was aged and badly in need of repair, but based on the clerk's assurance of a decent supper Josef took a room anyway.

The clerk looked on as Josef signed the register. "Novak," he said. "We got a Novak fairly close by—Andy Novak."

Josef nodded. "Yes, that is my brother. I am to meet him in the lobby tomorrow afternoon."

CHAPTER 49

They hadn't seen each other since Ondrej and his family had come to Chicago twenty years before, and Josef was stunned at how old his brother looked.

Ondrej was still bone-thin and wiry, but to Josef he somehow looked smaller. White-haired, his face deeply creased from sun and wind, Ondrej's hands trembled slightly and when he walked it was with a stoop to his shoulders.

"It is fine to see you again, *bratr*," Josef said, as the two men embraced. "Are you well?"

"Well enough for an old man," Ondrej said. "And you?"

Josef shrugged. "Some rheumatism, nothing more."

"And where is Lia?" Ondrej asked, looking around the lobby.

Josef stepped back slightly, took Ondrej by the shoulders and slowly shook his head. "Lia is dead, Ondrej. I lost her on Easter. It was a stroke."

"Ah, that is such sad news," Ondrej groaned. "I am sorry for you, Josef—my Irena will be heartbroken."

After they'd eaten breakfast and Josef checked out, he locked the Buick, and left it parked in front of the hotel. With his luggage in the pickup's bed, Josef climbed into the truck's seat for the drive back to his brother's farm.

"How is the wheat business these days?" He asked as the old Ford bounced back north along a dusty, unpaved road.

Ondrej shifted gears and shook his head. "My grandson farms the place now—Harland—that's Charley's boy. I mostly just sit on the porch and tell him how to do it.

"When I'm gone, the place will be his," Ondrej added.

"Lia and I were sorry to hear about Charley," Josef said.

Ondrej nodded. "I guess this family has lost its share."

Learning of Lia's passing, Irena *was* heartbroken. She served them supper, then went to the bedroom and closed the door. Josef didn't see her again until the following day.

Harland excused himself and went to bed soon after supper, and early the next morning, Irena's eyes were still red from crying.

"Joe, I'm sorry I was so rude last night," she said with a sigh. "Leaving the room the way I did. It was such a shock to hear about Lia. I started to worry a bit when her letters stopped coming—but I never said anything about it to Ondrej."

"What will you do now, Josef?" Ondrej asked, stirring cream into his coffee. "Will you keep the saloon?"

Josef shrugged. "It keeps me busy—and it's a living."

They spent all the next day in Great Falls, where Josef visited with his niece and her husband, and the following Saturday, Ondrej and Irena had a picnic in their yard, inviting the Jandas and their other nearby neighbors to meet Josef.

A few days after that, Ondrej took his brother in the truck and showed him all the improvements made to the farm over the years, and late that afternoon, with the sun turning the Marias the color of copper, they started north across the prairie.

"Now, there is something else I want you to see," Ondrej said.

A few miles later, the Ford approached a tiny, ramshackle old structure that Josef could see was almost falling down. It was a few hundred feet from the river, surrounded by grass and weeds, and as they got out of the truck, Josef noticed that much of the framing was exposed as pieces of dried out tarpaper had been torn away.

The plank door was hanging off its hinges and the structure's single window had only a dirty, broken piece of pane in it.

"What is this?" Josef asked. "An old shed?"

Ondrej shook his head. "No, it is a house."

"A house! I don't believe it."

"It's true," Ondrej told his brother. "This little place was my first home on the Marias River—I lived here through the winter of 1905 and 1906—alone."

"And it still stands," Josef said, as they ducked their heads low and stepped inside. "Amazing."

"It still stands," Ondrej offered. "Because a German built it."

"A German—was he a friend of yours?"

"Yes, a good friend—dead now many years."

As they rummaged about inside, Josef picked up a crumpled, yellowed sheet of newspaper that had been used as insulation. He carefully unfolded it and read the faded date: *June 18, 1905.* Under it was an article about riots in far off St. Petersburg, in Russia.

"I haven't been inside this shack since I abandoned it," Ondrej said, adding; "In 1906 I left it to the coyotes and the wolves."

After a bit, they went back outside and sat in the truck. Ondrej lit his pipe and Josef smoked a cigar. Both men sat silent, staring at the old tarpaper shanty.

"Do you ever think about the old country?" Ondrej asked. "Of our little farm in Třeboň?"

Josef shook his head. "No, not for many years. But what I do think about is if those Novaks who come after will remember us at all—and what we did once?"

Ondrej shrugged and shook his head. "Who knows? Each new generation have their own lives to live, and when they are old they may be asking each other that very same question."

They sat for a long time, smoking and saying little, as the sun started to set, casting long shadows behind the cottonwoods on the river. Finally, Ondrej tamped out his pipe and started the truck.

"It is getting late," he told Josef. "The nights are dark out here, not like in Chicago, and Irena will have supper waiting."

Epilogue

The Hillside

Lynn Novak found the message on her phone after returning home from dinner and a movie. "Your Uncle Harland passed away," her mother's voice was saying. "He's being buried on Wednesday—at the farm. Aunt Mae thought you'd want to know."

Going on the Internet, Lynn quickly made arrangements for flights to Montana—an early morning departure from Los Angeles, landing in Salt Lake City. Then, after a layover, a connecting flight into Great Falls. She'd arrive there Tuesday afternoon, rent a car, and be at the farm sometime after supper.

Uncle Harland, she thought sadly, such a shy, strong man. She could still remember him in that hot, stinking barn, wrestling a new calf into life. And now, almost two years later, she'd learned more about Harland Novak than she'd ever known then.

He's quite the old bull, ain't he? Lynn recalled Aunt Jo saying at the reunion that hot Fourth of July. Then she remembered him in the kitchen the evening Aunt Mae was gone, asking for her help—*this calf won't wait...can you help me, Miss?*

They wrote often after that, Harland and Mae telling Lynn the local news and gossip and answering any questions she had about the family. It was their help, more than anything else that allowed Lynn to write her book. As she packed, she carefully placed a copy of *The Novaks: An American Family* into her suitcase. Lynn had planned to send copies to all the relatives for Christmas—but Aunt Mae would get hers now.

A day later, and five hours after leaving Los Angeles, Lynn was waiting at the baggage claim area in the Great Falls airport. She collected her single suitcase and stopped off at the Hertz counter to rent a car. The attendant, a middle-aged man with a bald head and an ample belly, took down the information he needed and noted her name. "Novak," he said. "Novak's a Czech name. Quite a few Czechs around these parts—most of them farmers off in the baldies."

Lynn nodded. "I'm here for my uncle's funeral," she said. "He was a farmer—Harland Novak."

The clerk shook his head. "Name sounds familiar, but I can't be sure. I might have known him—was he an old fellow?"

"Seventy-five, I think."

"Well, seventy-five's a pretty good run," the counter man said, handing Lynn the keys to a blue Ford Taurus. "I guess I'd settle for seventy-five."

"Oh, Lynn, honey," Aunt Mae exclaimed, giving her a warm embrace. "It's wonderful you're here, but you needn't have come—and all the way from Los Angeles."

"I had to come," Lynn said quietly. "Uncle Harland and I were friends."

"Yes," Mae nodded sadly. "We've both lost a good friend."

Surrounded by sprays of flowers, one from Lynn's mother, the bronze casket had been placed in a corner of the parlor—draped by an American flag and Harland's framed service picture.

Lynn briefly knelt at the casket with her aunt, silently voiced a prayer, and then stepped back to say hello to others gathered in the room. Later, when Mae was alone, Lynn approached her.

"How did Uncle Harland die?"

"His heart," Aunt Mae said. "He was busy fixing a part on the tractor and I brought him a cup of coffee. Just as he turned to me, he give a sigh and dropped over. Harland was old and wore out, I guess, just like I'm getting to be."

Lynn reached into her purse. "I have something for you, Aunt Mae. I'd like to sign it before I leave."

"Why, it's a book." Mae said, sounding surprised. She put on her glasses and read the title. "*The Novaks: An American Family.* My goodness, honey—you got it published."

"I published it myself," Lynn admitted. "This first copy's for you—I wish Uncle Harland had lived to read it."

The crowd in the parlor had thinned. Most of them would be back in the morning for Harland's service, but Mae took Lynn by the arm and walked her to the door. "Take a walk with me, honey," Mae said. "There's something I want to show you."

They made their way out back of the barn, toward a low slope of hillside near the river. Mae needed some gentle help getting to the top, and when they reached it, Lynn found herself looking at a small, well kept graveyard, with one open grave freshly dug.

"Harland called this Burying Hill," Mae explained, pointing to the open hole in the earth. "That's where he'll be laid to rest in the morning—and one day I'll rest here next to him."

There were four other stone markers on the hill. Lynn went to each and touched them briefly.

"The men are all here," Aunt Mae said quietly. "And Irena as well. She's resting next to Ondrej. And over there, next to them, is Tom, their firstborn, who died of the influenza—and his brother Charley is buried next to him."

The next morning, Father McCombe drove in from Great Falls to conduct the service. When it was ended, Harland's casket was sealed and slowly carried to the top of the hill. The priest sprinkled both it and the gathered mourners with holy water and recited the twenty-third psalm—*The Lord is my Shepherd; I shall not want...*

As Lynn listened to the words, her gaze reached out past the family and friends. Beyond the low hill was the Marias, sparkling brightly on this fine summer morning.

Wiping a tear from her eye, Aunt Mae stood alongside her two sons, Fred and James and their wives, with her grandchildren and great grandchildren. Next to them were Harland's younger brother, Walter, with Aunt Jo, their son, Stuart, and his wife, Winnie.

Ondrej Novak's youngest daughter, Maria, taught high school for many years in Oklahoma, and eventually married a storeowner from Tulsa. She and her husband had a daughter named Laina who had died six years before.

But Maria Novak's grandson and great-grandson were there, their own wives and families in tow.

Scattered throughout were many neighbors and friends. A few Jandas had come, as did those relatives by marriage whose family names were Trask and Purvis, and off to one side, Lynn saw young Curtis Purvis, the little fellow she'd first met at the reunion. Curtis was two years older now, but his freckles were still there, and so was the mischievous glint in his eyes.

For reasons of which she wasn't quite sure, the land no longer looked barren. The sun felt warm on Lynn's face. Below the hill on the surrounding prairie, she heard meadowlarks singing and saw tiny wildflowers in bloom.

Standing behind them was the still solid old house that Ondrej Novak had bought from Ernst Koeller's widow all those years ago. Two years earlier, the same house had depressed Lynn, appearing weathered and forlorn—rising up from a stark, featureless land that seemed to offer its inhabitants only solitude and loneliness.

But now it seemed different—now the house felt a part of her. Sitting silent and almost empty, within its walls it guarded a piece of her history, a part of her heritage. Blood ran through that house, Lynn knew. Her family's blood, back to Valentyn and Janicka, flowed through this homestead on the stark, wind scoured Montana prairie, just as the same blood ran through the sturdy brick two-flat on Chicago's gritty southwest side.

As Harland Novak's casket was lowered, Lynn saw Aunt Mae go faint and fight to catch a breath. She was quickly supported and comforted by her sons and daughters-in-law.

In the end, Lynn told herself, it's family that matters most. She watched as the mahogany casket slowly disappeared into the earth, and listened as the meadowlarks sang their song of open country.

0-595-29441-3

Printed in the United States
62447LVS00003B/34-39